DRAGONS OF A DIFFERENT TAIL

17 Unusual Dragon Tales

Marx Pyle, J.C. Mastro, Victoria L. Scott, Anne C. Lynch

Cabbit Crossing Publishing, LLC

Dragons of a Different Tail: 17 Unusual Dragon Tales

Published by Cabbit Crossing Publishing LLC

This is a work of fiction. Names, places and incidents are either products of the author's imagination or used fictitiously. Any resemblance to actual persons, living or dead is entirely coincidental.

Cover Design by Shayne Leighton

Edited by Marx Pyle, Anne C. Lynch, J. C. Mastro, Victoria L. Scott

Illustration used in "Tiny Hearts" is by Lara Klein, Digital Artist @laarakln.illustration

Illustration used in "Poisoned Water" is by Sen R. L. Scherb https://linktr.ee/SenRider

"Chasing the Dragon" Copyright © 2021 by Sean Gibson

"A Wild Beast of The West" Copyright © 2021 by Marx Pyle & Julie Seaton Pyle

"Big Dreams" Copyright © 2021 by Victoria L. Scott [Latin teacher]

"The Brooklyn Dragon Racing Club" Copyright © 2021 by Katharine Dow

"Resorting to Revenge" Copyright © 2021 by K.W. Taylor

"Spirit of the Dragon" Copyright © 2021 by J.C. Mastro

"The George" Copyright © 2021 by Timons Esaias [mentor]

"Mouth of the Dragon" Copyright © 2021 by J. Thorn

"Mastering Aesthetics" Copyright © 2021 by Heidi Miller

"Catalyst" Copyright © 2021 by Kevin Plybon

"A Friend Called Home" Copyright © 2021 by Francis Fernandez

"The Last Hour of Night" Copyright © 2021 by G.K. White

"Witherwillow" Copyright © 2021 by Carrie Gessner

"Tiny Hearts" Copyright © 2021 by Sophia DeSensi

"Wei Ling and the Water Dragon" Copyright © 2021 by Jeff Burns

"Poisoned Water" Copyright © 2021 by Sen R. L. Scherb

"Forgiveness" Copyright © 2021 by Colten Fisher

All rights reserved. This book or parts thereof may not be reproduced in any form, stored in a retrieval system, or transmitted in any form by any means—electronic, mechanical, photocopy, recording, or otherwise—without prior written permission of the publisher, except as provided by United States' copyright law.

CONTENTS

Dedication	1
Introduction	2
1. DRAGONS OF ANTIQUITY	8
Chasing The Dragon	9
A Wild Beast Of The West	27
Big Dreams	49
2. DRAGONS OF NOW-ISH...& BEYOND	66
The Brooklyn Dragon Racing Club	67
Resorting to Revenge: A Sam Brody Story	83
Spirit of the Dragon	102
The George	119
Mouth of the Dragon	137
3. DRAGONS OF THE STARS	147
Mastering Aesthetics: An Ambasadora Story	148
Catalyst	163
A Friend Called Home	182
The Last Hour of Night	200
4. DRAGONS OF OTHER REALMS	225

Witherwillow	226
Tiny Hearts	239
Wei Ling and the Water Dragon	257
Poisoned Waters	277
Forgiveness	293
5. BONUS: BEHIND-THE-SCENES	300
A Potent Cocktail: "Chasing the Dragon"	301
A Wild Story Of The West: "A Wild Beast of The West"	303
Behind-The-Scenes: "The Brooklyn Dragon Racing Club"	306
Inspiration, Background, and Context: "Resorting to Revenge"	310
Behind-The-Scenes: "Spirit of the Dragon"	313
Dragons, Lists, and a Dragon Entering the Lists: "The George"	316
Behind-The-Scenes: "Mastering Aesthetics"	318
Behind-The-Scenes: "Catalyst"	320
Behind-The-Scenes: "The Last Hour of Night"	322
Behind-The-Scenes: "Witherwillow"	325
For my sister: "Tiny Hearts"	327
Behind-The-Scenes: "Wei Ling and the Water Dragon"	329
Behind-The-Scenes: "Poisoned Waters"	332
Behind-The-Scenes: "Forgiveness"	335
ABOUT THE EDITORS	338
ABOUT THE PUBLISHER	341

For all of those that dream of dragons.

INTRODUCTION
By Marx Pyle

Here, there be dragons!
There may be no greater mythological creature than the dragon. One of the greatest challenges faced by players in *Dungeons & Dragons*, is a fearsome dragon. The *Dragonlance* books—and accompanying role playing game—was one of my favorite book series and earliest exposure to dragon stories. And I still remember my little-kid heart nearly stopping as I watched Smaug search for Bilbo Baggins hidden among his treasure in The *Hobbit*.

I mean, everyone says unicorns are perfect, but how many unicorn stories do we have in comparison? If Beowulf had fought a unicorn, it would have been a very different tale. (Actually, now I want to write *that*...)

My point is few other magical creatures have inspired such creativity in every corner of this awesome planet, from the oldest legends to the most modern of stories. Whether it is the legend of Saint George and the Dragon, the moon-swallowing dragon Bakunawa of Philippine folklore, the "Mother of Dragons" Daenerys Targaryen's dragons in *Game of Thrones/A Song of Ice and Fire*, or Puff the Magic Dragon, we humans love stories with dragons.

The idea of this anthology was born in my last term of Seton Hill University's MFA program, but I planned to save it for at least another year. Two things changed my mind, however. First, pandemic-induced isolation made me eager to work with other people again. I mean, I love my wife, but even *my* super-introverted self craved interaction with other humans after a few months. The other catalyst was the unexpected death of a filmmaking friend. I worked with James Wallace Jr. off-and-on for years. He had always been supportive, and was probably one of the biggest supporters of the KWC FilmFest which I had directed for two years at Kentucky Wesleyan College. James and I made short films together and, although the two years spent at SHU kept me too busy, I had always expected to create more films with him in the future. Like many filmmakers, he longed to make a feature-length movie. Sadly, that dream died when he did. And I lost a good friend.

When a friend passes away, it's hard not to reflect on your own life—to think about what you'll be remembered for and what things you wish to do before your story ends. I realized I was guilty of what so many writers do: procrastinating. Making an anthology is hard, and I thought I needed more experience before I could tackle such a monumental project, but the reality is, you are never fully ready the first time you attempt something. It's the experience that makes you ready—the wins and the mistakes. So I needed to stop making excuses and dive in.

I reached out first to my graduating class from Seton Hill University and was pleased that nearly all of them jumped at the chance to participate. Then I called one of my mentors, Heidi Ruby Miller. She not only said yes, but decided to write a short story set in her science fiction Ambasadora-verse. Next I contacted another teacher, Timons Esaias. He has won or been nominated for a number of awards, so I wasn't sure if he would be interested. He was, and his story about a dragon boxer definitely fit the "unusual dragon tale" requirement.

Although I love SHU faculty and students/alums, I wanted to avoid the temptation of making this an entire SHU collection of authors, so I reached out to good friends from web series and YouTube: Jeff Burns and Francis Fernandez. They brought some fresh voices with their creative stories. I also happened to interview prolific author J. Thorn on our podcast GenreTainment, and was lucky that he was game, as well.

Finally, I reached out to other SHU students and met new author friends through them. Our talented cover artist, Shayne Leighton, suggested Sean Gibson, who created a very unique dragon story set in Victorian London.

I co-wrote a Wild West dragon story with my supportive wife, Julie.

The rules were simple: "Short story will include a dragon and either an unusual setting and/or a twist on the classic dragon archetype (i.e. not a classic European dragon, doesn't hoard treasure, etc.)"

I hoped for a collection of stories with dragons as we've never seen them before, and I wasn't disappointed.

Thinking outside of the box is sorta my addiction, so aside from the concept, I also tried some other unusual things: two rounds of critique groups between the authors and optional behind-the-scenes essays. The critique groups helped polish the stories and hopefully built some new friendships. As for the optional behind-the-scenes essays—I don't know about you, but when I love a story I've read, I always want to learn more about it. So, in the spirit of a Blu-ray commentary, you can look at the back of the anthology to learn more about the authors and their stories.

When I direct a film festival, I create themed blocks of films. In that spirit, I've broken this anthology out into four parts: Dragons of Antiquity, Dragons of Now-ish...& Beyond, Dragons of The Stars, and Dragons of Other Realms.

Dragons of Antiquity are stories set in a past that could have been.

"Chasing the Dragon" by Sean Gibson: When two Victorian detectives investigate a rash of dead bodies at an opium den, they learn that "chasing the dragon" is a much more literal—and far more dangerous—activity than they had previously thought.

"A Wild Beast of The West" by Marx Pyle & Julie Seaton Pyle: When the government outlaws the capture of wild dragons, the domestically-bred are worth their weight in gold. In this Wild West setting, Sarah and her dragon-riding posse confront a ruthless band of rustlers in an attempt to prevent a range war.

"Big Dreams" by Victoria L. Scott: Two dragons create an Earth-bound portal, but nothing goes right planet-side and they're stranded. As Earth's atmosphere poisons them and the humans plot their deaths, will the dragons find a way home before it's too late?

Dragons of Now-ish...& Beyond are stories set in the present and possible future...sort of.

"The Brooklyn Dragon Racing Club" by Katharine Dow: An elderly man, worried Brooklyn has changed forever, teams up with a young woman from his Dragon Racing Club to push back against the anti-dragon bias of his newest neighbors and a hostile city.

"Resorting to Revenge" by K.W. Taylor: A telekinetic dragonslayer goes on vacation in the woods with his girlfriend, but it turns into anything but a relaxing stay. A Sam Brody story.

"Spirit of the Dragon" by J.C. Mastro: Heavy metal superstar band DragonFraggen create a brand-new song using ancient writings they discovered in a cave in Wales, but guitar-wielding rockers shouldn't mess with magical forces they don't understand.

"The George" by Timons Esaias: A dragon holds the Heavyweight Boxing Championship of the World, and some folks have decided that this is unacceptable.

"Mouth of the Dragon" by J. Thorn: In a post-apocalyptic tomorrow, a dragonslayer must make a difficult decision.

Dragons of The Stars takes us on a journey out into space.

"Mastering Aesthetics" by Heidi Ruby Miller: "What can bring life can also destroy it." A story set in the Ambasadora-verse.

"Catalyst" by Kevin Plybon: When his sleepy space dragon gets boarded, a stargazing farmer must wake the beast to drive out the invaders.

"A Friend Called Home" by Francis Fernandez: When catastrophe strikes a budding planet, the people of that world find hope and a friend.

"The Last Hour of Night" by G.K. White: A space orphan on a backwater planet takes on one last job to escape a crumbling city and her dark past.

Dragons of Other Realms takes us to fantasy worlds very different from our own.

"Witherwillow" by Carrie Gessner: In a city divided between humans and dragonfolk, P.I. Iris Kane takes a simple case and ends up with more than she bargained for.

"Tiny Hearts" by Sophia DeSensi: When a sassy, ring-sized dragon binds himself to Lovlet, she's dragged to a magical creature shop where she finds family in unexpected friendships.

"Wei Ling and the Water Dragon" by Jeff Burns: Young and adventurous Wei Ling gets help from an unlikely source when she journeys to retrieve her village's sacred idol: an aquatic dragon who shares a special bond with the irreverent and feisty warrior.

"Poisoned Water" by Sen R. L. Scherb: As dragon deaths spike, Rayns enters his partner dragon into the illegal fighting ring to secure a meeting with the leader.

"Forgiveness" by Colten Fisher: A girl and a dragon watch the sky during Christmas and try to understand each other.

I hope you enjoy this wonderfully creative collection of dragon stories. - Marx Pyle

One
Dragons of Antiquity

CHASING THE DRAGON
BY SEAN GIBSON

"THIRD TIME THEY'VE PULLED a body out of that place this week. It's becoming a right epidemic. Celare? Did you hear me?"

"Yes. Curious."

"That's understating it a bit, mate. All everyone's talking about."

"Indeed."

"And this chap, John Johnston, they call him, though I suspect as that's not his given name because, well, you know... right at the center of it all, he is."

"So it appears."

"Chief Inspector Wiggins wants us to pay Johnston a call, shake him down a bit."

"Of course he does. Strictly by the book, our beloved Chief Inspector."

"Blimey. Doesn't seem as if you're taking this very seriously, Celare."

"I suspect it seems that way because I am *not* taking it even the *slightest* bit seriously."

"And just why bloody not?"

"Because, my dear Stanley, I believe the opium den is—if you will indulge the play on words—a smokescreen."

Inspector Hugh Stanley raised two thick eyebrows and pursed his lips in characteristic puzzlement. "You've lost me."

"You'll find yourself in due time, I've no doubt. Now then, you are a true-blue man of the Yard and right to suggest that we proceed as Chief Inspector Wiggins commands. Fetch your coat and let's be off."

Inspector Alistair Celare, trim and lithe even in an Ulster, cut through the early evening fog with a confidence and grace the lumbering Stanley couldn't hope to match, though the latter's considerable bulk intimidated in a way that complemented his partner's purposeful stride. Despite the throngs of people intent on seeking a meal, entertainment, or simply escape from the close confines of uncomfortable working environs, not a soul impeded the pair's progress.

A half hour's brisk walk brought them to their destination, a ramshackle dwelling in the East End. Celare smiled wryly. "Naturally. Couldn't have drawn it any better if we'd commissioned Cruikshank himself."

"East End, isn't it?" Stanley gestured to the surrounding buildings, which slumped in similar states of decrepitude. "It's all like this."

"Yes, but they have taken great care to make it painfully obvious to even the most unobservant passer-by—not that I would place you in that category, of course—that this building is an especially dubious place of iniquity, and undoubtedly the kind of sordid house of ill repute that so frequently graces the headlines of our most disreputable but, sadly, widely read tabloids these days: the opium den.

"Note the details, carefully cultivated to make us believe it is so, but each off the mark in some way. For example, you see the sleeping man next to the stoop? We are to assume he is Chinese, but I would wager that he is Korean, based on the Hangul letters tattooed on the inside of his left wrist. Note, too, the bluish haze that hangs about the doorway. It would take a very intentional effort indeed to maintain that smog despite the stiff easterly breeze, which means someone wants us, and all who walk by, to see it. No one here truly fears discovery. And mind the dapper but very agitated young man who is now making his second pass behind us, clearly wishing to gain entry but not so foolish, even in the throes of his addiction, as to enter when two of Scotland Yard's finest stand near the door. No, this place is not akin to the surrounding dereliction—the byproduct of true neglect and lack of financial means—though they would like us to believe it is."

"They?"

"All in due time, Stanley. Let us give a firm rap to announce ourselves, shall we?"

Inspector Stanley nodded and strode to the door, causing the well-dressed dandy lurking nearby to turn on his heels and retreat. The inspector raised a fist the size of a sheep's head and pounded three times, rattling the rickety door in its splintered frame. Long moments passed. Stanley turned back toward Celare and shrugged.

Celare motioned for Stanley to have another go at it. Three more times he pounded, the last blow threatening to dislodge the door from its protesting hinges. At last, a young Asian woman answered the knock. Her eyes widened with convincing surprise as she took in Stanley's uniform. "May I help you, sir?" she said in an accent that sounded, oddly enough, vaguely French.

"Inspectors Stanley and Celare, Scotland Yard." Stanley doffed his cap. "We need to speak with Mr. John Johnston."

The woman shook her head. "No such man resides here."

Stanley looked over his shoulder at Celare, who stepped forward. "I suspect, madam, that you speak the truth in a technical sense—I have little doubt that Mr. Johnston does not, in fact, call this make-believe hovel home. But that does not mean he is not currently inside."

"Seems like a pretty real hovel to me, Celare," said Stanley as he rapped gingerly on the warped doorframe.

"Authentic, even."

Celare smiled. "So it appears."

The woman shook her head once more. "He is not in the building."

"Another half-truth, undoubtedly," replied Celare. "Well, then, we shall wait—inside. It's too cold to stand about cooling one's heels, wouldn't you say, Stanley?"

"I could use a nice, warm cup of tea, sure."

"That won't be possible," the woman said.

"That is unfortunate. I suppose we will just have to round up some Bobbies and force our way in then, eh?" Celare gave Stanley a meaningful look.

"Right-o, guv. Chief Inspector Wiggins said not to come back until we meet with Mr. Johnston, so I don't see as how we'll have any problem finding lads with the right level of enthusiasm for the job, it being such a high-profile matter and all."

The woman turned away from the door as a harsh, clipped voice called out to her from inside. She looked down and stepped aside, opening the door wide. "You may enter."

"Wise decision," said Celare, stepping inside. "Now then—how about that tea? Two sugars, if you please."

The woman led the inspectors through a vestibule showcasing a tall, cracked vase adorned with a dragon, and then down a small corridor that opened into a larger chamber. Threadbare Persian rugs lay strewn haphazardly across the floor. Men in varying states of consciousness sprawled atop them, some staring at the ceiling with wide-eyed intensity, others curled in the fetal position with their eyes clenched so tightly that the flesh around their temples seemed permanently contoured. Stanley paused, aghast, and opened his mouth to speak, but Celare squeezed his right arm tightly and guided him through the maze of bodies to a doorway on the far side of the room before he could utter so much as a syllable.

"Note the smell," said Celare.

"I don't smell anything," replied Stanley.

"Precisely."

They passed through a gauzy silk screen patterned with plum blossoms and emerged into a small sitting area. The woman motioned them toward a small, low-set table in the middle of the room. An elderly Asian man with long, flowing mustaches sat cross-legged on the floor on the opposite side of the table, and before him rested a tarnished silver tea service, three mugs, and a dented tin bowl half-filled with sugar cubes.

Celare looked at the woman with raised eyebrows, but she motioned again for them to be seated. Celare shrugged and sat gracefully, mirroring the old man's pose. Stanley looked dubious but managed to lower himself to the floor, though he crouched on his haunches rather than attempt to contort his long legs into a position he doubted he could achieve with any degree of comfort.

The woman departed and the old man served the tea. He poured slowly and deliberately, spilling not a single drop. He picked up a small pair of tongs and placed two cubes of sugar gently into Celare's tea before turning toward Stanley and gesturing to the sugar bowl.

"Let's make it three, shall we?" said Stanley. "Been a right odd day so far. I could use a bit of a pickup."

Three sugar cubes plunked softly into Stanley's cup, causing a small drop of tea to leap over the edge and spatter the table. The old man frowned, covered his hand with his long, flowing sleeve, and meticulously wiped the spill. Then, he picked up his own cup, gestured toward the inspectors, and raised it to his lips to take a brief sip.

Celare and Stanley followed suit, though Celare, feeling the immense heat radiating from the cup, paused to release a cooling breath. Stanley, whose awareness lagged his partner's, grimaced and gasped. "Bit hot, that."

Celare nodded. "Curiously hot when it should be merely warm. Yet another of the artfully placed trappings intended to fulfill the expectations created by a very imaginative press and literary community. Though it appears as though vividly rendering such lurid descriptions is far more important than authenticity."

The old man simply continued to sip his tea, his face impassive.

"What do you mean, Celare?"

"This place is no more an opium den than you are a fluent speaker of ancient Greek," replied Celare before turning to look intently at the old man. "Where's Johnston?"

The old man drank from his cup once more.

Stanley looked back and forth between his partner and their host. "I say... is this not Johnston?"

Celare smirked. "No, this is not the man called John Johnston. Our garrulous host here can likely confirm, but I suspect Mr. Johnston is—what is that charming expression? Ah, yes—'chasing the dragon.'"

Stanley pursed his lips. "Do you mean to say he's one of the chaps passed out in the room we just walked through? Them as has smoked a bit more than they ought?"

"I am not convinced those gentlemen have smoked anything at all, but that's the thing about such colorful metaphors, Inspector Stanley. You can interpret them in more ways than one."

"You've lost me, mate."

"I suppose you could ask him for an explanation." Celare nodded toward the old man, who had not moved, had not even blinked, since his last sip of tea.

"Don't think I'd have much luck ringing that bell."

"No, I don't suppose you would."

Stanley removed his hat and scratched his head. "So, what do we do?"

Celare stared at the old man, who finally blinked, then stood and began to pace, head down and hands clasped behind his back. After two full trips around the room, he stopped before the door through which they had entered and raised his chin. "If you, too, wish to chase the dragon," he said, his voice slow and raspy, "the way is down. But know this: it can be hazardous to your health." He bowed and backed out of the room.

"What's he on, that one?" asked Stanley. "Maybe spent a bit too much time in pursuit of his own dragon, if you take my meaning."

"I do indeed. You have many superior qualities, Inspector Stanley, but subtlety isn't one of them." Celare stalked slowly around the room, eyes darting everywhere. "'The way is down...'"

"What are we looking for?" asked Stanley as he heaved himself to his feet and stretched.

"We are looking for... ah. Yes, of course." Celare smiled. "Saint Lucy."

"You really need to start spelling it out or I'm going to think you've gone fully 'round the bend."

Celare moved to stand before a small painting on the north wall of the room. "Too clever by half."

Stanley crossed his arms and raised an impatient eyebrow.

"This lovely lady," Celare gestured to the painting, "is the patron saint of virgins, and so not someone I expect you would be well acquainted with."

"Thank you."

"She hails from Syracuse, Sicily, where she's known as Santa Lucia."

"And?"

"Think about the phonetical pronunciation."

"I'll get right on that soon as you tell me what 'phonetical' means."

"Loo-sha. To the ear, analogous to the Chinese 'lóu xià.'"

"Get there faster, mate."

"'Downstairs.' That's what the Chinese phrase means."

"That's a right lovely bit of pudding, but I don't see as how it helps us."

"It will." Celare carefully removed the painting from the wall and, with a flourish, gestured to the spot behind it. "Behold."

"It's a little button."

"Your powers of observation remain as sharp as ever."

Stanley rolled his eyes as he extended a meaty finger and jabbed at the button. He stumbled back as a panel in the floor slid open beneath his feet.

"Stairs!" crowed Celare.

"Your powers of observation remain as sharp as ever."

"Touché." Celare peered down into the darkness. "Don't suppose you've got a torch on you?"

"Not presently." Stanley rummaged through the drawers of a bureau that sat on the opposite side of the room. "We can fix that, though." He hefted a walking stick that leaned against the bureau and began to wrap the end of it in a bundle of rags he had pulled from a drawer. He found a small bottle from another drawer, removed the cap, and sniffed. "That's the stuff." He doused the rags liberally with the contents of the bottle. Then, he reached into his coat and withdrew a small box of matches. "Hold this, eh?"

Celare took the makeshift torch tentatively, holding it as far away as possible. "I would prefer not to have my face burned off, if at all possible."

"Well, say a little prayer to Santa Lucia, then, and let's get on with it."

"Spoken like a man who's been with many a virgin."

Stanley ignored his partner and withdrew a match, struck it on the side of the box, and touched it to the torch. "Problem solved, mate," he said with satisfaction as the rags lit immediately.

"To the victor go the spoils," said Celare, passing the torch to Stanley. "Down we go." Celare stood aside.

Stanley cocked an eyebrow, then shrugged and stepped in front of his partner.

They descended slowly, each taking great care to ensure that their footing was firm before taking the next step. "Stairs must be positively ancient," muttered Stanley as a cracked bit of stone crumbled beneath his foot.

Celare ran a hand gently along the wall. "Not sure what that makes you then, my dear friend."

"What do you mean?"

"Judging by the color and thickness of the mortar in the wall and the extraordinarily precise angles cut into the stairs, I'd posit that this passage to hell couldn't have been carved out more than a decade ago."

"Huh," replied Stanley thoughtfully.

"'Lasciate ogni speranza, voi ch'entrate,'" intoned Celare wryly.

"'Abandon all hope' and such, isn't it? Even I know that one."

"You are the stalled clock of literary allusions."

Stanley grunted.

The pair continued their descent. The flickering light from the torch skittered across the walls, stretching their shadows into demonic parodies that capered and japed gleefully with each step they took. "You've never looked better, Celare," said Stanley, watching the grotesque parade.

"Stay sharp, Inspector," replied Celare. "I doubt we're alone."

They came to the bottom of the staircase, which ended in a narrow corridor that curved slightly to the right. "Arms," said Celare quietly, drawing a Webley.

Stanley nodded and unholstered his own revolver. They crept forward around the curve, their vision limited to the small halo of light that extended from the now-guttering torch.

The corridor ended in a chamber. The two looked at each other. Celare nodded.

Together, they burst into the chamber, weapons raised. The feeble torchlight touched neither the ceiling nor the walls of the chamber, suggesting a size far larger than seemed possible given that they had not descended to any great depth. Their torch flickered once, then again, and then smoldered into a softly glowing ember that failed to illuminate even Stanley's face.

"Hullo?" said Stanley, his voice echoing in the silence.

Light flared. Both inspectors cried out and raised their arms to shield their eyes. Celare blinked away tears and looked around the chamber. Lit torches, dormant just seconds before, lined the walls, spaced at six-foot intervals. Two stone pillars flanked a large dais. A lone figure stood before it, head bowed.

Celare squinted until details gradually began to resolve. A large wicker basket sat atop the dais. Three bulging, ovular objects the light pink of a young boy's dress sat nestled within it. The chamber otherwise stood empty.

The man in front of the dais raised his head and fixed his eyes on Celare's. Long white mustaches flowed from his face down to the top of his blood-red changshan. Crow's feet marked the corners of his eyes as he smiled, an expression utterly devoid of warmth.

"Your curiosity does you credit, Inspectors," the man said, his voice heavily accented—again, strangely enough, with a French inflection. "It will also be your death."

Stanley looked unimpressed. "And me having such big plans tomorrow—a bit disappointing, that. My death, I mean. Not the part about having plans." He turned to his partner. "Though I don't suppose as you've got much on your calendar, have you, Celare? Not so much of an inconvenience for you, I'd wager."

"John Johnston, I presume?" said Celare. "Or, at least, that's the nom-de-plume you've adopted in this... guise."

The man bowed. "John Johnston is as good a name as any for you to call me in the few precious moments of life you have remaining." His nostrils flared, causing his mustaches to ripple.

"Have a care, Celare—something about this doesn't seem right," said Stanley, suddenly jittery. "Didn't mean for that to rhyme," he added quietly.

"Your instincts are correct," said Celare, who began pacing back and forth. "I think it's safe to say that Mr. Johnston is more, far more, than he appears to be." Celare paused and looked at Johnston. "This is your home—you would be well within your rights to make yourself more comfortable."

"You presume much. You are in enough danger as it stands," replied Johnston.

Celare smiled coldly. "Occupational hazard, I'm afraid. Show us your true colors, won't you?"

Johnston moved slowly, hands clasped behind his back, toward the pillar on the right side of the dais. "True colors," he mused. "An interesting phrase. We all have our secrets, do we not?"

"I don't particularly like my wife's shepherd's pie, but I don't see as what that's got to do with anything," said Stanley. He looked at Celare and said, quietly, "Don't tell her I said that, eh? She's like to murder me in my sleep."

Johnston circled behind the pillar. Stanley tensed, finger tightening on the trigger of his Webley, but Celare's face remained impassive.

Only the top of Johnston's head remained visible as he moved behind the dais. "Some of us, for example, choose to live in the shadows because it's the only way we can be what we truly are—isn't that right, Inspector Celare?"

Stanley flicked a glance toward his partner, but Celare's eyes remained fixed on Johnston.

"Whereas some of us," said Johnston as he passed behind the second pillar, "are forced to live in the shadows."

"Come out where we can see you!" shouted Stanley as he raised his weapon.

"Be careful," replied Johnston in a raw, strained voice, "what you wish for."

A high-pitched scream echoed behind the pillar, one that quickly descended to a deep growl that suggested both pain and pleasure.

"Celare!" cried Stanley.

"Hold fast, Inspector," replied Celare calmly. "Arms at the ready, though I'm not sure they will do us much good at this juncture."

"What does that mean?"

"I mean precisely *that*."

A feral, lizard-like face emerged from behind the pillar, followed by a long—impossibly long—neck. Snow-white whiskers bristled and bulged from either side of the slender head and the cracked and receding gums could not conceal a series of stiletto-like teeth that ran the full length of the creature's extended jaw. The beast moved forward, and Celare and Stanley could see the point where its neck met a body that was only slightly wider and just as long, set atop four powerful legs that each ended in a blunt foot tipped with three spiky claws. Its body gleamed in the bright, flickering torchlight, scaly skin glistening in the full spectrum of the rainbow. The creature wrapped a short, thin tail around the lower half of its body and, as it came fully around to the front of the dais, stood up on its slightly longer hind legs.

"Good *God*!" shouted Stanley, stumbling backwards away from the monster.

Celare appeared fascinated, transfixed, even, eyes locked on the creature's own hypnotically yellow orbs.

"Celare!" called Stanley, rushing over to his partner. He gripped Celare by the shoulders. "Get hold of yourself!"

"I'm in full possession of my faculties," replied Celare calmly. "I'm simply taking a moment to observe that which I've never had the opportunity to see before."

"What the bloody hell is it?"

"A dragon," said Celare softly. "Or so it would like us to believe."

The beast's nostrils flared, and it breathed in deeply. It looked toward the side of the chamber and puffed, emitting a steaming stream of liquid that, when it hit the wall, melted the rock instantly.

Stanley quailed. Celare chuckled.

"Once again, to the untrained eye, the appearance is convincing. But, the devil, as they say, is in the details. And there, once again, you have failed miserably."

The dragon lifted its head, smoke puffing from its nostrils. It did not appear pleased.

"I don't think now is quite the right moment to be lobbing insults, mate," said Stanley.

"One should not find truth insulting."

"Truth," rumbled the dragon, "is malleable. You, Inspector Celare, should know that as well as anyone."

Stanley cocked an eyebrow at his partner. "Something you need to tell me?"

"You're a detective, aren't you?" snapped Celare.

"Yes, but—"

"Now is not the time." Celare glared at the dragon. "In Chinese culture, the dragon is a symbol of strength and power, yes, but it is also a symbol of good luck. It is not a destructive force; it is a paragon of excellence and virtue. You have sought at every turn to make it appear as though the Celestial Empire is infiltrating Britain, but in each instance, you've betrayed that your understanding of China is informed by penny dreadfuls."

The dragon growled.

"Show us your true self."

"A strange request, coming from you."

"I suppose it is at that." Gently, Celare peeled off the thin, well-manicured beard affixed to her face. "Satisfied, are we?"

"You're... you're not a man!" shouted Stanley.

"You can clearly see," said Celare to the dragon, "how Inspector Stanley has achieved such lofty rank and the high regard of his peers."

"But...but..." sputtered Stanley.

"Now, your turn," said Celare.

The dragon turned away from them, growled softly, and began to morph into something else entirely. Ripples flowed through its back as its body shifted from shimmering scales into a domed carapace. The beast grew two more legs and the claws at the end of each thickened until they became bear-like. Its tail remained serpentine, though grew three times longer. As the creature turned back toward them, Celare and Stanley stared at its most significant change: it now had a leonine head adorned with a scaly mane and long, straggly strands of hair. As the beast opened its mouth and roared, they could see that despite the changes, its teeth remained formidable weapons.

"Bloody hell... Now what is *this*?" asked Stanley, exasperated.

"Still a dragon, of a sort. I believe the French call it the 'Tarasque,' though they also refer to respiratory distress as having a cat in one's throat, so I don't place much stock in their linguistic prowess."

"French dragon—absolutely bloody fantastic," mumbled Stanley.

"A common English misconception," retorted the beast in a low, rumbling, French-accented growl. "It is not 'the' Tarasque, singular. It is 'a' Tarasque—as in one of many."

For the first time, Celare looked concerned. "Many?"

The beast smiled and gestured to the basket on the dais. "Our numbers have never been large, but a promising young occultist at Trinity College has discovered certain esoteric means of enabling us to reproduce more quickly."

Celare shook her head. "But why all of this... this theater?" She gestured to the building above their heads. "How does China factor in?"

The Tarasque snorted. Small wisps of smoke curled from each nostril. "You English and your obsession with the exotic. Your newspapers, such as they are, would much rather obsess over the sensationalist possibility of an invasion of illicit narcotics from China. A cultural attack intended to lure Britain's upstanding gentlemen into a haze of unthinking debauchery, than the possibility of a much closer, and much more dangerous, threat." The creature laughed. "Your customs officials are devoting so much attention to inspecting arrivals from the 'Far East' that they overlook far more dangerous imports from the north." The creature nodded toward the basket.

"I'm not nearly as sharp as Celare," said Stanley, "but I'm pretty sure that France is to the south." He looked at his partner. "Right?"

"It doesn't mean France," said Celare. "It means Scotland."

"The Auld Alliance didn't end with the Acts of Union," said the Tarasque. "It remains strong to this day—and it will at last bring about England's downfall."

"These are your eggs?" said Celare.

"In a sense. Birthed in France through arcane means and sent to Scotland, then imported here. I have fertilized them, and soon they will hatch and take their place among your people."

"There's a disturbing thought I won't soon forget," said Stanley. "The fertilizing part, I mean."

"Come now," scoffed Celare. "You can't possibly expect this absurd scheme to work. The gradual infiltration of our society by Tarasques? That's your grand plan? It would take years, and you could never place them in positions of authority. The French accent alone would give them away."

The Tarasque shook its head. "We have been at this for quite some time, Inspector. This final batch of younglings represents the culmination, not the beginning, of our efforts." The beast smiled, revealing every one of its deadly teeth. "And do not assume that we all have French accents—like humans, how we speak reflects where we were raised. I am aged, but many of our younglings have been brought up in the bosom of our Gaelic allies. Just imagine how much a Scottish accent might ingratiate one of us with your beloved Queen Victoria."

Celare turned pale. "Stanley, we've got to—"

Before Celare could finish, the creature roared, shaking the walls and causing the torches to flicker. It wrapped its slithering tail around the basket of eggs and lifted them easily from the floor. "It is far too late for your actions to make a difference. Our victory is imminent."

The Tarasque raised its snout and spewed a gout of molten magma. The ceiling ignited and exploded in the same instant. "Adieu, Inspectors," growled the creature as it leapt into the air, debris bouncing off its impenetrable bulk as it easily cleared the distance to the street above. Shrieks and screams filled the air, audible even over the collapse of the building as the people of East End witnessed the terrifying beast's emergence.

"Celare—down!" bellowed Stanley as he sprang toward his partner, who quickly dropped to the ground. Covering her with his body, he rolled them into the alcove beneath the stone dais.

It seemed like hours but took only minutes for the sky to stop falling. The shattered remains of the building came to rest above them, muffling the yells from the street above.

Celare drew in a shallow breath. "Well then," she said, "it would appear we've got our work cut out for us."

Stanley nodded as best he could from his contorted position. "You can say that again. Won't be easy shifting all this rubble."

"I was referring to saving the Queen's life."

"You think she's really in danger?"

"Connect the dots, Stanley. John Brown is a dragon."

"The Queen's personal attendant?"

"The very same."

"Bloody hell."

"It certainly will be if we don't get out of here quickly."

Stanley pushed gingerly against the shattered wooden beams that trapped them beneath the dais. "Our report to Chief Inspector Wiggins would make a stuffed bird laugh. I'll wager he won't be pleased."

"I won't let his podsnappery deter us," replied Celare.

"Never have before, have we?" Stanley began carefully shifting rubble. "This is going to take a while."

"Best move with alacrity, then."

"Aye." Stanley grunted as he wrestled a particularly large chunk of wood to the side. Some debris tumbled away, allowing a bracing blast of cold, fresh air to reach them.

The two worked in silence for several moments before Stanley spoke. "Hey, Celare—why did you never tell me dragons are real?"

"Because I learned the truth of that fact at the same moment you did. I didn't figure you needed it spelled out for you just then."

"Well, then, why didn't you tell me that you're a lady?"

"Why is it that you never noticed?"

"Noticing things is your job, isn't it?"

"Well, *I* did notice."

Stanley tilted his head to the side as if to concede the point. "Bet your real name isn't Alistair though."

"Just dig, Stanley. We've no time to waste."

"Right-o, guv."

Sean Gibson, "author" and slackonteur, is not a professional mini biography writer (if he were, this would be much more compelling). Instead, he's a professional guy by day, hangs out with his amazing wife, son, and daughter by night, and writes somewhere in between. He holds a Bachelor of Arts in English Literature from Ohio Wesleyan University and an MBA from the Kelley School of Business at Indiana University, though rumors persist that he also attended mime school (he is silent on the subject). Sean is the author of several stories starring Heloise the Bard, including "The Part About the Dragon Was (Mostly) True" (which inexplicably received a starred review from Publishers Weekly), "You Just Can't Hide from Chriskahzaa," and "The Chronicle of Heloise & Grimple." He also wrote the Victorian-set fantasy thriller *The Camelot Shadow* and its prequel short, "The Strange Task Before Me." He has written extensively for Kirkus Reviews, and his book reviews have also appeared in Esquire. Learn more about him at seangibsonauthor.com, but only if you're really bored and a bit of a masochist.

A Wild Beast of the West
by Marx Pyle & Julie Seaton Pyle

THE SPRINTING HERD OF wild dragons rolled over the gentle hill, plumes of dust rising in their wake as they rumbled into the sunset. The fading light danced brilliantly across their brown and black scales.

"Beautiful," I whispered.

"Yes, very," agreed Aaron, yet his focus was on me as he said it.

Clearing my throat and pointedly ignoring his implication, I pulled my eyes from the hilltop cowboys of our employer tending their cattle (the bait) to my men (the unforgiving steel jaws of our trap). Staring hard, I could barely make out their wagons hiding just out of sight.

"Not to doubt you, but are you sure this will work?" Aaron's question broke through my concentration.

I suppressed a sigh as I sized him up again. He was definitely overdressed for a bushwhack (and God knew how he could stand such stiff leather gloves in this heat). The man's habit of second-guessing everything was getting old, but his strong chiseled chin and light blue eyes that somehow twinkled even in the day's fading light served to soften my response.

He was the son of James Lucian, one of the richest ranchers this side of the river, who hired me and my team to take down a band of rustlers that had been either capturing or outright killing his cattle. I don't think he would've bothered hiring us, except they'd also taken nearly all of his dragons in the last raid. Since the government outlawed capturing the wild ones, the domestics were worth their weight in gold. Lucian also suspected this was all at the behest of another wealthy rancher with whom he'd been engaged in a series of escalating battles—a situation that threatened to break out into an outright range war.

Aaron had done little to hide his infatuation with me since we'd arrived. Not that the attraction *wasn't* reciprocated. However, our lifestyles mixed about as well as dragon fire and coal oil.

I flipped onto my back and leaned against the large rock to get more comfortable before I explained our plan to him. Again. As I spoke, I gently stroked my dragon lying next to me.

"This is the highest spot in the area." I pointed to the branches above. "The tree line will cover us when they fly in. The fading daylight, contrasted with the light from the large bonfire, will hide us until we want to be seen. My men are top-notch. We normally go after poachers, but rustlers ain't that different."

"Except they are ready to shoot it out," Aaron said.

I grinned. He'd obviously never been in an all-out battle with a group of cornered poachers.

Instead of arguing, I figured a demonstration was in order. I drew one of my shooting irons, then twirled and re-holstered it before he could even blink.

"Just makes 'em more fun to send to Boot Hill."

"He one of your 'top-notch men'?" Aaron nodded to Harvey who, for some unfathomable reason, was rising from his hiding spot next to us.

I turned and slapped him on the leg. "What the hell, Harv? Get down."

Harvey's eyes widened and he plopped back down. "Sorry, Sarah. I got to staring at the dragons..." he gruffly explained before his voice trailed off and his eyes once again settled on the beasts below.

I shrugged at Aaron. "I told you Harv's one of the best riflemen in this whole country, but I never promised stealth."

Baby purred his amusement, and I affectionately stroked his head, enjoying the familiar sensation of his cool scales beneath my hands.

"Your dragon is very well behaved," Aaron said approvingly.

I glanced at his own lying dutifully next to him. "And yours is very...obedient," I searched for a word that would sound complementary.

He chuckled. "Rock is a good dragon, but I can tell you two have a strong bond. What's his name?"

"Baby Blue, but I usually just call him Baby," I said, happy to wobble jaw about one of my favorite topics.

Aaron's eyebrows shot up. "He doesn't look like a 'Baby.' Rock isn't small, but yours is downright fierce. Except when he looks at you, he's just a puppy gazing at this mommy. I see the 'Blue' part, though. I have never seen one with that color scales."

"His herd's unique coloring," I said with a hint of sadness. "Very rare."

Aaron gestured to the parasol secured on my harness. "If you're expecting rain here, you are going to be disappointed."

I winked. "Oh that, it's my secret weapon."

"We will be here a bit if the rustlers stick to their usual plan. I bet there is a story behind you two."

"Fine." It wouldn't hurt to yarn away the hours until the rustlers struck. Harvey also loved the story, so I hoped it'd keep him from getting distracted again. "Nearly five years ago, I was hired to stop White poachers from killing the local wild dragon herds by a tribe who had a special relationship with the animals."

"I bet so," Aaron said. "It's the only thing better than riding a good horse."

"No, this tribe believed they were equals, not transportation. They even had legends about the dragons protecting them from enemy tribes."

"Were the stories true?"

"Maybe, maybe not. I like to think every legend of the West is true enough to believe in, like the ones my father told me. That's how the tribe knew about me: we once lived in the area during our travels."

"Oh yes, your parents took you all over the frontier, didn't they?"

"How'd you know?" I asked, surprised.

"Well, at the risk of inflating your ego, I've heard of the infamous Sarah Storm—hunter of poachers, dragon rider of legend, and slayer of the hydra." Aaron grinned shyly from beneath long dark lashes.

"Pfff, everyone brings up the stupid hydra." I tapped the back of my head lightly against the rock and huffed in frustration. "Not proud of killing it."

"But it had killed *hundreds* of people."

"It was just an animal being an animal. Not sure if it was sick or just sick of hiding from humans. I planned to capture and rehome it at the Zoo, but it had other ideas. In the end, it was him or me. Anyway, I don't like talking about it."

Aaron raised his palms in surrender. "Sorry to bring it up."

"That's okay. And to answer your other question: yes, I spent my childhood traveling the frontier with my parents. In fact, that's where I learned Cherokee, or *Tsalagi*, which is what I use to command Baby. Mom was on her griffin quest while Dad did his fieldwork on the *Yunwi Tsundi'*, the little people of Cherokee folklore."

"That was before they founded The Wild Beast Zoo, right?"

"Yeah, they retired from traveling and opened the Zoo in Lexington to protect and heal rare animals. I, however, still make the wide-open West my home."

Aaron leaned back and stared at the evening's first twinkling stars peeking through the swift clouds as the last rays sank below the horizon. I did the same and breathed in the rapidly cooling air, savoring that magical twilight moment when the unforgiving Western sun surrenders to the softer charms of the sparkling night sky.

"I've heard only good things about your folks," Aaron broke the silence. "They are *almost* as famous as you."

"Don't know about that. They're legends."

"Your mom is a biologist and your dad an anthropologist, right?"

"Wow, should I be flattered or..."

"My father is spending a small fortune for your services." Aaron chuckled. "I had to make sure he spent the family money wisely."

"He have a habit of not?"

"No, but this has become very personal for him, and that kind of passion can lead to mistakes. Enough about him. Tell me more about your parents."

"They're curious, adventurous. Taught me everything I know." I didn't know what else to say.

"Tell how they met. I love that story," Harvey said.

"Well, I have to hear that now," Aaron responded.

"Fine, you big saps," I teased, winking to soften my words. "My mom traveled the West documenting the rarer animals: dragons, griffins, and-"

"I heard she was the first to discover chupacabras," Aaron interrupted.

"Yeah, nasty little critters. Anyway, she saw Dad speak at Transylvania University regarding legends of an animal with a lion body and the wings and head of a bird. A griffin. She hoped to find clues that would lead her to a live specimen, or at least signs that it once existed."

"And it was love at first sight?"

I laughed. "Not even close. They argued. He tried to stop her from searching the Appalachian Mountains. After she left, however, he couldn't stop thinking about her. So, he eventually tracked her down just in time to rescue her from some weird cult. That's when Dad said he fell in love and asked her to marry him."

"And she said yes?"

"Nah, gave him the mitten. She said, I quote, 'I am a wild beast of the West and will not be tamed.'" I tried my best impression of Mom's posh English accent. "She left, following yet another clue to a griffin nest, but Dad refused to give up. He got a grant to travel the frontier studying Native tribes and tracked her down. Told her he could travel now, wherever she wanted. Instead of taming her, he became a wild thing himself."

"Ahhhh, I love that story. Mr. and Mrs. Storm—the perfect couple." I had to smile. Harv said that every time.

"I would love to meet them someday." Aaron stared deeply into my eyes. "Maybe they could teach me how to find my own wild soulmate."

I averted my eyes, careful not to unfairly encourage him. "Well, you can see them anytime at the Zoo."

Before he could reply, a rifle crack pierced the air. The bandits' flyers descended on the cowboys.

They were early.

I mimicked the call of a great horned owl, beginning the series of signals we'd perfected over the years for night jobs. Next was Harvey, and so on down the line, each with our own identifying nocturnal bird sounds, which tonight told my team to hold. We needed to strike at just the right moment, no sooner.

The rustlers fired upon cowboys below, visible by their muzzle flashes and the patchy light of the nearly full moon as it fought for dominance in the leaden sky. Thunderous hoofbeats reverberated throughout the canyon—right on schedule. If the pattern held, their horsemen would wrangle the cattle under the chaotic cover and watchful guard of their flyers.

Tonight, however, we'd shred their blueprint.

Their dragons' flames encircled the panicked bovines, providing only one route on the ground. I scanned the sky and located our plant, Erik (stationed down there to keep up appearances), on his dragon just as they were struck by a formidable figure from above. Another gunshot penetrated the night and he crumpled to the ground, followed by his dragon's blood-chilling scream as it was engulfed in flames. We'd just witnessed the death of a good man and his dragon, by...*a griffin with a rider?*

"How is that possible?" Aaron gasped. "A white man has never ridden a griffin."

"I've heard stories of three tribal warriors who have," I said, still in shock. "But no, no whites."

My parents had eventually found proof of griffins, the natural predator of dragons. Their high-altitude nesting and fierce personalities made them blissfully rare, but the oil they produced made them fireproof, dragon-killing machines. The one that took out Erik's dragon had pierced the throat with its beak, causing the combustible gases to erupt instantly upon exposure to air.

"We need to get down there." Aaron started to mount his dragon.

"No, we stick to the plan." If we allowed ourselves to react rather than act, to abandon our plan, we risked getting more killed. I silently vowed to send the varmints to hell across lots, but I had a responsibility to everyone under my command, and my steely resolve was why these men followed me into battle after battle.

The rustler's horsemen galloped into the opening, as expected. On my command, Harv aimed his trusty rifle at a bell hanging in a tree below. Anticipating a night attack, we'd hung a jar of lightning bugs exactly one foot to the left of it—more than enough of a guide for a crack-shot like him to find his target.

Ding!

Our men hidden in bushes near the fire released Chinese sky lanterns, with balloons hanging a foot beneath the glowing orbs. We'd ensured the rustlers would arrive downwind.

"Show Aaron what you can do, Harv."

He nodded and swiftly shot each balloon.

The moon and the dragon fire provided enough light to see that the released fumes had the desired effect. The riders chewed gravel as the panicked horses lit a shuck out of there.

"Damn." Aaron scrunched his face, waving his hand in front of his nose. "The wind picked it up just right. What *is* that?"

"Family secret." My family kept our discovery of the Sasquatch secret. It wasn't hard to imagine that those mostly gentle, intelligent beings would be treated far worse than the Native Americans. Gentle as they preferred to be, their musk terrified most animals. Horses and bears wouldn't go anywhere near it.

Our waiting gunmen poured out of the wagons and picked off the stunned, unmounted rustlers.

"Hyah!" I jumped on Baby Blue. Without hesitation, he leaped off the cliff and unfurled his "wings," which were really flaps of skin between his front and back legs, similar to those of *Glaucomys volans* or other types of flying squirrel. Dragons used them to catch the heat generated from their throats, as well as any naturally heated air in their environment like condors. When not in flight, the flaps folded into their bodies as added protection from predators, jagged rocks, and other dangers. While these fire-and heat-producing abilities were still a mystery, many scientists (including my parents) continued to study the chemical and biological processes. I, however, preferred to simply enjoy the experience. And I would never grow tired of the thrill of the flight.

Static electricity danced across my skin as Baby's heat mixed with the cool night air. I secured myself in the harness and tested that my legs were secure in their thick leather straps since I mostly stood in the stirrups. I breathed deeply to center myself and connect with Baby. Unlike most white horse riders who relied on bits, reigns, and spurs to communicate, I preferred the method of the accomplished horsemen of the Plains Indians, whose bareback equestrian acrobatics were legendary. Without such accoutrements, they used their entire bodies and emotional ties to move as a seamless single unit, often with weapons occupying both hands. So, too, must we connect with our dragons.

"Hyah!" Verbal cues also helped.

We gained altitude as we sailed around the cliff and circled behind the rustlers, trusting my men would follow and have our backs. God must have smiled on us, because the sky's leaden cover cleared, illuminating our prey. We descended on them from above.

"*Atsila!*"

Baby's stream of fire was joined by nearly a dozen others. The rustlers didn't stand a chance, either dying in their saddles or from falling to the earth below. Their dragons could withstand far greater heat and escaped unharmed, just as planned.

A smiling Aaron pulled up to my left. "Well, that went swimmingly!"

"Be ready. That wasn't all of 'em."

His smile dissolved as he scanned the horizon for a counterattack. Just then, his hat flew off as the sound of a rifle shot pierced the air. He swerved.

Dragon fire streamed out of the darkness as the gunman I was searching for rushed Baby and me.

Baby rolled, protecting me with his wings. Flames licked at my clothes, but my dragon shield held.

When the rider dipped to avoid collision, Baby flipped us upside down. Relying on my straps to hold, I carefully aimed my pistol. Three quick shots left the rider slumped partially out of his mount.

Suddenly, three more rustlers appeared in another surprise attack. I called out to my crew for support.

"Harv!" I pointed to them.

He nodded, leaned back, and calmly fired his rifle. The dragons pulled up as two riders slumped lifelessly and another fell off his dragon. Must have been an amateur, not knowing how to properly secure his harness. Before I could celebrate, however, a bullet whistled past my right ear. More whizzed past, but I couldn't locate the shooter, which meant he was behind us. Baby grunted, blood spilling out of his right wing.

Dammit, where are you?

Baby and I spun and dove, then swerved left and shot back up, still searching for our pursuer in the smoke-filled sky. More shots rang out, and a searing pain tore my pistol out of my hand. I sighted the shooter just a moment too late—he had me dead to rights, but before he could finish me off, another gunshot had him slumped lifelessly in his mount. Out of the murky haze, Aaron emerged with a wave and a triumphant smile.

I hissed in pain as I grabbed my backup pistol and searched for more rustlers, spotting what appeared to be the last four as they fled. I didn't have time to waste on a flesh wound.

"Harv, leave at least one to follow, but take out the rest," I yelled.

He nodded and again took aim.

Confident he'd handle it, I looked desperately for the griffin, which had disappeared once the shooting started. With each passing moment, I grew more nervous—that was one dangerous creature to lose track of.

In a blur of fury and feathers, the griffin slammed into Harvey's dragon, plummeting them into a death spiral.

"No!"

Harv's dragon, too stunned by his injury and already traveling at such a high speed, couldn't recover. They plunged to the ground with a shattering thud.

Baby and I dove, following helplessly as the griffin continued its vicious attack, clawing and pecking at the lifeless dragon. Harv must have managed to pull himself out of the harness because he was crumpled nearby. Yet, before I could act, the griffin rider shot, causing us to swerve as I returned fire. Nothing landed, but they beat a hasty retreat. The griffin's ferocious roar echoed in my ears.

As soon as Baby's feet touched ground, he quickly closed the gap on our prey. We continued exchanging fire, finally getting close enough to recognize the rider, a no-good snake I knew by reputation. The bastard grinned and pulled his reins, causing the griffin to leap high in the air. I fired a few more hopeless rounds—griffins could gain altitude from a running start far easier than a dragon.

I grabbed the loaded crossbow from my saddle. Releasing a deep breath, I pulled the trigger, and the arrow slammed into one of the griffin's rear legs. This was no flesh-piercing arrowhead, however. Rather, the glass vial attached in its place shattered.

Baby and I hightailed it back to Harv.

I leaped off and knelt over Harv, shaking his shoulders. "Harv, talk to me!"

Aaron landed and ran to us.

"Is he okay?"

"Okay? No, he's not okay. They crashed!" I knew I was being unfair, but I couldn't help myself. I'd known Harvey since I was a teenager; he was the little brother I never had. Sure, our work was dangerous, but somehow along the way, I'd convinced myself that Harv was just too big, too tough, and too formidable to ever really get hurt. Yet as he laid so still, broken and covered in blood, he suddenly appeared so very *human*. And just as vulnerable as the rest of us.

Aaron squeezed my shoulder. I didn't shrug him off.

Harv came to, coughs racking his body. Painfully squinted eyes bore into mine as he whispered, "We get 'em?"

Aaron knelt down. "We got 'em."

"How're you feeling, Harv?" I kept my voice light and steady.

"I—" Another excruciating coughing fit interrupted him. "My arm and at least one leg are broken. I... think I might...need to rest. Just for a bit," he tried to reassure me before another agonizing rasping episode.

At least he didn't spit up any blood. I tried to convince myself he just got the wind knocked out of him. Plus the air was smokey. Hopefully, that was it.

Please, be it.

"We'll get you back to camp, have Doc look at you," I told my fallen brother.

Aaron yelled to some of his men, "Round up any surviving rustlers." Then he turned to me. "Maybe we can get them to tell us where the rest ran off to, and who their leader is."

"We don't have to wait." I grabbed one of his pistols to replace mine. "I scent-marked the griffin. Baby can track 'em, but I have to leave now."

"You can't go alone." Aaron squared his shoulders resolutely.

"Tell Silas I marked the griffin with the pineapple scent. They can follow, he'll know how, but I gotta go."

Aaron stepped between me and Baby and stood his ground.

"Out of my way," I ordered, barely containing the urge to punch him.

"Hold on just a second, okay?" A few of his cowboys on horseback joined us. "Austin, get this man to Ms. Storm's camp and tell a man there named Silas to follow us. The griffin is marked with pineapple scent."

The cowboy looked puzzled. "Pineapple?"

"Yes," Aaron said firmly. "Fast as you can, or all this death was pointless. Understood?"

"Yes, sir!"

Aaron turned to me and nodded. "Now, let's go."

"You don't have to—"

"You need backup. I'm coming." He jumped onto Rock, ready once again to follow my command. "Lead the way."

I climbed on Baby, pulled a piece of dried pineapple from my pocket, and waved it in front of his nose. "*Tsutsayosdi svgata*," I said.

Baby purred, excitedly yipped twice in anticipation of his favorite treat, and ran to the hillside, already heating up. It would take time to gain altitude, but we'd find the griffin and get payback for Harv.

We flew twenty minutes before I spotted a light on the ground. I whistled to Aaron, and we landed on the highest spot.

"Did we find them?" Aaron asked, searching for signs of life below.

"That's an abandoned flint quarry. I saw a campfire, they're hiding down there."

The quarry had been owned and mined by Native Americans for centuries. Recently the government relocated them further west, and the mine, unknown to most whites, was abandoned. The high, curved peripheral ridge created a natural barrier on three sides, leaving only a small area that needed fencing to create a large, hidden corral, perfect for hiding illegal activities.

"Now what?" The campfire suddenly surged, and a bright burst of light interrupted my response. "What are they doing? Do they want us to find them?"

I was at a loss, then I caught a whiff of the smoke: a familiar, pungent mixture of herbs. "Luke must have figured out I scent-marked his griffin, so he's trying to confuse any dragons following the scent. With the winds scattering this smoke, we may be on our own."

"Luke?"

"Yup, Luke the Lightning," I explained. "No mistaking that unique scarring on his face."

"Damn, no offense, but I hear he's one of the best dragon riders alive."

"And, apparently, griffin rider, too. Whoever's behind this must have a lot of money to afford him. I need a minute to think."

After several moments of silence, Aaron spoke up.

"I got you off-topic earlier with your parents. You never told me how you got Baby."

He must've thought I was panicking—maybe I was a little—and wanted to calm me.

"It was a tough fight, but we killed or captured most of the poachers. Last I heard, they never returned, but sadly, Baby was the last of his herd. I tried to find 'em, but they either left their territory, or more likely, were slaughtered by other poachers."

I stroked Baby's scales, holding back tears at the memory of his heartbreaking loss.

"The last of his kind," Aaron whispered reverently as he patted Baby, too. "Ordinary greed killing extraordinary grace."

The seconds ticked quietly by as we continued to pet Baby, as if our affection could make up for all he had lost.

"I'm mad, Aaron. Right mad enough to start a fight with a rattler and give him the first bite."

"Me too, but how can the two of us take them?"

"With a little planning and a lot of luck."

As the sun peeked over the horizon, my men still hadn't joined us, confirming my fears about the herbal smoke screen.

We were on our own, but we had a plan.

Aaron started a campfire, letting the smoke announce his presence. As I'd hoped, Luke and his griffin came to investigate. Any dragons they still had would need time to gain altitude, ideally giving our dragon riders time to strike. They'd have no chance. And that plan would have been great.

Instead, it was just us.

Aaron and Rock sped off to a nearby rocky overhang to take cover. Spotting only Aaron and figuring he had easy pickins, Luke pursued.

Meanwhile, I circled undetected, high above on Baby Blue. As soon as they were out of sight, I targeted a group of dragons tied to a fence. At my command, Baby created a flaming barrier between the dragons and their riders, catching one man who had already reached his.

"*Atsila!*" I yelled when we landed, and Baby lit up the fence, freeing the dragons. As they scurried from the quarry, Baby and I merged with them, heading for a large, elevated rock formation so we could take flight. I heard gunfire, but doubted they could spot us in the crowd. Yet when we leaped from the ridge and flew, I glanced back and spotted a form closing in.

Luke and his griffin must have heard the pandemonium and circled around, because they now bore down on us with a vengeance.

Just as I'd hoped.

We stayed with the herd, which began to panic due to the encroaching griffin, as we spiraled to gain altitude. Luke continued to fire, so I pulled out Harv's rifle and shot back as I split off from the herd. We passed each other, taking shots and missing before stopping to reload.

I could imagine Luke smiling, thinking he had me, because the sun was to his back and I was effectively blind.

"Come on, Baby, let's show him how it's done."

We charged and I shot randomly to keep Luke from aiming. I grabbed my parasol, held it in front like a medieval jousting lance, and opened it. The sunlight bounced off the special reflective coating, blinding Luke. We swerved to avoid a collision.

"*Atsila!*"

Baby's fire stream caught the griffin's side when we passed, hitting Luke's legs. While he desperately patted at the flames, I exchanged the parasol for Harv's rifle. Twisting around, I released a deep breath and squeezed the trigger. Luke rocked back, his limp body sliding halfway off the griffin.

"That was for Harv." Damn, that felt good to say. "Okay, Baby, let's get back down there." We arced down to the flint quarry, detecting gunfire as we approached. The few rustlers who were left had Aaron pinned down and were closing in. I wasn't sure we'd reach him in time, but then Rock charged forward, rushing the men. They fired in response, but Rock sprayed them with fire.

Blue and I landed, ready to fight, but the rustlers were all either burned or crushed to death. I dismounted and ran to Aaron, who was trying to soothe Rock whose front leg was bleeding.

"Stupid guy," he said shakily as he gently stroked Rock's face. "Got himself hurt bad when we charged."

The cry of another dragon in pain pierced the relative silence.

I ran to investigate some cages near one of the rocky sides. They contained dragons—some with the Lucian brand, some who appeared to be wild.

"Move and you're dead."

I froze at the woman's authoritative command and spied the shadow of a shotgun pointed at my back.

"I don't care how fast you think you are," she continued. "You ain't that fast. Drop your guns, kick them away, and turn around slow."

I complied and found myself facing a well-dressed, distinguished-looking woman in her forties.

"So you're the one behind all this," I said.

"Damn right, and it was going well until you and your men showed up."

"No," Aaron's voice boomed behind us, near the cages. "You lost, Lenora. I know our families have always fought in the past, but this is insane. So many people dead."

She smirked. "Killing a Lucian will make it worth it. *Ignis!*"

"No!" I screamed, turning just in time to see a dragon charge the cage door and set Aaron ablaze. Before I could rush Lenora in a blind rage, however, Baby did. Wide-eyed, she stumbled backward and shot at him.

I grabbed a handful of dirt and a rock, rushed her, and threw the dirt in her eyes before she could fire again. Then I parried the barrel with my forearm and slammed the rock into her head. She tumbled gracelessly to the ground.

"Baby!" I ran to his side as he got to his feet, bleeding a little from one leg where the bullet grazed him, but thankfully otherwise unharmed.

I shifted my attention back to Aaron, who was rolling on the ground, engulfed in flames. While I desperately searched for blankets or water to help, he stood up and threw off his flaming duster, hat, and gloves.

"Aaron, wh- I- how?" I stammered, confused and relieved that he seemed unscathed.

He smiled and huffed out a deep breath.

"My family pays an alchemist for special fire-resistant oils to coat our clothes," he managed to say before I crushed him in an embrace and kissed him. "Expensive," he said and chuckled after our lips parted. "But after you get burned once by a dragon, you'll pay anything to avoid it again."

That's when I noticed his burn-scarred hands.

We were interrupted by a noise I'd never heard Baby make before, so we joined him by the caged dragons.

"It's okay, Baby." I unlocked the cages, keeping an eye on the dragon that attacked Aaron. He must have been the guard dog, but with his master unconscious, he seemed unsure of what to do. I led him out first before releasing the others. Aaron gathered those with his family's brand.

Then Baby rushed inside and rubbed excitedly against another dragon. Curious, I followed him, and that's when I saw them: six dragons with nearly identical markings as Blue. When he continued to caress the female's face and side, I knew she was his long-lost mate.

"You found 'em, Baby, your family." I smiled, tears tickling my cheeks.

As we led the herd away from their confinement and I prepared to say my painful goodbyes, Baby seemed to hesitate. The selfish part of me hoped he would stay with me, but I knew what I had to do.

"Go on, Baby Blue," I encouraged him, kissing his nose and rubbing our foreheads together. "You remember me, okay? Run free like the wild beast of the West you are, and be with your family."

Baby cooed and rubbed me one more time before dashing to his mate when she called. He spared one final glance before they all took to the air, his cries of joy joining the rest as they disappeared into the sunset.

"His family?" Aaron asked softly. I nodded and allowed his gentle embrace to comfort me.

"I'll miss him," I mumbled into his shoulder. "But this is what I've always wished for him."

We remained that way until we were blanketed by the shadows of dragons overhead. We looked up to see the cavalry had arrived—my men had finally located us.

Back at the Lucian ranch, a large barn served as our hospital where Doc did her best to patch up both humans and dragons.

I immediately located Harvey, already bandaged and splinted.

"How's he doing?" I asked Doc quietly.

She sighed, lifted her hat, and scratched her head like she always did before giving her unfiltered diagnosis.

"He'll heal up, but he needs time." Her tone brooked no argument. "Some of the other men have gunshot wounds and minor burns, which will also take time." She looked pointedly at me, as if daring me to try to move her patients. "Luckily, except for poor Erik, we didn't have any more deaths. You were lucky this time. Again."

"A few of *my* men weren't as lucky," Aaron said softly, eyes downcast.

I patted his back. "It's not your fault."

"No, it's Lenora's." He practically growled in the direction of the handcuffed woman, reaching for his pistol.

I grabbed his forearm, moving between them. "There was enough killing today. Leave her to the marshals. She'll get hers."

Sighing, Aaron nodded, gun hand drifting free.

"Well," I said, "I'm off to buy a new ride. Doc, tell Harv and the others to meet me at the Zoo in a week. First round's on me. You think Harv can ride second on one of the bigger dragons in a week?"

Doc scratched her head.

"Any normal person, I'd say no, but he's an experienced rider. Plus, the Zoo's got more resources for him and the injured dragons."

"Good. I'm headin' out."

Before I could, however, Aaron grabbed my shoulder and whispered, "Can I talk to you?"

I followed him out of the barn and the silence stretched uncomfortably between us. I steeled myself for the inevitable.

"Sarah, I feel a connection between us." Hopeful eyes searched mine. "I've never met a woman like you. I know I'm far from perfect, but I'll do my best by you. And with my family's money, I can give you anything you desire."

Unless I desire freedom.

I searched his eyes, picturing our life together: gentle dragon rides around the ranch, fashionable high-necked dresses, a high society wedding attended by strangers, years of birthing and raising children. And finally, growing old on the same patch of land, never again flying over the furthest hill just to see what's there.

I squeezed his hand, kissed him, and shook my head, smiling sadly as I repeated those fateful words, "I am a wild beast of the West and will not be tamed."

Aaron watched silently while I shouldered my saddle and began my trek down the winding dirt road. Perhaps he realized arguing was pointless. Deep down, I think he knew he was too tame for my wild life, too.

I'd reach the nearest town in about a day with plenty of money to purchase a dragon. However, finding a suitable one would be a challenge in the dwindling market caused by the wild-caught ban. While a blessing for the indigenous populations, it was yet another burden on a way of life already threatened by the encroachment of so-called civilization.

Perhaps extinction was the eventual fate of all wild things.

Something large landed in the thick foliage of a nearby tree. Pistol in hand, I crept forward to investigate when it suddenly descended and thundered straight at me.

Moment of truth: shoot or stand my ground?

I listened to the wild beast in me, holstered my pistol, and stared down the charging form as it slid to a stop mere feet away.

A griffin.

No, *the* griffin. Its markings and mount instantly identifiable as Luke's.

While the creature continued to aggressively posture—perhaps determining my worth—I confidently patted my saddle.

And smiled.

Marx Pyle is an author, screenwriter, filmmaker, podcaster, adjunct professor, and martial artist whose journey has been as complex as his characters and the worlds in which they live. His first degree was to save the world (Psychology), and the next to pay the bills (Computer Information Systems). His third degree (Film Production) helped him follow his storytelling dreams, but his final (Master of Fine Arts in Writing Popular Fiction) allowed him to do so without budget constraints. In addition to urban fantasy, he dabbles in science fiction, fantasy, and horror because he can't filter that "what if" voice in his head. Marx's new urban fantasy/thriller, *Obsidian Monsters* was recently released. He enjoys relaxing at home with his supportive wife, their two cats, and albino rabbit who, while mostly cute and cuddly, occasionally seems to thrive on human flesh and blood. (We suspect she's related to The Killer Rabbit of Caerbannog). He can be found online at https://marxpyle.com/ and on Twitter as @MrMarx.

Julie Seaton Pyle attended the University of Southern Indiana where she majored in Print Journalism/Computer Publishing. In addition to writing, she has done a fair amount of acting--both on screen and voice work. She's also the co-host of the podcast *GenreTainment*. When not writing or editing, she enjoys folk dancing, belly dancing, jewelry making, and roller skating. However, she especially loves spending time with her hubby (Marx Pyle), two cats (Veronica and Teddy Bear), and bunny (DeeDee).

BIG DREAMS
BY VICTORIA L. SCOTT

> A.D. 793. This year came dreadful forewarnings over the land of the Northumbrians, terrifying the people most woefully: these were immense sheets of light rushing through the air, and whirlwinds, and fiery dragons flying across the firmament. These tremendous tokens were soon followed by a great famine...

Anglo-Saxon Chronicle

THE TERRAN HUTS WERE on fire.

It was, unfortunately, Cadet Sansho's fault. The illness came on so suddenly, there had been no time for him to get away from the settlement before the damage was done.

The small bipeds screamed and ran as their homes blazed. Sansho felt awful. Why had the primitives built their dwellings out of dry plant material, for Thasyn's sake?

And why did he feel so sick?

"Gah! Go left! Go left!" Cadet Pulian shouted, banking to the side, flapping his wings to get more elevation.

Sansho followed him, but his spasming gut wanted to expel more of his stomach contents. The caustic vomit burned the back of his throat and filled his nose with the scent of brimstone. He knew he couldn't hold in the liquid flames for long. Aiming at a cultivated field away from the panicked bipeds, he set it on fire with a whoomp. No homes were hit, but there was more yelling and sounds of alarm as the flames in the field spread outward. He hoped the natives hadn't been growing something important there.

"Back to the camp," Pulian said, swooping down to Sansho's level and pointing his head toward the afternoon sun. Their shelter capsule was thirty oscills away, obscured in a gathering of trees. Most of their leaves were a vibrant green, but some had started to turn red, yellow and orange.

Sansho, exhausted and feeling another episode of vomiting coming on, nodded and followed his friend. The smell of smoke and the sounds of the natives' wails faded as the two Drecre dragon cadets flew away.

They landed on the shore of a large pool near their capsule and the trees that obscured it. Sansho vomited into the water, which hissed as the substance boiled and emitted steam. He pulled his left wing up to shield his face, feeling miserable. He hadn't been this sick since he'd eaten a bad batch of Lithonian Cragua. That time he'd spent the better part of two days in the infirmary and missed the promotion ceremony from second year to third year cadet.

Once the steam subsided, Sansho watched fish and other creatures he couldn't name float to the top of the liquid, obviously dead. It seemed a bad omen.

Pulian settled his wings on his back and paced, scanning the area for attackers. His kind, the Ystri, were smaller dragons known for their intellects, clear-headedness, and rapid flying speed. Sansho's clan, the Ter, were renowned for their size, bravery, and the ability to spit fire. The two types complimented each other. Sansho valued Pulian's no-nonsense disposition, and Pulian appreciated Sansho's go-getter attitude.

They'd worked together well their entire time at the Academy, and had even been accepted into the officer training program. But, despite their skills and Commander Dareban's praise, they'd been kept off even the simplest of missions because they were 'too young and inexperienced.'

"By Thasyn's Ass! Why didn't you tell me you were sick?" Pulian said, his blue-green tail swishing in agitation.

Sansho moved away from the side of the pool, his red wings and tail dragging on the ground. Why hadn't he been able to control his vomiting? He didn't want to think about how many natives he'd injured. But, even though he'd emptied his stomach, he wasn't better. If anything, he was more fatigued and out of sorts.

"I didn't know I was ill until we were in the air. And then..." Sansho shrugged, his wings moving up and down as he shifted his shoulders. "I couldn't stop myself. I've never heard of portal sickness striking so late—"

Pulian shook his head, looking up to meet Sansho's eyes. "We came here to prove to Commander Dareban we can handle ourselves on an off-planet observational mission. What are we going to say about this in the log?"

"It was an accident?"

His friend was unimpressed. "I told you we needed to be careful what we did here. There's a reason the portal coordinates were so hard to get. This is a hazardous place."

Sansho burped and exhaled smoke. The infocell he'd snuck out of the Academy database hadn't stated why

Terra was off-limits to Drecre level cadets, just that the planet was dangerous. The rumor was that Clutch Commander Dareban had been to the planet a few times, but hadn't really explained why he thought the planet was treacherous.

Sansho certainly couldn't figure it out. Though it was different from that of their home planet Zorix, the Terran environment was temperate and full of life. There were no predators larger than him and Pulian. The planet's technology level was so low, any attack would be easily repelled by the energy of the portal's walls. On top of that, the sentient bipeds didn't look all that menacing.

Therefore, Sansho and Pulian decided to visit the planet. They'd reasoned that if they did a survey of a Terran island and returned unscathed, Dareban would see they were ready for new challenges. The Clutch Academy welcomed initiative in its cadets. Sansho and Pulian wanted to be the youngest dragons to become Ondyr Sub-Commanders. This was the first major step on that path.

Sansho pointed a clawed hand in the direction of their portal capsule, which sat near the place where they'd arrived on the planet. "We managed the trip, arrived here successfully, and set up our camp so that the portal powers the capsule. So far, so good. All of that will show Dareban we can handle ourselves in a hostile environment. Once we finish here, he'll see we're ready to go on missions with the upper Itre Clutch cadets. Big dreams require big risks."

"We're only supposed to observe. Burning native dwellings was not part of the plan. You might have killed some of those bipeds!"

Sansho thought of the chaos he'd caused, the screams of the bipeds ringing in his mind. He hadn't wanted to hurt anyone, and had no idea how he'd explain what happened to the settlement in their report. How could a simple observational flight result in such a mess? Sansho said the first thing that came to mind. "I know. Maybe we can go back after the sun sets and see if there's something we can do to help—"

"Like what? Due to their primitive ocular systems, they can't see us. So far as they know, random infernal destruction just fell out of the sky. Terrifying to happen. The sentient life here is not going to help our case with Dareban. It'll get us demoted, or worse."

Sansho shifted from foot to foot, looking at the ground, his tail twitching behind him. Pulian, as usual, was right. "I know. I'm sorry. I didn't do it on purpose."

His friend flapped his wings. The bitter scent of anger hit Sansho's nose. "The result is still a disaster. There's no way we'll make Sub-Commander if these sorts of things continue."

"Look, I don't want to argue. I think I'm done horking up fire. Let's go back to the capsule, all right? I'll rest. You can work on our mission log and check the readings on the equipment. Then I'll take the first guard duty, and you can sleep."

Pulian stomped off into the trees, tail up and flicking right to left. His backbone defensive spines glowed a deep red color, signaling his annoyance. Sansho followed, doing his best to hide how tired he was.

Sleep would help, he was sure. He entered their capsule and fell into his bed.

Sleep didn't help. If anything, Sansho felt more tired than before, and his guts squeezed so hard he thought his intestines had cut themselves in half. He had nothing left to expel, but that didn't keep his belly from twisting in pain. The back of his throat tasted like smoky bile.

Pulian was in better shape, but not by much. His blue-green spines drooped and his scales were pale, his wing membranes ashy. He slumped over the instrument panel of the capsule, concentrating on a readout. Pulian had been fine before Sansho rested. Why was he unwell now?

Pulian took Sansho in with a glance.

"You look like shit," Pulian noted.

"You don't look so good yourself."

"Yeah. About that. I've been checking the atmospheric readings," Pulian said. He swallowed hard. "There's a problem. Actually, there's more than one problem."

Sansho sat down in the chair next to Pulian, swinging his tail to the opposite side of his friend's. "What's up?"

"The information we stole—"

"—borrowed—"

"—about this planet wasn't right."

Sansho's stomach roiled. Something inside tightened up, pulling painfully, and he worked to keep his voice even when he said, "That can't be. I got it from the Academy database directly. What isn't right?"

"The atmosphere is 78% nitrogen, about 21% oxygen—"

"Like the infocell said, and well within our tolerances—"

"—and .93% argon."

Sansho shut his snout with a snap. He didn't know much about argon, but he did know it was toxic for dragons.

"One of the first symptoms of argonic poisoning in Ter dragons is...uh...extreme digestive distress. That's why you vomited fire. In Ystri dragons, like me," he sighed, "it's what's causing my increased body temperature. The progression of the symptoms is based on exposure. The longer we're here, the worse it gets."

That was not good news. A frisson of fear went through Sansho's mind, but he willed himself to stay focused. "We'll break out the medical kit and give ourselves the antidote." He stood up. "Where is it?"

"While the condition is treatable, the standard capsule medical kit doesn't include an argonic poisoning treatment. I checked. There are some fever reducers and stomach ailment meds, but I don't know how well they'll work. Argonic poisoning causes breakdowns in the body's organs. Drugs to control the symptoms could exacerbate that deterioration."

"Like?"

"Making our lungs fill with blood? Slowing our heart rates until we pass out?"

"So, a short-term remedy would cause worse problems."

"Yup," was Pulian's grim reply.

That meant Sansho's guts would continue to rebel, and then what? Burst? Would he shit flames and torch his own innards? He sat back down. Pulian's body temperature would continue to increase. How long would it take for his friend to get heatstroke, or worse?

"Then let's pack up and go right now. Once we're back home, we can—"

"The portal is unstable and damaging the local area," was Pulian's flat reply. He made the console display show the visual feed on the portal. "I reduced its size to lower the energy expenditure, but I'm not sure it helped."

Sansho opened the capsule door and looked outside at the interdimensional doorway, which was now the size of his clawed hand. It crackled with yellow portal energy, but it flickered in and out. Black-green cracks and jagged pits lined the doorway's edges.

The area around the portal was another matter. Where there had once been leafy green growth, a grey wash covered everything. The damage spread out in all directions, a destructive wave of interdimensional poisoning.

"The environmental effects have stopped, but I can't reverse the damage," Pulian said.

It was classic portal decay. They'd confirmed the integrity of the device before they left and it had been fine. This sort of major malfunction made no sense.

"I triple checked the integrity of the portal before we left, Pulian," Sansho said, wiping a hand down his snout. "This shouldn't be happening. Is there something in the Terran atmosphere that would cause this?"

"Not so far as I can tell. Then there's the last thing," Pulian replied, panting a little. He brought up the visuals on the village they'd flown over earlier.

In the center of the settlement, surrounded by burned huts, three bipeds lay on the ash covered ground, unmoving. One of the natives rocked back and forth in obvious grief with a corpse in its arms, while a couple of others attempted to comfort the distressed one.

Sansho's stomach griped and writhed. He knew it had nothing to do with the argon in the air. Even if it had been unintentional, he'd killed those bipeds.

Pulian pointed at the image of the grieving bipeds. "I think we were wrong about the natives not being able to see us."

He switched the visual feed to show a group of Terrans standing in front of a large stone structure on the outskirts of the group of huts. The building had a pointed spike jutting from its roof with crossed sticks at the top. They'd thought it was used as some sort of gathering place due to its size. Pulian believed the crossed sticks had some sort of religious function.

A native in front of the open doors of the structure brandished a stick with a large metal fork on the end, while the others waved fists and other strange, pointed instruments in anger and agreement. At their feet in the dirt was a crude rendering of Sansho and Pulian in flight. They'd drawn flames coming out of Sansho's mouth.

"They've been at that for a while," Pulian said, wiping his face with a forearm and slumping on the console. "They saw which way we went, and I've noticed more native activity on the outskirts of this large area of trees."

"The infocell said the visual field of Terrans didn't include the energy wavelengths of our body colors."

"At this point, I think we should call it a dis-infocell," Pulian said. "It should have told us about the argon and the natives. Why didn't it?"

"I don't know," Sansho said. "The seals on it—everything looked official and legit. I have no clue why this is happening."

"It's like the Universe is playing a nasty trick on us. It isn't the planet that's the danger; it's what we don't know or were misled about that's causing the problems."

"Let's leave," Sansho said.

They'd get in massive trouble when they returned, but even a demotion was better than argonic poisoning and dealing with angry Terrans. If they'd known the natives could see them, they'd have confined their flying to night time. Technically, they weren't supposed to engage with the natives at all.

Pulian laughed, but there was an edge to it. "There's only enough energy for one of us to pass through, assuming the interdimensional facets are still operational. If they are, then whoever goes through and gets back to base can get another portal established."

Sansho's squirming innards went cold. "And if they aren't?"

Pulian turned off the visual feed. "That dragon becomes the newest vaporized resident of the interdimensional void, which would at least be a faster death than argonic poisoning."

"Yeah, but there has to be a way out of this that's less...erm...lethally dispersive. How much time does the portal have?"

Pulian waggled a clawed hand. "Another planetary rotation before it collapses completely."

Sansho looked around the capsule. They'd used the smallest one that could accommodate them, but it was meant more for excursions to uninhabited planets than it was a fortress against attack. The energy holding it together came from the portal, exploiting the unique nature of the dimensional opening to give them somewhere to live and gather data. The walls were built to withstand rough weather, made of material spun from the energy of the void between dimensions. It was larger than any of the Terran shelters they'd seen, but it wasn't made of stone like the religious building in the Terran village. If the natives attacked, Sansho wasn't sure how long the capsule would last. But, when the portal flared out, so did their capsule, leaving them exposed to the bipeds.

Sansho's guts twisted, forcing a groan out of him. He asked, "How long will it take for the poisoning to make us incapable of flight?"

"I estimate we have half a Terran day for the poisoning to become that severe."

"Can we filter the argon out of the air in the capsule?"

Pulian put his forehead on the console next to the visual display of the angry Terrans.

"Negative. The infocell hadn't mentioned argon in the atmosphere, so we didn't include air filters."

That meant they'd be ill, on the ground, and unable to fight back when the natives found them. The primitive iron weapons they had were a lot more dangerous in that scenario.

"Well," Sansho stood and, gripping his belly, shuffled away from the console. "Let's make it colder in here to counteract your fever and see what we can do to stabilize the portal so both of us can leave."

"And when the natives come?"

"If the natives come, we'll have a plan." He sounded more confident than he felt.

They sent three distress beacons through the portal, hoping one would reach home, but weren't counting on it. Nothing Sansho did helped to stabilize the portal, though lowering the capsule temperature made Pulian feel better. Sansho's cramps continued unabated, but at least he wasn't vomiting fire. They were both growing weaker, their bright scales and wings turning black-grey as time passed.

When night fell, Sansho lay under the opened command console, panting, trying one last time to fix the portal to return them to Zorix. He'd reprogrammed energy parameters and dimensional coordinates, then resorted to a 'claws-on' approach as a last resort. Tools lay strewn around him on the floor while the conduits inside the console pulsed with less and less power.

It was Pulian, wheezing in his bed, who brought up using the self-destruct function.

"We can't leave, we're too ill to escape the Terrans, and it'd keep them from accessing our technology," Pulian said. "It may be our only option."

Sansho crawled out, scattering tools, and checked the readout. He chuffed in surprise. "Pulian, one of the beacons made it home. Something's coming through."

Sansho widened the portal, turned, and headed to the capsule door, one arm over his abdomen and stars in his visual field. He punched the button to open the door, revealing the now half-black dimensional opening. Leaning against the door's edge, Sansho watched as another dragon stepped through the portal, his scales on fire. He dropped to the soil and rolled, putting out the flames. As tendrils of smoke rose from the dragon's body, the portal behind him winked out. The capsule disappeared, leaving the three dragons alone and unprotected in the small clearing, surrounded by gloomy trees, with the full moon shining down and distant stars twinkling overhead.

Sansho stumbled over to the smoking dragon while Pulian groaned and tried to stand up. The moon bathed everything with grey light, and Sansho realized just how deeply in trouble they were when he saw the distinctive three-pronged head crest and artificial leg.

Clutch Commander Dareban, singed and obviously in pain, glared at him. Sansho's nostrils filled with the stench of burnt scales.

"So, Cadet Sansho," the older dragon said through gritted teeth, "what in Thrasyn's dark heart made the two of you think coming to Terra was a good idea?"

Sansho swallowed, nausea boiling in his guts. "We...ah...wanted to impress you, sir."

"I'm impressed you're still alive, but that's as far as it goes," was the commander's deadpan reply. "Once we get back to Zorix, you'll have a great deal of explaining to do."

Then they heard the shouts of the Terran bipeds and saw the bobbing flames of torches at a distance.

Dareban looked over his shoulder at the incoming natives. "Making friends wherever you go, as usual, I see," he said. "We'll need to get out of here quickly, then."

With a grunt, he stood. Scorched scales ruptured and dropped to the ground as Dareban moved over to Pulian, whose eyes were rolled back in his head as he struggled to breathe. The commander knelt and moved his hands over the downed cadet, then checked the reading on the subcutaneous display on his wrist. He did the same thing to Sansho, who tried and failed to keep his face from showing the agony he felt.

"Argonic poisoning? Why didn't you treat it?"

Sansho watched the approaching points of torches moving through the trees. The natives shouted at one another in a guttural language. They'd nearly reached the clearing where the three dragons were. "The medkit...didn't have anything...for argonic poisoning."

Dareban shook his head, seemingly unconcerned about the coming bipeds. "Well, fine. Get out the spare portal, and we'll head home."

Sansho stared at him. "Spare portal?"

Dareban's gaze was furious. "You didn't bring a spare portal generator?"

"No, Clutch Commander," he said, ashamed. They'd only been able to get one, and it had tested out fine before they'd left. They hadn't felt the need to get another.

"Without permission, you took all the trouble to come to Terra, a planet rated beyond your rank, and didn't bring a spare portal?" Dareban stood and scowled at him. "I don't know which is worse, your stupidity or your hubris."

"Yes, Clutch Commander," was the only reply Sansho could make. He doubled over and spat flaming green bile on the ground.

Dareban stamped it out with his clawed prosthetic foot. "None of that, Cadet."

"No, sir," Sansho choked.

The commander popped open a panel on his metal leg and pulled out an emergency portal generator, handing it to Sansho. He pointed to where the prior portal had been. "Set this up, and we'll get out of here—"

There was a dull thud. Both Sansho and the commander stared in surprise at the iron-tipped wooden shaft that jutted out of Dareban's chest. He let out a gurgle and fell over on his side. He groaned as dark blood seeped from the wound.

The Terrans stepped into the clearing, the flickering light of their torches illuminating angry, determined faces, rough clothing, and crude weapons.

Sansho's stomach heaved, but this time he was glad of it. He stumbled over to the crowd and vomited a thin stream of flaming bile at their feet, forcing them back and creating a tall perimeter of fire around the three dragons. By the light of the burning circle and despite the screams of the Terrans, Sansho activated the portal Dareban had given him. More iron-tipped wooden shafts flew at the dragons, this time spearing Sansho's left wing. He pulled it out with a roar as his wing membrane tore, shooting a stream of liquid fire into the sky that set one of the trees ablaze.

Sansho's body burned from within as his digestive tract destroyed itself. He thought he felt a line of caustic acid roll down the inside of his right leg, showing just how much internal damage there was, but he still took the time to verify the portal's destination. Then, satisfied it would take them back to Zorix, Sansho stumbled over to Pulian. He dragged his limp, incredibly fevered friend to the portal and slipped him through in a jumble of limbs and tail.

The circle of flames was starting to burn out, but the tree he'd set on fire caused the neighboring trees to ignite. The burning trees and the yellow energy of the portal illuminated the clearing, causing the natives to scream in terror and run away, some of them dropping their weapons.

Sansho forced his limbs to work, shaking Dareban. The emergency portal wouldn't last long without a temporal anchor, and Sansho' had no time to establish one.

"Commander!" he shouted. "Commander, can you walk?"

Dareban didn't respond.

Black lines and cracks formed around the edges of the yellow rectangle that was their way home. Sansho lifted the commander and felt something tear inside his body. The pain was excruciating, but he set it aside to put Dareban and then himself through the portal. As the dimensional energies sucked him home, Sansho's mind shut down. He welcomed the darkness.

"Is there anything else you'd like to add, Clutch Commander Dareban?"

General Steros, the judge of the misconduct trial, leaned forward, giving Sansho and Pulian a stern look. The courtroom was austere, in grey stone, with no decoration save the crest of the Clutch Academy under the emblem of the Zorix Empire. Two Itre dragon cadets stood by the door, staring off into space as if they weren't paying attention to the proceedings, but it was all for show. Their numerous mistakes on Terra had been described, examined, and discussed in excruciating detail in that courtroom over the past two days. Sansho and Pulian's massive failure had been the talk of the Academy.

The Drecre cadets sat in silence in the defendant's booth, exhausted and embarrassed. It had taken several days for them to recover from the poisoning and injuries they'd sustained on Terra. Sansho's torn wing graft ached and itched as the court proceedings wound down. Their advocate could do little to help and simply sat there, waiting for his chance to make a final plea for leniency. Sansho doubted it would work.

"No, General," Dareban said. "Sansho's efforts at the end did save both Cadet Pulian and me. It was an impressive show of courage and strength, but their actions were the direct cause of their being in danger in the first place."

"I see," said General Steros."Cadet Sansho, can you give me any reason why I shouldn't kick you and Cadet Pulian out of the Academy?"

Sansho glanced at Pulian, who made a slight nod. They'd discussed the answer to that question while they'd recovered in the sickbay.

Sansho cleared his throat. "With respect, Sir, I cannot. I accidentally killed Terrans. We risked our lives and the life of Commander Dareban. We were poorly prepared for the planetary excursion, and beings suffered as a result. If we had not been so focused on going up in rank, this would not have happened." He drew himself up to his full height. "Cadet Pulian and I are fully prepared to take responsibility for our actions. We made a grave mistake and should face the consequences."

Sansho sat down and waited for the verdict.

General Steros looked thoughtful. "Advocate, do you have anything to add?"

Their advocate, a spindly bureaucratic Secha dragon, stood up and bowed slightly. "General, these are young dragons with their whole life ahead of them. Their marks and performance reviews at the Academy have been outstanding up to this point. They've participated fully and earnestly in the investigation of the incident. As they have said, they are ready to accept the consequences of their mistakes." He sat.

"Cadets Pulian and Sansho, please rise to receive your sentence," the general said.

They stood at attention.

"You are both demoted two ranks. You will spend the next year working with the incoming dragon cadets. It will be your job to help them avoid the mistakes you made by going to Terra on your own. At the end of that year, your conduct shall be re-evaluated, when a decision will be made about your continued presence in the Academy. You are dismissed."

The two cadets left the defendant's booth and exited the room, flanked by their cadet guards and followed by their advocate.

General Steros watched them leave and turned a sardonic eye on Commander Dareban. "I see your Terran Trap worked again," he said. "It was a spectacular failure, just as you intended."

The commander shrugged. "It was easy to sabotage the portal and plant a faked planet dossier on the infocell. These two at least figured out why they were becoming sick. The other victims didn't."

Steros shook his head. "Last time you lost the leg. This time you came close to losing your own life."

Dareban chuckled. "It looked worse than it was. Had to play it up for the cadets."

"Nevertheless, this deception is very risky for all involved. Sansho and Pulian were reckless, arrogant, and careless. They would have perished at the hands of the bipeds if you hadn't intervened. You really think those two are potentially top-level command material?"

Dareban smiled, showing teeth. "They weren't before, but maybe after this, they will be."

Steros stood up and came around from behind his judge's station. "I don't know why you bother."

"Well, General," Dareban said, "big mistakes teach important lessons. Let's hope those two learned theirs."

Five words describe **Victoria Scott**'s knowledge base: "How hard can it be?" This can-do attitude inspired her to learn to speak Latin, to quilt, and to operate a blueprint machine. Sometimes what she tries can be damn hard, like learning Ancient Greek, studying karate, and taking Calculus. Those...were not as successful. Victoria writes Contemporary Fantasy, usually while hanging out with her dog, Red. She teaches Latin by day and earned her Master of Fine Arts in Writing Popular Fiction at Seton Hill University. Her bucket list is simple: drive a Zamboni, cruise down the Nile River, and get a book published. How hard can it be?

Two
Dragons of Now-ish...& Beyond

THE BROOKLYN DRAGON RACING CLUB

BY KATHARINE DOW

IT WAS ANGELO'S TURN to share at the monthly meeting of the Bay Ridge chapter of the Brooklyn Dragon Racing Club. He pulled himself slowly to his feet. The other members watched with sympathy while he straightened his back with a soft grunt. His formidable body, once as strong and solid as a fire hydrant, no longer obeyed him.

"I blame the friggin' umbrellas!" He wiped his callused hands across his belly. "It used to be normal to walk down the street, just minding your own business—"

"That's right, Angelo..."

"And then out of nowhere you'd feel this blast of hot air come at you. Remember that? It'd blow you off your feet half the time. You'd look up at the sky and see a whole flock of dragons fly past at 100 miles an hour screaming like a bunch of teenagers on the Coney Island Cyclone. So what if you were about to get rained on by buckets of guano? It didn't smell so bad. You could even dodge it if you moved quick. Besides, chicks used to swear it was good for the complexion. Remember how they'd scrape it off cars and sell it in those cute little jars? Remember that?"

Angelo looked around the room. Karima, the newest and youngest member of the club, gave him a thumbs-up. Angelo cleared his throat. "Well anyway, like I said, with all these friggin' umbrellas in the neighborhood now, no one looks up at the sky anymore. If they're not hiding under 'em, they're covering their roofs with 'em so the dragons can't land anywhere. Dragons are out on the street like they're nothin'. They got no place to live now. Nothin' to eat. These people don't care about the friendship you can have with the dragon, the companionship. They don't care about the freakin' beauty of a dragon's scales, the way they catch the light. All people think about is not getting pooped on—like that's some kind of life achievement."

He sat back down and crossed his arms. "They hate dragons," he muttered. "It ain't right."

But it wasn't just the new people's animosity toward dragons that broke Angelo's heart. It was everything. His neighborhood had changed around him, and he hated all of it. He wanted his childhood back. He wanted to go back to a world where dragons perched on every flat surface in the borough and sheltered beneath every tough little tree that dared to punch its way through the concrete. He missed opening his bedroom curtains in the morning to the sight of a dragon's inquisitive face squished against the window, wondering why he wouldn't let it into his home. He knew where he stood in that world. He knew what life was about.

Karima, the new member, spoke next. She had just bought a female dragon from an old timer in Queens— her first. She named her dragon Yellow Hook, the name Bay Ridge used to go by until everyone decided to try and make the neighborhood classy back in the 1850's. It was a good name—he'd give her that. But what she thought she was supposed to do with just one dragon, he had no idea. Every dragon needed a family. They just didn't fly right if they tried to go it alone.

He moved closer to look at the photos on her phone of Yellow Hook launching herself into the sky; Yellow Hook dive-bombing a chooch; Yellow Hook stretched out in the sun, some human's keffiyeh draped artistically across her back. She had a powerful chest and great wing structure. She was young, but she looked like she could be a champion already. Angelo looked a little closer. With a sick feeling, he understood why the old timer had let go of such a promising young dragon: she was sick.

The scales around her nostrils were brown instead of gold. With that kind of damage, Yellow Hook's radar would be so stunted she wouldn't be able to find her way from one end of the block to the other. He looked around at the group to see if any of the other guys had noticed. A couple of them were smirking. One made eye contact with him and shrugged his shoulders. Karima showed them another photo of Yellow Hook, her voice bursting with enthusiasm. None of them said a word.

Angelo shuffled over to the club's jury-rigged vending machine and kicked it until it spit out a can of beer.

Luis, the club president, cleared his throat. Karima put her phone away and sat down.

"Before we wrap up for the day," he said, "an announcement. Representative Alcidas, that moron from Staten Island who thinks she represents us, is tryin' to pass a federal urban dragon ban and she wants to open up upstate New York to dragon hunting."

The room erupted into jeers.

Luis scratched his chin. "I guess she hoped we wouldn't notice, or maybe she thinks even if we do, that not enough people care. There's people who will pay a lot to hunt a dragon. I guess that's who she's working for now."

"We'll vote her out—"

"She lied to us—"

"My father fought against people like her in the war—"

"What about dragon racing?" shouted Angelo, his voice breaking through the noise. "Will this mess with that, too?"

Luis fixed his gaze on the ceiling and took a deep breath. "That will be banned too, at least in Brooklyn." He ran a freckled hand over his face. "Look, we should all talk later about what to do, when we've each had a little time to think about a plan."

The club members finished their beers in sullen silence and filtered one by one out of the club, all except for Karima, who sat down at a corner table and pulled out her phone. A picture of Yellow Hook in flight filled the screen. Standing underneath the dragon was a small child, arms thrown wide, his face turned up to the sky. Angelo drifted closer to get a better look.

"Nice picture."

Karima looked up at him with a bright smile. "Thanks. I'm a photographer. Weddings are supposed to be my bread and butter, but lately, all I can think about are dragons. I think I'm in love."

"The guy who sold you your dragon, did he tell you why he was letting her go?"

Karima pulled her hair back in a ponytail and gave him a quizzical look. "He said he was retiring and needed to start finding new homes for his dragons."

"So, he sold off all of his dragons?"

"No, I think just Yellow Hook so far."

"You pay a lot for her?"

"He sold her for like 20 percent of what he said a dragon normally goes for. He said he liked that a young person was getting into the dragon racing business, and a young woman at that. Made him feel like he was contributing to the future."

Angelo wondered if he should say anything. It wasn't really his business. "The thing is, Karima," he said. "I don't think he was being straight with you. You're not gonna win any races with Yellow Hook."

"You noticed the brown scales, didn't you? Don't worry. My grandmother has a recipe for that, from her grandma back in Palestine. I started treating the scales right away and the problem is almost cleared up."

Angelo paused, his beer halfway to his mouth. "You sure? I've never seen a dragon recover from that condition."

"You ever raised dragons outside of New York City?"

"Why would I do that?"

Karima laughed. "I guess I can't argue with that. Why don't you come over and meet Yellow Hook?" she asked. "I could really use some advice about how to train a dragon in Brooklyn. My grandma remembers a lot from her childhood, but she isn't familiar with raising urban dragons and my neighbors have started hassling us, so I'm feeling a lot of pressure. I don't want to give up Yellow Hook. I mean, I just got her, so I'm trying to figure out if there is a way I can be more discrete about having her. People have been doing this here for generations, right? It can't be that hard to pull off."

Angelo studied her face, so alive with enthusiasm and hope. For the first time in years, he wondered if it wasn't over in Bay Ridge, not yet anyway. "I would love to meet Yellow Hook," he finally said. "When do you want me to come over?"

"You free now?"

Angelo finished his beer and walked with her down the street as the sun slid into the bay, bathing the Verrazzano Bridge with the last of its soft, golden light. They passed a cluster of stray dragons huddled around a trashcan, nudging it hopefully. He recognized one of them: Odysseus. He had been a decent flyer at one point, huge at almost six feet in length, until the scales around his nostrils turned brown and cracked, and the jerk who trained him stopped feeding him. No point in racing a dragon that can't find its way home. Angelo made a note to himself to stop by later with a bag of meat.

As if sensing his thoughts, Odysseus lifted his head to look at Angelo and allowed his scales to glow for a moment. Angelo nodded back, his heart heavy.

Karima lived only three blocks away from his place, in the sort of squat brick row house common in his part of Brooklyn, complete with decorative silver bars lining the balcony and covering the front door. A single air conditioning unit leaned precariously out of a second-story window.

"My parents moved out of the city a couple of years ago, but I decided to stay here with my grandma," she said. "I like it here. It isn't the sort of neighborhood most people pass through—not on purpose, anyway. So, if you live here, you're that special type of person who would choose to spend the best years of your life going back and forth on the world's slowest subway line. It's next-level stubborn. I admire that."

"The mighty R train, defender of Bay Ridge."

"Exactly. Plus, as a photographer and an artist, I kind of like that this neighborhood belongs to me. I like that I can walk the streets and no one is shooting a music video or making a student film. In fact, the only film ever made here was about a guy desperate to leave. This place is so deeply uncool, it's perfect. As a photographer, I don't have to share the streets, and now that I have Yellow Hook in my life, I feel like the sky belongs to me, too. I know this is all in my head, but there's something romantic about the idea and I don't really care if it's real. Anyway, here she is."

They emerged onto the flat roof of her home and came face-to-face with the most powerful young dragon Angelo had ever seen in person. At least five feet in length, the muscles covering her short forelegs were knotted and lean. In a year or two, they would bulge with muscle. Her chest was wide, and her snout was covered in dozens of tiny scales, indicating a powerful radar. He leaned down to examine her scales. Unlike when the photo was taken, the brown was barely visible. She wasn't going to get lost in the middle of a race anytime soon. She tilted her head to the side, staring at Angelo with an unsettling intensity.

She waddled over to him and butted her snout against his palm.

"She likes you."

"She's curious," he responded. "My hands smell like dragons and raw meat."

Karima knelt next to Yellow Hook and scratched her underneath her chin. Angelo studied the muscles that rippled under Yellow Hook's scales every time she shifted. The jerk who tried to rip off Karima would die when he realized what he had done. The thought filled him with delight. He wondered if Karima's recipe could help Odysseus too, or if it was too late for the old dragon.

"You start training her yet?" he asked. "I'm taking one of mine out this weekend. You can come if you want. Since she's alone, it might help her learn how to find her way home if she trains with one of my dragons, in case her snout is still a problem."

"That would be amazing. I would love that."

"They should probably meet first to make sure they get along. Mine's named Smokey. He's big, like she'll be. He's been depressed since his mate died, so I've been trying to spend more individual training time with him."

"I'm sorry to hear about that."

"It was a freak accident. She bounced off one of those new extra-reinforced windows those anti-dragon jerks are installing everywhere. Broke her shoulder and fell about a hundred feet. There was nothing anyone could do."

"How horrible."

"You wouldn't believe how many dragons can't figure out those new windows. The old ones think they can just smash through them like the old days, and the young ones don't know they should fly around instead of through. They don't realize the danger until it's too late."

Karima ran her hand slowly over Yellow Hook's scales and Angelo noticed that a fist-sized patch on her side was crusted with blood. Yellow Hook opened her eyes and stretched. "I worry about her safety, Angelo. The neighbors have been hassling her. Throwing things at her when she leaves my roof."

"What do you think about that, Yellow Hook?" Angelo asked.

Yellow Hook's scales thinned to a translucent sheen, and she shrank before them, her body bunched into a tight, compact knot. A sooty puddle of guano appeared underneath her belly and spread across the roof.

Angelo chuckled. "Looks like she doesn't like your neighbors, either."

Yellow Hook expanded back into her natural form and lifted into the air. She slowly circled the roof and then dive-bombed a neighbor's parked car.

"That's it, Yellow Hook! You show 'em," he said.

Yellow Hook swooshed right past a living room widow. The faint sound of a family screaming reached them on the roof. Angelo cheered.

"Don't encourage her, Angelo. I taught her how to do that last week, but I've been feeling bad about it ever since."

"Hey, she's got as much right to this city as we do. You know dragons don't migrate. They stay put. Yellow Hook's family has been around here longer than mine has, longer than any of us."

"I know, I know."

He glanced at his watch and his stomach grumbled. "How does 6 a.m. sound?"

"For training? Wow. That's early."

Angelo didn't wait for her response. He was late for dinner.

Angelo pulled up in front of Karima's house in a white windowless van. He opened the van's back door and was immediately enveloped in a cloud of smoke. Coughing and squeezing his eyes shut, he gestured to Karima to bring Yellow Hook over.

Karima stared at his van, wide-eyed, while Yellow Hook gracefully flew toward the smoke and landed with an ominous thud somewhere inside. Angelo slammed the door shut and hurried back to the front.

"Hurry up, we don't got a lotta time before Smokey burns another hole in the floorboard and falls underneath the van again."

"Doesn't he realize what he's doing?" Karima asked, buckling in.

"I ask myself that question every day."

"Where we going?"

"Coney Island. We'll let them out at the beach and then see if they can make their way home. The trip to the beach should give them enough time to get acquainted, but not too much time, if you know what I mean. Should be just enough time for her to be desperate to follow him home. They'll probably head to my place, not yours, but we can get Yellow Hook home from there, no problem. You got her tagged?"

"Yes. I can follow her path on my phone."

"Good. Back in the day, we didn't have that technology. We'd lose 'em all the friggin' time. Sometimes they got confused and went the wrong way, sometimes they found some food and forgot what they were supposed to be doing, and sometimes people stole 'em. It was anarchy. Loved every minute of it."

Angelo found a spot near the aquarium and ran to the back of the van. He opened the doors and the dragons hopped out onto the road. A car swerved around them, tires screeching. Smokey and Yellow Hook ignored it and sat down in the middle of the road.

"This is the tricky part, getting them to fly after they've spent this much time smoking and cuddling."

"Have you thought about getting a van with windows?"

"I don't want the competition to see who I'm training. That's one of the reasons I like getting out here early."

"What's the other reason?"

Angelo looked away. He thought about meeting up with the guys for coffee before they trained their dragons. He thought about how empty of dragons the beach was now. He thought about how awkward it was, to be the only person still out there doing this most of the time.

"Smokey," he bellowed, ignoring her question. "Get it together. It's time to train the new kid." He turned to face Karima. "Watch what Smokey does first, all my best dragons have learned how to do it. If Yellow Hook is smart enough, she'll mimic him."

Smokey arched his back and launched himself into the air, his spackled scales blending into the dim morning light. For a minute, they could follow his movement through the sky, a faint smudge against clouds. Then he disappeared.

"What is he doing?" asked Karima.

"They usually release around twenty or thirty dragons at a time. A dragon that learns how to blend into the sky can slam against a couple of the others and scramble their radars without anyone noticing. Of course, it only works if he does it right at the beginning of the race when it's real chaotic and it's hard to keep an eye on individual dragons. Smokey knows he's got to be visible to the judges again before the dragons start spacing out."

"Has he ever been caught?"

"No, but one of the other dragons I used to race got caught once. Problem was the entire group of dragons decided to play the same trick, and they all disappeared from the sky at the same time. Imagine a big blue empty sky mysteriously filled with the sound of dragons colliding. All of us owners were banned from racing dragons for an entire year. Would have been worse except for the fact that hardly anyone was left to race after that."

Yellow Hook sniffed the air and shuffled closer to Karima. Smokey snapped back into sight and she launched herself into the air after him. Smokey dove to meet her, his body streaking through the air like a falling star. Yellow Hook hovered in the air, then whipped her body around his, like water circling a drain, her body flashing in and out of sight.

"I had no idea they could fly like that," Karima whispered. "I mean, I've seen them racing before, but this is really something else."

"She's a natural. I think you've got yourself a champion."

Angelo whistled at Smokey. The older dragon pointed his body in the direction of Bay Ridge and began to fly home. Yellow Hook followed closely behind.

"So, what now?" Karima asked.

"Smokey knows the way home. Looks like she likes him enough to follow him, so we don't have to worry too much about her getting disoriented along the way. You only need to try this a couple of times from a few different locations, a bit farther away each time, before Yellow Hook will learn all the landmarks she needs to get home. When she's finished healing, if that thing your grandma knows works like it's supposed to, her radar will make sure she knows what direction to fly in if you enter her in any really challenging races. Just try not to move too much, or maybe ever."

"What's the farthest Smokey has ever flown in a race?"

"Chicago to New York."

Karima whistled. "How much did that make you?"

"Back in those days, you could make a lot more than you can now, but let's just say it was enough to buy me and my wife our house."

"What's that race worth now? Enough to pay off my student loans?"

"Enough for a car, maybe."

Karima watched as the dragons disappeared behind an apartment building. "Should we get going?"

"They'll get home a lot faster than we will, so there's no point in rushing."

"Want to grab a coffee, in that case? We passed an open bodega on the way here. I can barely keep my eyes open. Not a morning person."

"I know that place. Last time I got a coffee there, I found half a cockroach at the bottom of my cup."

"When was that?" Karima asked, laughing.

"Forty years ago. I guess I could give them another chance."

"You sure? I don't want to rush you." Karima pulled out her phone. Yellow Hook was already halfway home.

"Hop in the van. We can drink horrible coffee on the drive back."

While they drove, Karima pulled out her phone and watched Yellow Hook's progress across Brooklyn. She had less than six miles to fly. If she and Smokey kept up their pace, the whole trip would take ten minutes.

"I think they went to my roof," Karima said.

"No kidding? That's incredible. I didn't think she would manage to find it, since she's not quite healed yet."

"I know, right?"

They waited for a light to turn and sipped their coffee in companionable silence. Angelo pulled off the plastic cover and tried to look through the brown liquid to the bottom. "Found any cockroaches yet?"

"I've decided not to look."

The light changed and Angelo put the cover back on. "That's not the worst idea."

They turned on her street and were greeted by the sight of flashing lights and at least three police cars. An elderly woman wearing a long billowy dress stood in the middle of the street. "My grandma," Karima gasped. "They're surrounding my grandma."

Angelo slammed on the brakes and stopped the van in the middle of the street. "Let me handle this. I know one of those guys. He's my cousin's kid."

"What is this about? What are you doing?" Karima shouted, ignoring Angelo.

Angelo hurried to catch up with her. "Jimmy, it's me, Angelo. What's the problem?"

"Got a call from the neighbors, a noise complaint. Apparently, they got some dragons here."

"It's legal to own dragons."

"Yeah, I know, but maybe the lady might consider keeping them somewhere else or something."

It was then that Angelo noticed the extraordinary series of noises coming from the roof, loud chuffing followed by low growling roars.

Karima looked over at him, her arms around her grandma. "Is that what I think it is?" Her grandma covered her ears with her hands. The old woman was shaking with laughter. "Is that why the neighbors are complaining?"

"I think our dragons have fallen in love, Karima."

"Oh, no. I'm so sorry."

Angelo shrugged. This wasn't the worst thing that could happen. Maybe they could even be a team. With Smokey's experience and Yellow Hook's strength, he and Karima could make some decent money.

"Jimmy, you wanna tell us who made the call?" Angelo said.

"Can't do that, Angelo."

He saw a curtain twitch from a ground floor apartment across the street. It might not mean anything. He would probably look, too, if there were a bunch of cops in front of his place.

"If no one is doing anything illegal, there's not much point to this visit, is there, Jimmy?"

"You know we gotta check things out."

Angelo pulled out his phone. "I'm calling your mom."

"Oh, come on, Angelo. I'm just doin' my job. Don't call my mom."

"Since when is hassling people about their dragons your job?"

"We got a call—"

"Hey! Mary, how you doin'? Guess who I'm standing here with? It's that missing son of yours. Exactly, the one who never calls anymore. Hey, Jimmy, your mom's on the phone." Angelo looked around. Jimmy was already in his car, frantically trying to make a U-turn in the narrow road, his lights flashing. The other cops were ambling back into their cars.

"Mary, I gotta go. Just realized my battery is almost out. But Jimmy wants to talk to you, definitely. He told me he did. I heard he's finally ready to propose to that girlfriend of his. No, not that one, the one with the hair. Yeah, the one you don't like. You should probably call him right away before he does it. Take your time. He needs his mother to talk some sense into him. Okay, good. Talk to you soon."

Karima's grandma had gone back inside the house. Karima sat on the front steps alone, shoulders slumped.

"You okay?" Angelo asked her.

Karima pulled herself to her feet. "It felt so good, taking Yellow Hook on her first training run. But what if it's like this all the time? My poor grandma."

"How many dragons can you afford to own?"

"Maybe one more, that's all. Why?"

Angelo made a face. "What if someone paid you to keep more on your roof? You got the time?"

"Like, how many more?" Karima angrily wiped away her tears.

Angelo shrugged. "I'll be back this evening. I've dealt with neighbors like this before. I know what to do."

"What does that mean?"

"Don't worry about the noise up there," he shouted over his shoulder. "Smokey's just trying to sound tough for her. He'll get tired eventually."

"Angelo, what are you planning? I think we should just let it go."

Angelo got back in the van and leaned out the window. "You gonna let these people push you around? Who do you want to win this thing, you or your lousy neighbors?"

"I don't know."

Angelo gave her a hard look.

"Me," she said. "I want to win."

"Then get in the van. We got some work to do. The first thing we gotta do is get you some more dragons. Immediately. Then, we're gonna get you another dragon every time they call the cops. Don't worry about the cost; that's what the Racing Club is good for. Whenever a member is in trouble, the others will step in."

"Will that work?"

Angelo looked up at the desolate sky. His heart racing, he dared to imagine it full of dragons.

"This is Brooklyn," he said with confidence. "Of course, it will work. At least one more time."

Odysseus had never had it so good. Whenever the rain fell, his new human had a tarp he could sit under, cuddled up with lots of other dragons. When it was sunny, he could stretch his body out on her hot flat roof, far away from moving cars, and sleep for as long as he liked. Comfortable in a nest on the roof was a cluster of eggs, guarded by another old-timer.

He lifted his head and watched a flock of slightly lost young dragons fly past, training for their first race. Yellow Hook and Smokey flew on either side, keeping them in loose formation. He heard his human, Karima, calling to them in her clear voice, guiding them home. It wasn't time to eat yet, though, so he launched himself into the air and circled past the diner he used to beg from, just in case there was anyone he knew there.

He flew in a wide loop and released a load of guano on top of the neighbor's car, just like his human had asked him to do. Then he flew straight toward the Verrazzano Bridge, his scales glowing softly in the light, to join the dozens of others who shared his roof.

Katharine Dow is the author of "The Funeral Company," a short story in *Working Futures: 14 Speculative Stories About the Future of Work*. Dow is a graduate of Seton Hill's Master of Fine Arts in Writing Popular Fiction program. Raised in Kenya by U.S. born parents, and a subsequent resident of six other countries, Dow currently lives in Brooklyn, New York with her spouse and a cat. You can visit her at her blog, katharinedow.com or find her on twitter, @suggestionize.

RESORTING TO REVENGE: A SAM BRODY STORY

BY K.W. TAYLOR

"WHEN YOU AGREED YOU needed time off and that we could go on a vacation, you also agreed I was in charge," Heather said. "And a weekend at this resort lodge was within budget and driving distance."

"But the *woods*? Where the bears live?" I asked.

"Are you afraid of bears, Sam?"

"I'm not *not* afraid of bears."

"You do realize you are a telekinetic, dragon-slaying badass with supernatural powers, right?"

The road took a sharp, winding curve, and I tried not to let my stomach lurch as I steered. "To be fair, I have never technically battled a bear. How do we know they're not deadlier than dragons?"

"Because dragons have evil intent. Dragons' main objective in this world is to kidnap, abuse, and kill humans, all the while masquerading as regular people."

I gave Heather a sidelong glance. "And you're saying bears don't do any of those things?"

"You also battled interdimensional monsters and ghosts," Heather said, completely ignoring my stupid comment. "I can't believe what a weenie you are about nature."

"Nature is less predictable than dragons! As you yourself said, dragons are pretty single-minded and pure evil. And it's my job as the chosen modern-day knight to slay them before regular folks know they secretly walk among us. Bears, though? Nature? My powers are no match against that stuff!"

"Mmkay."

"Besides, on this trip, we're not magically enhanced types, obviously," I said. "I am a radio show host, and you are my producer, and we're just a normal couple who met at normal work. No telekinetic superpowers for me, no newly-emerging ESP empathy type skills for you."

"I mean, those *are* our actual jobs, Sam."

"That's why it's a great cover."

Despite the lighthearted tone of our conversation, I couldn't help harkening back to what the first dragon I ever encountered had done, how it had posed as a coworker and nearly destroyed the woman I loved. This pain nagged at me more often than I cared to admit, and so I maintained the façade of an asshole, even as I constantly feared for Heather's health and safety. I gave her a smile, which she returned, and I told myself nothing bad could possibly happen on this getaway. It would just be a few days of peace and quiet.

As I was about to give up on ever finding our destination, the curves in the road straightened out, and over a hill, a huge log cabin rose as if from thin air. It was beautiful enough to make even my cynical heart sing at the prospect of a weekend here.

The sun shone on grass so green it looked almost surreal. The air smelled clean, pollution-free, and floral. The lodge itself was long and low, with a wall of floor-to-ceiling windows at the front behind a row of wooden rocking chairs on the porch. Some of these were occupied, and as I pulled myself out from behind my steering wheel, one of these occupants rose from his seat and came down the steps.

"Hello!" the man called. "I'm Ned, you two must be Heather and Stan." He had an Australian accent and a very strange fashion sense that looked as if he were auditioning for a music video in the mid-1980s. His pants were bright red, and he wore a skinny leather tie over a white dress shirt. Not exactly hiking-in-the-woods attire.

"It's Sam," I corrected.

Ned cocked his head to one side. "I'm sorry, what?"

"Sam, not Stan," I said, this time with a little edge in my voice. Heather shot me a look. "What?" I said. "Sorry, I prefer it when people get my name right."

Ned laughed. "Forgive me. *Sam*. Of course." Ned pulled one of our bags from the back without being asked. "I'd be so delighted to show you two to your cabin. Most of the other weekenders are here already." He nodded to the porch. "You'll meet everyone at dinner, but from left to right is Val, Drew, Roger, Lexi, Merin, and Gemma." He laughed. "Did I get that all right, everyone?"

The porch rockers all laughed and waved. "Good job, Ned!" a man called out.

"Hey, you two!" one of the women said with a wave.

I glared at Heather. "I thought this was a *romantic* getaway," I muttered.

"It was supposed to be," Heather stage-whispered.

"And it will be!" Ned announced. "We just like to take our meals family style. It is a bit social here, I admit."

I tried to smile, but I suspected it came out more like a grimace.

"Your cabin! Let's get to it!" Ned announced. He took two of our bags, I took another, and Heather was left free as a bird as we trudged behind the lodge to find several smaller buildings. Ned led us to the second one in the half-circle, a cabin with mauve curtains.

Ned unlocked the door and pushed it open, and I had to admit it was nice: one big room, but spacious, with high ceilings. There was a fireplace in one corner and a huge bed against the far wall. The bathroom was glass-walled and sported a huge shower. Everything smelled of cedar. "Your hot tub is on the back porch, and then as I said we take meals in the lodge. On your first night here, you *must* join us for cocktails and board games after dinner."

Heather poked me in the ribs when she caught my less-than-thrilled expression. "Cocktails," she repeated. "You like cocktails."

"I hope they're strong," I said.

"That's the spirit!" Ned said. He handed me the key. "I'll leave you to it. Dinner's at six! Tonight is a pasta buffet."

As soon as Ned swept out, I dropped the bags and collapsed on the leather loveseat at the center of the room.

"Please don't make me go to this game night," I implored Heather.

She responded with a raised eyebrow. "I can try to make it worth your while."

The next half hour's events caused me to be in her debt, and that's how we found ourselves in the main lodge's enormous great room after a decent dinner. Ned cleared the dishes away, replacing them with several boxed board games. Our end of the table got a Scrabble set. Heather set it up as two people nearby slid in closer.

"Mind if we get in on this?"

I looked across the table, and a man around my age—mid-thirties—with a scraggly brown goatee going slightly silver held out his hand. "Hi, I'm Drew."

I shook. "Sam. This is Heather."

"And I'm Val." His companion was seated next to me, a woman with a tidy bob dyed a shade of green matching the frames of her glasses. Both had elaborate tattoos winding down their arms. "Big fan of word games, so if you'll have us, you might lose."

Heather laughed. "We'll see. I'm pretty good, too."

We played amiably enough, but about halfway into the game, my head started pounding. I wasn't sure if it was the shock of being in unpolluted air for the first time in decades, or some kind of sixth sense associated with my powers I'd just started to understand, but either way it didn't feel great. I excused myself to make a cup of coffee, hoping maybe I was just under-caffeinated. "Skip me this turn," I said, making my way to the ample kitchen connected to the great room. I passed two other groups of people huddled over games. My head pounded a bit more.

Coffee, I needed coffee.

I set about operating the single-cup brewing machine that used little eco-unfriendly pods instead of honest-to-goodness loose coffee. After struggling with it for a moment, Ned took over for me, giving me what was supposed to be a good-natured mocking for not understanding the brewer, which of course made me dislike him even more.

"Decaf?" Ned asked.

"No, regular."

Ned seemed offended. "But it's almost eight o'clock! You'll be up for ages!"

Yeah, and you'll be up all night nursing a black eye if I don't get my caffeine, I wanted to say. "Hey, what can I say, I'm addicted!" I punctuated the overly cheerful sentence with a hearty fake laugh, which Ned joined me in.

"Whatever you say, old chap." He finished making my coffee and asked how I took it.

"Black," I said.

"I read a study saying people who take their coffee black are often sociopaths." Another chortle from old Ned, and the stabbing pain in my head pulsated.

"Yep, that's me, a sociopath." I sipped the coffee, which tasted strong and bitter and absolutely perfect. I decided I was done dealing with strangers and returned to Heather to announce I was turning in.

Heather pouted. "But you were doing so well!" she said, pointing to my feeble score.

"Avenge me," I said.

I waved goodnight to Drew and Val and trundled off into the sunset with my sociopath coffee and a spring in my step. Getting away from people was a real mood-lifter indeed.

I opened the lodge door to find myself greeted with a green, scaly snout. "I'm hiding in plain sight." The words came out of the gaping, sharp-toothed mouth of a reptile so large it took up the entire first floor of the building, based on what little I could see through broken windows and fire-ravaged holes in the wood. "I'm in your midst, and you don't even know."

I backed up. A dragon followed me here. Big, bad, nasty things tended to follow me everywhere I went, but that was exactly what I was trying to get away from on this vacation.

I held up a hand, directed all my focus and will into my palm, and a huge log came out from the pile of rubble from the lodge and shot directly at the dragon's face. Before I could see where—or even if—it landed a blow, I sat bolt upright in bed. Heather slept soundly beside me.

Our cabin was fine. There was nobody here. But I knew this wasn't just a nightmare.

I smelled coffee and stirred to find Heather putting a cup on my nightstand.

"Breakfast soon?" she asked, ruffling my hair. "I'm going to hop in the shower. Feeling better?"

My head wasn't pounding anymore, but I wasn't feeling better, not while I knew there was a monster nearby. "Sort of," I said. I took her hand and eased her to sit down on the bed next to me. I sat up against the pillows and relayed my nightmare.

Heather gave me an indulgent smile. "I don't sense anything bad here." Then she exhaled a short laugh. "Well, maybe the fashion sense on that one chick, Lexi. Like, those barrettes are huge and ridiculous. Nobody wears those outside of a reality show, especially not to spend a few days in the woods. Is she one of those influencer people? Ugh."

Most of the words she said didn't make sense, but I assumed this was me being a luddite. "No, but it was very vivid," I explained. "Totally like the dreams I had the last time I found out someone nearby was a dragon. It's part of my whole dragon-detecting skill set."

Heather could sense the emotions and intentions and—to some degree—thoughts of otherworldly creatures. It wasn't a psychic skill, not quite, and it was newly acquired, so she was still feeling out how to use it to our advantage.

"I've been kind of passively reading people," she said. She carefully laid out her lack of sensing anything bad. "Nobody is a dragon. At least I doubt it, based on what I've been able to tell so far."

"I hope you're right."

Somehow, I found myself roped into a hike I was assured was "not arduous," yet the trek from the lodge to the actual wooded path itself seemed to take forever. I had barely quit smoking, and my blackened, thirtysomething lungs were not used to exercise of any kind, even the gentle variety. Still, I was trying to appease Heather and trying to shove the memory of the nightmare out of my mind, and so here I was, tagging along after the couple we played Scrabble with the night before. They were talking with my girlfriend while I staggered along, wondering if I should have put on sunblock, bug spray, or both. The air was crisp, hovering between summer and fall, and I had to admit this nature thing might have some nice things about it. Back home, it would be hotter and smellier just due to the mix of smog, concrete, and random strangers' BO as people crowded the sidewalks. This...this was better. I didn't dare admit that, though.

Val seemed very quiet but sassy when she did speak up, but Drew was a blowhard. Not as bad as Ned, but still cocky and irritating. I was supposed to be the only cocky, irritating jerk in a crowd, so someone stealing my thunder annoyed me. I tuned back in to the conversation he was having with Heather, talking about "ley lines" and the benefits of sleeping inside of a pyramid.

"Like a literal pyramid?" Heather asked, frowning.

"Anything shaped that way will do." The way he laughed made it seem like Heather's question was the stupidest thing he'd ever heard.

I was starting to loathe him.

But was loathsomeness evidence he wasn't human? If that were true, lots of people might assume *I* wasn't human, and despite having some nifty things I could do with magical energy, I was not a dragon, monster, alien, or general creepy crawly. Drew, though...Drew had a chaotic demeanor.

Suddenly, Val stopped and looked at the sky. "I think I felt a raindrop."

The clouds moved swiftly overhead. I glanced back toward where the lodge should be, but now everything was behind the rise of a hill, and we were only halfway to the hiking trail.

"Do we turn back or forge ahead?" Heather asked. She nodded at the woods. "We'll get some natural cover there, and it might ease up."

A crack of thunder sounded, and I flinched.

Drew shook his head. "The likelihood of getting struck by lightning is astronomical." He shoved his glasses up his nose.

"It's reduced even more if we're inside," I pointed out. I turned and headed back. "I'll make cocoa!" I called, hoping that would entice at least Heather to follow me.

Before I could get partway up the hill, though, the sky seemed to unzip itself, and the rain was immediate and torrential. I looked back to find everyone following now. I broke into as fast a jog as I could. I shook myself out on the welcome mat before opening the door.

Behind me, Heather looked a lot worse for wear. "I'm going back to our cabin," she said.

"I'm making something hot to drink, and I'll meet you back there once this lets up," I said. I wanted to interrogate some folks, feel them out, and see who might be stalking me, if it wasn't Drew. He and Val didn't even stop at the lodge and were already hightailing it to their own cabin next to ours.

Heather pulled her jacket over her head and made the sprint across the lawn. I shut the door and could smell something coming from the kitchen. Dinner already? It seemed early, but if Ned was making a complicated dish, maybe he had to start.

But maybe it was a potion. A spell. Something magical.

I took a step from the foyer to the kitchen to find that indeed Ned was there, puttering and humming. "Good smells in here," I remarked.

Ned spun around. "Stan! Sorry, no, Sam." He laughed. "I don't know why that's so hard for me."

"I don't know either." I shrugged. "But whatever you're doing would definitely be outside my wheelhouse, so different things are hard for different people."

Ned didn't seem to take my comment as the thinly veiled insult I intended it to be, so much so that when I offered to help with dinner he accepted. It turned out to be a stew, a cheese sauce, and a complicated bread, none of which appeared to be magical. I gently grilled him as we worked, but the only thing Ned seemed to be hiding was a love of midcentury musical theatre, the versatile properties of yeast, and a tendency to get flour on his shirtsleeves.

The rain died down as we finished, and I helped Ned get the dinner set out for serving. Other guests trickled in, grabbing bowls and plates and glasses. Heather wasn't back, and I reached in my back pocket for my phone to call her, only to find it wasn't there. I pictured it sitting on my nightstand.

"Hey, save back some for my girlfriend," I said to Ned. "She's probably taking a nap."

"Of course." Ned filled a plastic bowl with stew and popped a lid on it. "Take this with you if she sleeps through."

"Will do." I joined the others at the table. Everyone took a place there, and as we dug into our food, the storm ratcheted up, culminating in a crack of thunder, followed by sudden darkness as the power went out. There were groans and surprised gasps. It was still early enough that a sliver of light came through the floor-to-ceiling windows, but it was muted and growing dimmer by the minute.

"Does anybody have a phone?" I asked. "I want to make sure Heather's okay."

"Here you go," the man seated next to me said.

"Thanks, uh—"

"Roger," he reminded me.

"Right, yes." I tapped at the phone icon and punched in Heather's number, but the phone let out a series of beeps and informed me it had no service. "Do you not get a signal here?"

"I forgot I wasn't using data, just wi-fi," Roger said. "Anybody else got any bars?"

Val and Drew shook their heads, as did others. "Ned, your internet isn't on the cable system?" asked one woman. I remembered her from the night before; she had long, stringy brown hair and was extremely thin.

I couldn't recall her name, but when Ned answered her, he called her Gemma. The conversation devolved into technobabble that I couldn't parse, but basically because the power went out, we were all cut off from communication.

There was a cracking sound, followed by a loud crash. I jumped to my feet and hurried to the front door, heedless of any danger and focused on making sure Heather was okay.

"Whoa, slugger, come on." Someone pulled at the back of my shirt, and I swung around to face Drew.

"I have to make sure Heather's safe," I said. "I can't call her, she's not far, but if something fell out there, I can't sit here and wonder if she's trapped under a log!"

"Man, you're gonna get *yourself* killed if you go out there," Drew protested. He turned back to the group. "Nobody's got bars? We can't call out at *all*?"

Ned snapped his fingers. "I think I remember a CB in the cellar." He scurried off.

"What good's that gonna do?" I demanded. "It's not like she has a CB in our cabin!"

"We can call the park ranger," Roger said. "He can go out and look. He'll be a lot more equipped than we are in an emergency."

While Roger had a good point, none of them knew I was a one-man arsenal of telekinetic power. If Heather was trapped, I could help her faster than any dopey ranger with nothing but a radio, a golf cart, and a set of khakis. As I was about to come up with a way to leave the lodge, the door sprang open to reveal Heather, ensconced in a drenched poncho.

I hugged her tightly. "You're all right!"

"Yeah, but a big oak tree isn't." She wound her arms around my waist. "It split right in half. I saw it happen from our cabin, and it fell right across the only road off the property. The power is out everywhere, from what I can see."

"Do you have any bars?" Drew asked her.

Heather pulled her phone from her pocket and checked. "Nope." Another discussion about the internet ensued, and Ned reemerged from the basement to report that the CB's batteries were dead.

"I guess we're stuck here," Heather said.

"We saved you some dinner." I steered Heather into the kitchen and retrieved her serving of stew. "Might as well eat if we're stuck."

Heather gave me a peck on the cheek. "So is everyone here at the lodge, then?"

I shrugged. "I guess I was focused on making sure *you* got here."

Heather noted the people still milling near the front door and those talking in semi-panicky tones around the table. "Where's Merin?" she asked, plucking a piece of bread from the plateful on the kitchen island.

"Who?"

"Merin," Val piped up. She was still sitting at the table, tapping away at her phone screen as if it should be doing something. "You know, she almost went hiking with us earlier? She's a political scientist at State College?"

I shook my head. "Doesn't ring a bell."

Heather whapped me lightly on the arm. "You know her," she said, her tone accusatory. "You told me at breakfast she looks like Vanessa Williams."

"Oh, *her*!" I thought back fondly on my brief notice of the woman who was statuesque and striking. I hadn't caught her name or even paid attention to anything she said, though. "No, I haven't seen her since this morning."

"She's staying here in the lodge," Val said, "not in a cabin."

"There's a couple of suites upstairs," Roger said. "We should all check."

"I'm sure she's fine," Heather said. "Weather like this can sometimes be great for sleeping. She probably grabbed a good book when the hiking didn't pan out and then took a nap."

"And missed dinner?" I lifted one shoulder in a half shrug. "Ned and I were loud, and then food smells, and thunder—it would wake me up is all I'm saying."

Heather put her bowl down, and people split up into loose teams. Ned assured us the basement was empty, but Heather checked anyway, and I followed Roger upstairs. He went left, I went right, and it wasn't long before I found a half-open door. I knocked and called Merin's name. When I got no answer, I pushed it the rest of the way open.

Merin was on the floor, her hair flowing out around her head like a dark halo. She appeared to be unconscious. I immediately called out to Roger for help. I patted her cheek.

"Hey, are you okay?" I leaned in and felt a trickle of breath against my face. Roger joined me and began first aid, assessing if she needed CPR. He instructed me to get Merin a bottle of water from her mini fridge. When I stood, I noticed a set of marks across the wallpaper—long, jagged, and in a set of three, as if a reptile had slashed it with gigantic claws. There was also a faint tinge of gray on the otherwise-pale surface, almost like smoke damage.

There was a dragon here.

I tried to keep the others from looking at the wall, because I was honestly not sure how to explain the state of it. Remodeling, maybe? I'd have to hang something up to hide it before we all checked out, so that at least Ned wouldn't notice it later.

I gave Roger the water, and Gemma joined us and began helping. It took a while, but soon the patient seemed to come around. "She's okay," Gemma announced. Soon Merin was sitting up, propped against a pillow.

"Who did this to you?" Roger asked her.

Merin shook her head. "I don't know. I came in here to get something, and then everything went black."

Whoever did this did it as a warning to me. There was even a scent in the air reminding me of the dragon I fought not so very long ago, a sort of charred electricity, mingled with a distinct dampness having nothing to do with the storm raging outside.

I couldn't wait any longer. "Roger, come with me. We have to get everyone together."

"But Merin..." Roger protested. "Someone should stay with her."

"I'll stay," Gemma said. "I'm a volunteer firefighter. I have some basic EMS training."

I nodded. "Okay, good." I swept out with Roger at my heels, and as I passed through the kitchen and dining area, I urged everyone to join me in the theatre room across the hall. It was the only room where I could address everyone facing me. The sound of the rain was muffled due to the lack of windows, and the low ceilings might offer a modicum of protection against a dragon actively shapeshifting. Roger found some candles, and soon the entire collective was seated in comfortable chairs while I paced in front of the blank movie screen on the wall.

I gave a brief rundown of what I thought happened to Merin, leaving out the supernatural elements and couching the incident as merely a physical attack. "Where was everyone?" I asked. "I know Ned and I can vouch for each other in the late afternoon, and Heather, Drew, and Val and I were out together earlier in the day. It's unclear when it happened, so please give your whereabouts from breakfast onward."

Heather sat in the front row but looked all around the room. I knew she was trying to get an empathic reading on everyone as they rattled off their alibis. I tried to tamp down my natural instinct to be snarky and instead adopted a calmer, more persuasive demeanor. That seemed to help everyone get comfortable talking.

Not everyone had an airtight alibi. Heather was alone in our cabin, and Val and Drew could only corroborate they'd been alone together. Roger and Lexi had been watching a movie in this very room, though, and they were able to describe a good portion of the plot while claiming neither of them had seen it before today. The fact that they were relative strangers and not a couple who had reason to stand up for each other had me convinced.

"Let's take five," I said after a bit. "I want to check on Merin again."

People began talking amongst themselves, and Heather pulled me into a corner. "Everyone seems normal and not up to anything," she whispered to me. "But, Sam, there's one person absent." Heather raised her eyebrow at me. "If it's really what you think it is, I think it's obvious who did this."

"You think Merin faked it?"

Heather rolled her eyes. "No, it was the other one. Gemma."

"Gemma only stayed with Merin because she has emergency training," I said.

"Gemma's also the only one nobody said they were with," she pointed out.

Damn. How could I have been so stupid? I raced out of the room.

As I rounded the staircase landing, I focused my energy, searching through the dim light for things I could use as weapons. I held out my palm, and half the bannister railing off the top of the staircase flew into my outstretched hand.

Before I could reach the guest room, I was halted by the hulking form of a dragon in the middle of shifting between its human glamour and its real size and shape. The face was still somewhat human. I recognized Gemma's angular features in the rapidly elongating snout covered in green scales. She wasn't yet too large to fit in the hallway, however, nor was she even much bigger than me. This helped, as I was able to send the railing flying through the air, giving her a good knock on the side of the head.

She grimaced, but then the expression turned into a sickening smile. I was barely able to dodge out of the way before a plume of hot smoke rushed from her nostrils into the stairwell. I flattened myself against the wall, my attention darting around to find another weapon, but Gemma rushed down the stairs. I could sense a kind of frenetic energy about her, as if she were on the verge of shapeshifting.

There came a loud crunching sound. I raced downstairs and straight out the front door, which she'd burst through rather than bothering to open. There on the front lawn, visible as lightning flashed around her, was a creature taller than the entire three-story building. I thought back to the last time I fought a dragon, and I didn't remember him being so large.

The creature let out a deep, guttural laugh and sat down on huge haunches.

We can communicate just our thoughts. The voice in my head sounded like Gemma, human and calm. *You're thinking about my brother.*

I wiped dripping rain out of my eyes. "Your brother?" I asked aloud. "What are you talking about?"

"You killed him," she replied, still inside my head.

"The only thing I ever killed was a dragon two hours from here and lots of months ago," I said. "That was your brother?"

The dragon bowed her head.

Doug had pretended to be my coworker. He'd kidnapped Heather. He'd tried to kill me. Of course his family wanted revenge, but I wasn't going to let another creature put the woman I loved in danger. I focused on a nearby tree and shoved together energy and power, focusing all anger and rage and passion and fear. The tree's roots ripped out of the ground, and in a swift motion of my arms swooping through the air, the tree mimicked that movement and sailed across the lawn at Gemma.

The attack wasn't fast, though, and Gemma predicted the tree's trajectory. She unfurled two huge wings and fluttered a few feet in the air. The tree landed safely behind her with a percussive thud. Rain continued to pour down, nearly blinding me, but the smoke coming out of Gemma's nose fizzled out as soon as it touched the air.

I might not be able to attack her with my telekinesis, but she also couldn't set me on fire, not in this deluge.

"We're at a standstill," I yelled up to her. "Give up, and I won't call the cops on you. You might be a dragon, but the police don't know that. They'll be on your human disguise in a heartbeat, and you won't know a moment's peace. Especially if Merin dies."

The wings retracted, and the dragon's entire body shifted so quickly the movement was blurry and indistinct. Now it was just a small woman standing in front of me, her hair lank and drenched around her narrow face. She moved closer but still kept some distance between us, knowing she was much more vulnerable in this form.

"You let me go," she said, "I'll let you go. Everybody will be safe, but you won't call the cops."

"That's what I propose," I said.

"I know where you live. If you come after me, I'll kill you in your sleep."

I wondered if I could somehow harness a bolt of lightning and send it straight into the woman's heart. But that was just it—she was a woman, not a dragon, and I didn't murder people. She wasn't human, but she certainly looked like one right now. Did I want to make this deal?

I held out my hand, rainwater streaming off the sleeve of my shirt. I was freezing, terrified, and without options.

Gemma shook my hand. Her grip was firm, her skin freezing and somehow scaly, despite looking like regular skin. She stepped back, and moments later she was back in her dragon form, wings straining against the sky, punching her way through clouds until I could no longer see her.

When I came back, everyone was huddled around the dining table. I was pelted with questions, and I obfuscated as best I could. Not everyone was buying what I was selling, but I had a few convinced that Merin fainted, Gemma left to find a park ranger, and the front door was ruined because of wind. I was momentarily concerned about what would happen when Gemma didn't return, but it was highly possible she registered at the lodge with a fake identity and any attempt to track her down would be met with paperwork roadblocks.

When the lights came back, people drifted off to their own cabins. Heather and I were left alone. I told her what really happened. "I didn't trust her, but I took the deal to protect everyone."

"Are you going to go after her later?" Heather asked. "She only has one human form, after all. You could find her."

I weighed my options. We could go home and plan for battle. We could plan for battle immediately. Or we could...

"We go," I blurted out.

"Not home."

"No." I shook my head. "Probably not."

K.W. Taylor's first science fiction novel, *The Curiosity Killers*, was published by Dog Star Books (2016). She is also the author of the *Sam Brody* series of urban fantasy works, including the recent novella "The Skittering" (2020). Most of her over fifty short story publications have been in the horror genre. More recent anthology appearances include *555 Vol. 3: Questions and Cancers* (Carrion Blue, 2018), *Ink Stains* (Dark Alley, 2017), and *A Terrible Thing* (555/Carrion, 2016). Taylor holds a Master of Fine Arts in Writing Popular Fiction from Seton Hill University, a master's in literature, and recently completed a Ph.D. She co-hosts the podcast *PosPop: Positively Pop Culture* and is currently at work on both a new science fiction novel and her first full-length nonfiction book. She also appears on the actual play RPG podcast *The Cast Perilous* and teaches college English in Ohio.

SPIRIT OF THE DRAGON
BY J.C. MASTRO

TO SAY THAT DRAGONFRAGGEN took their motif seriously would be quite the understatement. From flame-throwing guitars and ground-pounding drums, to scale-patterned leathers and draconic set pieces, the band invented the dragonmetal genre. Yet, overused imagery and tired mythic tropes could entertain the headbangers only so far. After three platinum-selling albums of a similar tone, it all felt a bit stale. The band needed a hit single for the latest record. Something different, something heavier, something...ancient.

It is why the bandmates went skulking through a dark, off-limits side tunnel in what was known as King Arthur's Labyrinth, located in the hills of Snowdonia, Wales. A spelunking river boat attraction, albeit kitschy, replete with dramatic smoke and lighting effects and tales of the legendary king vanquishing dragons. A must see for such a band. A certain treasure trove of material to write the hit they sought.

"I dunno, Johnny. That boatman was just playing the part." Drake Williams shook the remnants of the waterfall they'd splashed through from his ears for the third time. "There's nothing down here,"

"No, dude," Johnny Hellfire wrung the water from the Celtic-patterned bandana he'd purchased at the gift shop and tied it back on his head. "I slipped him a hundred to give me the inside scoop. It's down here."

"*Vhat's* down here?" Gunther Wyvern coolly flipped his leather jacket over his shoulder. "Zat vaterfall killed my buzz."

"You'll see."

Johnny ducked through a pitch-black portal in the cave wall and pulled out his phone's camera light.

"You boys whine too much. This shit's badass," said Tommy Draconis as he slapped out a drum fill on the low ceiling.

"Ja," Sven said.

The bandmates turned their phone lights on and reluctantly followed the optimistic lead singer through the dank gloom. Rivulets of water seeped through the stone. A chill draft whistled over the rocks. It was easy to envision knights of old hunting the fabled beasts by torchlight through these carved tunnels. Or, for the less imaginatively inclined, the nineteenth century Welsh ore miners who'd actually dug them.

"It's opening up. I can see a light ahead," Johnny said.

The narrow passage widened into a cavernous chamber. Massive stalactites nearly touched the floor like the fangs of the beast the band adored. At the far end, bathed in a shaft of light from an unknown source high above, hung a tattered and faded Arthurian dragon banner. And below it sat a single stone pedestal with an open book atop it.

"That's it! Holy shit..." Johnny stowed his phone and rushed over.

"Whoa." Drake spun slowly to take in the scene.

"Zat's so metal."

"Ja."

The band followed Johnny over and encircled the pedestal. The book, an illuminated manuscript with yellowed and smudged parchment pages, rested peacefully upon it. Certainly, there was no way for the members to tell its age or authenticity. They were rock stars, not archaeologists.

"Dudes, this is what we've been looking for!" Johnny said.

"That's some History Channel, Illuminati manuscript shit right there," Drake said.

"Look at the dragon artwork on the page... and the writings..."

Flowing script filled the intricately bordered pages, blocking out two faded color illustrations. One of a rearing, fire-breathing dragon wielding blunt weapons, and the other fully subdued and clapped in heavy irons and chains.

"That's so my next tat," Tommy said.

"Ja."

"Vat's it say?"

Johnny leaned in closer and hovered his finger over the lines, taking great care not to touch the delicate pages. He muttered the words he could make out, unknowing of most of their meaning. Tommy and Drake debated which tattoo artist they knew could do justice to the dragon depicted.

"I think it's Latin," Johnny said.

"How do you know zat?"

"I'm not stupid, dude. It says 'spiritus,' like religious sermons and stuff. And 'draconis,' obviously..."

"Spirit of the dragon," Tommy said reverently.

"Hell yes!" Johnny belted out his best rocker whoo and high-fived his mates.

"Ja." Sven flashed the universal rock on horns gesture.

"Everyone snap a pic." Johnny pulled out his phone. "We'll find someone to translate this."

"Ah... I see you've found it."

The band spun in unison at the new voice. A dark-cloaked figure stood directly behind them. His hands were crossed and hidden in the flowing sleeves of his rope-tied robes. Only the lower half of his hooded face could be seen in the misty light from above. The slightest grin pushed deep wrinkles at the sides of his mouth.

"What the hell, dude? Don't be sneaking up on people like that," Drake said.

"My apologies. You seem to have found what you came down here to find. The book... Perhaps it will serve your purpose?"

The man's voice was low and relaxed, a lulling mumble to his accent.

"Who is this guy?" Tommy said.

Drake gave his friend a deadpan look. "It's the boatman."

"Yeah, I know. I mean what's his deal?"

"He sounds like Robert Downey Jr. in zat movie vhere he stuck his hand up a dragon's ass."

"Ja." Sven chuckled.

"When did Iron Man ever—"

"I'd certainly not recommend that action." The boatman's grin widened.

"What is this place, this book?" Johnny said.

"No one truly knows. This cave is millennia old. The tunnels leading to it not so much. Who wrote the book, put it here and when I cannot say. Or, perhaps I can. But won't."

The last part of his statement had no effect on the band members, be it their irreverent lack of focus or inability to comprehend his flowing speech. They merely stared at the enigmatic boatman.

"In any event, it too is ancient. I understand from Mr. Hellfire here—quite the name I might add—that you young men are musicians with a fascination for dragons?"

"Damn right, man. We're DragonFraggen!" Tommy threw his arms wide to indicate the entire band in the enthusiastic gesture. "Haven't you heard of us?"

"Afraid not. I presume you seek the book to create new unholy melodies? You will not be disappointed. The words on those pages tell of the magical imprisonment of the dragon beast Tympanagon. The incantation used to shackle its raucous spirit for all eternity. And... how to release it."

Drake cocked his head and raised an eyebrow. "Layin' it on pretty thick there, dude."

The boatman simply shrugged.

"He's playing ze part, Drake. It's just a story."

"Well, whatever." Johnny put his arms over Drake and Gunther's shoulders. "We've got our new song, guys. Let's get outta here and get this translated."

"Ja."

"And thanks." Johnny nodded to the boatman.

The band made for the cavern exit, discussing as they went whether their roadie Big Stan could use his college Latin studies to translate the text.

The boatman turned and called after them, "Good luck to you. May the dragon's spirit awaken the fire you seek."

His eyes glowed a pale green from under the heavy, black cowl.

Three months later and ten new tracks recorded, DragonFraggen huddled around the studio mixing board somewhere in the neighborhood of midnight. Calloused, string-creased fingers ached, vocal strength hung on the edge of cracking, and the recorded track under review reduced to incongruous sounds through uncountable listens. The band had poured their souls into this album, and confidence rode high at its potential success. If only they could find the missing element to push the final song into dragonmetal perfection.

"It's so damn close." Johnny ran his hands through his curly long hair.

"What more does it need?" Tommy said. "The verses are great, the chorus a crowd pleaser, it's heavy as shit..."

"Ja." said Sven, head down on the edge of the mixer.

"I wanna use the actual stuff in the book about Tympanagon," Johnny said. "It'll make it feel real, you know?"

"Well, you could use this part here," said Big Stan, who was studying a tablet, swiping his finger over a zoomed-in picture of the book they'd discovered. "Incantatio, or incantation. It's what supposedly summons the dragon. Otherwise, there isn't much else about him."

You wouldn't think by mere appearances that Big Stan was only a handful of credits away from attaining a master's degree in Classics. The bulky six-foot-two, ponytailed and tattoo-covered guitar tech had eschewed his formal education for his love of heavy metal music. A concept very few could wrap their heads around. To those confused, he'd simply quip, "When you gotta rock, requirite vibrare."

"I like zat idea. Ist very metal."

"What's it say, Stan?" Johnny said.

"Do you want the Latin, or in English?"

"Try the Latin," Drake said.

"It's a simple quatrain after what seem like instructions," Big Stan said. "Canendus est pluribus voces, verbenta tympana... The incantation says, 'Spiritus Tympanagon de somno exsuscitat, ex carcere te liberamus umquam excitosa optundit.'"

Though no one heard through the soundproof glass, a wave of vibration rolled over the cymbals on Tommy's drum kit.

"That's kinda badass," Tommy said. "You know where that should go? Breakdown."

"Breakdown," Drake and Gunther said in unison, nodding slowly in total agreement.

"Ja."

"I like it, but no way I'm getting all that out. Not tonight, anyway," Johnny said.

"You could record the English, and save the Latin for live shows," their producer suggested.

"Zat's perfect. Vhat do you think, Johnny?"

After a moment of quiet thought, Johnny stood and drained the last of his water bottle. He crinkled the plastic and tossed it hard into the corner trash can.

"Let's record that breakdown."

"We're coming to you live from Castle Donington in Leicestershire, England, where DragonFraggen is set to close out this multi-day Metal Mayhem event just moments from now. Nearly 100,000 fans have camped out and headbanged this week here at the home of the original Monsters of Rock festival in the 80's and 90's, and the energy is high waiting for DragonFraggen to take the stage. The band will debut live for the first time the title track of their latest album, *Spirit of the Dragon*, due out tomorrow."

The stage for DragonFraggen's performance was the largest and most elaborate they'd ever designed. Its black cloth backdrop and steel lighting rigs towered above the packed-in crowd. It was flanked on either side by two massive video screens currently showing a feed of the cheering fans. Onstage, risers for the drums and dynamic movement of the band members were covered in a façade of weathered stone, also concealing the numerous pyrotechnic effects for the explosive show.

The centerpiece, however, was a ten-foot-tall animatronic dragon suspended above the drums. This creature of metal, latex, and mechanized guts boasted wings that stretched across the stage and eyes that glowed a menacing red. Blue-gray smoke curled from the sides of its clamped-tight jaws. Taloned hands and feet flexed open and closed. The dim preshow lighting gleamed off its realistic greenish-brown scales.

Backstage, Johnny stared up at the dragon in wonder. His heart was pounding from the adrenaline he always felt before a show. The power of the anxious fans hummed through his feet, feeding the energy inside him. He adjusted his open leather vest and squatted to stretch his scale-patterned pants one last time.

Tommy stepped beside him and clapped him on the back. "You ready, dude?" he yelled over the din of cheers.

"Hell yes!"

"Then let's do this shit!" Tommy signaled across the stage to the other band members waiting there. Then, he whipped off his t-shirt, tossed it aside, and jogged onstage up to his drum kit, the new dragon tattoo across his chest radiant in the lights.

Sven, Gunther, and Drake strode out confidently, their guitars slung low over their shoulders, long hair waving gently behind them.

The crowd roared.

Johnny held back, waiting for his cue once the first song began. Tommy pumped his kick drum three times, the booming sound of which shook the very ground of Donington. The guitarists cranked the volume knobs on their axes to ten, the frequency buzz of the amplifiers drifting palpable static through the air.

In unspoken unison, the three guitarists launched into the harmonious opening melody of their first hit, "Fury's Fire." Two bars in, Tommy stomped two marching beats on the kick drum, repeating through the harmonized intro until Sven broke free with a chugging low B power riff. Johnny walked onstage as the lighting gradually shifted from dim blue to yellow. He strode to front and center, stepped up to the slightly elevated platform jutting out into the crowd, and assumed a ubiquitous wide-legged, rockstar power stance.

"Fury's Fire" paused, save for a sustained chord from Sven. The lights went dark for just that instant before blazing to full as pyrotechnic pots exploded clouds of fire into the air. Johnny leaned his head back and belted a war cry over a wall of distorted sound and beat that carried like a shockwave through the frenzied crowd.

One hour into the thus far blistering set, Johnny was backstage with Big Stan taking one last look at the Latin verses of "Spirit of the Dragon" while Gunther plucked and slapped a groove metal bass solo onstage.

"It's encarcere te liberamos, right?" Johnny said.

"Almost. *Ex* carcere te liberam*us*," Big Stan corrected.

"Ok, got it. They're gonna love this."

"Damn right. I had the engineers rig up the words to go on screen, too. Really get them into it."

"You rock, man!" Johnny high-fived Big Stan and walked back out on stage as Gunther's last note buzzed to feedback.

"This next song," Johnny announced, "is the first single off our new album coming out tomorrow!"

The fans screamed.

"Yeah? You wanna hear it or what?" He raised his arms wide in an exaggerated questioning gesture. The crowd cheered even louder.

"Good! We're excited to play it for you!" The rest of the band took their places behind him. "We discovered some of the lyrics for this song in an ancient book found deep in a cave in Wales." The crowd continued to cheer but didn't react to the story. "No shit, man, we really did! Isn't that right, Sven?"

Sven stepped up to a nearby microphone. "Ja."

"See, Sven was there. We all were. You may have noticed our new friend up there." Johnny pointed to the animatronic dragon. "That's Tympanagon, the dragon from the book. Say hi, Tympanagon."

The mechanical monstrosity raised its head and unleashed a stream of fire high into the air that blew over at least the first three rows.

"Damn!" Drake said over the mic.

"Right?" Johnny flipped his hair back. "Well, this song is about him, a terrible dragon imprisoned for eternity. Maybe we should let him out?"

The crowd cheered again.

"Are you ready to hear it?" Johnny yelled.

They cheered an affirmative.

"It's called 'Spirit of the Dragon!'"

The band launched into the song's heavy, double-pedal bass driven tempo led by a long chord rhythm layered with a syncopated lead melody. Light gimbles spun and flashed, Tympanagon's wings flapped. Tommy's arms flew in a blur over his drum kit. Drake's hair whirled in a mass of head-banging perfection. Gunther pounded away at his bass hung low between his knees. Sven stood atop a back riser, his face calm save for a snarl of lip, his guitar's headstock pointed straight up. Johnny stood still in his center stage place, legs wide, head down, and one arm raised to the sky.

Eight bars in, Johnny lifted his head and unleashed a long, guttural scream as the song's rhythm bounded into double time.

> *"Dragon born of wrath and fire,*
> *Who cursed the land with death and pyre.*
> *Destructor of the souls of all,*
> *Buried deep in granite hall."*

Johnny ran to stage right and leaned back to belt the chorus.

"Dragon, rise!
Take flight and scourge the land again.
Dragon, rise!
Spirit free to terrorize!"

The crowd was a churning cauldron of heavy metal bliss. Not an arm was down, not a voice was silent. The moshers flailed in their primal dance of mayhem.

"We strip thee of thy power thus,
Quench thy thirst for killing lust.
Binding wings in chains of steel,
Claws ground down and brought to heel.
Dragon, rise!
Take flight and scourge the land again.
Dragon, rise!
Spirit free to terrorize!"

Johnny ran the full length of the stage to underneath the far-left video screen. His sweat-glistened face twelve feet tall above him. Sven jumped down from the riser to take center stage for a guitar shredding solo that defied the dexterity of the human hand. Drake paced the stage, whipping hair in constant motion. Tommy's arms and feet never stopped their wailing onslaught upon his drums.

Johnny smiled in appreciation of what may have been the greatest metal masterpiece DragonFraggen had ever produced. Time for the final verse, and the epic breakdown to bring it all together.

"Trapped by magic ages old,
The incantation never told.
For speaking thus brings certain doom,

Free thy spirit from its tomb."

Johnny strode back to center stage as the band hit the breakdown. The drums slowed to a standard backbeat. The guitar rhythm chunked in muted, drop-tuned chords punctuated by staccato leads. The band let it grind on for several bars before dropping it down so Johnny could speak to the crowd.

"This next part," he said through heavy breaths, "is directly from the book. It's the incantation to release the spirit of Tympanagon. But we're gonna have a little fun with it just for you. Whaddya say?"

One hundred thousand agreements overpowered the music.

"We'll do it first in English, then we're gonna chant the original Latin all together. The words will be up there for you. Awaken, Tympanagon!"

The band kicked the breakdown back to full. Johnny leaned over and growled into the mic.

"Spirit of Tympanagon,
Awaken from thy sleep.
We free thee from imprisonment,
Thy destructive rhythm ever beats."

He repeated it once more, then stood up to address the crowd again. "Hell yeah! Alright, here we go, all together in the original Latin!"

"Spiritus Tympanagon,
De somno exsuscitat.
Ex carcere te liberamus,
Umquam excitosa optundit!"

After the first recitation, the very ground of Castle Donington shook, though imperceptible through the cacophony of metal and chants. The lights of the stage flickered for just an instant, also escaping notice.

Upon the second, a hot wind blew across the concert grounds and fluttered the backdrop of the stage. The animatronic dragon swayed from its suspension lines. Its red glowing eyes blazed brighter than ever before. Had the music not been so loud, the echoing booms of distant thunder—or was it drums, perhaps—would have been heard.

As Johnny and the DragonFraggen fans began what would have been the final time through the chant, the breakdown rocking on as heavy as ever, the dragon reared back its head and released a jet of superheated fire. Its wings retracted, its arms reached up and grabbed the lines holding it above the stage. An arc of blue-white energy struck down from the heavens and flashed against the upper stage truss. It coursed along the dragon's lines and erupted in a shower of sparks from its back.

The animatronic Tympanagon crashed down behind the drum riser as the lighting flickered and pulsed across the stage. The crowd screamed in delight and excitement. The band stopped playing and looked at each other in utter confusion.

Gunther ran over to Johnny. "Is zat supposed to happen?" he yelled over the crowd noise.

"I don't think so!"

Sven, who now stood stage right with Drake, tossed his light-blond hair back over his shoulder and shrugged.

Tommy rose from his drum kit, looked back behind him, and spread his drumstick-holding hands out wide to indicate his cluelessness, as well. The Donington metalheads didn't get it either and continued to relish in the spectacle.

Backstage, Big Stan was frantically yelling over the walkie to any of the crew to assess the situation and the damage. He turned to head out on stage for a better look, and nearly ran into a dark-hooded figure.

"Who the hell are you?" he bellowed.

"My apologies, good sir. I came to see the show. And it is about to get quite interesting, it seems."

"You don't belong here. Out of my way."

"Oh, but you see I do. I assisted those young men in finding the incantation to release Tympanagon." The boatman's wide grin creased his cheeks. "He's been dying to come out of imprisonment to play."

A horrendous squealing of metal and a thunderous roar burst from the darkness behind the drum riser.

"Ah, and here he is now."

Johnny and Gunther turned to see first a pair of wings burst up behind Tommy, followed by taloned hands that slammed down and pierced the drum riser. A hulk of greenish-brown flesh and scale preceded the rise of glowing red eyes and jaws packed with the fangs of what was now the real Tympanagon. The beast blew a fireball over the heads of the band and roared. Tommy spun to look, yet had no time to react as Tympanagon dropped its head, grasped him from above, and lifted him into the air.

"No!" Sven screamed.

Tommy's body flew like a ragdoll as Tympanagon tossed him backstage without care. The crowd cheered yet again, believing this horrific display to be a stunt show for their entertainment. Johnny, Gunther, and Drake knew better by this point, and had gathered together at the front of the stage. Half paralyzed by fear, half contemplating how the saying, "the show must go on" could possibly be applied in this scenario.

"Vhat do ve do?" Gunther was clearly on the edge of full-blown panic.

"I don't know!" Drake shrieked.

The band mates looked to Johnny. The first inkling of his personal responsibility for all this chaos was tugging at the back of his mind, yet he knew it was not the time to bow out in shame. Johnny sent a hopeful prayer to the gods of metal that Tommy was alive, that the band and these hundred thousand people would survive. Then, he decided to try something.

"Hey, Tympanagon!" he called out over the mic. "What do you want?"

The dragon growled and spat a fireball that ignited a monitor at stage left.

"Dude, don't piss it off more!" Drake said.

Johnny didn't listen. "What do you want?" he repeated.

Tympanagon then took a step forward and stood behind the drums. Its eyes blazed as it appeared to survey the double kick drum kit. One deep bass drum thump reverberated throughout the venue. Then another. The dragon's fanged jaws seemed to gleam in a smile.

"Is he-" Gunther began.

Tympanagon double kicked the bass and hit the snare. Then another drum fill, and another ending in a cymbal crash.

"Ja..."

"You have got to be f—" Johnny's exclamation was cut off by a renewed wave of cheers from the crowd.

Tympanagon roared again and beat out across the kit what is perhaps the most famous drum fill of all time, hitting the skins at the edge of their tolerance. He kept on playing the beat, laying down the tempo for the 80's iconic hit.

"Did he seriously bust out Phil Collins just now?" Drake said.

"Zat is so metal."

"He wants to play?" Johnny said. "Fine. Let's play. Guys, "Spirit of the Dragon," final chorus, now!"

The band members spread out and Drake kicked it off with the driving rhythm guitar of the song. Gunther dropped in the low end with his bass, and Sven brought lead melody. Tympanagon didn't sync up with them at first, but after pausing to roar and breath a stream of fire once more, he found it. The double thumping madness that once belonged to Tommy Draconis, now provided with the drum skills of ages by the dragon.

Backstage, Big Stan stared, mouth agape, at the utterly unfathomable scene onstage. Medics wheeled an injured but very much alive Tommy past the grinning boatman who stood next to Big Stan.

"Those are my drums, bro," Tommy managed through the oxygen mask.

"I told you things were about to get interesting," the boatman said.

"How... What..." Big Stan had no words.

"I'm surprised you didn't pick up on it, wordsmith. In your translations, it didn't occur to you the meaning of the word tympanum? Drum? The dragon's name? A bastardization of tympanum and dragon."

"Drum dragon," Big Stan said.

"Precisely."

"You're behind this? But, why?"

"Come now, you translated the incantation instructions as well? Pluribus voces, verbenta tympana? Many voices and beating drums? What better way to unleash him than such a cacophonous gathering! Do enjoy the show."

The boatman's eyes glowed pale green from under his hood.

Rocking heavier than ever before, thanks to Tympanagon, DragonFraggen jumped into the final chorus with improvised lyrics inspired by their new drummer. The crowd was in a heavy metal frenzy.

> *"Dragon, rise!*
> *Take the stage and pound the drums.*
> *Dragon, rise!*

Tympanagon shall terrorize!
Dragon, rise!
Dragon, rise!"

J.C. Mastro grew up in California in the 1980's. As a child, he enjoyed science fiction and fantasy, spending sunny days outside battling invisible aliens and flying through space in oversized, cardboard ships. Evenings and lazy afternoons were spent consuming 1980's TV and movie favorites like reruns of *Star Trek*, and *Star Wars* on worn-down VHS tapes. In his teens, J.C. discovered a love of reading sci-fi and fantasy novels by authors such as Frank Herbert, Michael Crichton, Timothy Zahn, Anne McCaffrey and even Stephen King. His goal is to entertain readers through fun action and relatable characters, and to stimulate their imaginations--just like his was growing up. J.C. earned a Bachelor of Arts in Creative Writing and English from Southern New Hampshire University, and a Master of Fine Arts in Writing Popular Fiction from Seton Hill University. He is currently a visually impaired stay-at-home-geek-dad seeking publication for his first young adult sci-fi novel, *Academy Bound*. Connect with J.C. at jcmastroauthor.com or Instagram @jcmastroauthor

THE GEORGE
BY TIMONS ESAIAS

I'D BEEN MINDING MY own business, training at Jimmy's gym, when my manager showed up with a limo. "They want us down at Pope's," he says.

Azi—everybody calls him The Hawk—doesn't bother with details like who 'they' are. One of the reasons he thrives in the boxing game is this ability not to let information slip. Lot of folks in boxing prefer to stay behind the curtain.

Another thing Azi doesn't care much for is dragons. Most of his clients stick to the gendered Humans' Divisions, but I have a title, and the All-Species purses are the biggest, so he lowers himself to managing my career. He's got two kids in college and a third on trial in the Federal system, and I pay for all that.

The limo pulls up outside Pope's, and it's the front entrance rather than the real entrance. Sure enough, the Press is waiting.

Looks like they found another George. Another Great Human Hope.

Payday.

Pope's is the top training facility on the whole continent, fancier even than the Mexico City powerhouses. Boxing, kickboxing, mixed bullshit, they cater to all that. When I'm doing a title fight we do media events there, under bright lights, with brand-new equipment. Never more than half an hour sparring, half an hour posing for pictures. Then it's back to Jimmy's, because dragons aren't really welcome at Pope's.

We stink, we scuff the equipment, we scar the floors. We are unacceptable.

If I cared, I'd have been listening carefully to the reporters and their questions, or looking for banners, to try to figure out who the guy is. I do not actually care. There will be film, I'll be watching him for hours, and I've probably already seen a few of his fights.

To me he's just another George.

They plan to give him my title, with a big upset victory. They've let me build up the stakes for two years now, but it's time to cash in, time to restore order, time for a human to be on top.

Alas, I don't plan to let that happen.

***

Back at Jimmy's I'm watching the new George's fights on my phone, and on a borrowed pad. Yeah, I've earned 327 million bucks in my career, but it's all being held in trust, because I'm an animal. I'm a dragon, and shouldn't have a right to property, money, or any of the ladies who keep circling around.

So, yeah, the facilities aren't the best. This latest George, Belissaro, is a tall heavyweight, and they're counting on his reach. I've got long arms for a dragon, but they're only good enough for inside work against a human. My jab is usually shorter than the George's hook, which isn't optimal.

My edge is my stride. I'm outta reach and then one step we're chest to chest. If I could breathe fire, that would be it, the guy would be toast. That's all myth, though, so I have to settle for the uppercut, or the hook to the liver.

The film is pretty clear. He's tall, he's heavy, he's convincing, and he's got the chance of an ice cube on molten lava.

Which means they're going to be cheating.

When other dragons ask me what the big difference is between human opponents and dragon opponents, my answer is simple: humans cheat.

We don't have much of a life out on the reserves, or in the animal parks, but human cities are horrible places for dragons to live. They're afraid to let us boxers train in the mountains, for fear we'll fly away. The smells are overwhelming, and useless when you're not allowed to hunt. Humans are all cooking oil and tobacco, in my actual experience. And those damn perfumes. The zoos are the only relief, but they won't let you at the merchandise, so it's more a tease than anything.

I'd love to just pack my nostrils with clay, but that wouldn't be wise. When they finally decide to come for me, I want to smell them first.

They keep the fighting dragons in a couple of converted warehouses down next to the canal. Part of our spending money goes to air filters, to keep things tolerable.

Communication between us is monitored, since they don't want us conspiring. They also don't let us duel, so the only way we can establish relative status is our rankings, and none of us believe in the rankings.

I expect the humans know that this works on our minds, and they see that as a good thing. I see it as a really stupid idea, and likely to lead to unauthorized duels with humans.

Humans don't duel well with my kind, unless everybody is sticking to Marquess of Queensbury Mark

IV rules.

Even then they have to cheat to win. Which, of course, they try to do all the time.

The food sucks, too. I'm a millionaire, at least in theory, so what do I get to eat? Sixty burgers a day, and two bales of hay. Not the treetop canopy leaves that our bodies evolved for, but damned cut Timothy grass. And four gallons of some popular, inexpensive beer.

I have one dream in life. Just one. I want to meet the person responsible for IPAs, and slit their belly open and drag their organs into the sun. If they're already dead, as they should be, I'd like to dig up the grave and urinate on the coffin.

My eyes are made to see details forty miles away. Looking through a window makes me nauseated, something about distance vision being interrupted at close range. So ever since I first went into training, I've been feeling half-blind.

My eyes are also best at distances under about twenty feet, to help with precision snatching. In a boxing ring, that's an edge. I can't punch as fast as a human, but I can see the muscles tensing before the guy decides to throw. I can see his footwork before it happens. On an average day I can always be where he doesn't want me, and I never have to be where his punch is going.

That's boring in the ring, though, so they make us wear a jaw-snaffle that cuts down the field of vision. Can't trust those nasty dragon teeth, you know. And our wings are netted tight 24/7/365, so we can't use those.

I can't be dwelling on the negatives, or the damn rules that are out of my control. I've got a George to deal with. A George who thinks he's going to win.

We have no facilities for road work, so my legs are never in great shape. There's no track at Jimmy's, because it was built for humans, and humans could run in the streets. They have a couple of worn treadmills, but no dragons allowed.

That's not unfair. We're hell on equipment.

What's unfair is they won't let us run or climb. We get to jog around a warehouse floor, which is polished concrete.

So I get a plan, once. *Can we have heavy wire mesh mounted on the wall and ceiling, for training purposes, in the warehouse?*

Sure, they say, if it comes from my funds. Good enough.

But it had only been up for three days when the Feds show up to inspect our living facilities. They see three of us hanging from the ceiling, and that's it. It all comes down, at my expense.

Having strong thighs is bad for us. Dangling from heights might make us regress, might make us go all atavist.

With six weeks to go before the fight, it's back to Pope's for a presser. I'm suspicious, because they're having us pose side-by-side, which doesn't typically happen until the weigh-ins. Usually it's all about the George. Even though I have the title, the press is getting *his* family story, getting *his* life history, looking for street brawls in *his* youth, and all that.

Reporters never ask where I grew up, because viewers might find that disturbing. They assume I don't know whose egg I hatched from. They assume that family means nothing to dragons. Especially modern, "semi-domesticated" dragons.

Belissaro reeks of bay rum aftershave. They should have shaved his chest and back. He's walking proof that humans are not-so-great apes.

Right away, I get his game. He starts leaning into me, to push me aside in front of the cameras, to show how powerful he is. What a pushover I'm going to be.

He's trying to get me disqualified. They pulled this on "Tornado" Tarask when he was the Number One contender, got him to shove the human aside during the weigh-in. It's okay for a human to misbehave, to shove the dragon; but if the dragon pushes back, oh, then it's wild behavior. Unmanageable animal. Automatic disqualification.

Tarask is back at the breeding farm now, in a cage, getting his sperm extracted. Once they think they have enough, he'll be cut up for gumbo and andouille.

For all I know, they've done that already.

So I let him move me 18 inches, and then I hold position. After half a minute, he pushes again. This time I step away to the side quickly, and he stumbles into my shoulder, which makes it clear who was doing what.

Belissaro is furious at being made to look foolish, so he pushes his privilege. He throws a hook at my head.

Hadn't expected that one, but I let him connect, and roll it off. I do not sweep his legs from under him with my tail, I do not hit him back.

I could kill him right there, because he is so sure that I'm helpless that he dropped his hands while he yells defiance at me. I calm myself by counting the deathblows he is open for. It would be so simple, that it's not worth the bother.

Not worth dying for.

They make a show of pulling him away, and we leave the facility immediately. Azi is hopping up and down in the car, because he knows a publicity coup when he sees one. "That prick just sold like half a million tickets! His followers think he was tough, your followers will be wanting revenge in the ring. Brilliant side-step, by the way. Nicely done."

This is maybe the second time I've heard a compliment from The Hawk, so that's the big surprise of the day.

They brought this guy along kinda quick, so there is less film footage on him than I would have liked. He had two draws and two no-decisions to start with, which is kinda odd, and then the unbroken string of knockouts that suggests arranged outcomes. Fixed fights aren't much good for studying a fighter, because everything but the footwork is fake. They had given him a couple of tests, though, once he got a bit of a record. He scored a second-round TKO in the first one, getting a horrible cut over the guy's eye. The other fight took him into the fourth round before he scored a legitimate knockout. A nice jab, followed by a left hook to the head, and a very solid right to the belly. One, two, three.

So into the practice ring I go, working on counter-jab tactics. Some while back I learned the trick of hitting the guy's elbows if he's jabbing. The jabbing elbow if he's staying outside, the other elbow if he's coming in. Dragon hands seem to be built for that kind of thing, and the Georges are never used to it.

I've had one of the gym rats go through the film for illegal punches. You can tell a lot about your opponent by the number of illegal punches. One or two per fight is inaccuracy. Unless they always come when the referee is out of position, then it's strategy.

Our new George is a cheater. 45 hits below the belt, 21 rabbit punches, some 50 attempted kidney punches, and he doesn't have all that many rounds in his history.

He also didn't seem to care who was looking, but the refs only occasionally interfered. He'd had exactly two points taken away for his behavior, and one of those was to make a fight look real.

I smell a new champion.

All of us in the dragon boxing game are hoping that our successes will break down the walls that keep us prisoner. Right now, we're like the bears in the old bear-baiting rings. What we hope for never happened for the bears. The bulls in bull-fighting have never made it either.

Still, we train, we fight.

Figuring that they want this to be my last fight, I've been going over those few useful snatches of film, and trying to think up new tactics.

The problem is that I can't actually try those tactics in sparring sessions, because I assume they're being taped and shown to the other side. Instead, I work the heavy bag for half-hour stretches, imagining the moves, imagining the punches. I keep my feet planted and square, to avoid giving anything away. I expect Belissaro is now expecting me to go flat-footed to throw hard, and is preparing accordingly.

What would work best is to coldcock him with the first real punch. That's not a thing you can count on, but I'm known for letting the other guy work for half a round before I start hitting. So maybe that'll surprise him.

Another idea I toyed with is shifting behind him repeatedly, and catching him on the turn. I've made a career from side-stepping and then closing, with a hook from whichever hand is closest to belly or chin. It makes them nervous. But what if I sidestep, then step forward right into the punching arm, and then step around? Like

I'm going to throw a kidney punch, but I don't. A heavy shot to the shoulder, maybe? A hook to the near side as he tries to face me, maybe? And if he makes the mistake of grabbing, uppercuts to the armpits, my signature tactic.

Ali used to step through punching range, and I watch those films several times, mixed in with some other stuff so nobody realizes what I'm about.

I'm doing a lot of visualization. One of the scenarios I'm preparing for is if they actually decide to tell me that the fix is in, and that I have to throw the fight.

This is unlikely, because dragons respond badly to fraud like that. When Quetzl had the Dragon Middleweight belt, they had a little conversation with him: his agent, his trainer, two of the commissioners. They told him he had to go down in the sixth round, and let his opponent rule for about six months. Then there would be a rematch. Bigger money, that way.

He ate three of them before he got hit with tranquilizer darts. The commissioner he'd only emasculated, who was next on the menu, spilled the beans. The commissioner was later shot by the mob for his contribution to justice; Quetzl ended up sausage, despite his recent dietary choices.

But it will be awkward if they tell me, because I'll either have to refuse or lie. If I refuse, they'll shut down this life I have, because humans live in a perpetual snit. If I lie, then I have no honor.

So the most notable thing in the lead-up to the fight is that I don't do any interviews, and they never take me to

Pope's again for publicity shots. It seems they're using old film, hinting at secrecy on my camp's part. Nobody's ever allowed to come into Jimmy's, ever, since they started letting dragons train there. That rule doesn't change.

They also decide that the weigh-in the day before, at Pope's, will be in separate rooms. No side-by-sides, no press conference, just half-hour documentaries on Belissaro's home life and family. And his cute kittens. The world is gonna feel so good when he wins.

So good.

Except the dipshit doesn't make weight.

How can you *not* make weight for a heavyweight title fight??? It seems he's been a bit lazy, is what I hear from the guys at Jimmy's this afternoon. He's naturally a light heavyweight, and hasn't been spending hours at the training table putting in the calories, and then hours of weight work turning them into muscle. So he comes into the room as a cruiserweight, which violates the title rules and the contract.

The six sanctioning bodies and about three cruise shipfuls of lawyers huddle in a ballroom for most of the evening. The result is a split decision.

Four of the sanctioning organizations change their rules to allow a cruiserweight to win a heavyweight title. There's history behind this, because it used to be just fine, back when boxing was just people; but there were safety reasons for why they got rid of that. Anyway, for those four the fight is still on. One group refuses to change the rules over one fighter's screwup, so they pull their sanction, and their belt is no longer on the line. The last group announces that they're pulling their sanction, and that if I go ahead and fight, they're pulling my title and taking the belt back.

We send it to them by special courier first thing in the morning.

What I like about a fixed fight is that you know it's hopeless. That takes all the pressure off.

There's a hiccup with the limo this morning, so they send an SUV instead. You'd think they'd want all the trappings of reigning championship to enhance Belissaro's victory, but that's not how they're playing it.

My agent isn't in the locker room, and neither is my trainer, at first. Only Lucas, the glove man, seems to be taking his job seriously. The ref watches him wrapping my claws with only half his attention, chatting with one of the judges about where they'll eat after. No press. No fans.

One title is already gone, one is in limbo, and the other four are clearly moving on.

Lucas was acting like a mother cat, unhappy as hell. "Protect yourself at all times, out there," he says, a couple of times.

"Plan on it," I say. "If they let me."

With the big fights they pull out all the stops as far as fanfare. The challenger's entrance took a good twelve minutes, and I'm rude enough to not even leave the dressing room until minute five.

You can learn a great deal just standing in the tunnel, though. A lot of expensive cigar and pipe tobacco is being burned in the arena, and some high-grade dope, as well. More than the usual amounts of heroin sweat and cocaine sweat, so the organized betting folks are here in force.

I figure my chances of leaving the building alive are near zero. That's good to know.

Who else is here? There are paralyzing amounts of perfume in the arena; male, female and none of the above. Three dragons and a basilisk, too, but I have no idea why. And there's Belissaro, and his trainer, and one of the cheapest cut men in the business.

They're cutting corners on a title fight, which isn't a good sign.

I make my entrance slowly, because it's in the contract. I ignore the pyrotechnics because that stuff is annoying, and I ignore the "models" who walk you into the ring. They put these four ladies in tiger-striped swimsuits or something, and they look too ridiculous even to eat.

What I pay attention to is Belissaro's smell, and the funny way he has with his arms.

He does not smell of anger or of fear, which is weird in a boxing ring. Fixed fight, and he is in on it, obviously.

A decent fighter comes into the ring with relaxed shoulders, and tends to roll them to keep them that way. I'm doing it, and I'm a dragon. But Belissaro has his tight and raised, and he's doing this thing where he thrusts one forward a bit, then back, one at a time. His arms are slightly bent, not dangling.

He has trouble touching gloves after the instructions from the referee. I check his eyes, but they aren't glazed or unfocused. He stinks of booze and weed and whatnot, but nothing recent. It tells me, though, that they aren't going to be testing his blood or urine. So the rules are already out the window.

So, yeah, what am I to do when there are no rules?

At the bell I leave my corner walking to my left, because I'm supposed to move to the right. That makes him have to rethink, and that's when I see what they'd been working on, his footwork.

In the tapes he always sorta strolled to his right, then lunged to start his jab. But now he's squared up, shuffling from side to side, with his hands wide and low.

I slide to the right, staying just beyond the reach of his jab. He shuffles toward me, hands still wide, like he intends to herd me into the ropes with the threat of a jab from either side.

Which might work against a human. I step right through his range, and hit the inside of each elbow when he tries to react, then a hook to the ribs as I move through his left arm and out of reach.

We do that two more times before he gives up on the new plan for the moment, and goes back to his regular stance. He hasn't touched me yet.

He pumps two jabs at the air.

I can see what the deal with his arms is, now. The jabs sorta hang for a moment at full extension, and he pulls them back with his elbows, palm facing him, not me.

He has weights in his fists.

I let him touch me twice with the jab, to make sure, though I crack his elbows for revenge. Then I let through a hook to the ribs, rolling it just a little, and sure enough. I've fought champions, and nobody throws that hard.

I slide to the ref, but never turn my back on Belissaro, and say, "He's got weights in his gloves."

There is no reaction.

There's about a minute left, and I have to think, so I keep sliding under his jab, throwing little uppercuts, to back him off.

Nobody bothered to tell me which round I was going to lose in, which makes it hard to plan. He's frustrated, but not trying very hard, so it must not be this one. I'd been hitting him half-strength, even on the elbows, because I'll need to surprise him later.

The weighted gloves tell me that they plan to have him deliver damage, and then the ref will go for an early stoppage. I have to make my move first, then.

I decide to confuse him, by sliding to the left, and hitting him outside the elbow when he jabs. It ruins his footwork, because he keeps expecting me to come in close, and he's loading up for an uppercut. Basically nothing happens, because I'm killing time. I let a couple of the jabs to the ribs get through, which stings, but he needs to think he's scoring.

He still wasn't giving off fear.

The bell rings and I get right in the ref's face. "He's got weights in his gloves. What are you going to do about it?" He gives me a cold stare, the you're-not-human stare. The clear answer is Nothing.

I step to the ropes above the judges' table and timekeeper's bell, and say, "He's got weights in his gloves." Two of the men are embarrassed enough to keep their eyes down. The state commissioner just looks daggers.

"Get back to your corner," the ref orders, behind me.

I approach my corner and they slide the bench in for me, but Lucas has been elbowed away from the pillar, and I smell deception from the other two. I quickly decide that I can't trust them, and if you can't trust your own corner, there's nothing left.

I remain standing, facing the corner, gloves on the ropes. Okay, it has to be this round. What do I do?

I don't want my corner to even see me thinking, so I turn to watch the George. Okay. It's gotta be quick and final. And before they get a chance to disqualify me.

I try not to think about how disappointing this match is, fighting this sad cheating clown. Not much honor here, even if I win.

The bell rings, and he takes four steps forward and then goes back to that sideways sidle thing. They'd reminded him of the plan, I guess.

Once again, I step to the left, and he tries to jab and step right at the same time, but I'm not there. I'm already going the other way, right, and hit his elbow hard with a right hook, and that took him off balance.

What would have been his left uppercut ends up jammed against my side, and I pivot hard and hit that elbow with a left hook so tight it breaks something. That's the price of carrying a weight in your glove, human.

His arms are both out of position. He decides to grab hold. Expects a right to the chin.

Humans are quicker with their hands, but slower with their feet. I step just enough back so he can't reach around, but not far enough to let him hit me. Both his gloves are uselessly extended, and he's bracing his arms to carry the weights.

My right goes just below his ribs, and I put absolutely everything I've ever had into that punch. Coaches had taught me to punch through the target at something further in, like the spine. The ref was behind him and off to my left, so I tried to nail the ref's testicles with the punch. Belissaro comes up off the ground a bit, like I had made a heavy bag bounce.

That's the One, but it takes at least two.

The Two is a left uppercut, meant to break his jaw. I don't worry about his next punch, or the ref, or anything else. Break his jaw, I think. Drive his teeth through his mouthpiece. Break his jaw forever.

Then the ref is in my face, stopping my gloves, pretending that he's breaking up the hold that never happened. This confuses me, so I step back, which you don't want to do, and I briefly wonder why he's looking at me and signaling us to separate. A few seconds later I realize he's protecting Belissaro from punches, by pretending there was a hold.

None of that matters. While the ref is facing me, Belissaro crumples to the canvas. He goes down like a tree the last bit, and his head bounces. He is clearly out.

I slide toward a neutral corner, and the ref can't figure that out, but the crowd reaction makes him turn. As I lean against the corner post, expecting maybe a bullet from the stands, my opponent convulses briefly on the canvas. The ref stands over him for at least a count of six, forgetting that he is supposed to be counting, but the ring doctor rushes in to take care of things and the ref's knockout signal is lost in the commotion. It isn't very convincing, anyway.

I walk to my corner and tell them to cut my gloves off. We usually do that in the dressing room, after, but I want my claws ready for whatever is coming. Lucas has the scissors, and he pushes the assistant trainer aside and does the job. "You need to get straight out of the building," I mutter to him. "Protect yourself at all times."

He reaches up and slips off my jaw snaffle, and then he's gone.

I can smell anger in the stands, but you get that anytime a fight ends. Things are too chaotic to sense an actual hunter.

By the time I've turned around, gloves off, tape unwrapped, they've already whisked the latest George out of the ring and out of sight. Along with his illegal gloves, of course. There is clearly confusion at the judges' table, because they were planning for one thing and got another. I could guess that they are trying to come up with a way to call it a No Decision or to disqualify me, but there's the slight problem of International Television and that there've already been about sixty slow-motion replays of the knockout. They are playing it on the overhead screens, even as I stand here.

Finally the announcer waves me over, and the ring gets cleared. I only half listen as he gives the time and round of the knockout, and lifts my arm as though I've actually won something.

The young ladies are draping the four belts over my shoulders. They aren't very good at it, but then my claws are out. I'm not helping much, because I've already stepped through the wrong door, where nothing has any value anymore. Where fights are all fixed, titles are meaningless, and prize money never shows up in your wallet.

I'm standing here with no plan, no allies, and four belts that can be taken away for any technicality whatever. I won a fight that was supposed to go the other way. My people had known, so there is nobody important I can trust. My lawyers seem to be in my corner, but they've never actually won me anything.

Besides, lawyers don't protect you from bullets, they just help with the estate afterward.

But what was I supposed to do? Lose? I'm the Bipedal Heavyweight Champion of the World. It's all I've got. It's all I am.

What the heck was I supposed to do?

Timons Esaias is a satirist, writer, and poet living in Pittsburgh. His works, ranging from literary to genre, have been published in twenty-two languages. He has been a finalist for the British Science Fiction Award, and he won both the Winter Anthology Contest and the Asimov's Readers Award. His story "Norbert and the System" has appeared in a textbook, and in college curricula, so yes, he is required reading. He was shortlisted for the 2019 Gregory O'Donoghue International Poetry Prize. His full-length Louis-Award-winning collection of poetry -- *Why Elephants No Longer Communicate in Greek* -- was brought out by Concrete Wolf. He teaches in Seton Hill University's Master of Fine Arts in Writing Popular Fiction program. People who know him are not surprised to learn that he lived in a museum for eight years.

MOUTH OF THE DRAGON
BY J. THORN

JAKU WATCHED AS THE flames engulfed Senkfor, the skin dripping from his body. The dragon, massive before the burning man, reared back on its hind legs and belched another ribbon of fire, which silenced Senkfor forever. The beast then turned to Jaku, its eyes sizzling.

Jaku sprinted, trying not to gag on the reek of roasted flesh that hung over the weed-strewn parking lot. He ran up the hood of what might have once been a Ford sedan, leaping off the roof and landing behind a cinder block wall as a blast of fire roared overhead.

The dragon shrieked, its wings beating at the humid air in what could only have been June or July had calendars still existed. It circled over the parking lot like an immense hawk, the creature's shadow darkening the land below.

Jaku bolted across the pedestrian causeway that stretched over the aqueduct. The wide man-made river beneath him sluiced through the concrete channel as it flowed toward the settlement.

After stumbling down the causeway's stairs and rolling through a ditch, he ran for the nearest structure. Jaku scrambled down into the old building's basement stairwell littered with blue shopping bags and plastic water bottles—artifacts that would outlive the civilization that had created them.

"C'mon, Dragonslayer. Find your honor." Jaku spoke the words to himself as a form of self-consolation after watching the beast burn his friend alive.

Holding his dagger to his chest, Jaku picked through the debris until he came to a rusted steel door. It sat ajar but not wide enough for him to enter. He yanked on the top of the door with both hands, pulling it open just far enough to squeeze through.

Another shriek found its way into his subterranean hiding place. Senkfor's killer wouldn't give up so easily. Jaku had seen dragons circle their prey for hours before going in for the kill.

"But he can't follow me down here," Jaku said, though somehow his own words felt like charcoal lies.

Jaku clambered deeper underground until total darkness engulfed everything. He flicked his lighter three times before a small flame revealed the rest of the room to him.

Jaku found himself in what was once a subway station. Having never lived in this city nestled on the shores of the great lake, the stop held no particular sentimental value. He'd been a boy when the dragons had returned in an attempt to burn humanity off the planet. So, in that sense, he shared little of the nostalgic doom of his fellow Dragonslayers—older men who harbored a hatred for the creatures that ended civilization. In many ways, that hatred was all they had left.

Nobody could remember things any longer. Jaku knew he'd been alive for at least two decades, but even for him, specificity beyond that was impossible. But while certain things remained in the fog of memory, the scar that ran from his left eye to his chin stood steady as a warning, a reminder of the imminent mortality they dealt with every day.

Jaku tossed his braided hair over one shoulder. It landed in the middle of his back on a leather jacket weathered by several winters. He stood up straight, standing well over six feet and yet with a frame much like a coiled spring.

He pulled the map from his belt pack, holding the lighter high enough that he could see the edges of the yellowing paper.

"Yes, not far," he said, dragging his finger from the subway platform on which he stood to the tunnel entrance that led into the lair. Less than a 2-minute walk through the tunnels, as the rat crawls.

The lair. It's what the Dragonslayers called it, but the dragons didn't live there. Not even the wisest shaman in the clan knew where the dragons came from or where they nested. Their only hope to stave off complete extinction was to bait the dragons into a cave-like place with the lure of shiny objects—some gold bullion from an old bank vault, but mostly scavenged copper and brass polished to sparkle.

All that glitters is not gold.

Jaku couldn't remember where he'd heard that phrase, but he was happy the dragons couldn't communicate with humans. Otherwise, they might understand the old adage and realize the treasure was merely bait.

He put one hand on the wall's smooth ceramic tile as he headed east on the platform and deeper into the tunnel. Several minutes later, Jaku felt the air current shift as he entered the cavernous room. Here, trains used to meet to exchange passengers during the rush hour.

A stroller sat on the edge of the platform, tilted on its side and missing a wheel. To his right, Jaku saw a mess of cardboard boxes discarded by their occupants long ago. The old ticketing machines stood on the far wall like silent sentries with nothing left to guard.

The first Dragonslayers had set the traps down here, catching several dragons over the years, which seemed enough to spare the settlement from total annihilation. But recently, more dragons had filled the skies above the old city, and fewer became ensnared in these traps below.

Sulfur, burned copper—the dragon stench had become unmistakable since Jaku started trapping them. He slid the bandanna up and over his nose before pulling a dead rat from his rucksack.

While the adolescent and more brash Dragonslayers preferred to pierce the beasts with a spear to the eye, the wound to Jaku's own face had taught him the dangers of proximity. His mentor encouraged him to use his brain. To outwit the dragon rather than overpower it.

Jaku spent the first few days of each month hunting rats in the tunnels, slitting open their bellies, and stuffing them with a concoction of deadly poison. After a week or two caught in the trap, the hungry dragon would gladly and unknowingly accept a meal of tainted rat from a slayer, felling the creature without so much as a single stroke of a sword.

He hadn't been in this tunnel for several weeks, which meant the creature might have been snared many days ago. The dragon caught in Jaku's trap would be starving. If he fed the beast two or three poisonous rat carcasses, the thing would be dead by sundown.

When Jaku turned the corner, he saw the silhouette of the dragon against the tunnel's wall. The creature's exhalations had lit some rubble, and its smoldering cinders cast a faint campfire-like glow throughout the cavern.

Fending off the stench that breached his face covering, Jaku moved in closer with a dead rat in each hand. He stopped several hundred yards from the dragon, mentally calculating the range of his fiery breath.

The dragon turned to face Jaku, a sneer of pride and defiance showing before the beast cocked its head sideways and looked at him like a stray mutt.

"What? Hungry, eh? I'll bet you are, you son of a bitch."

Jaku drew his right arm back, ready to toss the first rat when the walls shook. Plaster and dust floated down from the ancient ceiling, and Jaku had to stagger to keep his feet beneath him. But it wasn't an earthquake that shook the tunnel. It was the dragon. The beast had spoken.

"I don't want your tainted offerings."

He shook his head. It wasn't possible. The Dragonslayers had never captured a beast that could speak. The creature's voice came to his ears upon rusted gears, but despite that dry, metallic tone, Jaku could understand the dragon's words.

"Huh?"

"Keep your rats."

Every time the dragon spoke, it shook the tunnel with a bellowing reverberation.

"That's not possible. You can't talk."

"And yet we converse."

Jaku looked at the dragon's talons, confirming the steel spring trap had completely ensnared the creature. It had to be legitimately caught. Otherwise, the dragon would have left the tunnel by now.

No, this beast stood before the Dragonslayer, speaking in words Jaku understood.

"I'm a Dragonslayer. I'm bound to—"

"I care not of your oath."

Jaku moved closer, putting both rats back into his rucksack before pulling his sword.

"You'll break that on my scales. But you already know that."

He looked at his sharpened blade before looking back at the dragon. Jaku's eyes watered, the stench even more potent the closer he got to the beast.

"Tracking the sun, are you?"

The question knocked Jaku back on his heels with almost as much power as the dragon's odor. Why would the beast ask such an odd thing?

But then it struck him. The dragon knew that the settlement closed the gate at sundown. Of course, it knew. If they didn't close the gate, the dragons could firebomb the village. The first settlers had steel-plated the rooftops, which protected the people from an aerial assault.

Jaku needed to return to the settlement before sundown. No Dragonslayer had ever survived a night alone in the ruins.

"I have time."

The dragon's massive head moved up and down, its eyes alight. "Waning…"

"I can come back for you tomorrow. I can return every morning and watch you starve to death."

It lifted one large talon, wagging it at Jaku with a grin. "My brothers. I know they have been searching. Will discover my predicament. Soon."

The dragon may have been speaking slowly and with an odd cadence, but it did little to hide the creature's intellectual prowess. The clan, the Governor, the Dragonslayers—they'd all underestimated the beasts.

"Then I should stab you in your eye now and be done with it."

"Or… alternatives."

The dragon folded its wings onto its back, dropping its jaw low until it could look Jaku in the eye. The creature had supplicated itself before Jaku. He hadn't said as much, but the gesture was unmistakable.

"Like what?" Jaku asked.

"Influence. I have it. A truce between *Draco* and your clan."

He had never heard a dragon talk, nor had he any idea how to translate dragonspeak. But the context made it clear. This dragon commanded others, and he wanted Jaku to know that he was open to negotiation.

"I cannot trust a dragon."

It huffed, blue flame spitting from both nostrils. "How do you know you cannot?"

He didn't.

Jaku folded his arms across his chest and nodded once at the dragon. "Go on."

The dragon sat back on its haunches with an unblinking stare. It grumbled before speaking. "Free me, and I promise my brethren will not incinerate your colony."

He stepped back and giggled, shaking his head at the dragon. "Or what?"

"Or we wait for my brethren to arrive. And then..."

The beast trailed off, not needing to explain to Jaku what would happen once they took to the skies above the settlement.

"How do I know you won't burn my home to the ground even if I let you go?"

"You do not." The dragon smiled, its tail sweeping across the rubble-strewn floor, chattering like a gigantic rattlesnake.

Jaku felt the decision roiling in his stomach, the first question coming like heartburn in the back of his throat.

What would the other Dragonslayers do?

Of course, it depended on the slayer. Still, they'd all sworn an oath to protect the settlement by eliminating the dragons. But which part of that oath was most important?

Jaku understood the simple logic involved in keeping the clan protected. If they did not, everyone would die. And yet, what of eliminating the beasts? He was a Dragon*slayer*—the only safe dragon being a dead one.

Some of his comrades would have already stabbed this creature in the eye, while others would take hours debating the offer. Jaku didn't have hours, and he didn't have a spear long enough to pierce the dragon's brain through a socket.

"The sun." The dragon slowly nodded at a burning pile of rubble as if it represented dusk.

"I know," said Jaku. "I need a moment to think this through."

Would this creature keep his word? The decision came down to this single question. Could Jaku trust the fire-breathing demon to aim his flames elsewhere?

Jaku looked down at his old wristwatch, and those little hands confirmed the dragon's intuition—night was coming. If he didn't leave soon, he'd most likely never see his family again.

"Okay."

"Yes?"

Jaku looked at his boot, kicking an old bottle deeper into the darkness. "Yes."

"Splendid."

"You're giving me your word. You will not burn the settlement to the ground."

"I promise. We shall not."

Jaku walked to where the chain from the trap met the steel bracket. He took the crescent wrench from his belt and loosened the bolt holding the trap's bracket to the wall. He turned it to the left several times until he could hear the bolt rattling behind the ceramic tiles.

"I'm leaving. I imagine it won't take you more than an hour to work that bolt the rest of the way out."

The dragon nodded, its eyes never leaving Jaku's.

"You gave me your word."

And with that, Jaku turned and ran back down the corridor, sprinting through the tunnels until he reached the exit door and the path leading him back to his people.

"It's Jaku!"

He ran through the gate as his fellow Dragonslayers gathered around. Jaku saw Senkfor's shield hanging from the top of the wall surrounding the settlement. They'd incorrectly assumed it had incinerated him as well, not expecting Jaku's return.

"I come bearing good news."

The Governor stepped forth, placing a hand on Jaku's shoulder. "Share with us."

Before Jaku could reply, someone cranked the old foghorn, alerting the clan of an imminent attack. The men in the watchtower had spotted dragons overhead.

"No, no, that's not right."

He ran past the Governor and across the main thoroughfare that cut the settlement in half. Jaku sprinted up the steps of the watchtower, taking two at a time. When he arrived at the top, he could see for himself that the northern skies were littered with dragons. But they flocked at a distance of at least ten miles, appearing like a cloud of gnats on a humid summer day.

"What are they doing all the way out there?" one of the watchtower guards asked.

Jaku didn't know. He stared at the horizon, waiting like the rest of them.

The dragons descended, but they didn't come closer. Jaku looked at the guards. The one with a pair of binoculars spoke first.

"Oh my god."

Jaku grabbed the binoculars from him, speaking as he did so. "What do you see?"

"The dragons. They're lining up on the lake's shore. Over the aqueduct."

It was then that Jaku heard the rhythmic flapping of their wings, hundreds of dragons swelling the water in the lake—and pushing a lethal tide south down the aqueduct. Directly at the settlement.

Jaku whipped the binoculars over the wall, swearing to himself.

"What is it?" asked the guard.

"Never trust a dragon."

"Never trust a dragon."

J. Thorn has published two million words and sold more than 185,000 books worldwide. He is an official member of the Science Fiction and Fantasy Writers of America, the Horror Writers Association, and the Great Lakes Association of Horror Writers. Thorn earned a Bachelor of Arts in American History from the University of Pittsburgh, and an M.A. from Duquesne University. He is a full-time writer, part-time professor at John Carroll University, co-owner of Molten Universe Media, podcaster, FM radio DJ, musician, and a certified Story Grid nerd. jthorn.net

Three
Dragons of the Stars

MASTERING AESTHETICS: AN AMBASADORA STORY
BY HEIDI RUBY MILLER

What can bring life can also destroy it.

*S**HUILONG QUADENSIS.* That was the fossil's scientific name.

Xin Clayton's gaze meandered up the skeleton of an ancient creature embedded in the wall of her laboratory. It and its many kin were more affectionately referred to as great silica dragons, even though silica accounted for only a small percentage of the fossil's mineralization. The dragon's powder blue, luminescent remains coiled and twisted up four stories embedded within the gray walls of the original matrix. This specimen was one of the little ones.

The megafauna buildings in the main square of Rushow Territory reached a hundred floors of alternating slate walls and windows. The dragons were remnants of a world long-extinct by the time Tampa Quad had been terraformed. Because of the animals' uniqueness among the Intra-Brazial's six-moon system, the fossils became objects of immediate desire.

The process of petrification and mineralization, which scientists like Xin still didn't understand completely, had left the departed creatures as hard and durable as the fabricated synthstone used to build everything else in the system. That's why all available fossils had been harvested and used for Rushow's beautiful architecture.

Substance matching aesthetic had since been the prevailing architectural style of the territory. The motto of all life in Rushow, in fact. Rumors persisted of slabs being shipped off-world to wealthy collectors, but none were ever publicly displayed due to the hefty fine it would incur from the Embassy, the system's ruling body.

The gargantuan cuts of glowing fossils were all the embellishment necessary for Rushow's edifices inside and out, save for the glass domes which topped the territory's behemoth structures and the soft blue lighting shining from inside each one. No wonder early architects used mostly glass or transparent synthstone for the remaining walls, elevators, and skybridges, which connected the whole city center. Some of the windows had abstract patterns of blue in every hue.

Once thought to be invincible because the remains survived the violent terraforming process a millennium ago, the fossils had become unstable, somehow losing their luminescent quality. After today's inspection, Xin feared it was because they were decaying.

On her watch.

Not one year ago, Xin became the most recent in a long line of directors. Her official title—because titles were quite important in the system—was Director Geological Observer, which made her both proud and embarrassed.

The recent breakdown of the fossil's luminescence became Xin's puzzle to solve.

Her scientists had made little headway in their investigations because samples of the sea-dwelling fossilized creatures were difficult to acquire. At least the theories so far supported marine life, even if there had been no water here before the terraforming. The serpentine curve of the body and powerful legs, which folded back to streamline their bodies, would have allowed for loss of drag and forceful propulsion through liquid. The fossilized remains often appeared to be swimming up and down the walls of Rushow.

"Is it that bad?" Olivia Ludivico asked before passing a cup of chai to Xin and stroking her long pink and black hair.

"It may be nothing." She took a sip and allowed its cream and spice to soothe her almost as much as the touch from her Prime Amour. Xin never asked for affection, and didn't always offer it up, yet Olivia seemed to know when she needed it, especially after three years of marriage.

"You may be the resident stoic to everyone else, but I'm not everyone else." She dipped her head for a kiss. "What's going on?"

Xin held up the steaming chai. "Something like this."

"Is my choice of beverage causing you grief this morning?" Olivia could quip through a supernova.

"It's the steam, not the chai." Xin used her wrist reporter to throw video onto a holographic airscreen. "Have a look at the latest footage from the voyeurs flying around Mammoth Two during a scheduled dome cleaning."

Mammoth Two was the first building to start fading. Since it housed the living quarters for all the quorum government and other wealthy families in the region, it was the tallest in Rushow.

"Wait." Olivia stepped closer and sipped from her own cup. "The fossils are steaming. Or smoking. There's a white cast to the vapor when seen from a certain angle."

The normally off-white sky had made detection difficult until a slight downdraft had concentrated the steam around the dome's blue glow.

"If I didn't know better," Olivia continued, "I'd say the fossils might be...."

"Sublimating."

"Yeah. Exactly. Looks like sublimation. Is that possible?"

"Considering we know very little about these fossils or how they survived the terraforming, I would say many things are possible."

"You think there's a correlation with the waning luminescence." Olivia manipulated the airscreen to zoom in on a patch of steaming wall.

"It's no coincidence that the fading fossils are the ones sublimating," Xin said.

"That could be a problem."

"If "by a problem", you mean the fossils are decaying, which could lead to catastrophic structural breakdown, then you are correct," Xin said.

Olivia swore. "Half the edifices we've checked this month show signs of luminescent degradation." She swore again. Her excitement at a new finding was often akin to outrage.

Xin admired her passion. That's why they were so well-suited, both as work colleagues and personally. Xin's emotional variability displayed as a smile or a frown with little in between. One of Olivia's favorite games was trying to get Xin to raise her voice. On more than one occasion, when Olivia was despondent, she would say that she wished her personality would allow her to feel nothing, too.

But Xin *did* feel things, at least she thought she did—just maybe not in a way which others could understand.

"Have we discovered the cause yet?" Olivia asked, a slight flush to her fair skin.

"Maybe," Xin said. "I've used every examination tool at our disposal." She paused, knowing when she revealed this next part, it would become real to another person. "I detected an alien substance."

"More alien than the creatures these fossils once were?"

"Alien *to* them."

Another series of curses flew from Olivia's mouth.

"Though I only have a theory what the substance is," Xin said, "it's definitely the cause of the degradation."

"Have you checked the Archives?"

The corner of Xin's mouth dipped ever so slightly at the mention of the sacred History. "I tried first thing but have been locked out of that part of the Archives."

Olivia snorted. "Figures."

This wasn't the first time they'd been denied access to data concerning the terraforming. Security about the volatility of the process remained high.

What can bring life can also destroy it.

"Have a look at the radio-molecular results from a sample I managed to obtain."

"From here?" Olivia scanned the room as though she might find one of their walls missing.

"From the very top of Mammoth Two, thanks to a favor from one of the dome cleaners."

Olivia had already pulled up the report on the airscreen and read as she conversed. "How did they get a sample?"

"A chunk fell on one of them," Xin said.

"Yikes. That stuff is almost indestructible." Then, "Was it a big chunk?"

"The size of his fist."

"Big enough." Olivia rubbed her head as though she could feel the cleaner's pain. "There's a substance bonded to the mineral. Or there was. It's breaking down."

"The byproduct is what's escaping through sublimation. Have you identified it yet?"

"Yeah, but it has to be a mistake."

Xin already knew what Olivia was seeing, and that there was no mistake.

Still, Olivia opened multiple airscreens to recheck the findings. Her pale, deft fingers manipulated each display the way a synth spider floating over Carey Bay spun lines of light in time to music. On Xin's rare trips to the Hub on the other side of this giant moon, she had always marveled at how graceful those machines were. Olivia possessed that same boisterous grace—at once a whirlwind of movement, loud excitement, and perfect rhythm.

When Olivia stilled her hand mid-swipe, Xin accepted the tranquil moment was gone. The chaos of truth would now drown out everything else.

"It's pruithium," Olivia whispered.

A trail of goosebumps sprouted along Xin's arms and legs. "Yes, that was my conclusion as well."

They both remained quiet for a moment.

"If this really is pruithium—"

Xin eliminated any doubt. "We both know that it is, likely from a ship's leaky propulsion system never picked up by the scanners or purposely evading the scanners."

"The radiation," Olivia said with a little hitch to her voice as they both stared at a spot where the floor to ceiling window met the wall, a wall so close to them that they could discern the fine bone structure of a once noble animal glowing in coiled mockery of what it hid.

"My best estimate," Xin said, "is that we have six months before there will be too much radiation in the atmosphere to scrub it out. That's if all the fossils continue to degrade at their present rate and only the spots with luminescence contain the pruithium. If it has somehow spread through other parts of the fossil slabs, we'll be looking at an accelerated rate of decay with no reclamation of the region possible for many decades, perhaps centuries to come."

A snort drew her attention back to Olivia. "Or maybe we'll all just glow blue. We'll be as novel as those poor residents on Deleine whose reactions to their vaccines produced coral-colored eyes." Olivia pondered a moment. "Actually, everyone would forget all about them if we were walking around with patches of blue, glowing dermis."

Xin wished she could muster some levity, but she remained lost in silent contemplation.

After a deep breath, Olivia asked, "Well, what are our options?" She swiped away the airscreens as though they were a physical impediment to a solution.

"The fastest and easiest is injectable synthstone," Xin said. "They've made progress with that on Tampa Three after the Tredificio disaster."

"Good, good. We seal the remaining pruithium into the existing rock."

"For now."

"Hmm. But it's not the preferred solution, especially if the fuel permeated the rest of the slab." Olivia was already on the same track as Xin. "Plus, it only buys us some time."

"Perhaps a decade. Then, the decaying pruithium will eat through the synthstone just like it is the rock."

"Okay, what's plan B?" Olivia smiled conspiratorially.

Its radiance in the face of this catastrophe made Xin hate her next words. "I don't have one."

Olivia's positive veneer remained in place. "Fair enough. Like you always say, 'When you don't know your next step, go back to the research.'"

"Research which is banned from us in The History."

"Not necessarily," Olivia said. "There's a rumor the terraforming data was archived V-side."

"In the virtual world? That seems unlikely since the Embassy can't regulate it as well as they would like."

"It might not have been put there by the Embassy."

"I don't think it would matter who put it there now that there are so many new security measures in place after the Palomin debacle a few months ago."

"Oh, yeah, Palomin. That *was* a debacle." Olivia's voice quickly lowered. "Sorry. I know you lost some people in that battle."

"Distant relatives who could care less about a woman who chose science over life as a cender-toting contractor," Xin said. "I was never interested in my violent birthright."

"True, but still, genes are genes, which is what makes a family, family, violent or not. Speaking of...our way into the V-side is with a fragger contingency set up on the outskirts of the city."

Xin's breathing hitched. "No."

Olivia held up her hand in placation. "I know, I know. It's a lot to take in, asking anti-Embassy radicals to help a government-sanctioned organization, but only the fraggers can access the V-side Archives undetected. I've heard they're the ones who put the terraforming data in there to begin with."

Before Xin could protest again, Olivia hurried on with her argument. "Honestly, it makes sense. Rushow was originally envisioned virtually, and I theorize that's how they knew to plan it out this way. They had the same knowledge of the landscape and the creatures that the original terraforming teams did."

"It's still a bit difficult to believe. In any event, you're right. There is no other way to access that data." Xin took a deep breath and followed the tail vertebrae of an animal forever captured in her desktop. "Set it up."

Xin would be thankful to see clearly again. The lenses she and Olivia were sent to wear by their fragger contact blacked out her vision as soon as they entered the small, silver transport vehicle. The only glimpse of their driver had been of auburn hair streaked in dark green. Xin couldn't even tell if it were a man or a woman.

Xin kept her anxiety in check by drifting into the soothing beats and tranquil melodies streaming through the co-coms inserted into her ears. Given fraggers propensity for mind-altering substances, she was just glad the contact hadn't decided to drug them. It would seem Olivia could have used some stims or drops to help with her anxiety as she crushed Xin's hand in a death grip the first hour of their long ride.

They could have simply been circling Rushow Territory most of the night, or maybe the fragger contingency was really that far away. In any event, when they were whisked out of the vehicle, there was a brief moment of daylight as their lenses left blackout mode before an arm at each of their elbows guided them through an open door of a small, white building.

Before Xin could get a closer look at the green-streaked redhead, they disappeared back through the door, and it snapped shut, leaving Olivia and Xin in a bright white area the size of a boardroom.

The music faded out as a voice spoke to them directly through the temporary co-coms.

"These are your insertion tubes." The voice interrupted.

Xin stared at the only objects in the room—a half dozen silver pods lined up like so many shiny coffins.

Olivia squeezed Xin's hand tightly again. As their gazes met, Xin gave her a small nod and a smile in reassurance. Olivia returned the gesture, but it looked as forced as all of Xin's expressions usually felt.

"Have you both used a pod before?"

"Y—" Olivia's voice cracked. She cleared her throat and rolled her shoulders back before speaking up. "Yes, in V-parlors in The Hub."

"No," Xin said.

Olivia showed surprise. "You've never been to the V-side before?"

"Will that be a problem?" Xin asked.

"No, but the insertion process can be disorienting for first-time users. Choose a pod. Your time here is limited."

Olivia didn't let go of Xin's hand immediately. "Better together, right?"

"Always," Xin said.

Olivia gave her a quick kiss before jumping into a pod as though she might lose her nerve if she didn't do it that instant.

Xin lay down in the one beside her Prime.

The lid slid over her, and she experienced the slightest sense of claustrophobia as the white lights arcing around the sides dimmed before going out completely.

She closed her eyes against the darkness. They had been told in the package that the lenses needed to be worn at all times, including for insertion. Little sparks appeared randomly, as if testing her pupil dilation.

The voice came through the co-coms once more. In the darkness, it sounded like someone lying next to her, whispering in her ear.

"Please remember that this is a favor because we have a mutual interest in understanding the files you are about to encounter. Should you try to insert a data miner or expose the insertion point at any time, you won't be leaving this facility."

There was an emphasizing pause.

"Prepare for insertion in three, two, one."

"It's an ocean," Xin said, struggling with her balance on the small boat where she and Olivia stood. She crouched down to rest on her knees and gripped the edges of the craft. "Is this...wood?" Her virtual fingers slid over the carved rim. "It feels like wood. The tactile sensibilities in here are astounding. I had always heard the V-side was immersive, but that description seems inadequate now that I'm inside."

A rush of exhilaration left her breathless. Breath. "Am I breathing?" She felt silly asking a question she knew the answer to, but this wave of emotion was as unbalancing as the purple ocean waves around them. She laughed.

Olivia flinched beside her, then laughed as well. She sounded like Olivia, but her avatar only resembled her in the fact that it was blonde with blue eyes and had a similar chin.

"Do I look like me?" Xin asked, trying to see her reflection in the dark, choppy waves.

"Not a lot." Olivia laughed again.

Then Xin had a realization. "I can't smell anything."

"The only thing the V-side architects haven't been able to simulate or improve upon."

The absurdity of their situation spurred Xin into a raucous outburst. She laughed until tears streaked her face and her abdomen hurt. Never in her life had she felt this giddy, or at least, ever openly expressed this kind of emotion. It was addictive. She wanted to be this way all the time.

Olivia gathered her composure first and spun around in the boat. "There should be an invitation waiting for us." The little vessel rocked with her movement, and she staggered along with it. "Do you see a sphere somewhere? It would be bright blue and as big as my head."

"You won't need an invite today."

The words came from a humanoid with distinctly dragonesque features who sat cross-legged on a wooden raft several meters behind their boat. The voice sounded female but the avatar's form, which was covered in glittering green scales, was androgynous.

"We were granted permission to enter the Archives for Rushow," Olivia said.

"Which is why you do not need an invite," the dragon-person said. "The lobby of the entire V-side is based on the original oceans of Tampa Quad. It is a point of pride because my many-great-grandmothers designed it."

"It is truly amazing," Xin said, "and immersive. I feel...everything, things I've not ever felt."

"Was it the data we're here for today which allowed your grandma-great to theorize the color or was that simply her aesthetic?" Olivia asked.

"It's what she saw aboard the scout ship."

Olivia used one of her more colorful words to emphasize her disbelief.

"Olivia means that the oceans would have already been long gone by the time of contact," Xin said.

The dragon-person mimicked Olivia's voice perfectly as she used the same obscenity in response. "And before you comment further, look at what you came here to see. Then, you can tell me what is true and what is not."

A swell of water lapped over the bow of their small boat. Exhilaration spread through Xin as a water dragon slid beneath them. She crawled to the other side to see it reemerge. The animal rolled onto its side and peered at her with a glowing blue eye.

"It's exactly as I had imagined it," Xin said. "They...they look so real." Tears fell from her eyes, her cheeks flushed, and her hands trembled. Unprepared for these virtual sensations, Xin rolled into a ball on the boat's bottom.

"Hey, you okay?" Olivia rubbed her back.

"I can feel you," Xin said. "Like you're right next to me."

"I am, technically. The V-side is its own kind of real."

"No. You don't understand. For me, it *is* more real than our world." Never had Xin been able to express her emotions in such a way. It was like only being able to see in black and white then suddenly putting on lenses and encountering a rainbow.

"That happens sometimes," said the dragon-person. "We use the V-side for therapy among the fragger organization."

Xin sat up. "Does it work?" Her words were on a whisper of hope.

"Almost always. But after many immersive sessions."

Olivia squealed, breaking into the reverie of this new possibility of expression for Xin.

The squeal became a curse and a laugh. "Someone was clever about hiding this data."

"What do you mean? I don't see any data." Xin scanned the watery world. No blocks of words overlaid the lavender sky. No encrypted symbols floated among the ocean waves.

"It's not just about seeing in the V-side," the dragon-person said. "You should know that by now."

"Here." Olivia took Xin's hand in hers and placed it onto one of the dragons.

She marveled at the feel of its slick skin. The warmth of true bliss spread from her fingertips throughout the rest of her body along with a sensation that tickled her mind. She held her breath, that fake breath with no capacity to smell, that existed only in her mind. Just like the data now flowing into her from this animal.

A rumble in the distance drew their attention to the skies.

"Has someone else entered this part of the V-side?" Xin asked.

"It's a simulation of the data," the dragon-person said. "A static rendering—non-interactive."

"Is that an exploratory ship?" Olivia asked.

"Yes, the first one with my ancestor aboard," the dragon-person said. "These are images taken from primitive voyeurs of the time. We've mixed and painted the footage for V-side resolution."

"The ships aren't due for another millennia," Xin said.

"They are right on time."

"There's still water...." Xin let her words drift off, but the dragon-person finished her chilling thought for her.

"And still dragons."

"Are they venting some sort of exhaust or water vapor?" Olivia pointed to a faint, blue contrail following the silver ship.

Icy awareness stabbed into Xin's reverential state.

"Pruithium." The word stuck to dry lips. She licked them, no longer marveling at how real the sensation was.

"They—*we*—brought it here while the creatures were still alive."

A sob choked her.

Not even as a child did she cry like she did now. Several massive sea dragons swam in and around the boat. They raised an eye out of the water or an entire head as if showing concern for Xin. Their kindness, whether a programmer's whim or not, was almost too much for Xin to take. "Our ancestors poisoned these creatures. Killed them. All of them."

"Now, you understand why I have devoted my life to protecting this data," the dragon-person said. "As have all in my long line before me."

Xin spread her arms wide and hung over the side of the boat to embrace part of the giant sea dragon's head. "I'm so sorry," she whispered.

"I've been waiting for the right moment and the right people to help me bring this to light," the dragon-person said. "It is the beginning of many lies exposed. There had to be a reason for the rest of the Intra-Brazial to care—or even believe—the corruption of the Embassy. Your findings and your passion show me there is hope."

No one had ever relied on Xin for her passion.

"It won't be easy to share this ugly data," Olivia said, stroking the animal's back.

"Truth isn't always very pretty, but it is still built upon a substantial structure," the dragon-person responded.

Xin was struck by a harsh irony.

No longer was *substance matching aesthetic* in Xin's world. To show the ugly truth, substance must now master aesthetic.

"How can we do this?" Olivia's voice was quiet. "It's so much to take on. How...?"

"Together," Xin said. "We're always better together." She leaned over to kiss Olivia with the passion she had always felt, with the passion of a woman reborn with the gift of purpose and all the wonderfully terrifying emotions which came with it.

THE END

Heidi Ruby Miller is a travel writer turned novelist. She uses research for her stories as an excuse to roam the globe. Her books include the popular *Ambasadora* series (Dog Star Books), *Man of War* (Meteor House), which is a sequel to Science Fiction Grandmaster Philip José Farmer's novel *Two Hawks from Earth*, and the international award-winning writing guide *Many Genres, One Craft* (Headline Books Inc.). In between trips, Heidi teaches creative writing at Seton Hill University, where she graduated from their renowned Writing Popular Fiction Graduate Program the same month she appeared on *Who Wants To Be A Millionaire*. Follow Heidi's writing journey with her husband, Jason Jack Miller, and their two cats in the newsletter *Small Space, Big Life* and find her on YouTube, her website, and Instagram all as Heidi Ruby Miller. Find her online at www.heidirubymiller.com.

CATALYST
BY KEVIN PLYBON

THE WEED FROM THE belly of the dragon, that was the stuff.

Selway Bhak took a long drag on his vaporizer, twiddling its intensity dial. Smoke stung the back of his throat and he coughed.

This belly batch was chill. It had a bite, but it wasn't harsh like the crop from the kidneys. Sweeter, too, than buds from the shoulder cavities. He'd snuck a few primo leaves from a silo this morning and flash-dried them.

He needed a damn smoke today, because apparently the world was ending.

From his orbit around Daianos, his uptight yellow world, he could see the red glow of lasers on the horizon. The fleet of the glorious Hidran Empire had finally arrived this morning after a decade of suspense. Rank after implacable rank of pyramid-shaped battleships and zippy fighters appeared out of the black Void, bent on annexing their latest planet. He had watched the fight on his work tablet, and it was ugly. The defensive cloud of drones that the brass had bragged about was shredded already. The Hidrans advanced like a storm. Daianos was getting creamed.

Ten years to prepare and the brass had fucked it up, just like they fucked up the rest of the world. Good for nothing.

Bhak puttered his lips and tried to relax into the weed, letting it dull his anger. The invaders might come for his dragon, but at least he'd be high.

He stood at the edge of one of the larger cavities inside Kaoat, this damn beautiful, sleepy worm he was blessed to farm. Above him, the gentle curve of a rib lined the fleshy ceiling. Glowing pustules poked from the meat and bathed the whole place in green light. Long pools of ichor —dragon juice, Bhak called it—dotted the sticky ground, and stalks of crimson bore-weed grew out of the juice. Bhak dragged a hand through the leaves of the nearest patch, sniffing the fresh pollen. Odd that there was nothing between him and the Void but a few yards of beast.

Lately, he had the feeling that Kaoat was warming to him, waking up. Giving him sublime weed. He brushed his fingers on the wall, wet with dragon juice, and felt the worm say hello: a tickle at the base of his spine, an intuition that Kaoat had more for him.

Yeah, it was a shame the world was ending.

Bhak took another long toke and blew the smoke against a transparent membrane in the creature's flank. When it cleared, he saw other worms making their lazy ways around Daianos, multi-colored spines on their backs gleaming in the dark. Unbelievably massive things, miles long, just like Kaoat.

And there, coming around the planet, was the vanguard, a grim pyramid: a Hidran battleship.

Trembling, Bhak turned his back. There was nothing he could do—but at least there was weed to bale.

He trotted toward the center of the cavity where a metal shed housed all his tools. A harvester rig with man-sized tires rested beside the shed. He clambered up a ladder and took a seat in the cab. The windows opened, the fruity dragon air rolling in. After a second of hesitation, he strapped on his seatbelt. He was pretty high, better be safe.

He docked his work tablet on the control panel and powered up the harvester. Pistons hissed, blades at the rear began to churn, whining up to speed. He throttled the rig gently forward, puffing on his vaporizer.

He was relaxing a bit more. There was a war outside, but in here it was just him and the weed and the worm.

An alarm beeped on his tablet. Something blocked the way.

"Custodian Bhak! Custodian Bhak!"

A woman stood in front of the harvester with upraised arms. Standing in the nearest bore-weed patch, in fact, crushing precious buds. He almost shouted at her to move her ass, but realized who it was: General Tillian Fare, head of research, the brass who owned all the dragons. The weed was too valuable to entrust to a bunch of farmers.

Gold trim and tassels marched across the shoulders of General Fare's dark blue uniform. Normally a pillar of confidence, she slouched today, her eyes wide and bloodshot. Understandable. She didn't even have any soldiers with her—they probably needed everybody against the Hidrans.

That tickle in Bhak's spine again. The dragon nudging him. He always got the feeling that the big guy did not like the good General.

Fare craned her neck, lips peeling back. "Custodian Bhak, come with me."

"You look stressed."

"Daianos is falling," she snapped.

"Want a pull? It helps." He gave a leisurely salute with his vaporizer. It was a mark of how harried she was that she hadn't noticed it.

"Do you care at all?"

"I have a crop to bale."

Her eyes rolled. "High command is desperate. Our only chance is to try to wake the worms. Bring them into the fight."

Interesting. Bhak had seen two dragons duke it out once, the only ones you could really call "awake." Quite a sight, and they did have big claws. He clicked his teeth, chewing imaginary ships.

"Don't your scientist people say they've been sleeping for like a thousand years?"

"If we can wake them," she said, "the bore-weed serum will let us control them. It works perfectly for the drones."

For years, the brass had touted the big guns on their defensive drones, and a mind serum distilled from the bore-weed that let the pilots fly them. Super deadly combo, they claimed. A direct mind link guaranteed to toast those primitive Hidrans. Bhak glanced out the membrane window into the Void again just in time to see lasers flash, a half-dozen drones go up like candles.

"Doesn't look like it's working."

Fare's voice ticked up an octave. "Yours is the most intelligent, the most empathic. We injected him with a small amount already, but something is missing. A catalyst. Perhaps you can help us understand."

Bhak stared. "You what?"

"It's a simple procedure. We introduced the serum into the dragon's brain stem. From there it's a matter of closing the mind link. That's where you come in. The psychologists say you have an unusually strong relationship."

An overwhelming urge to pancake the General surged through his hands, and he very nearly jammed the harvester's throttle forward. He held back at the last second.

"Get off my worm."

"You *must* help me."

Not likely without her muscle around. "You aren't gonna move?"

Bhak grabbed his empty lunch pail from the floor of the cab and chucked it at General Fare. She stumbled out of the bore-weed patch and he motored forward, spitting out the window as he passed. In his wake, naked stalks snapped to attention, shorn of buds.

"Your planet needs you," she screamed.

Ten years to prepare. Icy Void, these people.

"Go lose your war, General," he called.

Hours later in his sleeping cavity, Bhak washed the crusty ichor from his body. Odd to be sudsing up with the apocalypse going on. But the bore-weed harvest was done, baled and stacked by the shed to be shipped out. No doubt thousands of Daianos soldiers would be in need of a smoke. Not to mention new limbs.

His own limbs ached from the labor, but it was good. After he toweled off, he added a bit of dragon juice to a bowl with some spare leaves and ground them to a paste. He rubbed the paste on his arms and sighed, the fatigue dripping away. Minty vapors tingled up his nostrils. Bore-weed was powerful stuff.

It was funny that no one had thought to make use of these dragon things until recently. Mammoth lizard oddities floating in the Void like moons, that's all they were for hundreds of years. Until somebody discovered the cavities inside them and the miracle weed. The brass, already stretched thin with the Hidrans incoming, pounced on the worms like starving cats—here was an advantage the enemy didn't have.

At the time, he was living in Garmoria, a town near the equator. A sleepy little place in the yellow-dust desert where the local pastime was to smoke as much as possible. The war effort vacuumed up most of the food, so that new dragon grass took the edge off. But then the brass sent word that they needed space farmers, and the stoned, hungry mayor finally had enough. Told them to fuck off. The next day, sleek military cruisers appeared on the horizon, shimmering in the heat, and vaporized half the town.

Bhak yanked a clean shirt over his head, stuffing down memories of pulverizing lasers and collapsing walls.

Wonderful people, the brass.

He took a saucer from a dragon-bone cupboard. He pinched the tip of a pustule sticking out of the wall and watched a sweet-smelling goop squirt onto the saucer. The stuff had grossed him out when he first came on board nearly a year ago, but it tasted fine. Like warm plums.

Warmth sparked inside him, the meaty room resonating. Kaoat was happy that Bhak liked his goop. Maybe it was all the weed Bhak smoked, but these past few days the dragon had been intruding more and more on his thoughts.

You there, wormy? he thought.

The base of his spine tickled.

Hope the General isn't doing anything too painful to you.

The tickle became a flame. Rage so hot that Bhak stumbled against his wardrobe. For a second he thought he might pass out, but the feeling faded, becoming blessedly cool.

You really don't like her.

Bhak had to admit, not all that rage had come from the worm. The thought of General Fare jabbing Kaoat with a syringe in some dark cavity made Bhak want to run her over again.

The walls undulated with pleasure, agreeing with Bhak's murderous thought. Bhak was surprised. The dragon had never done *that* before, reacting physically.

He took a pull on his vaporizer and glanced out a membrane window to check on the end of the world.

The Hidran fleet had advanced through the first ring of spidery drones on this side of the planet, battleships nosing toward the second. A few of the ships burned, drifting hulks, so the brass had scored some victories. But there were way too many left.

Not far away, a glittering Daianos command cruiser was giving the Hidrans hell, torpedoes flying. An oversized bridge sat like a glass wart on its swooping hull. All the damn Generals in the vicinity were probably on that thing. Well, except Fare.

Bhak didn't know who to root for, honestly. Which was worse: getting conquered, or getting your ass pasted like Garmoria?

On his belt, his tablet beeped. He tapped it. "Bhak."

"Custodian Bhak, there are Hidrans on board!" It was General Fare, whispering.

Bhak's heart thumped despite the weed. He should have blocked the entry membranes in Kaoat's neck. "That was fast."

"I barely got away," she hissed. "I heard one say to shoot anything that moves."

"I told you to get out."

"You have to help me."

She sounded genuinely terrified. He puffed on his vaporizer like a man suffocating. "Where are you?"

"The left dorsal."

Literally miles away—she'd never make it. Bhak considered hanging up. Nobody would ever know. The Hidrans would eventually find her and toss her into the Void, and maybe he could convince them that he grew good weed.

"Bhak!"

A memory: those cruisers coming out of the desert, shimmering in the Garmorian heat. He remembered being so damn high on bore-weed that he thought the dragons themselves had come down from the heavens. He remembered wishing, after the town had been burning for a while, that he could have stopped it.

Damn it all.

"Can you get to the belly? Kaoat can expel you from there. The command ship is close."

"I think so."

"Take the northwest passage, it's the quickest way."

The line went dead. Not a word of thanks.

He clipped the tablet back onto his belt, then flung open his wardrobe. He shoved his planting suits aside until he felt reassuring cold metal. From behind the suits, he pulled his gun. A silvery automatic with a wicked muzzle. A souvenir from Garmoria.

Out the window, a Hidran battleship exploded, and Bhak jumped.

He packed dried bore-weed into his vaporizer and took another drag. If he was doing this, he was gonna be fucking stratospheric.

Kaoat's belly was a fun place to visit because you could die if you slipped. The "ground"—the inside of Kaoat's stomach lining—was sunk in acid a quarter mile deep. Bhak had built a network of catwalks over the stuff, and platforms held aloft by thrusters. That's where he grew the good weed in man-made ichor pools. Something about the belly fumes made it grow thick and tall and delicious.

He took another puff when he arrived at the valve-door to the stomach, a circle of hardened flesh. He pressed on a pustule beside the door and the circle shivered and split apart, trailing strings of mucous.

Humid air washed over him, a cloying stomach funk. He stepped onto the first catwalk, gun to his shoulder. Far below the metal slats at his feet, orange liquid bubbled. His stoked brain grappled with the strange gravity that all the dragons seemed to generate internally—just one more thing nobody could figure out about these crazy beasts. It was almost like they had evolved for humans.

Bhak edged toward the first floating platform. "General Fare," he called.

A valve-door on the other side of the belly slurped open and Fare dashed in. Her pristine uniform was torn, a scorch mark across her face.

"Here!" Bhak called.

She sprinted across the catwalks and platforms, closing the distance in a few minutes. She crouched beside him, behind a crate of fertilizer. "They're on my ass. I had a few men but they're dead." She glanced at his weapon. "A farmer with a gun. Fantastic."

"It's great to see you as well."

"Just get me out of here."

Bhak knelt and slung off the canvas bag he was carrying. He unzipped it and rolled out a crinkly plastic planting suit. Fare's ticket out.

As soon as he laid the suit on the catwalk, the stomach cavity around them shook and he had to steady himself. The base of his spine itched.

Kaoat felt... sad? That was sweet.

"I'm not leaving, wormy," he muttered. "She is."

"Who are you talking to?"

He ignored her and held out the clear plastic. "This has a radio and life support on the inside. Not exactly rated for the Void, but it'll do for the acid. Look for the intestinal passage at the bottom, Kaoat will fart you out from there. You can signal the command ship."

Her face was tinged green. "You aren't coming?"

"I'll take my chances."

"They'll never leave you alive."

Bhak hesitated—and a laser bolt flashed over his shoulder, burying itself in the flesh wall beyond. He spun, raising his gun, just as pain from Kaoat lanced through his mind.

His vision went double and he stumbled. That *definitely* hadn't happened before.

A half-dozen soldiers jogged in through the nearest valve-door. Shaved heads and all muscle, they could almost be from Daianos, except for the crimson uniforms of the glorious Hidran Empire. And the half-dozen glorious muzzles pointed right at him.

"Duck," he shouted, pulling the General down.

She slapped his hands away and already had two pistols out, blasting shots over the crate. Two Hidrans dropped.

"Nice."

Her eyes flicked, frantic. "Where's that suit?" She felt the catwalk behind her with a hand and glanced back.

Bhak peered over the edge and saw the plastic suit falling, swinging in the hot air. It landed on the acid lake and floated like a flower.

"Sorry, General."

"That was the only one?"

Her voice was climbing, panicky. He held out his vaporizer. "I strongly suggest you take a hit."

A hail of laser fire ate away at their crate, and they had to bail, crouch-running through the red stalks of a boreweed patch to get away. Leaves tickled his face. They took cover behind a harvest shed.

"You said you'd take your chances with the Hidrans," she hissed. "Would you actually betray your world?"

"Maybe they'll let me keep the gig."

"They're merciless and you're in the damn navy."

"You could surrender. I'll put in a good word."

She groaned. "How did I get stuck needing rescue from a traitor?"

Traitor? Whose military had incinerated half a city to make a point?

That murderous urge from before swept through Bhak again, this time to shove General Fare right off the platform. He saw it clearly. She'd make a nice splash beside the floating suit, and then her body would melt down, food for Kaoat.

Bhak shook himself. Get a grip. It wasn't Fare that had destroyed Garmoria.

The base of his spine tingled. Kaoat was disappointed.

"If you want to help," Bhak muttered at him, "get these Hidrans off our backs."

General Fare's eyebrows rose. "You *are* talking to the dragon!"

The cavity rumbled again and the catwalk tilted. Fare tumbled into Bhak, both of them falling against the railing, clinging to the steel.

"Kaoat!" Bhak shouted.

At the other end of the cavity, a fountain of acid erupted from the lake below. It arced high into the air and came down as orange rain—directly on the Hidran soldiers. The drops hit a few of them and they screamed, their bodies twisting.

The rumbling subsided and the catwalk righted itself. Bhak struggled to his feet.

"Now's our chance," he said.

"You controlled the worm," General Fare hissed. "How?"

His fingertips tingled. He stared at the dying men. One of their buddies knelt beside them, opening a med kit. "I didn't do anything. Come on."

A harvester rig sat beside this shed, just like in the other cavity. Bhak sprinted to it and hauled himself up the ladder into the cab. Fare toppled in behind him.

"We can't go back," she gasped. She was right. Another squad was piling through the door behind them.

Bhak docked his tablet, cranked up the machine, and flung the throttle forward, sending them roaring toward the opposite exit.

Right at the first group of Hidrans.

The ones that had dodged the acid rain dove out of his way onto one of the platforms. The rest were still screaming, their skin giving off orange smoke. Bhak might have swerved if he could, but he was on the catwalk now. Nowhere to go.

One chunky man shrieked, "For the eternal renown of the emp—"

Bhak ran him down.

Weird gurgles bubbled up as the harvester and its enormous tires rolled over, pulping the soldiers. Bhak looked back to see gore dripping through the grates. His stomach churned, but his awareness of Kaoat surged, the worm rejoicing.

Bhak shook himself, struggling against the feeling and the bore-weed fog. Damn bloodthirsty beast. First he wanted Fare dead, and now these fools—

When Bhak looked up, the valve-door was coming fast.

"Open up, wormy!" he shouted.

The hardened meat ripped and split just in time for the harvester to blast through.

"I'll get you another suit," he said to Fare.

She was staring at him, mouth slightly open. He'd seen that look before on the faces of some of his more excitable friends back in Garmoria, when they found out there was a whole depot of military rations in town. No food lines if you were brass.

Hunger.

Fare's eyes sharpened. A smile brightened her dirty face. "They're hurting him," she said quietly.

"Huh?"

She grabbed his tablet from the cab's dock, dialed up a video, and shoved the screen in his face.

"Sure, log right in."

"Look, this is live."

The feed showed a harvest cavity in Kaoat's left shoulder, bore-weed patches dotting the floor. A group of Hidran soldiers had surrounded one of the patches. They slid a machine into position, a cylindrical steel housing that lay on a carriage with tires almost as big as the ones on the harvesters.

Bhak squinted. What was it?

An enormous blade extended from the housing and started to hum. Its edges blurred with power. Bhak watched in disbelief as one end of the machine tipped up and the blade plunged into Kaoat's flesh, cutting around the patch.

The walls around Bhak radiated fiery pain, and he could have sworn he heard Kaoat shrieking in his mind. He clenched his fists and took three long drags on his vaporizer. He offered the weed to Fare again, but she waved it off.

"If I have you and the worm on my side, we can fight our way out of this," she said.

Kaoat was in pain.

"Tell me how."

Bhak goosed the throttle, speeding through the sticky passageways that webbed Kaoat's innards. Tight corners, but that was nothing new for him. He remembered a hot night in Garmoria, whipping down an alley in a hovercraft with the boys, riding low with flour they boosted from the generals' private depot. Shouting insults at the dark sky where those stupid defensive drones twinkled. The brass were worthless. All that weaponry and still the town went hungry.

The next day, after they'd stolen the food, the cruisers of death came buzzing out of the desert.

This time, the pain in Bhak's chest was his own. Never knowing if it was his raid that brought the fire.

"Pay attention!"

General Fare had her guns out the cab window. There were way more Hidrans around than Bhak had thought, shouting as the harvester sped by. General Fare dropped a few.

"Take a left!" she shouted.

Bhak swung the rig around, bowling over a pair of crimson grunts. "We should be stopping that machine." He could feel that the cutting was done, but Kaoat still hurt—a memory of pain.

"We have to wake him and find the catalyst. Stop here!"

Bhak hit the brakes so hard he almost flew out of his chair, but he'd clicked in his seatbelt. General Fare wasn't so lucky and splatted into the front window. She groaned and wiped a trickle of blood from her forehead.

Bhak caught himself licking his lips—Kaoat's reaction or his, he wasn't sure.

She jumped out of the cab, touched a pustule on the wall, and ran through the valve-door that slurped open.

He knew that door. What had she been saying hours ago, about the serum?

Kaoat's brain stem was at the back of his neck, up a long, slimy shaft that held a dragon-bone ladder. Fare and Bhak climbed, and by the time he reached the top, his arms were screaming. He dragged himself into the brain stem cavity behind Fare.

It was dark, the gloom lit by arcs of electricity. Sacs of grey matter hung from the walls, flashing when the arcs hit them. Why, exactly, were they here? The electricity made growing weed up here a no-go.

He took a long, deep drag on his vaporizer. "What do you even mean by 'catalyst'?"

"The bore-weed serum," she said, breathing heavily. "You already have some connection with the beast, so we figured all we needed was to give the worm itself a little dose. But I don't know how to complete the mind link. It's like he wants something else."

"What should I do?"

"Ask him what he needs."

Bhak frowned. *You heard her. Something special to connect us?*

An image of startling clarity filled Bhak's mind: his own silhouette, kicking General Fare to the ground and shooting her through her left eye.

The real, live General watched him, one undamaged eyebrow trembling.

Bhak licked his lips.

Wormy, maybe you didn't understand.

"Well?" Fare said breathlessly.

"Well—"

There was another flash of lightning, and Bhak gasped in horror.

Someone had driven an enormous steel spike into the brain sac nearest him. The sharp end was buried in spongy flesh, and the other end had a screen with flashing lights on it.

Fare saw him looking and touched the screen, calling up a beeping chart. "I don't know why it's not working. The team assured me the dose was enough."

The fire that filled Bhak was equally his and Kaoat's.

"That's your damn serum?" he said. "You're hurting him."

She tsked. "It's a splinter."

The rage and the bore-weed in his system were a weird, boiling combination. The murder image came again: Bhak's boot in the General's gut, her arms raised in fear, the laser burning through her brain.

"Stop," Bhak hissed.

Fare watched him. "He's saying something, isn't he? What's he saying?"

The itch in Bhak's spine went suddenly cold, and he saw something else. One of his own memories—the worm was digging around in his mind.

He was standing in Garmoria, in the blackened remains of an amphitheater. A dozen meathead generals stood lined up, telling the survivors their fate: farm a dragon or pay a ridiculous tax to stay. Bhak felt the desert heat on his back.

Like a video on his tablet, the image zoomed in, focusing on a woman at the end of the line. Her back rifle-straight, her golden tassels pristine.

He gaped. That was Fare. In his memory. He hadn't known her at the time.

"You were at Garmoria?" he whispered.

She frowned in surprise, then chuckled. "Got a lot of recruits out of that one. Got you."

"You destroyed half my town."

"For the good of the world."

Bhak's fists tightened.

"You think I'm the bad one?" She grabbed for his tablet again, dialed up a video and thrust it at him. "This was one hour ago."

There was Garmoria—you could tell because the western neighborhoods were bombed-out ruins. But as Bhak watched, a light grew on the horizon. A ship?

No. The light came closer. It was fire.

A wave of destruction passed over the city, roiling like the sun, and when it was gone... Nothing. All of Garmoria was a burned patch in a yellow wasteland.

Gone.

"What happened?" he said dumbly.

"The Hidrans bombarded the southern continent."

Bhak didn't know what to think. The bore-weed was thick in him. He shook himself, scrubbed his eyes, tried to get the images out of his head. Tried not to think about the people who didn't run off to farm a dragon like him.

General Fare regarded the big spike in Kaoat's brain. "As I said, the Hidrans have no mercy. You see what happens if we lose."

Bhak clung to his vaporizer. Hidrans before him, the brass behind.

The worm around him.

Desperately, he cast a question to the air: would Kaoat fight?

One pure dragon feeling cut like Garmorian sunlight: *murder this murderer.*

Okay, but why, wormy?

More from Kaoat: aching loss. Dragons betrayed by their riders long ago. The last true rider granting a request from the worms, altering their minds so they could never be ridden lightly again. Not without a sacrifice.

What do you mean, riders?

Kaoat strained against his sleep, the catalyst near at hand.

Murder this murderer.

"We could afford to lose Garmoria," Fare was saying. "At least it wasn't the capital."

Bhak gave in to the worm.

He dove at her legs and the two of them went down hard on the juicy floor, Bhak punching and scratching.

"Cease and desist!" Fare shrieked. She pulled a hooked knife from a sheath on her hip.

Bhak slapped it aside, then lifted her with a grunt and slammed her into the wet brain sac beside the spike.

An arc of electricity came zapping through the air. Bhak smelled ozone and stepped back, watching General Fare's eyes go wide, her frizzy hair stand on end. She jerked once, screamed twice, and collapsed.

A roar thundered in Bhak's head. The itch in his spine became a flame again, but this time spread down his arms to the tips of his fingers. He fell to his knees and shut his eyes.

Wormy, what the hell?

Exultation pounded through his skull, the bore-weed thrumming.

Bhak opened his eyes and saw the Void.

Miles below, Daianos burned. Hidran battleships stretched into the dark as far as he could see until they were no more than stars. Fighters zipped around his head.

Bhak flexed his claws, wiggled his tail. He opened his maw, felt stiff joints crackle.

What's happening to me?

He brought his awareness back to his body, his human body, and the smoking corpse in front of him.

The catalyst...

You knew she was at Garmoria the whole time, he thought.

He felt Kaoat pulling at him, guiding. Casually, he swiped at a passing Hidran fighter with a massive claw, slicing the ship clean in half. Others took notice and swarmed.

Bhak felt himself surge, sacs of gas under his arms propelling him forward. His teeth closed, ripping at the tiny ships. A battleship trained its guns on him, but he zoomed toward it and got there first. His fist closed around the bridge and tore it off in a spurt of atmosphere.

It's not nearly enough, he thought in despair, looking at the endless line of battleships.

Kaoat flooded Bhak's mind with more images.

Those generals standing in a merciless line in the amphitheater back in Garmoria.

That glittering Daianos command ship, not far away, where all the generals were probably huddled.

Other dragons orbiting Daianos, their stoned Garmorian custodians inside chatting with the sleepy worms in their minds. All needing catalysts to wake up.

Suddenly, Bhak understood. In his human body, he dragged deep on his vaporizer.

Damn bloodthirsty worms.

He turned the leviathan, caught sight of the command ship, and accelerated. Maybe they could win this.

The brass *were* good for something after all.

Kevin Plybon is a technical writer and author based in New York City. "Catalyst" is a prequel to his unpublished novel, *Dragon Star*. You can find him on Twitter @kevilknc and find other published work at kevinplybon.com.

A Friend Called Home
by Francis Fernandez

Nathan showed Lucy the telescope cube in his hand. He reached out for her, an excited smile spread across his face.

A giggle escaped Lucy's lips as he pulled her up from the grass and onto her feet. "Why are you in such a hurry, Nathan? We have time," she said, brushing the back of her dress.

Nathan's eagerness and impatience was etched in his furrowed brow, only making Lucy giggle more. "But we need to get a good spot! The whole village is going to be there for the meteor shower and I just don't want a...bad spot."

"Okay, space boy, let's go."

The two walked along the paved walkway of Nova Terra, street lights blinking on to guide their way, as the sun slowly crept closer to the horizon. It did not take them long to make it to the hill where families sat around on blankets, ready to witness the big event.

Nathan and Lucy found a spot near the top where the scientists had already set up their telescopes. Nathan quickly put the telescope cube on the ground and gave it two firm taps.

A soft whir wafted in the air as the cube expanded with gears and springs. Silver and gold metal warped and transformed into the tripod, and then into the telescope itself. Nathan looked into the eyepiece to get it ready. "So," he asked casually, "did you tell your parents about this weekend?"

Lucy blushed at the thought of their upcoming first date. They had been fond of each other since they were children, and Nathan had finally asked her out so many years later. She was embarrassed, but she'd been waiting for that moment in what felt like forever. "Yes, I told them."

"Awesome!" he said, looking back at her. The smile on his face was affectionate, and it always had a way of making Lucy's heart beat a little faster. Nathan turned back to the telescope to make more adjustments. "I'm so excited," he said, looking up from the telescope to wink at her. "I have everything planned. I know a couple of places around Nova Terra you haven't seen yet. I know it, it's going to be..."

A murmur grew amongst the scientists nearby. The mounting tension seemed to flow out and fill the still, evening air. The other villagers must have felt it too, as they all looked up at the darkening night sky. Lucy watched as Nathan turned the telescope toward the stars, trying to find what had everyone so interested.

Nathan tapped the top of the telescope to produce a second eyepiece. "Lucy, come here. I need you to see this." Lucy got up quickly and looked through the viewfinder. "What do you think that is?" he asked. She instantly saw what all the fuss was about. In front of the sun was something she'd never seen before.

Lucy focused the telescope and gasped. Two creatures the size of the moon were fighting, silhouetted by the backdrop of their sun. One was lizard like and appeared to have a skin of red. The other was a dark shadow that moved and struck like a ferocious beast, but had a body like murky oil.

The scientists scrambled between looking at the spectacle and arguing over what was happening. The villagers got up, trying to see the moon-sized shadows in the sky, their mood a mix of worry and wonderment.

"Maybe we'd better go," one father said to his family. Others agreed, and picked up their things. There would be no meteor shower show tonight.

Nathan and Lucy watched in rapt interest as the two creatures clawed at each other, flying through the vacuum of space before striking again with tooth and nail. It was vicious and frightening, and like nothing they had ever seen before. The nearby scientists, who vehemently searched through their wrist computers, proclaimed they were baffled that there were no records of these titans.

A brilliant light suddenly filled the emptiness of space, shining brighter than their sun. Every person on that hill shaded their eyes as the light grew stronger and more intense. Then it was gone. Nathan and Lucy looked back into the telescope and saw that only one creature remained.

The large, red beast seemed to be floating lifeless.

The villagers picked up their pace, obviously aware that something was happening they did not want to stay for. Scientists enthusiastically typed in data on their exciting new discovery. Nathan and Lucy shared a knowing look that something felt wrong.

A sound like a droplet hitting a pool of water reverberated throughout the hillside. Looking once more into the eyepiece, Nathan and Lucy watched the beast begin to move closer. It did not take long for the figure to grow bigger as it hurtled itself toward their planet.

The village Elder stood up with authority and calm, bringing the panicked people to silence. In a voice that demanded attention, he ordered everyone to go back to their homes. The pods that had come from their ship almost a thousand years ago, were built to withstand the harshness of space, and could endure what was to come.

Nathan and Lucy stared up into the night sky, trying to find the creature with the naked eye. They scanned every star until they located a patch of darkness in the shape of the beast. It was moving fast.

No one else seemed to notice this. The village scientists were too busy fervently talking amongst themselves to notice that the Elder had spoken, and the people hurried down the hill.

The noise was almost deafening when the creature entered the atmosphere. The villagers broke into a run, their screams drowned out by the ever-increasing sounds of crackling and popping as the moon-sized being plummeted toward the planet.

Lucy ran alongside Nathan away from the chaos, but it was too late. The impact threw them off their feet, pushing their faces into the dirt. Dust and debris hung in the air as another rumble came from the crash site.

The ground beneath their feet shook.

Nathan looked up from where he lay, unable to see anything. His vision blurred and his eyes watered and stung from the dust.

The earthquakes grew more violent, as did the panicking from the villagers. Screams seemed to blanket Nathan in fear and uncertainty. His heart beat like a drum in his chest as he tried to move his legs to get up. He could feel his brain telling his legs to move, but something was stopping them. He reached down and discovered the massive rocks on top of him. "No!" he screamed, desperately trying to push himself out from under the rubble.

His body went from numb to feeling like it was on fire. Nathan grabbed at the boulders on his body, but his sweaty fingers could not get a firm grip. He frantically looked around for help, but the dust was too thick. "Help!" he shouted into the madness.

The sounds of running villagers fleeing the chaos were all he could hear. He clawed wildly at the rocks that pinned him down.

"Nathan!" It was Lucy. "Nathan!" There was a pause and Nathan feared the worst. She suddenly slid to his side, pulling and pushing at the rocks on his legs.

The ground shook again, loosening beneath him. Eyes wide, Lucy held onto Nathan's arms and desperately tried to pull him up. It was not enough. Earth and soil gave way into an endless pit.

Nathan's body disappeared into the emptiness below.

She almost fell in with him, but the Elder's large hands took hold of her wrists and pulled her to stability. "Let's go!" he screamed, and yanked her to her feet.

Lucy ran with a numbness she had never felt before. She'd abandoned Nathan. Her final memory of him was watching him fall into an abyss, a darkness she could not see through. Before she was pulled away, she saw his face. While hers was racked with fear and dread, incredulously, his held a smile of relief. Nathan seemed happy that she would be safe.

Lucy stared blankly at the mountainous ball of jagged rocks resting silently on the plains in the distance. This was the creature they'd seen fighting amongst the stars. Now, it was a lifeless moon that had torn their world apart.

She hated this rock. It had taken months for her to come to that conclusion, but now she hated it with every fiber of her being. She loosened the fist she had subconsciously made, wishing she could punch the rock to death. But how do you get revenge on a rock? How do you get back the home this piece of dirt had taken away from you?

Behind Lucy, the villagers continued to rebuild Nova Terra. The pods that they'd thought could withstand a monster lay in pieces among the broken streets and uprooted trees. Villagers had built makeshift houses and salvaged what technology still worked. Miraculously, everyone survived the tragedy, save one. So much had been destroyed, their planet a victim of this lifeless beast.

Lucy stared into the distance at the disaster on the other side of this fallen moon. On the other side of the stone monster was nothingness. Through some magic or technology that neither herself nor the scientists understood, they were being protected from the vastness of space. When the creature had crashed, their planet was fractured, yet somehow the village remained intact.

Nothing made sense.

It was difficult not to let the talk from the villagers enter her mind at that moment. The loss of hope, the acceptance of inevitability. There was no escape plan, and no means off the planet. Lucy only listened in on the conversations, letting the older and more experienced take the lead. That only frustrated her more. There were no answers, no big solution. Just yelling and screaming and pointing fingers. She hated it.

She hated everything. She missed Nathan.

Eyes watering, Lucy walked toward the massive rock she'd never touched, never visited. Even miles away, she could not see the top of it. What felt like seconds, though could have easily been hours, she found herself standing before the enormous piece of space debris. She mindlessly looked around it. Its bulk just went on forever. Nathan would have been so excited to learn about something so new, so different. Nathan...

Lucy shook her head to clear the thoughts rushing into her mind again. The feelings of anger and loss seemed to cover every inch of her body, like a cold bath. It was almost too much to bear. Finding her breath, she forced herself to sit against the space rock.

The surface was warm and oddly soft against her back. Her hands pressed up against the jagged scales. It seemed to hum with life. Her eyes narrowed as she felt every inch, trying to figure out what this was.

Then, a familiar noise echoed against the body of the beast. One she'd heard on that fateful day so many months ago. The sound of a droplet hitting a pool of water.

A growl rumbled across the valley. It was deep, yet almost melodic. There was a sharp pain in her chest as the thought of death reminded her of...

Nathan...

Lucy's breath caught when she heard the voice. Scrambling to her feet, she looked around the empty field, trying to find a source.

Poor Nathan. I am sorry...

The voice again. It was deep and warm, elderly and comforting. It was like the voice of God.

I am no god, young one. I apologize for not warning you. You have wakened me from my slumber, and for that, I must thank you. But also, I am immensely sorry for the hurt that I have caused you and your people. I saw what I had done before I fell into my sleep.

Lucy scrambled away from the space rock, afraid she was going insane. The rocks in front of her flexed and moved, and the ground beneath her feet shook. She fell to her back, no longer questioning her sanity. Villagers arrived to the scene on their hover bikes. Some helped her up, while others pointed lazer guns and vibration swords at the moving mass.

Please Lucy. Tell your people to stand down. I do not wish to harm them.

"What? Who is that? What's going on?" Lucy asked, gathering her courage. "Who are you?"

The earthquake intensified, but the people stood their ground, unafraid of what was in store.

As far as the eye could see, the wall of stony scales extended out, growing larger than was thought possible. Arms, legs, and wings made themselves known. Yet, to anyone up close, all they could see was the thigh of this creature.

The shape of a head emerged from the center. Lucy's rescuers screamed. She looked up at the shadow of what could only be the chin of a lizard.

"Are you the monster in front of us?" Lucy called out. The nearby villagers simply gaped in awe.

Yes. I am the Dragon who landed here. Again. I am so sorry...

"Sorry for what?"

I did not mean to land here. I have caused you and your people so much pain. I can feel it and see it in your mind, young Lucy.

"You're in my mind? Can no one else hear you?"

Yes. Only you and I may speak to each other. No other being may communicate, for it is the way. You were the first to make contact with me, and thus, you are my new bonded. For that I apologize, as well. You were never meant to touch me.

"I don't understand," Lucy said, somehow sensing the unease the Dragon was experiencing. What even was a Dragon? She was so confused.

I will try to explain...

Little prepared a person for a Dragon to delve into their brain. Connery, which was the Dragon's name, became connected to Lucy's mind the moment they'd touched. It was the will of the Dragon. The will of his kind. They are protectors of the universe. Their nature is to bond with a species, to understand them, to learn from them, and thus grow stronger and more resilient from that knowledge. It was their only weapon against the oncoming threat to the galaxy.

Often times, the person on the other end of a bonding was weak-willed or weak of spirit and could not handle the intense, emotional bond that would present itself. This led to madness and erratic behavior as the two learned that they could read and enter each other's minds.

All this information flooded Lucy's head through images and thoughts that were not her own. She did not feel her body fall to the ground. Connery knew the potential trauma of the bonding, and did his best to soften the blow. He had absorbed her knowledge when they'd bonded, of her life on the planet and her love of Nathan. Of the tragedy that was Connery's arrival, and the calamity they faced today.

Lucy was living a second life in mere moments. She learned of the war in the stars, the battle for the planets, and the need for this bonding. She also learned of how Connery had lost his previous bonded in that heated battle she'd witnessed through the telescope. When his bonded was killed, the Dragon lost consciousness and crash landed on the planet. The impact turned unconsciousness into slumber as Connery grieved for the bonded that he had lost, and awaited the bonded that was to come.

Tears fell from the Dragon's eyes like buckets of salty water. Lucy lay on the ground, her eyes wet from sorrow and loss. They were both grieving for someone dear to them. Miraculously, they had found each other.

The sadness was then overtaken with centuries of knowledge and experience filling the young girl's mind. Lucy was in awe as she witnessed the passage of time and the rise and fall of planets. The Dragon, in turn, saw Lucy's imagination and creativity, the possibilities, the hope and ingenuity that lacked the cynicism of age. Lucy understood that this destruction was not Connery's fault, and that maybe there was a way to save the planet and its people.

Nathan panicked, blinking rapidly and feeling for his body. The shock faded quickly when he realized he was standing in the middle of a pavilion. In front of him was a tiny animal that stood on its hind legs and reached to about his waist. It was cute, and kind of welcoming.

"Hello!" the creature said. Its black, beady eyes seemed to take Nathan in. It had dark yellow fur, and what looked like dog ears on an otter's face. Somehow, the mix worked well together. Its hands were human-like with opposable thumbs, and it was not wearing any clothing.

"Hi," Nathan replied hesitantly, trying to figure out what the creature was.

"Welcome to the After Life. I was just about to go over there," it said, pointing to a building that resembled an ancient diner from the twentieth century. "Since you just got here, you wanna join me?"

"Sure," Nathan said with continued trepidation. "My name's Nathan."

"Good to meet you. My name is..." the words that came from the animal's mouth sounded like seals barking.

"I don't know if I can even make those sounds. I think I'll just call you Otter Dog, if you're okay with it."

"I have no idea what that is, but I like it." Otter Dog smiled up at Nathan in approval.

The two walked into the diner, which had a beautiful view of the city below. Ringed tiers of platforms rose from the center of the city, reaching into the heavens with no end in sight. On each ring were shops and parks and restaurants.

"So," said Otter Dog, "what does the After Life look like to you?"

"A lot like ancient Earth."

"Huh. Earth. Haven't heard that word in a while. So, you're an Earthling."

Nathan was even more confused than before. The last thing he remembered was Lucy's face, and the relief he felt, knowing that she was safe. But that also meant... "Am I dead?"

Otter Dog laughed the cutest laugh he'd ever heard, like birds playing a harp made of kitten purrs. "Everyone here is dead. That's why it's called the After Life."

"I thought it'd be different."

"I've been here a long time, kid," Otter Dog lamented. A server rolled up to them in roller skates, but their face was not human. It was gelatinous with small tentacles writhing about.

"Don't be afraid," Otter Dog said, "we all have to find a way to pass the time." It turned to the server. "I'll take a number 4 special, and the kid here will take a milk." The server nodded and sped off.

"Pass the time until what?" Nathan said.

"Rebirth, kid." Otter Dog stretched its arms and legs before continuing. "We may be dead, but we don't stay here forever. Oh, no. A time comes for all of us, whether it be days or centuries, where we get to go back to the world of the living!" Nathan perked up at the idea of being able to go back home.

"That doesn't sound terrible. You just wait and then you go back to the world of the living?" he asked.

"Well, you go back as a baby, and you usually forget everything. Your past life, your time here in the After Life." It puffed up its chest with pride. "I'm one of the lucky ones that remembered everything the last time I was reborn. No one believed me about my previous lives! Can you believe that?"

The food arrived. Otter Dog's plate contained vegetables that Nathan did not recognize, and his milk was ice cold to the touch. He took a sip and was surprised by how refreshing it was. Food tasted better when you're dead, he supposed. Otter Dog ate his food with nimble hands. It was cute to watch.

"I'm going to forget my life on Nova Terra? My family? Lucy?"

"I don't know. But honestly, you may be here for a while, kid. So, I'd suggest you don't worry about it. I mean, you just got here." Otter Dog shrugged sympathetically.

Nathan sighed, still settling in with the thought that he was dead. The life he'd known was gone. A sense of despair enveloped him. He just wanted to cry. He'd never get the chance to grow up. Never have a chance to have a life. Never have a chance to be with Lucy.

While Otter Dog was finishing his meal, Nathan stared out into the skies of this strange city. In the distance, he noticed what appeared to be a black hole, devoid of light or life. "Hey, what's that?" he asked the adorable little creature.

"Oh, those. Yeah," it frowned, rubbing its button nose with the back of its hand, "I wouldn't get near those. They've been popping up a lot over the last few centuries. The rumor is, it takes you back to your living world." Otter Dog seemed unimpressed by the black hole that hovered so high above the city.

"Isn't that a good thing?" Nathan asked excitedly, wondering if it was a way to go back to the living world, back to his life with Lucy and Nova Terra.

"I've seen people go through them, but then...well..." Otter Dog looked sad. "I've lost a lot of friends that way. They never come back to the After Life. Not in decades, not in centuries, not ever."

"Oh," Nathan decided to drop the subject. The two spoke a little while longer before parting ways, promising to meet again tomorrow.

Outside the diner, Nathan looked back up toward the black hole he'd seen earlier. It was still there, and it flickered and sparked like a venomous trap. He tried not to think about it. He was dead, after all. But what he wouldn't give to go back to the life he once had.

It had taken months, but Lucy was finally able to convince the Elder and the villagers that she and Connery had a plan to save them from this dying planet. Though they feared Connery, and could not speak to the Dragon like she could, Lucy was able to reassure everyone that he was not the monster he appeared to be. It quickly became apparent that the Dragon was the reason the planet had not fully collapsed on itself. The sheer size of the beast had a large enough gravitational pull to keep what was left of the planet in place, for now.

The villagers were strewn along the back of the dragon, preparing for their new lives. A cacophony of tools and wood rang throughout. Lucy could feel Connery fighting the urge to laugh as people hollowed out his scales with pick axe and hammer, which seemed to tickle him. These would be their homes soon. At least until they found another planet.

Lucy worked with whomever she could to get the process going faster. Those who were skeptical quickly warmed up to Connery and the idea of living on this Dragon for however long it took. Lucy was not a leader and still followed the Elder's words, providing any input and guidance Connery had. That proved to be fruitful, as the Dragon was transformed into a city, and not a moment too soon.

The magma core could not be ignored as the planet crumbled under the Dragon's feet. The people of the planet were already tucked away in their new scale homes amongst the supplanted trees used for oxygen, ready for the journey ahead. Connery had his own atmosphere that could not be explained, and no one really cared to.

Many watched as the remains of their planet was turned into an uninhabitable wasteland. Others cried in their beds and held each other for comfort. The massive wings of the Dragon moved against the vacuum of space, but no one felt a thing. Life continued on.

Lucy sat atop Connery's head. The expanse in front of her took her breath away. Her heart ached all the more as she thought of Nathan and how much he would have loved to see these stars up close. To be the traveler he always wanted to be.

The sadness welled up from her belly. She sensed the empathy that came from Connery. She felt relief being bonded to him, and grateful that he'd saved the lives of her people. "I know you know about Nathan, but do you mind if I tell you about him anyway?"

I would be pleased to hear your stories.

There was no concept of time in the After Life. It had been a long time since Nathan's good friend Otter Dog had found his rebirth into the living world. With no one to help guide him, Nathan had given in, and found himself in front of the infamous black hole.

Every time he'd brought it up, the cute little critter would try to convince him of what a bad idea it was. At this point, Nathan no longer cared. He found that the more time he spent in the After Life, the more he missed home. He missed the hill, if it was still there, that let him look up toward the stars. Most of all, he missed his family, and he missed Lucy.

Nathan looked cautiously around. Most of the other entities that inhabited the After Life kept to themselves. The few who did notice him, shook their heads in disapproval, but never made a move to stop him. "I really hope the rumors are true and you don't turn me into a bagel in the next life." Mustering his courage, he reached out into the bleakness of the black hole.

The pain was intense and unexpected. He tried to scream, but no sound came out. As quickly as the pain had come, it was gone. Nathan did not have time to notice the darkness that had consumed him before his body emerged from the other side. He looked down to see his skin was covered in whatever the black hole was made of. Slimy ink coated him from head to toe. No matter how hard he tried, he could not pull any of it off. It went all the way down to his feet. Feet that were floating in the nothingness of outer space.

The trip through space had been peaceful up until then.

What was once a leisurely cruise through the cosmos, turned into a fight between two behemoths. Connery explained to Lucy that these were the enemy of existence. Mindless, shadowy creatures who sought only to consume and destroy. Products of some malevolent being.

Lucy gripped the small spikes of Connery's head, as it swiped at a silhouette shaped like a tentacled lion. It was hard to tell against the backdrop of space. But Connery knew. He always knew where these things were.

The Dragon's claws slashed with purpose through the darkness, making contact with the creature before them. There was no sound in this deadly dance, only the occasional rumble along Connery's body, causing the people in the city below to scream when they shook.

The tentacles tried to wrap around the Dragon's body, squeezing the life from the noble beast. The villagers below scrambled to get away from the shadowy tendrils. Connery's jaws latched onto the mid-section of the tentacled lion, ripping inky flesh and smoky bone. Just like that night so long ago, a flash of light emanated from the center of the shady animal and pushed Connery and the city back. The Dragon braced itself, making sure to keep the villagers safe.

The mountainous mass was revealed to be a small animal Lucy had never seen before. A cat-like creature with tentacles for arms and legs. It lay lifeless in the emptiness of space.

I'm sorry you had to see that. We do not know where they come from. Only that they consume life like a parasite. They have existed since the beginning of time. We Dragons were brought here to fight them and protect those who cannot protect themselves.

As if on cue, another shadow appeared in the distance. Invisible to the human eye, it was Connery's awareness that helped Lucy see the creature manifest. "Here we go again," she said, "But, why is it so small?"

It starts at the size it was before its corruption. It consumes the lives of others to grow. Such is its curse. Though we know not where they hail, we know that they were someone or something, once. Corruption gives them this form that you see before you. It knows nothing but to feed its empty life with the lives of others.

We are fortunate that we found one in its infancy. It is harmless to me at this state, but we cannot let it go about to sew chaos.

Lucy understood.

She watched the figure float closer to them. Her eyes widened. Through Connery's keen sight, she was able to see that it was Nathan.

Connery heard this thought and became hesitant.

The Dragon flew toward Nathan and allowed him into his atmosphere. The shadow was able to land in front of Lucy. It smiled.

"Nathan? Is that you?"

"Yeah," said a voice that sounded like the rustling of leaves. "I came back to you. I missed you," Nathan said before suddenly gripping his midsection as if in pain. "Sorry. I'm hungry. And for some reason, you look like food." He chuckled.

"I know," said Lucy sadly, recalling what Connery had said. Her eyes watered. "I'm glad I got to see you again."

"Me too. As a matter of fact, I never got to tell you something."

The tears came this time, and she thought she could see them on Nathan's shadowy face, too. "I love you, Nathan."

Nathan laughed. "You beat me to it! I love you, Lucy. I'm glad you and the others are safe." He grabbed at himself again, though this time, Lucy could sense the pain. "I barely got here. What's happening to me?" Nathan seemed panicked.

Lucy took the inky hands of her childhood friend and squeezed them tightly. "I don't know. But this Dragon, Connery, and I are going to find out who's doing this and stop it from happening to anyone else." She hugged him. So tight and so warm that she did not want to let go. Lucy knew the risk and she did not care. She knew these would be their final moments together.

Nathan sighed happily, but found himself turning his head. The hunger consumed him like a need. It almost overtook all other thought in his head. He clung to the remaining thoughts he had of his life on Nova Terra, but the need became too strong. He felt the urge to bite into the soft flesh of the woman he had loved for so long.

Lucy could feel his body turning and before he could act, she pushed him out into space. She fell to her knees and sobbed.

There was nothing left to say. She knew what had to happen. Eyes shut tight, she felt Connery dip his head down and bite.

Nathan was given a second funeral. The only one to perish on that fateful day. From that moment on, the Dragon who had caused such calamity became an unlikely friend. That friend eventually became their home.

Francis Fernandez discovered his love of the written word at a young age, delving into fantasy and sci-fi novels during his early teens. In high school and college, he dabbled in long-form fiction writing, eventually starting a novel he would never finish. In his senior year, he joined drama and became an actor, and his writing evolved into scripts and screenplays. Francis wrote one successful screenplay which was used by the local movie theater he worked for to promote candy sales to the patrons. His love of the creative inspired him to become a podcaster. That eventually led to his one mic show, the *Online Friend Simulator*, co-host for *Points of Interest Podcast* and the geeky improv show, *Super Geeked Up*, where he enjoys telling the kinds of jokes that make you groan.

THE LAST HOUR OF NIGHT
BY G. K. WHITE

COLD, SLICK STEEL PRESSED against her back. Jammed into a dark tube, desperate and hungry, fire burning down her legs from holding her in place. Dark gods, she hated the Moon. Air vented in and the smell of ozone surrounded her, like ammonia, but sharper. The black strands of her hair whipped into her eyes. She didn't blink. The small oval of deeper black lay a few feet above her, and she couldn't lose sight of it. Scavengers who lost their exit in the VAC tubes... She shifted herself up an inch. Her legs and arms ached but still worked in unison. A little closer.

Emptiness lay below her. The bottom of the slide. Deep, frozen space. She shuddered against the chill on her skin. Small cries came from beneath her. Her feet touched against something soft, fleshy. She curled one gaunt leg inward. The air stirred again. She had to get out.

"Raia? Hey, Raia."

Raia rubbed her eyes. Pale earthshine beamed through the bar window to her left and shimmered against her sister's synth pocket knife in her hand. She was in Atom's bar at her favorite booth.

Across the table, her younger sister's small pink lips pulled into a firm line. "I said this place is a scrap-hole. That's usually when you tell me to take a walk outside the Hab."

"Sorry, Gim," she said, checking her limbs. They were no longer sickly but lean and muscled. Gods, she hated that memory. "I think I blacked out somewhere between 'synth sales are in the crater' and 'Agon is taking your lungs back.'"

Gim sniffled.

Raia twisted the knife's sharp point and scraped a tiny circle into the molded wood tabletop. Without looking up, she knew her sister's eyes had lowered and her teeth were gnawing the corner of her lower lip.

She rotated the knife again, harder this time. A little pile of sawdust formed around the knife's eternally sharp point. It was a birthday present she'd made for her sister. She'd modified it from the bar's synth cutlery, an exorbitant expense for a bar. A last-ditch effort to draw in wealthier customers and remain open. It hadn't worked.

The AC vent above her shuddered. A gust of warm air blew the flecks of wood down to the bar's dusty metal floor. The crater she'd dug looked the same as the countless others pockmarking the table at her booth.

Zhoomp. The vac-vent set in the wall near the floor sucked in some dust.

Raia fought to keep her eye from twitching. They were in trouble, they needed to focus, and her sister was rapidly falling apart. She ran both hands up over her forehead and then back down to rub her eyes, inhaling deeply through her nose.

Gim blew her nose into a dusty bar napkin. "I'm in trouble, huh, Rai?"

A pang shot through Raia's chest. "We're not dead yet, kid."

Gim snorted and rested her head on her own arms. "It's four hours till the Light comes and, with it, all the high paying jobs'll disappear. This year's Night didn't exactly present the scores of a lifetime, and we need to feed the gang all Light. The little ones..."

Raia dug the two forefingers of her left hand into her right palm and scratched vigorously.

"We don't have the money for me, and if we can't get it... My enhancements... They'll take... I'll be—"

"I know, kid." She glanced around the desolate bar for the rest of the children. The bar was quiet, but the large piles of smashed chairs and tables made it hard to see much of anything. Still, the kids were probably out picking the Storage Dome clean for the millionth time. She reached a hand over to pat Gim's slender wrist.

Tremors shook her sister's body, and her small hands tightened around Raia's arms. Gods, why did she suck so much at this? Time to pull out the big guns. "We'll be okay, little nut."

Gim gave a half-hearted chuckle. Then she sat up and wiped away the tears rolling down her cheeks. "Not often you quote mom, Rai."

Not like she had much choice. The nickname always worked. "For all her scrap, Grace had a way with words...sometimes."

Her sister rolled her eyes and ran a hand through her own brown hair that fell in waves down to the middle of her back.

Ew. "How do you get through ten months of the Light with all that stuff on your head, Gim?"

Her sister's smile grew. "You're just jealous because your neck's been freezing for all two months of the Night."

It was true. She'd spent the last two months relying on what little earthshine they got and the excess heat funneled through the vents from the mining plants to stay warm. But the Light was coming. She rubbed her bare neck.

Another warm gust shuddered through the vent above them. The few bar lights still working dimmed and flickered. Raia waited for the lights, and the whole Hab covering the city, to turn off forever. After a moment of sputtering, they returned to normal. She exhaled slowly, her shoulders slumping against the seat back.

A robotic voice sparked and chittered over the internal speakers. "Ding."

The familiar scrape of the front door sliding up against its metal inlays was followed by a hesitant male voice calling out. "Hello? Is this where I find Raia Steel?"

Well, shunt her scrap-hole. Raia drew her palm up from her neck, formed her hand into a fist and rested against her knuckles. And there she thought the last day of Night would pass by peacefully. Thank the dark gods she was wrong.

"We're back here," Gim called. She scrubbed her own face with a dirty sleeve. "Smile, Raia. People like smiles. It makes them feel comfortable."

Somebody shunt her out an airlock, please. "Now who's quoting Grace?"

Her sister shot her a look that was all raised eyebrows and judgment. "Grace? Still? Really Raia?"

She sniffed loudly and rubbed her thumb once across her nose in the customary gesture. "Shunt off, Gimmera."

Hurried footsteps echoed across the tile. The man stumbled his way through the broken bar stools and tables that littered the low-lit room.

Gim stuck her jaw out and looked up in a huff. "I'm not going anywhere till I vet the client."

"I don't need a babysitter, Gim."

"And yet, here I am."

Ugh, sisters.

She handed Gim the pocket knife, and pulled out her own rusted dagger. "Fine, sit next to me and try not to talk."

Multiple crashes sounded. The man was still struggling with the debris littering the bar. He was tall and somewhere between pudgy and fat. Well-fed. A freshly pressed gray suit clung to his body, desperately trying to contain his mass while he pushed aside a broken table. His suit, plus the graying short-cropped hair recently cut, said banker or factory owner. To eat that well in this city you either ran the money or the synth-factories, though since the invention of hyper-fuel the latter had been steadily closing. No need for synth suppressants to keep the body still if cryo-sleep wasn't necessary. The stuff was useless save for making eternally sharp cutlery.

One more stumble over a half-corroded drink dispenser and the man finally reached their booth. He wiped his brow with a thoroughly used handkerchief and perched himself on the far end of the torn-up seat cushion directly across the table.

Raia stared at the flop sweat already reforming on the man's forehead for a brief second before meeting his small, beady eyes. Fear or desperation. Maybe both. "What's the job?"

He shifted his perch on the booth, moving weight from one giant flank to the next. His gaze darted around the room before resting on Gim for a second, and then Raia herself.

"You're Raia Steel? The thief?"

"Yeah, that's me."

The man blinked and tapped his fingers together, nodding as he did like he was counting.

Definitely a banker, which meant somebody didn't pay their loans. It was the only reason she ever saw bankers.

He pointed to her sister. "But she looks barely 13. And how old—"

"Old enough."

Gim huffed. "I'm 14."

She was going to kill them both. "What. Is. The. Job?"

The banker smiled weakly. "Right then. Well, I work for the Luna branch of the First Galactic—"

"The job."

"Well, the thing is I need someone who can go outside the Hab, the city as it were—"

She slammed her left hand flat on the table.

The banker twitched back into the booth seat and clutched his kerchief. "I need you to rob a shipment of goods on the twilight surface train."

A familiar spark bloomed in Raia's chest. She lifted her head off her knuckles and nodded. Finally, the good stuff.

"Starting point?"

"The factories."

"Destination?"

"The mayor's palace."

Her foot drummed against the metal floor. Fat cat Mayor Agon. After the human race hyper-fueled their way across the stars, the Moon became the shunt end of the galaxy with way too many synth factories. And their illustrious mayor ran to his palace outside the Hab and stayed there. Probably ate better than anyone on the planet. If anyone deserved to be robbed... "A container? A whole car? One item? What are we talking?"

"One item in car 756." The banker held his hands shoulder width apart. "An egg-shaped thing about this big. It's made of synth so it'll shimmer. Don't let it touch your skin."

Her sister harumphed. "A synth egg? Don't you know synth is worthless now? And why can't—"

She waved her hand at Gim to shut her up. "Security?"

The banker's lips pulled tight in a self-satisfied smile that was likely to get him stabbed in this part of town. "I paid off the train workers. They'll turn the cameras off and leave the car empty, but..."

She squinted. "But?"

"I can't do anything about the automated security."

"Guns or Bots?"

"Bots with guns. A whole platoon."

She ignored her sister's sudden intake of breath. Security Bots were insanely dangerous, but that usually meant the client was willing to pay big, if you approached them right.

"Hmm." She rubbed the stubble growing on her neck.

The banker's brow furrowed. He leaned in, practically reaching his hand out to her. "I can pay extra. Please."

Her heart nearly skipped. Oh yeah, she had him. "How much?"

"50,000 credits."

She kept her face calm and her hands tight on the table to keep herself from jumping up and kissing the man's pale lips. Just enough money. Pay off Gim's lungs and give her a little extra to make sure she'd be okay. This was it.

Her sister whispered in her ear, "No way, Rai. A whole platoon? Shad-di Yi-reh. He'll take care of us. We'll figure it out."

The mighty provider. She rubbed the ache at her temple. That was Grace's delusion. Raia believed in whatever controlled the space outside, the emptiness. Unknown dark gods she'd never meet who had always been and always would be coming for her.

Still, a whole platoon... Her leg hover-bounced against the rough underside of the table. She brought her hands together and scratched at her palm.

Bing. The soft sound emanated from her temple. Somebody had sent a private message to the AR lens in her eye. She twitched her cheek to accept.

The LMS Sorrow launches at sunrise. $?

The text hovered in the air for a moment before she swiped with her hand to shut the AR lens down. Shunt. She lowered her head, avoiding Gim's eyes.

There was only one way off the slide.

"I'm in."

The stolen cargo van jolted as its mag-anchors attached to the side of the train car and locked in place. Five minutes till the Bots swept this area again. Raia took her hands off the wheel. The dash beeped at her, but the van stayed perfectly still, lashed to the side of a train rocketing across the rocky gray surface of the Moon. She twisted her helmet so it would seal and said a silent thanks to Lift for the mag-anchors. That boy could modify anything. Of course, she couldn't use the van's brakes anymore, but she never did that anyway.

She hopped into the back loading area, sat on the floor, and attached the van's cable to her belt. The other end was wrapped around an auto-crank bolted to the floor. She tapped her helmet a few times. The suit's HUD came up.

Oxygen 95%. The meter flickered. *0%.*

Her hand paused halfway to the airlock hatch in the ceiling.

Another flicker. *95%*

Seriously?

Dark gods, the only thing worse than stolen tech was old stolen tech. Her heart thumped against her chest. She was definitely going to have a heart attack. She sighed and popped the ceiling hatch. The cable pulled tight. Air rushed up her body, over her head, and out of the van, trying to fill the empty space. Her whole body felt like a blackhead somebody was trying to squeeze out. After a moment, all the air was gone.

She tapped the button on the wrist of her suit. Nothing happened. Her stomach did a little flip. She tapped it a second time. Nothing.

Shunting scrap sifting, plas-guzzling synth-hole. Why didn't I check this dumb thing?

She could practically hear Gim's voice berating her. *You said there wasn't any time. Night's almost over, Gim. Gotta finish the job, Gim.*

That kid needed a good spanking.

She jammed her finger onto the button. A whirring sound emanated from the back of the truck. She kicked off the floor hard. The metal of the hatch brushed against her slim shoulders as she squeezed through. One of these days, they'd steal something with a hatch made for humans, not delivery boxes.

The emptiness outside pummeled her suit. Turns out all you need to feel wind in space is a whole bunch of speed. She squeezed the metal frame of the van in a death grip. She'd given enough to this shunting rock. She wouldn't give her life, too.

The flashlights on her helmet kicked on, and her body switched to auto-pilot. Crawl over the top of the van, grip and move, shimmy up the frame between train cars, keep your legs spread to avoid natural knee-gripping, and be careful not to rip the back of the suit on the car behind. This part was easy. She excelled at climbing things, no matter the conditions. It was why she became a thief in the first place. She reached the plastic hatch on top of the car in no time at all.

A small group of grayed hills stood out on the horizon. It was more than she should be able to see. The Light was coming. Half a day away, maybe less. She imagined eyes watching her in the darkness. Creatures of the night waiting to see if she'd fall, if they could get one last meal before they had to run from the dawn.

"Not real, Raia," she spoke aloud to calm herself. "If you got stranded out here, you wouldn't be eaten. You'd just suffocate and then your body would be roasted by the sun long before anyone found you."

It wasn't working. It never really did. Space was an ancient horror movie—silent and creepy as hell. There's no controlling the fear, only distracting yourself from it.

She wedged one boot between the side railing and gripped the handle of the hatch fiercely. The pocket knife in the pouch on her belt made short work of the hatch's plastic safety catch. It popped open without a sound. She fought the shiver running up her spine and pulled herself into the car.

The lights on her helmet lit up a nearly empty white container. A single rectangular box lay against the back wall. Like a giant plastic coffin. She shook herself, pushed off the ceiling, and floated to the back of the car. It took her a moment to realize the box wasn't locked in any way. Strange. She snapped it open.

A large silver object lay inside against a soft purplish cushion. It shimmered and glowed as her helmet lights moved over it. She grabbed it with two hands and pulled it free of the box. It was slightly taller than it was wide as the banker had said. What he hadn't said was how it moved against her gloved hands, like it was a disembodied pregnant stomach, which...

Gross.

A green light flashed, lighting up the car and causing the object in her hands to wriggle uncomfortably against her fingers. Small bubbles of red floated across her vision. Some of them touched the silver orb in her hands, making tiny splatter marks against its shimmering surface. The rest slowly moved toward the back wall where a new scorch mark decorated the fiberglass.

Heat blossomed in her leg, and her helmet beeped at her.

Oxygen 50%

She gripped her thigh where it burned, and her white glove came away a dark red. A large bloody streak bordered by little orange embers had replaced her suit's egg-shell white. Shunt her, she'd been shot. The suit beeped again, and her arm lit up with more heat as the synthetic fabric mended itself over her wound.

She whipped around. A glowing robotic eye stared through a large plasma bolt hole in the front wall.

Scrap.

"Ding." The door to Atom's bar scraped against its inlay as it slid open.

She hazily registered the familiar counter at the edge of her blurry vision. How had she gotten to the bar? Her jacket poked her in the ribs. Her foot hit something light. A plastic stool clattered across the floor into a pile of broken bar furniture already stacked at the side of the bar.

"Raia? Are you back?"

Her lips parted. "Hnsm."

Pain blossomed in her throat. Shunt. A dim memory of a robot arm choking her swam in the muddy waters of her mind. She shoved aside a table bottom and stumbled toward her favorite booth. Her foot squished as it hit the floor, liquid swishing around in her left shoe. Had she stepped in a puddle? She focused on her leg. Blood, a small brook of it, ran from a deep gouge in her thigh, over her black leggings, and pooled into her dark blue flats.

Scrap. Her last good pair.

Her heart fluttered like a bird trapped in a cage. She pitched forward, hip checked a table, and sprawled across the floor, scattering a dozen bits of plastic and wood.

Her vision dimmed, but her heart hammered against her chest. The grainy scent of moon dust filled the air.

"Raia?"

The voice was hurried. Worried. Gim. Definitely, Gim.

Wood cracked and clattered.

"Oh, God," her sister yelled. "Stitch, get in here!"

Pain lanced through Raia's leg like a pulsing vein and cleared the fog in her head. Small hands clutched her thigh, putting pressure on her wound. Gim's hands.

Stitch, the member of their orphan gang who served as their doctor, cursed from behind a pile of broken server Bots to her right.

Her jacket poked at her ribs... No, no it didn't. The train ride, the car chase, the dumb relentless robot security. She'd had to hide the orb. Raia opened her eyes, unsure of when she'd closed them.

Her sister knelt over her with her whitened lips pressed into a tight, worried line.

"Don't worry, kid." Raia unzipped her jacket with a shaky hand. The dark silver and gray egg rolled over her stomach and hit the floor with a thud near her hip. "I got it."

Gim's eyes softened, and she let out a breath. "Not exactly what I was worried about, Raia. In case you can't tell—" her sister held up a gory hand briefly before putting it back down on Raia's thigh, "—you're bleeding out."

"Yeah," Raia nodded as her arm and leg began to tingle. "That's not good."

Her sister's mouth moved again, but the words sounded muddled and far away.

Tiredness stole over her muscles in waves, pulling every part of her back into darkness. "Get the money. Take care of them, Gim."

She pushed the words out before the last wave closed her eyes.

She wasn't quite asleep. Something cold pressed against her back like the steel walls of her childhood. And the smell, the awful stench of endless nothingness, it haunted her.

"...money... tell me... it? Any blood?"

Raia was lying on her back. She shivered. The bar's metal floor might as well have been a giant ice cube. A blurry figure swam into view. Big, meaty hands gripped the sides of her jacket and shook her violently.

"I've got your money." The banker's sweat soaked face clarified against the dark ceiling of the bar. "Did you touch the egg? Tell me."

Stitch shouted something about blood loss and laser burns that her mind couldn't quite track.

Her sister's little hands were pulling at the banker's flabby arms. She was shouting, too, but Raia couldn't make out her face. Everybody but the banker was a blob.

The banker shook her sister off with one arm, revealing a small metal briefcase that lay on the floor behind him, the kind bankers carried a credit stack in.

The suitcase consumed Raia's view. She summoned the energy to raise her hands.

"Gloves," she whispered against the pounding in her head. "All good. No touch."

The banker smiled. "Good."

He let go of her then.

Her upper body slumped back to the floor, and the room faded again, but a few sounds remained. Stitch saying, "Money's all there."

That was good. Gim was safe from the body mod recall. She'd keep her lungs no matter what Raia did, and their little gang of orphans would be okay.

The next two sounds happened in unison.

Gim said, "Stitch, what did she mean? Take care of them?"

Bing. Her AR lens chimed near her temple. A new message.

Sorrow's eta is 4hrs. $?

She fought to wrench her heart back into the hole that punched through her chest. She repeated "they'd be okay" until her emotions shut the hell up, and she drifted back into the quiet, suffocating steel walls of her mind.

Her leg hurt. A lot. She rubbed some smudges onto the bar window to keep from itching at her tourniquet. Outside, the domed ceiling of the Hab was lit up like a Christmas tree. The heat lights attached to the dome acted as their sun during the two long months of darkness, the Night. They kept the city warm and on a normal schedule.

As she watched, one of the lights blinked out. She closed her eyes. Lights only turned off on the dome for one reason: the energy got rechanneled to seal a hole in the fabric. A hole out into space.

Raia dug her rusted dagger into the table top. She wished she'd borrowed Gim's. The synth blade would go deeper than hers.

Her sister *hmm*ed across the table from her as she ate the last bit of chicken on her plate and stared out the window at the lights. "How many does that make?"

Raia sighed. The dome hung over them like a massive net with hundreds of dark spots. "I lost count a long time ago."

Gim tossed her chicken bones toward the vac-vent in the wall.

Zhoomp. It opened and sucked the bones into the tube connected to the building.

An acrid smell filled the air, like cleaning supplies. Raia clenched her teeth and rubbed away the goosebumps on the back of her neck.

"You never talk about it. When you were young..."

Dammit, Gim had noticed. She rested her water glass against her pounding head and tried not to itch where Stitch had...well, stitched it.

"What was it like growing up in the vac tubes?"

She shrugged. "Cramped."

The heat from her sister's stare warmed the side of her face.

Gim had asked before, but her voice was different this time. More determined.

Raia hated when they did this. "I don't want to talk about it, Gim. It wasn't pleasant. Groups of us would spend almost every day in there crawling around."

"Why?"

The sharp scent of ammonia lingered. Her lungs constricted. Dark gods, why couldn't her sister let it go? "Because that's where the scrap was. Not all of us were born in Grace's 'house of love and free food.'"

"But ever since the city planners left, the tubes vent to airlocks."

Raia rubbed her temple. A cold feeling had crept up her back like she was pressed against something hard. Sweat built at the nape of her neck. "The timing cycles. Tubes don't all vent at the same time."

"Wasn't it dangerous if you were caught in a tube that was venting?"

Memories echoed in her mind. The squish of flesh. The acrid stench. The crack of bones. She ground her teeth and barked, "Not for the kid on top."

Her sister laid a hand on her arm.

Raia had to focus not to break it.

"That's not who you are anymore, Raia."

"Isn't it? We're all dying, kid." She fingered one of the many holes she'd dug in the tabletop. "A settler's shuttle hasn't come to the Moon in 10 years." She trailed her finger up and over the wood until it dipped into another hole. "Water for the city is 100% recycled. Energy dipped below 50% this year, and the oxygen generators are 20 years old. And we've lost count of how many holes have ripped in the Hab." She put her palm flat and ran her hand across the splintered wood. "*LMS Sorrow*, that puddle jumper they're launching at sunrise, will be the last one they're able to scrape together. The light of civilization hasn't touched this place for years, and it's slowly freezing over. We're all trapped here, dying slow."

Her sister didn't understand. It showed in the soft-set angle of her eyebrows, the slight upward pull of her cheeks.

Shunt.

"The Confederate won't let the city die. And even if they did, it'd happen long after we're dead." Gim crawled out of the booth and stood. Then, her lips grew into a soft, sad sort of smile. "I'm sorry you feel like you're trapped, Rai. But you'll always have a place here, a home."

Raia grunted at the familiar words, Grace's words, and turned back to her window.

Her sister's soft steps receded and the door to the back room and side exit squealed a moment later as it slid open.

"You just don't get it, kid," Raia whispered to the empty seat. "Nobody cares. We're all just scrap sitting in the tube. The only difference is some of us have realized the airlock has opened. The tube's become a slide, and we're clawing our way to the exit."

"Ding."

Broken plastic clattered against the steel floor at the front entrance. Something big had crashed to the ground.

Raia pulled her knife out of the table and got to her feet gingerly. It'd been less than an hour since Gim left. No one should be here till the Sunrise meeting. She kept her footsteps light and crept down the path between the broken chairs, tables, and Bots. When she rounded the corner near the entrance, a soft gurgle reached her ears.

The banker lay on the floor beneath the front bar among several newly broken stools. Light reflected off his sweaty forehead and the large red stains in his suit which had been ripped in several areas, exposing rolling flabs of bloody flesh.

He wheezed. "Money...owed me money." Then his eyes locked on hers, and he let out a shuddering gasp. "You touched it."

Questions whirled through her head, a twister created by a million different winds. Her gut sank into the floor. "Who did this to you?"

He shuddered, and more streams of red liquid leaked out of the many scorch marks across his body. "You did."

Light flashed into the room.

The banker jerked backward against the bar. A new hole sizzled in his expensive suit jacket right over his chest. His gelatinous body slumped to the floor.

A hand wielding a light pistol emerged from the door.

Raia was already moving. She was a thief, not a fighter, but she was fast and adrenaline had numbed her wounds. She slashed the attacker across the wrist as she passed in front of the doorway.

Something hit her legs.

She fell, but rolled and came up with her knife ready.

The light from the heat lamps poured through the doorway silhouetting the woman standing there. Against all the rules of shadow, shards of light reflected off every one of the scales making up her skin. She pointed the gun still gripped in her hand at Raia.

Raia held up her knife. No blood. In fact, the rusted steel had broken halfway down the blade. "The hell are you?"

The woman moved forward into the light of the bar.

A shinier version of Raia's own face stared back her. The tornado swirling through her head ballooned.

The thing smiled. A wide, fearful thing. "I'm you. Just...better."

Light flashed, and everything went white.

The steel of the tube is cold, always cold.

And she can see the others below, but she is alone, always alone.

Jammed between the walls, the emptiness coming to consume her, and with one way out.

She almost welcomed the brutal light of consciousness when it came.

"...and you are my answer." The voice rasped in her ear. "Like that great, ancient creature. You will hoard all the knowledge and power of each of the worlds you are born on, and together, we will build a new galactic empire. An empire of dragons. Contact me, my pets, and I will lead you into the future."

Raia blinked her eyes open. Ropes chafed her wrist where they'd been bound together. The blurry fake-wood walls told her she was still in the bar. This was the stockroom. The actual stock for the bar had been emptied a long time ago, leaving nothing save four walls, two doors, and some lockers. She and the gang only ever used it for the side entrance, or for a place of quiet reflection. Of course, in the latter case, you usually only had yourself for company...which she did.

The shimmer version of her leaned against the wall across the room. A small, smug smile on her face.

The deep blue of her eyes held a specific coldness. A sliver of emptiness squirmed through Raia's heart.

A low sardonic voice cut through the cloud in her head. "Did you recognize the speaker?"

"Mayor Agon. Dumb, scratchy throat. What was that he called you? A dragon? Is that a pet of some kind? You're some sort of clone."

The Dragon tilted its head to the side and puffed air out of its nose. Its jaw jutting out like it was considering how to grind its next meal. "Call me a pet again, weakling."

The thing definitely had her temper. Someone else mimicking her go-to angry position was...bizarre.

It spat on the floor beside her. "Do I look like a mindless ghost of you, kid?"

A dozen panicked worms squirmed for cover inside her chest and her head was pounding like it was frantically trying to keep a beat. Even still, she chuckled. She'd always found herself funny. "I never realized how demeaning that nickname was until now. Dark gods, how does anyone put up with us?"

Bing. A message blipped onto her eye-screen. *Where the hell are you? Sorrow leaves in an hour.*

The smile returned to the Dragon's face. "Last hour of Night, Rai. Your ride off planet is leaving. Did you work up the courage to tell our—" It moved its nose in a circle as if smelling the air, then slithered the word "—sister?"

Her heart plunged into her stomach.

"I didn't think so." It chuckled through its nose. "To answer your question: Agon made the egg. You supplied the DNA. And I am no one's pet."

Nope, no way was this her fault. "I didn't touch—"

The image of a big bubble of her blood splashing over the egg flashed in her mind.

Damn bots and their lasers.

"In our defense," it kicked itself off the wall and walked toward her slowly, "the banker's instructions were a little vague."

She swore. Any chance of this being on someone else just got vented. A coal burst into flame somewhere between her stomach and heart. Shunt, she could be so stupid.

"Yes," the Dragon pushed her same, blue-tipped black hair out of its face. "You can be."

She fought the urge to kick her—its face.

Stay calm. Think your way out. Stall.

"Why did you kill the banker?"

It squinted at her and then shrugged. "Already took his company. He was useless."

She willed her sluggish brain to keep up. "You took over his company? He only got the egg a couple hours ag—"

It jumped the last few feet between them and got right in her face. "That, my stupid self, is what we can accomplish in a few hours—" it gestured toward her, "—without all this guilt and sadness paralyzing us. Without a bunch of kids pulling us down."

She rammed her head forward, but the Dragon danced back even before she'd started. Without her hands to brace herself, her momentum carried her face to the metal floor with a dull thud. Pain shot through her skull and stars exploded behind her eyes.

"Predictable," it chuckled through its nose again. "Relax, you won't ride the slide today if you don't want to. I've got a deal for you."

The ropes at her wrists loosened.

Her arms suddenly free, Raia rolled to the far corner of the room and came up in a short crouch. The stitch in her leg pulsed angrily. She shifted her weight.

The Dragon rolled its eyes and slid something metal across the floor.

The small object scraped along until Raia stopped it with her foot. It was her credit stack.

"Take your money and get off world."

She eyed the credit stack. Nothing came without a price. "And in return?"

"Just change your name and never come back. I'll even let the little gang of misfits live." The Dragon's smile faded into a tightened line. "The Moon is a nice, quiet little place to amass influence and silver. It is mine now."

Raia picked the credit stack up and ran her fingers over the hard edges. The weight was comforting. But it couldn't be that easy. It never was. "I don't understand. Why let me go? I'd be a threat running around the system. What's in it for you?"

The Dragon's mouth curled into a sneer, and it chuckled in its throat. "One little girl lost and desperate isn't any threat to me."

Okay, ouch.

"Think of it as a reward. You probably saved me from whatever Agon does to his dragons to make them obey his pathetic will. Besides, the thought of you out there somewhere, living your sad life with half the vigor and a quarter of my ambition will fill me with such joy."

Raia ignored the sting in her chest. "Gods, you are such a shunt face."

"Wonder who I got that from."

She huffed. "You aren't me."

"Oh, I am. Remember our last day in the tubes? Before Grace found us?"

An acrid scent filled the air like sulfur mixed with industrial cleaner. She sank to her knees and fought to keep the memory down. "Don't."

"Remember what we did to avoid riding the slide? What we did to our last 'sister'?"

The cold walls pressed in on her back. Like someone had put a weight on the paper of her soul. She clutched her chest where her heart trilled against her ribs. "Please, don't."

The wind ripped at her body. The crunch of bone reverberated through her heel. A harsh yelp of pain sounded from beneath her. But then her little fingers finally gripped onto hard steel, the entrance to another tube. She clambered in and her heart settled.

The girl below, her face so peaceful and still, even with a broken nose, slipped down the tube and disappeared into the dark with a soft scream.

Raia tore herself from the memory.

The Dragon's hand lay soft on her shoulder. "That's who we are. We're a survivor. And right now, you are on the slide. And we both know the only way out."

A rock settled in the pit of her stomach, pressing down the guilt and pain of what she'd done. It left a simple and hard truth learned in the bitter, crowded tubes. "Step on or be stepped on."

The Dragon's mouth curled. "I knew you'd understand."

The air grew colder, thinner, as if it was being pulled away. The room closed in around her. What little warmth was in her faded, leaving harsh steel beneath her feet and sharp air in her lungs. Her throat constricted by reflex holding in as much air as possible. She barely registered the dragon exiting into the bar.

She was suffocating, dying. She had to get out.

Her body crossed the room, gripped the handle of the side exit door, and pulled it open before she'd even realized she was moving. Just as she was about to leave the bar and the planet behind, a glitter of light touched the corner of her eye.

A little sliver of light shone through a brown paper bag resting in Gim's cubby. A present for the end of Night. Tradition. Stepping toward it warmed her. She carefully unwrapped the paper. Gim's small synth pocket knife lay inside. The one Raia always borrowed. A little sticky note was attached.

Thought you could use a new one. Besides, I want to be with you when you fight...wherever you go. You are a good person, Rai.

-Love, your sister.

Something soft and warm bubbled in her chest. She always underestimated how perceptive Gim was.

Go, Raia. It's okay.

The unspoken words lifted the weight from her back. The room expanded and that cold bite left the air. She gripped the knife in her hand and turned toward the front room where the dragon had gone.

Darkness, but not death. Death would've been better. The metal tube pressed in from all sides. She crammed her feet up and shoved herself forward, squeezing through the cold cylinder. Cold wind streamed down the slide, pulling at her clothes, stealing her breath. Gim yelped below her. Somewhere further down, Stitch cried out. Exhaustion washed over her bones. There was nothing she could do for them. She was barely holding on herself. They were alone. Every one of them.

Suddenly, the air lightened. It wasn't pulling her down anymore but filling her lungs again. A hand touched her back. Too big to be Gim, too warm to be human. Golden light flooded into the tunnel, and her body started to float upward, carried by the hand at her back.

A gentle presence snuggled up behind her like when Grace used to hold her after a nightmare. It whispered in her ear. Something soft, something sweet, something loving.

Bright medical lights shone down on her from the ceiling. Cloth was strapped over her right eye. She blinked the blurriness away. She was on her back in a bed, and worse yet, she recognized the room. Hospital.

Guess she won the fight with the Dragon.

A pair of arms wrapped around her side and pulled her into a fierce, rib-breaking hug.

Her little sister's long hair blocked out the lights. "Oh, Rai. You're okay. You're okay."

A shard of pain shot up her leg, along her right side, and all the way to the top of her head. "Doesn't feel like it, sis."

Gim nodded; her face still buried in Raia's neck.

Soft tears trickled down Raia's shoulder. Somehow it made her body feel a little less scrapped-to-all-hell. "I did okay, huh? What about the Dragon?"

Her sister sniffed and sat up. "You mean the other you?"

More than a few questions sprinted through her mind. The gang was working off such limited info. "How did you guys know which—"

"Um," Gim laughed. "She sparkled and she didn't have any of your scars. Anyway, she was dead when we got there. Stitch said to tell you that sparkle Raia took a ride down the slide."

They'd disposed of the body and carried her to the hospital. Probably saved her life. Something bright swelled inside her, a remnant from her dream. "Remind me to thank him."

Her sister's smile faded. "She did a number on you, Rai."

Her whole body pulsed in affirmation of her sister's words. With a trembling hand she reached up and touched her right eye. A little spasm of pain shot from her head to the middle of her gut. "How bad?"

Her sister's grip on her tightened. "We rushed you here right away. The doctor owed Stitch a favor, apparently. He said it's too early to tell."

A boulder sank into her stomach. Her thoughts teetered on the edge of the hole they'd lived in since she was a child. But she took her sister's hand in her own, and the warmth centered her. "Let's talk about something else."

"Well...the *LMS Sorrow* is taking off. I know you don't like to watch the shuttles, but—"

"No," Raia said. "I'd love to."

Gim snuggled up in the bed next to her and flicked her wrist at the vid screen on the far wall. The screen flickered for a second, and then a flat gray launch bay and a long triangle-shaped travel shuttle came into view. The *LMS Sorrow*.

Her sister smiled brightly. "Know what mom used to say she liked about launches?"

"No, what did mom say?"

"She used to say it was sad to see people go, but she was happy they were going in a group. Space is a dark place, she'd say, and the best way to bring light to a dark place —"

"Is to do it together."

A smile spread across Raia's face as she spoke the words. A warm, peaceful smile.

G. K. White was born in Texas in 1991 and raised by two amazing parents who, by reading to him, created a love for stories and myths. His parents worked hard to pry his hands off the latest *Redwall* novel, or a video game controller, and convince him to eat dinner. Both obsessions carried over into adulthood, becoming vital parts of his procrastination as he matriculated at the University of Houston-Clear Lake with a Bachelor of Arts in English. He continued on to earn his Master of Fine Arts in Writing Popular Fiction from Seton Hill University. G.K. currently lives in western China where he teaches English and writing when he isn't working on his debut fantasy thriller novel, *The Third Gift*.

Four
Dragons of Other Realms

WITHERWILLOW
by Carrie Gessner

"**F**UCK." THE WORD COMES from my gut as I twist to get a look at myself in the mirror and pain screeches through my body.

The cut over my left eye won't stop bleeding. I've been sitting in the cramped bathroom of my office for ten minutes now, a towel pressed over the wound. Each time I peek under the fabric, blood trickles out again. Each time I press it against my skin, a stinging sensation.

Being a P.I. is more trouble than it's worth. I definitely get more pain than money out of this gig. Not like there are a lot of options open to me, though. With the city torn between human and dragonfolk, I can't exactly go ask the dragon families for work. I'm not even sure I'd want to. Even from afar, families like the Everskies, the Sunblazers, the Riverwards, and the Moontenders are intimidating. Everyone's seen them flying the skies in their dragon forms. In interactions with human, elves, and everyone else, they shift into humanoid forms. That's all well and good, but give me the certainty of humanity any day.

I gingerly remove the towel, and this time, the blood's congealed enough that it doesn't start running down into my eyebrow. I slap a bandage over the cut without bothering to wash it and walk back into the main office to find a woman there. I try not to show my surprise.

She strides forward gracefully, hand extended. "Iris Kane, right?"

I shake her hand. "That's right."

"I'm Evangeline Starr. Two Rs."

Pretty name, pretty woman.

"I did knock," she says, lips curling in a smirk, and I have to remind myself to *let go of her hand*.

"Oh," I say, straightening my shoulders. "I was... occupied."

"I can see that." She studies my face intently, her confident expression turning into something too much like concern.

"Right." I veer away from her and behind my desk. The chair squeaks as I sit. I gesture for her to sit in the one on her side of the desk. "Well, Ms. Starr, what can I do for you?"

"It's 'Miss,'" she says, sliding into the armchair with effortless grace.

My mouth is suddenly dry. "Excuse me?"

"It's 'Miss Starr.' No need for the 'Ms.'" She extracts a cigarette case from her purse, plucks one out, and smiles coyly. "Don't suppose you have a light?"

I fish my lighter out of my trouser pocket, and she leans close when I ignite it.

"Thank you." Leaning back, she inhales, holds the breath, and exhales a plume of smoke that drifts lazily toward the ceiling.

I hold her gaze. I don't like having to ask questions twice.

Finally, she says, "I need you to locate something for me."

Sounds promising. "What sort of something?"

After another puff, she says, "A dragon egg."

The split lip and bruising eye probably help hide my shock. "That's quite the job. What for?"

"My fiancé...overstepped, let's say. He's not part of the family yet, but he acts like he is."

I chuckle. From the icy fury in Evangeline's eyes, he'll never be part of the family.

"It's a family trophy. He stole it from me and used it to pay off his gambling debts over at the Ivory Crown."

Bastard. I've seen a lot of women stuck in similar situations. Difficult, almost impossible, to extract oneself without a bit of help. "All right. You want me to do what, exactly?"

"Steal it back." She grins. "Or at least find out precisely where it is, and I'll do the stealing."

She is bold. Bold enough that she could do this without me. "Before we hash out the details, one question. Why me?"

I've thrown her for a loop, and confusion looks strange on her. "Excuse me?"

"Why do you want to hire *me*? You said you did your research. Then you must know no one takes me seriously."

"That's exactly why I want to hire you."

Huh. Kudos for honesty. "All right, Miss Starr. I'm listening."

The thing is—once Evangeline fills me in on the details, I start to regret taking the job. I'm in over my head just knowing certain details about the circle she runs with. The great families of the city, always bickering or brawling or boozing. Puzzles, though, I like those. But I gave my word, and that's one thing I don't go back on. Not anymore.

I take a drag of my cigarette as I walk across town. The smoke burns into my lungs, but I hold the breath until I can't. "Good" isn't the right word for how it feels. The sting matters, though, somehow.

Moxie's Club is full tonight. Not a surprise, but not even this level of chatter can drown out the canary on stage. Gorgeous voice.

Moxie herself is behind the bar, shiny auburn hair hanging over her shoulders, the neckline of her green sequined dress plunging low.

I tilt my head toward the stage. "New girl?"

"Yeah. Like her?"

"'Course. I like everything you do, Moxie."

"Don't try to sweet-talk me." She grasps my chin. "Not when you come in here all roughed up like that. You behind the eight ball with someone? Mitchell's boys do this to you?"

Mitchell and his goons have more to concern themselves with than a little old private eye. Most days. I wriggle out of her grip. "You don't have to worry about it, Mox. Vole around?"

"Corner." Frowning, she pours me a finger of whiskey and slides it over. "You know I got a soft spot for you, kid, but you don't make it easy."

"Where would the fun in that be? Thanks for the belt." I toss the words over my shoulder as I head to the corner table and slip into the booth across from Vole, an elf. His tall, lithe form is hunched, and his face is even more gaunt than usual.

"Vole," I say with a nod.

"Kane."

He's twitchy, restless, like always. Vole's an icebreath addict. Even has the ice-blue ring around his eyes from consuming so much. It's new, just hit the street a year or two ago. Came from the dragonfolk. Only it's a basic pain reliever for them. Gets humans high as heaven except, apparently, the comedown is nowhere near as nice as that place. I stay far away from the stuff.

I slide my whiskey toward him instead, which he gulps down without so much as a wince.

"I'm looking for a dragon egg. White and red. 'Bout that big." I hold my hands in a teardrop shape. "Would've been used to pay off debts at the Ivory Crown."

Vole scratches his patchy beard. "Yeah, yeah, yeah. Might've heard about something matching that description."

"Is it still there? Back room maybe?"

The Ivory Crown Casino's owned by dwarves, who, as a rule, tend to stay out of the human-dragon rivalry the city is infamous for. Maybe they're the smart ones.

"Nah," he says with a shake of his head. "More like it's headed to the Witherwillow tomorrow night."

Right. The elusive underground ring that auctions off dragon, elvish, and other magical artifacts to the highest bidder. To humans, they're a symbol of superiority. The more non-human objects a family has, the more power and influence. That's why Mitchell thinks he's unstoppable—and what makes him so insufferable.

"Where is it this time?" The location moved with each event. Part of the prestige. Only those in the know—or those who could pay well enough to become in the know—could stay in the loop.

"Ellington Alvenor's," Vole says.

I can't decide whether to laugh or groan. He's the patriarch of another prominent human family, one of the big rivals to Mitchell. If only they learned to work together, they might have a shot at driving out the dragonfolk for good. Lucky for everyone else, the human families are too busy outbidding each other on stolen goods to put their brain cells together and figure it out.

Still, I'll never get in there. Me—born to no money, secondhand clothes, doing a gig that's barely a step above the gutter? Yeah, they'll sniff me out in seconds.

But maybe not if I'm with Evangeline. The surname Starr doesn't ring a bell, so her family can't be as important as Mitchell's or Alvenor's or some of the others, but it's clear they've got money. Wealth can get through many a door otherwise blocked.

"Thanks," I say and move to stand up.

Vole clicks his tongue. "Uh-uh. Can't get in without a password."

"And I assume you know it."

"Sure, I do."

I hold his stare for a few more seconds before I take out a sawbuck and put it on the table.

He puts his palm over the bill and sweeps it into his fist. "When they ask you, 'What's inevitable?' you say, 'The day when the dragons swallow their own tails.'"

Good grief, how pretentious these people are.

"Thanks, Vole."

"Pleasure doing business with ya, Kane."

I wish I could say the same.

***

"You clean up nice," Evangeline says with a smile. Then she squints and runs her thumb over my cheek. "You could use a more even hand with the cover-up, though."

I swat her hand away. The fact she can see through my makeup under a dim streetlight doesn't bode well, but I'm counting on everyone looking at her instead of me. "I did my best, all right?"

"Suit yourself. But if anyone looks at you for more than three seconds—"

"They won't."

"Then they'll see evidence of that scrap you were in yesterday."

I shrug. No one ever looks at me that long, so it won't be a problem.

She arches a brow. "What, no return compliment?"

"You'll get plenty of those tonight without my help. Can we go now?" I'm antsy because I don't like bringing clients along on jobs, but I couldn't see a way around this one and Evangeline herself has no objection. All she has to do is be the center of attention while I grab the egg.

Ellington Alvenor's downtown mansion—as opposed to the one just outside the city—is disgustingly large. I've seen it from the outside, of course. The way it seems even bigger on the inside makes my stomach turn. I could palm a pair of fae-made candlesticks from here and be set up for life. Too bad I left that life behind me. It's hell to have a nagging conscience.

The crowd is exactly what I expected—rich, snobby, dressed to the nines in brightly colored gowns and monochromatic tuxedos. I couldn't afford a new dress, and none of the few I owned were up to snuff. I went with my brother's old suit, a bit shabby but safely nondescript. Evangeline, in a sparkly, floor-length crimson gown that hugs her frame, draws eyes from all around. Even if they clock me as not of their ilk, the fact that I came here with her should dissuade them from making a scene.

We stroll through the party. Guests mingle in every room on the first floor. The biggest is a ballroom. At the far end is a jazz band, and lining the other three walls are velvet-draped tables, where the items up for auction are displayed. The middle of the room is open for dancing, with many couples already taking advantage of the music.

"The auction begins at midnight," Evangeline says in my ear.

I nod. "So, I'll do it right before then." A little over an hour to kill until then. "Drink?"

She snags two flutes of champagne from a passing waiter, hands one to me, and says, "Maybe we should do it sooner. If we wait, everyone will be getting last-minute looks at the items."

I sip my champagne, tart on my tongue. She drains her glass, takes mine, and sets them both down.

"Come on." Taking my hand, she pulls me out onto the dance floor.

I'm not the savviest of dancers, but I can make do. Wish I could've finished my drink first, though.

"I still think I should do it," she murmurs as we twirl.

"Look at everyone." I flick my gaze around the crowd, make sure she follows it. "No one's paying attention to *me*. With you here, I'm practically invisible."

She rolls her eyes but makes no protest.

"Do you see it?" I ask, looking over her shoulder at the auction items.

After a moment, she nods. "There. Center table on the west wall. Lot 33."

She spins us so I can get a good look at it. From this far away, it doesn't look like much. I scan the room for exits. Besides the wide archway we came through, there are glass doors behind the orchestra that open into a garden courtyard and a servant staircase tucked into the corner.

There are also guards standing in corners and milling through the crowd. Not too many, but enough to discourage any funny business. I frown even though I'd expected nothing less.

Evangeline pokes the furrow in my brow. "We're at a party. You could *try* to look like you're having fun."

"Sorry," I mumble. "There are guards."

"What are guards to us when we're dancing?" Evangeline says cheekily. Most things she does are cheeky. Then she drops her smile, drops her voice, and asks, "Why's it called Witherwillow?"

"You know how the magical folk tend to revere nature?"

"Mm-hmm."

"This is in direct opposition to that. These human families, they're obsessed with progress and cityscapes and all that. Not only are they trying to prove they're more civilized, they're sending a message that if magic is natural, like a tree, a willow, they're going to destroy it, wither it."

"That's a lot of hate."

I nod. "Every time I start to believe in the inherent goodness of humanity, I experience something like this."

Evangeline hums thoughtfully. "It's people like you, though, who have the vision to change things."

"You mean people who have no money and no power?"

"Give it time," she murmurs.

When the song ends, Evangeline leads me off the dance floor. Hand in hand, we stroll along the auction tables, pretending to gauge our interest in the items. Despite Witherwillow taking place once a month, they sure do have a lot on offer: enchanted dice; a dwarven gun; a glass dagger of elvish make; a silk scarf that, according to the label, was once worn by a necromancer; a hundred-year-old book written in celestial; a goblin skull; a witch's eyeball. I have to suppress shudders at those last two. Actually, I can't imagine any of these items have been given up willingly. It's one thing to hear about events like this happening, quite another to see it in person.

We finally wind our way around to the middle table on the west wall. Up close, the egg is much more interesting. The white and red scales are shiny and have a marbleized look. I can see why the Starr family would want it back, although who did it belong to originally? All I'm doing is assisting in shuffling it from one human's hands into another's. Rightfully, it didn't belong to either of them.

Evangeline pokes me in the forehead. "What's putting that adorable frown on your face, huh?"

"Just thinking."

"What about?"

"Who these all belonged to originally. And what kind of sickos get off on stealing someone else's culture."

She spins me around so my back is to the table, her arms encircling my waist. "You, Miss Kane," she murmurs, "are quite the surprise."

She leans forward an inch, but then just as suddenly backs away, a weight dropping into my pocket as she goes.

"Wh—did you just..."

"Shh. Act casually. Eyes on me so you don't go bats, all right?"

She leads me toward the garden, and I have to use all my willpower not to look back at what is most certainly an empty pedestal now. Because the egg is in my pocket.

"This wasn't the plan," I hiss as we come out into the moonlight. The aroma of jasmine assaults my nostrils. "And you could've just bought it at the actual auction."

"Yes, but where's the fun in that?"

Shouting materializes from the ballroom, and the orchestra stops playing. A handful of Alvenor's goons emerge from the ballroom and rush toward us.

I glare at her. "That didn't take them very long."

"We can argue about my methods later, darling, but for now, there's nowhere to go but up!"

She jumps on to a trellis at the side of the house and climbs. I don't know how she does it in those heels, and I'm glad I have sensible shoes on.

"Come here, you no-good spiv!" one of the goons shouts.

My cue to haul ass up the trellis. The egg in my pocket plunks against my side as I go, and I'm not as skilled as Evangeline. He catches me by the ankle, yanks, and nearly drags me down.

I cling so tightly to the lattice that my knuckles go white and, for a wild second, I think my fingers might break off. I kick out blindly. My boot makes contact with something—hopefully the man's head—and his grip loosens enough for me to wriggle up and out of his reach.

Finally, I make it up to the top. The roof, thankfully, is flat. Evangeline looks cool as a cucumber.

Out of breath, I spread out my arms. "What the hell do we do now?"

"You," she says, "don't have to do anything. I really am grateful for all you've done."

Before I can grasp what's going on, she presses her lips to my brow, right where the makeup is covering my cut. When she pulls away, my skin is warm and tingly. It takes me a second for my brain to catch up to what's happening, and what's happening is that she's backing up toward the edge of the roof. The egg is clutched in one hand. She must have slipped it out of my pocket just as smoothly as she'd slipped it in.

"I hate to leave you like this, but I'd like to think this isn't the end," Evangeline says, still looking at me.

"What are you talking about?"

Then she jumps.

My heart leaps into my throat, and I race to the roof edge. All I see, though, is a dragon, scales shimmering crimson in the moonlight. She dips down before rising on the wind, and my breath catches in my throat. Her body is long and sinuous, built for power and grace. But her wings, her wings spread wide and blot out the moonlight. It should be a terrifying sight, but the sole thought resounding in my head is, "Magnificent."

Then my mouth falls open as I realize what—or *whom*, rather—I'm looking at.

Evangeline.

Well, fuck me.

One hand in my trouser pocket, the other pinching a cigarette, I drag my feet on the way back to my office. The goons didn't want to let me go, but when they saw I didn't have the egg on me, they assumed I was just a worthless good-for-nothing looking for a fun night out. At least they didn't rough me up before letting me go.

I sigh. Should've asked Evangeline for full payment up front. I only got half, and there's no way I'm tracking down a woman from a dragon family to get her to pay up. Can't even be properly mad. She fooled me good.

My body groans as I make my way up the stairs to my office. Yeah, I should go home, but the office is closer and between the fight yesterday and the chase tonight, I'm ready to drop. Once inside, I kick my shoes off, throw off my jacket, and lock the door behind me. I don't even turn on the light.

I shuffle past the couch and toward the desk to stub my cigarette. The hiss of it is audible in the quiet night.

I freeze. There at the edge of the desk, illuminated by slices of moonlight, is an envelope. Warily, I open it and have to catch my breath at the wad of money inside. It's way more than I'm owed, and I have a feeling I know who it's from.

Beneath the money is a folded slip of paper. Inside, in elegant, flowery script, it says:

No hard feelings, right, sweets? I knew you'd get away safely. One of the benefits of being "invisible," as you say, although it's their loss. I'm sure you've figured out by now that there was no fiancé, stupid or otherwise. I never lied to you about the egg, though. Not really. So it's a family heirloom, not a trophy. Almost the same thing. Only it truly belongs to us rather than a damned human clan who thinks getting their dirty mitts on something makes it theirs. Not that I dislike all *humans. Anyway, my siblings and I have been jostling for the position of Mama's heir, and I think it's safe to say recovering this will put me back on top. I never would have found Witherwillow without you. And yes, I could have bought it at auction, but why should I pay for something that's already mine? If you ever take a night off, darling, come see me at Scale's End. I'm sure I can find a way to repay you.*

XoXo

Alexandra Evangeline Sunblazer

I huff out a tiny laugh. Scale's End, the club across town owned by the Sunblazers, one of the most influential and intimidating dragon families. She really laid it on thick with the whole two-Rs-in-Starr act. I tuck the money and the note into a drawer of the desk, lock it, and then sink down onto the couch.

I reach up to swipe my bangs out of my eyes. My fingers brush against skin that's smooth where it shouldn't be. I go to the bathroom, pull the chain for the light, scrub my face clean of makeup, and examine myself in the mirror. There's no bruising to be seen, my split lip has healed, and there's no trace of the cut above my eye, right where Evangeline kissed me.

Well, I'll be damned. That's something to ruminate on in the morning, though. And hey, maybe tomorrow night, I'll find my way to Scale's End. For now, though, sleep.

Carrie Gessner received a Bachelor of Arts in English from Carnegie Mellon University and a Master of Fine Arts in Writing Popular Fiction from Seton Hill University. She writes speculative fiction and is the co-host of the *Positively Pop Culture* podcast. When she's not writing or reading, she likes to go for walks in the park with her greyhound.

TINY HEARTS
BY SOPHIA DESENSI

A SPOON FULL OF sugar may help the medicine go down, but that's a fable of the past. I take mine one gag-reflex-inducing gulp at a time. Because here in Granular City, magic and sugar are illegal. The Despots really are a dreadful, soul-sucking bunch.

But I just so happen to have a tiny ounce of the white gold. I untuck the glass vial from my sunflower stockings. No one will be back for an hour—they've gone to the market—so, I flip through the crinkled pages of a recipe book until I find a particularly sugary dessert just to spite the Despots' reign...Brown butter maple cake, drenched in caramel sauce.

Tap, tap, tap.

I pause, clenching the sugar vial and lean over the counter. There're no branches or brindles, just hay-colored weeds and dandelion fluff floating through the air. I wipe my sweater sleeve over the window, which doesn't do much of anything besides smear the dirt. Maybe I just imagined it.

With a shrug, I set down the sugar and twist the oven knob until it clicks, igniting blue flames.

Tap, tap, tap.

"Let me in. Let me in. Hurry," says an anxious, muffled voice. The glass rattles.

"Hello?"

There's no one, but I know I heard a voice.

I lift the windowsill. A waft of chrysanthemum and motes of pollen swirl inside in.

"Thank you. Thank you." A two-inch, chalk-white dragon scurries over the windowsill and across the counter. He's no bigger than a large strawberry, and round like one too. His tummy skims the worn wood as his claws click hurriedly toward the sugar.

"Reunited. Finally," he exclaims and clings to the jar with all four limbs. He tumbles backward but steadies himself with his tail. "At last, I found you." He smushes his stubby nose to the glass and smooches it.

"Uh, excuse me, tiny dragon, but if you think you're going to steal my sugar, you've chosen the wrong kitchen to rob." I pinch his barbed tail and lift him to eye level.

"I'm not tiny." The dragon bites my thumb, and I drop him. "Maybe you're just huge."

I'm insulted for a second, but then he scurries back to the sugar. His claws scrape shallow lines into the cork. He forces himself up by his tail, wiggling, and tumbles on his back. Good thing he doesn't have wings, or they'd be squished.

"Okay, not-mini-dragon, this is mine, so I'll just be taking—" I shake him from the glass, and he somersaults.

Just as he's about to smack into a knobby gourd, he leaps up and shuffles back toward me.

"You have to come with me. It's an emergency," he says in a tone that sounds like the world is about to end.

I glance up at the sky, just to be sure. Nope, still a pristine blue with puffs of cotton candy clouds. It's not falling yet.

He yanks my sleeve, and his claws snag the knit yarn.

"I'm not going anywhere, you crazy little lizard."

"But you bake the best sweets in the entire world. You have to come with me." He smacks his paw against the countertop. The thump not even big enough to stir a mote of dust. I wonder how much of the *entire* world he's actually seen, being that he's only two-inches big.

"Wait," I say.

His scales darken to blueberry, and he looks up at me with dewy doe eyes.

"Are you the little bugger that took a bite out of the plum cake and left the rest to rot. Plums are only in season for so long, you know." Not that I can be mad— it was Madame Fidgetstick and her wife who grew them. We both should apologize really, but that's beside the point.

"That should be a compliment," he says, licking his claws one by one with a forked tongue. "I couldn't contain myself. It was delicious." He hiccups and puffs a cloud of smoke from his scaled-lips.

"Well, you won't be stealing any sweets today." I grab two brown eggs from a wicker basket and crack them atop a stick of warm butter in a tin bowl. The bakers will be home in less than an hour; they can't catch us in their kitchen.

I uncork the sugar vial and breathe in the sweet scent. My magic prickles in anticipation. Sweet, life-giving sugar. I lick my thumb and speckles of gold glint up the pale patches of my arm. The magic fades just as quickly as if merely a ray of sunlight.

"You'll like my home," he says.

"Mhm." I don't even have a true home, unless you count graveyards or the rare occasion I find an abandoned cottage, but he doesn't need to know that.

"We have an endless supply of sugar."

I jostle, beating the mixture and flick butter and egg across the counter.

"Are you trying to get me arrested? Get out of here." I shove him toward the window, really wanting to flick him right into the weeds where he belongs.

"Wait. Wait. Wait." He digs his paws into the wood. "We have all the sugar you could ever want."

"Great. Then you don't need me." I poke his round belly.

"You don't understand. No one can bake. I need you. *They* need you. We all need you." He tugs at a tarnished silver band around his neck.

"Who's they?" I ask.

"Loren and Ruderick and the familiars. Loren's your age. Well, I think she is at least. You're not like, super old, like thirty or something, are you?"

"Okay, that's enough insults from reptiles for today. And I'm seventeen, thank you very much."

"Ugh." The dragon shoves the silver collar over his head and forces it onto my pinky.

"Ow. What are you—?"

"There. Now you have to come with me. We're bound."

He leaps onto the ring, curls in the empty setting, and hardens to ivory.

"What in the—?"

The stone changes color. Specks of olive-green tinge the edges and spread like watercolor, deepening to a rich emerald.

I tug at the band, but it's stuck. I can spin it, but it refuses to move past my knuckle. That sneaky dragon really did bind me to him with some sort of weird magic.

Slamming my hand on the counter, the vial of sugar rolls off and shatters on the clay tile. I don't have time for this. The bakers will be home soon and this is my only chance to bake a cake for my sister.

He's left me no choice. I'm going to have to take him home and hope that whoever his owner is can unbind us in time to be able to still bring something to my sister's grave.

"Fine," I say.

The stone cracks like the shell of an egg and he crawls out. His scales remain the same shade of mossy green.

"Really? Promise?"

"Oh, so you could hear me?" I ask.

"I'll take you there." He smiles with a mouth full of yellow fangs.

Just what I wanted for my Sunday afternoon, a trip to a rando's house by way of blackmail from a puny dragon.

There's a creak upstairs and then a jingle of the front doorknob. The bakers are home early.

"Fifty pounds. I said fifty, not fifteen," the baker's wife shouts.

"Hurry." I switch off the oven, heft myself onto the counter, and crawl out the window into the grass. The dragon leaps onto my head.

"You're tangling my hair." I pluck him from my pink strands.

"And you called *me* a thief. You don't live here either," the dragon says, righting himself and shaking an ant from his foot.

I kick the window shut. "Just—I know, okay? Let's go." I pick him up and run down the sidewalk, crunching dried maple leaves beneath my feet. "Which way?"

"There." The dragon points down the street of Victorian homes. A blanket of fog creeps over the gable roofs.

A chill prickles my wrist. I grasp my bare skin.

"My ribbon," I say, spinning to search the ground.

"We don't have time," the dragon whines. "It stunk anyway."

The frayed, tawny fabric clings to a crabapple shrub. I yank it from the bramble, jostling a berry to the dirt.

"No," I say, cramming it into my stocking. As the train horn sounded and iron wheels ground the tracks, my sister leaned out the window to wave goodbye. The wind tore the ribbon from her hair, and I caught it in a fist. That was the very last time I saw her.

"What's with that?" the dragon asks.

"What's with the color changing?" I ask, in an equally snarky tone.

"I'm a mood dragon." His scales ombre through the rainbow before settling on a deep periwinkle.

"As if I didn't already wear my emotions on my sleeve, now I wear them on my dragon. Great," I say.

"*Your* dragon?" His scales pucker to raspberry.

"I didn't mean it like that." The faster I return him, the faster I can get to my sister's grave.

"Yes, you did," he sings. "We're going to be together forever, eat all the sweets we want, then stay up all night and tell each other all our secrets—"

"None of that is happening. I'm just bringing you home so you can unbind me from your stupid spell."

"It's not a spell. It's a gift." He shimmies, puffing out his chest.

"Oh, thank you so much for the gift of your unyielding annoyance."

"You're welcome." He snuggles into the crook of my collar bone. His smoke tickles my chin. "Stop," he shouts. "We're here."

The dragon points to an ancient-looking house with murky stained glass bay windows and round turrets, trimmed in carved wood like lace.

"There?" I ask. It looks like it should be condemned.

"Yes. Go in. Go in," he says, climbing down my sweater.

The corroded porch steps groan as I step onto them. Sawdust trickles from the porch beams and the shiplap is decayed with mold. Hesitantly, I twist the doorknob shaped like an oversized key. Rust flakes into my palm, and I wipe it on my skirt.

I step inside onto the creaky hardwood and a baby phoenix squawks from where it's perched above a mahogany desk. A nest of hatchling griffins are tucked within a brass chandelier.

"We're closed. Don't come back," a girl says with pin-straight, corn-silk blonde hair down to her hips. She saunters across a second-floor balcony, trailing her fingers over the banister in a sheer, ebony robe. Fur snags in the wood and tears from her sleeve cuff.

"I'm returning your dragon," I say, holding it out in the palm of my hand.

"Divi. What have I told you?" She flings the gossamer skirt of her robe and it shimmers in the candlelight. "Divi." She stomps down the stairs and gives him this look that makes his scales blanch to a pale blue.

"No, no, it's different this time. I've found us a baker," Divi says, raising to his back feet on my palm. "I'm her familiar, so you can't part us." He spins, tangling himself in my hair.

"Stop that." I swat him. "He bound us without permission."

The girl snatches my hand and presses her finger to Divi's ring.

"Ow." I tug my hand away, but she tightens her grip, pressing her steel-tipped fingernails into my skin. She's just as crazy as the dragon.

"What is this?" she demands, shaking my wrist.

"Uhm. Excuse me? Hi, I'm Lovlet," I say. "The person whose arm you're pulling off."

"Loren." She drops my hand. "Family calls me Lore," she says to me, then turns to Divi. "Do you want to go back into the jewelry box? Apologize."

"Bleh. It smells like mothballs, and I'm allergic to sterling silver." He pretends to choke and then falls stiff on his back.

"You aren't allergic to silver." She turns on her stiletto, ramming her heel into a threadbare rug.

A shadow flickers in a tarnished mirror on the damask red wallpaper. Flames bloom across the glass, igniting impossibly from within, and singe the gilded frame.

The shadowy features of a man appear in the hazy glass.

"Cut it out," Lore says. "No one thinks you're scary. Get over it."

"She was almost afraid of me," the phantom says, patting smoke from his lapels. "I'm the house haunt."

Lore shrugs. "If you have to say it, Ruderick, then I don't think it really counts."

At the end of the hall, the door is kicked open. A girl—if I can even call her that, ghoul or spirit would be more accurate—carries a tray of steaming, blackened cookies with hardened worms jutting out at every angle.

"There was an accident," the ghost girl says. Her body blurs like vapor. I pinch my nose at the stench of charcoaled worm and burnt sugar.

"Mabel, If we can't feed the creatures—"

"I know. I know. Okay?" ghost girl says. "Oh, hey." She turns to me, smiling. The filigree of the wallpaper shines through her green eyes. "Divi finally found his match. Good for him."

Lore snatches the tray of burnt cookies from Mabel and stomps down the hall. "This is an issue, unless you'd like to become familiar food. Oh, wait, you're already dead. I guess they would just eat me then," Lore says.

"Uhm, hey, hello? I can't stay." I wave, but they're already walking toward the kitchen. "I'm just here to give you back your dragon," I shout after them. They don't hear me, too caught up in their bickering.

I follow them down the slanted hall, coughing on the scent of bird poop and stale hay. What looks like lava warps within an orb aquarium, hung like décor on the wall, and a black bat with wings of amber plasma swirls through the tank.

I've never seen creatures like this before. I've known friends to keep familiars—ordinary ones like black cats, ravens, and dragons. I always thought them to be rodents that mooch your magic, but these are different.

I walk to where a braided moss and ivory rug covers a depression in the wood floor.

"Be careful! Don't fall into the basement," Divi says, gripping the seam at my shoulder. "I'm afraid of the dark." He shivers.

What kind of dragon is afraid of the dark? Doesn't he live in stone? Or, he is the stone. I twist the band on my finger. I don't know. This is all so weird.

"Stop. Take your dragon back," I call from the middle of the hall. An electric yellow frog leaps onto the aquarium glass beside me and I startle.

Mabel and Lore turn toward me. Smoke spills out of their stove in the kitchen behind them. Jars of sugar are laid haphazardly over the counters. Tons and tons of precious sugar so carelessly unorganized.

"This is a familiar boutique," Lore says. "You found your familiar. Congratulations."

"No. You don't get it. I don't want him." Smoke continues to spill from the stove. I shove my way past them and thrust open the back door that leads to a rather lavish garden, but that's not important right now. I fan out the smoke with a rag. Sheesh, you'd think they never cooked a day in their lives.

Dim sunlight shines fractals of burgundy and amber across the hardwood, from stained glass jars filled with dried clover, coated in sugar. I'd have enough magic with that amount of sugar to cast any spell I wanted.

"Lovlet can cook. She's the best," Divi says in a high-pitched voice. "That's why I brought her here."

"Really? Good. We need the help," Mabel says, dropping the tray into the sink.

"What was in this?" I ask, picking up a black cookie that's harder than brick.

"Blood worms. There's more in the fridge, but not much more," Lore says.

I open the fridge. One side is labeled creature food, with containers of raw meat and dirt with who knows what else hidden inside. The other half is stuffed with soggy take-out containers and bottles of cream soda. Gross.

"I'm sorry, but I can't stay here. I need to get back," I say, sweeping the rag from my shoulder and dropping it on the counter between bottles of sugar. My mouth waters. I could pocket a small jar while they're turned away. I still need to bake something for my sister. If I show up without a dessert, she'd roll in her grave.

"What do you need to get back to?" Lore asks.

"My life," I say, shrugging because that really should be a good enough excuse.

"Do you have a life though?" Lore asks, eyeing my mismatched crocheted sweater, peony puff sleeve blouse, and tiered periwinkle skirt that flows over my sunflower stockings.

"Fine. I'm between homes right now, but still—" Divi rolls into a bowl of sugar and flour, licking powder from his paw. His scales pucker a shade of taffy.

"Why not stay here with us? You already admitted you don't have a home to go back to," Mabel says.

"And do what?" I ask. I don't even know why I'm considering this. I shouldn't be.

"Bake. Cook. Help us feed the familiars."

With this amount of sugar, I could bake a dessert for my sister and have enough left to use my magic for, well, forever.

"Okay," I say. I'll agree for now, but once my potion is ready, I'll unbind us and head to the cemetery with a dessert and my pockets full of sugar.

"Really?" Divi leaps over a small pumpkin.

"Finally," Mabel says. "I hate cooking."

"I'm hungry." Divi pouts. "I used lots of magic binding us." Divi huffs a trail of smoke and turns a shade of blue.

Mood dragon? Guilt trip dragon is more accurate.

"Ignore him. Blue's his favorite color," Mabel says. "And he already ate."

"We'll be back. Shout if you need anything. Recipe book's over there," Lore says already walking out of the door. "Whip up something sugary. The familiars need it."

"Do you have a recipe book?" I ask.

"Right—over—" he pauses to gulp breath as he pulls himself up the cabinet's knobs. "Here." He hefts himself up and lets out a long sigh, puffing his round cheeks.

I open the cabinet, and he points. I pluck the book from a stack and flip through the crinkled pages. Spells work best when bathed in it, but if Divi ingests the potion, it'll still work.

"How about strawberry shortcake?" I ask.

Divi wrinkles his nose. "I don't know. Sounds healthy."

"It's not healthy," I laugh.

"Fruit? I don't know."

"You liked the plums enough," I say. Why am I even arguing with him? "Just sit over there quietly, until I get this done, please."

"What about cupcakes?" Divi pierces the parchment with his claw. An illustration shows a chocolate cake with cocoa shavings, atop fudgy frosting. My mouth waters. That would be enough sugar to fuel my magic to its true potential *and* enough for the unbinding spell.

"Okay, let's do it," I say.

I grab a bottle of sugar and begin cooking based on the instructions from the book. Divi curls up on the page. He snores softly and hazy smoke trickles from his nostrils in the shape of a cupcake.

I place the batter in the oven, slip in my potion, whip the frosting, wait for the cakes to cool, shave the chocolate, and frost the cupcakes, all while Divi sleeps completely unaware. I shove a little strawberry in the center of each cake before I frost them.

"Hmm," Divi murmurs. His eyes blink open, and he stretches.

I lick my fingers and feel the sugar thrum through my body, energizing the cells that have been napping for far too long. The lace curtain in the window flutters. Between branches, the sky is smeared in marmalade. My stomach grumbles. Wow. I must be hungry if the clouds look tasty.

"Try one?" I ask, sliding a cupcake across the counter.

"You betcha." His tail wraps around the cake, and he plunges his face into the frosting. Crumbs fling around him.

"Don't forget to breathe," I say, plucking his face from the fudge.

"Mhm." His tiny, snake-like tongue flicks over his face, wiping the frosting from his nostrils. "Tastes kinda like sage, and, bleh, lemon," he says with a smack of his lips.

He's smarter than I thought. He can taste the extra ingredients. I thought the chocolate would cover it.

"Yeah, thought I'd experiment a little. How'd you like it?" I ask. Time for my bite to break the familiar bond. I reach for a cupcake—

He coughs. "It's delici—" A tear swells in his eyes, and he grips the pale scales at his gut.

"Is there—" He coughs again, choking on his words. "Strawberries?"

"I put one in the center of each." I scoot the cutting board forward. Pink juice sloshes over the plastic.

"Allergic." His scales brighten, speckling in purple, green, and blue.

I cradle him in the palm of my hand. His scales feel cold. "Lore!" I shout. "Mabel! Help!"

Divi's body puffs like a swollen toad. He spits up the cupcake. Chunks of chocolate and strawberry fall from his lips.

Mabel filters into the kitchen. Her form is hazy for a second and then she comes into focus. "What's with the shouting?"

"He's allergic to strawberries. I didn't know. I'm sorry. Hurry. Please, he's swelling."

Mabel plucks him from my palm and drops him on the recipe book. "Stop being dramatic, or I'll get Lore," she says in a serious tone.

"What are you doing? He's sick."

"Divi isn't allergic to strawberries. He's playing you."

"What? He's playing me?"

"Yep. Divi, you are Lovlet's familiar. If you didn't want to be partners, then you shouldn't have bound yourself to the poor girl."

He wipes a tear from his eye and sits up. His scales blink to a solid lime green—guilt. "She was trying to unbind me. She filled the cupcakes with a spell. I can taste it." He wipes his tongue with the back of his paw.

Mabel looks from Divi to me. "You two need to work out your own problems. Whether you like it or not, you're bound. No more poisoning each other."

"I wasn't—" I say, but Mabel cuts me off.

"Work it out." Then she walks through the wall and disappears.

"I can't believe you. I was actually scared for you," I say. I should have seen through his façade—I've been tricked before.

"Hmph." Divi turns away, thumping his barbed tail on the counter.

I am not taking any more attitude from him. I tap him right on his forehead.

"Excuse you," Divi says, scrunching his nose slits.

"You're a little brat. You forced this binding on me, dragged me here, and tricked me into thinking I'd almost killed you," I shout.

He turns around and taps his paws on his side. "I'm almost three hundred years old," he whispers. He brushes the recipe book with his foot, scraping a thin line across the page. "Every familiar found their person, but not me. Never me." His foot pauses on the scribbled word, *sift*. "Each time I stole a bite of your desserts, I tasted your magic and knew your magic was like mine. Sad. Lonely."

His scales darken to a deep cerulean.

I rub my elbow. "You could sense that?"

"Mhm." He tucks his chin, avoiding my eyes.

"You're right." I swallow a scratch in my throat. I've been lonely so long, I feel numb.

"You can have all the sugar you want here," Divi says. He climbs a cabinet, hanging from the knob.

"I wasn't always like this—sad, angry. My sister used to love sugar—we both did, but she liked it a little too much." I swallow, gripping the edge of the smooth wood. "I thought she was like me, but I was wrong, and it cost her everything."

Divi's tail flicks around a glass bottle filled with candy-coated rose petals. I pluck one from the glass and place it on the top of a single cupcake.

"What's taking so long?" Lore shoves herself into the doorway of the kitchen. "Are the desserts ready?"

"Uhm," I say, glancing at the cupcakes. The spell won't be complete until I take a bite.

Divi steps forward. "Almost. Just working on the finishing touches of our magnum opus." He chef-kisses the air.

"What? There's not time for—oh, those will work." Lore spots the cupcakes and struts forward with determination.

"They can't eat those," I say, stepping in her path.

"Why not?" Lore places a hand on her hip. "Doesn't matter the form of the sugar. " She rubs a thin pink line on her elbow.

"They're toxic," I blurt.

"Isn't that kind of the point?" Lore asks with a humph.

"No, no. What our simple Lovlet here is trying to say is —"

I clear my throat.

Divi shifts and continues, "It's a funny story actually." He laughs. "Really. Poor, naïve, sheltered Lovlet knows nothing about magical creatures—"

"She gets the point," I interrupt, ready to flick him off the counter and into the flour sack.

"We forgot the sugar. What she means is that it's actually *not* toxic at all. That's the problem." He waves his finger and paces the counter. "Yeah, that's it. And now we have to make a new batch."

Lore pushes past me and dips her finger in the frosting. "Tastes sugary to me."

"But—" I say. They're not meant for her.

"It's fine." She picks up the plate and whips her hair off her shoulder, sending a waft of jasmine through the air.

"Hurry." Divi gives me a shove. Well, a shove for him. It feels more like a poke, but I get the message. I hurry after Lore into the hall. A flurry of batting wings, jostling cages, and tiny roars erupts from the hall filled with creatures.

"Here. Make yourself useful and hand these out to the birds." She shoves the tray into my chest, before walking down the hall and into the greenhouse in the front parlor.

Divi crawls up my skirt and says, "Let's go."

"*Now* where do you want to go? We're supposed to hand these out." Maybe I can stuff a few worms in the frosting real quick.

"But they have a spell in them," Divi says. "They can't eat that." He sticks out his forked tongue, "They'll never be able to bind with their one-true person. And without *them*...their magic can never grow."

"Wait." I shift my weight and regrip the silver platter. "Familiars can do that?"

"Why else would you bind to a familiar if not for protection and increased magic?" Divi flicks the tip of his tail with a claw.

"I wouldn't," I say. "I didn't choose this, remember?"

"Forget feeding time at the nursery. Let's go to the cemetery. You can bring the cupcakes." He leaps onto the platter and faces me. "What's Lore going to do, kick us out? You don't want to be here anyways."

"You sneak out a lot, don't you?" I ask.

"Mhm," he says, looking proud of himself.

"Okay. Quick, before she comes back." I run down the hall carrying the tray of cupcakes and a mood changing dragon, wondering how my Sunday turned into such a mess.

Dew-dampened grass smushes beneath my toes, wetting the hem of my skirt. I place a cupcake in front of my sister's headstone.

She deserved so much more than this. I pull out her ribbon and weave it around my fingers.

Divi curls up beside my ankle. I trace the engraved letters of her name. It's too polished, too fresh.

"I can't do this life without you. I can't do this alone." Hot tears roll down my chin and tumble against my chest. "Thank you for this," I say to Divi.

"I didn't do anything."

"You did."

"In that case," he sits up, "you can repay me by showing me your magic."

The cupcake's frosting is a deflated puddle of fudge, and it drips over the sides of the cake. I smear my finger in the chocolate and lick it. I haven't felt my magic since my sister passed away. Golden pinpricks speckle my fingertips that then grow and glow, sending gleaming patches of illumination up my arms. Divi runs down my hand and scrutinizes my skin. I revel in the warmth, in the rightness of my magic. A magic I used to share with my sister.

"Beautiful." Divi clings to my ring finger; it glows with speckles of neon purple bioluminescence. "It's like mine." Divi shivers his brilliant magenta scales.

The color fades, and we're left in darkness. A mockingbird chirps from one of the many branches draped in moss.

"She taught me to bake so I could use my power," I say. "But then she became addicted, and the Despots killed her for it."

Divi cuddles my foot.

I stroke Divi's back, tracing my finger along his spines. He curls his tail around my finger. Hazy plumes of smoke dissipate in the breeze.

"The bakers we lived with fired me shortly after and kicked me out of my home. I only sneak back to use their oven," I admit.

"Why?" Divi asks. "Why do you bring her sugar?"

I pluck a blade of grass, pinch it in half, and pull the filaments apart. "I believe she can be revived." I've never spoken my greatest wish out loud before. "She has soul magic. She's harder to kill than most, and I believe if I can feed sugar to her soul, she may come back." I sniffle and chuckle. "It's dumb, just my grieving mind, grasping at any hope."

"I don't want to be unbound," he whispers. He scoots away from the cupcakes. "I'm your familiar. We're family," he says from the bristling blades of grass.

I smile and grab the tray of cupcakes, leaving one by Karma's headstone.

"I knew it," Divi says, sitting in the dirt.

"Knew what?" I scoop him into my palm.

"I knew we'd stay up all night and tell each other our secrets," he says.

"You don't know anything." I place him on my shoulder. Gooseflesh rises along my arms as I trudge up the hill past my sister's stone. I guess not all bonds are formed by blood. Some blossom all on their own. And in this world of tiny hearts, all we have is each other.

"Let's go home."

"Hopefully the synx hasn't taken a bite out of Lore yet," Divi says.

I laugh. "I guess we better tell her we don't need that spell anymore and cook another batch of bloodworms."

Sophia DeSensi holds a Bachelor of Arts in Creative Writing from the University of Central Florida, and a Master of Fine Arts in Writing Popular Fiction from Seton Hill University. She has published nonfiction with Entertainment Benefit Group, the *Palm Beach Daily News*, and has taken courses at the Editorial Freelancers Association. She is a member of SCBWI and APSS. She currently works as an editor at The Parliament House Press and is the founder of FiC the Monster novel software. Sophia's active on social media via Instagram at @sophiadesensi and Twitter at @desensisophia.

WEI LING AND THE WATER DRAGON
BY JEFF BURNS

I SPLASHED THROUGH A puddle from yesterday's storm, running for my life.

The scummy guys chasing me were soldiers of Li Fan. She was the most feared warlord in Shanhou, the Queendom my village was in. She was also really hot. So it might not be the worst thing if these guys captured me.

But what I carried was too valuable: the sacred dragon idol of my village. The sunlight shimmered along the small crystalline statue in my hand, bathing me in a soft light that made it look like I was running underwater.

The warlord's men had stolen it from my village. Then I stole it back. Which they didn't like very much. Hence the very fast running.

I knew my parents would be furious when I returned. They had called me a foolish girl as I fled their shouts and pursued the bandits. But if I stayed home, I'd just have to help clean up the mess these goons made and then do boring chores. This was way more exciting. And the idol was way too important to my village. My parents had prayed to it after I was born as part of my naming ceremony. I had learned to fight under its steady gaze. I even had my first kiss under the pavilion where the idol rested, the bright moonlight shining through the dragon's eyes and casting me and Jia in a sea of nighttime bliss.

I poured on the speed through the tall grass, the Qiying Mountains glistening in the distance, the Jandu Forest ahead of me.

The warlord's goons hurled shouts and curses as they closed in.

But it was too late. I had reached the sanctuary of Jandu.

I tore into the lush woods and immediately disappeared.

My trackers entered right behind me. And came to an abrupt stop when they realized their quarry had seemingly melted into the trees.

It was darker here, the thick canopy only permitting sporadic shafts of sunlight to peek through. The soldiers spun in circles, reacting to the sounds of wildlife. The forest had a mystical quality, spooky to some but majestic and calming to me.

I leapt from the tree I was perched in, appearing like a phantom, and kicked in opposite directions, striking two of the warriors solidly in the chest.

I landed in a horse stance, my arms flowing around me and settling into fighting position. I had studied Shou Shu, the style of wushu taught in my village, from the time I could walk. I had taken to it immediately. My grumpy shifu even raved about how talented I was, which I'd hoped would convince my parents to let me train more and scrub the floors less. And maybe even make them proud of me.

The remaining four warriors rushed at me. I twirled my body, my arms moving in smooth circles as I brushed their blows aside and sent them stumbling. Shou Shu was a quick, graceful style: flow like water, strike like the wind.

After a few moments, it was over. Six unconscious bodies littered the leaf-strewn forest floor. One of the warriors had blood pouring from her nose. Probably because I had rammed my elbow into it.

I plucked some jinjin plants and shoved them in her nostrils. She came to and yelped. It was like she wasn't used to strangers sticking weird things in her nose.

"It will stop the bleeding," I informed her.

She stared at me, apparently surprised by my kindness and trying to figure out if we still needed to be enemies.

Before she could make that decision, the air whistled. I dove on top of her as an arrow flew through my splayed locks. My lips landed a hair's breadth from hers. She gazed at me like she thought I might kiss her. Well, she was kind of cute.

Bolts sunk into the ground around us. More of her compatriots were crashing into the woods.

I stole a look at Stuffy Nose. "Sorry, maybe we can make out when you stop being all evil and stuff. Oh, and keep that plugged for at least a half hour and get plenty of rest."

I scampered off, leaving her with a bemused look. Well, it's not every day you get to meet Ling Wei, Shou Shu Master and Medicine Woman Extraordinaire!

I retrieved the idol from the small hollow of a tree I liked to take naps under and took off deeper into the forest. Arrows hissed through the leaves, splinters of bark obscuring my view as the metal points ripped into the trees.

A rumble permeated the greenery, and Silk Ribbon Falls came into view. The cascading water spilled into the Sichou River and emptied into the Great Sea.

I cut diagonally through the woods and emerged where the river met the top of the falls. I swore a prayer to every goddess I knew, closed my eyes, and leapt off.

Arrows whizzed by my ears. Luckily, I didn't feel any of them penetrate my flesh.

I think I screamed. It was hard to tell with the sound of the rushing water.

As I plummeted, I realized just how high the waterfall was. And that this was definitely the stupidest thing I had ever done.

The dragon idol slipped from my grasp. I opened my eyes and saw it tumble end over end, seemingly in slow motion.

As I reached for it, the world returned to normal speed. And this time I definitely screamed as the idol and I plunged into the depths below.

I pierced the water and opened my eyes to dazzling blues highlighted by shafts of sunlight.

One of those shafts sparkled off the idol sinking right in front of me.

I grasped for it, but a current of water pulled me away. I frog-kicked against the strong tugging, desperate to get the sacred object. My fingers brushed it. My eyes lit up. Until the current pulled me farther underwater. Bubbles emerged from my mouth as I screamed in frustration.

I twisted and turned as the raging vortex sucked me into some kind of tunnel. I was completely at its mercy, twirling like an underwater acrobat.

Just as I thought I couldn't hold my breath any longer, the current stopped. The water was dark. I swam in the direction I hoped was up. I broke the surface, sucking in the beautiful air.

I spat out a bucket of water and surveyed my surroundings. I was in an underground cavern. Some strange flora cast the walls in an eerie blue.

I slicked my hair out of my face and stared in wonder. I had no idea this was here.

Something bumped against my back. I jumped, afraid it was some slimy eel or something else gross. I turned: it was the dragon idol! I snatched it up, whispering a thankful prayer and wondering how it suddenly had more buoyancy.

I swam to the shore and pulled myself onto the rocks, shivering from the cool air in the cavern.

I placed the idol on the ground, and my clothes soon followed. I spread them out in a beam of sunlight streaking in from a hole in the cavern ceiling.

I closed my eyes and bathed in the warmth as droplets ran down my body. I was relaxing into a nice state of meditation when a gust of warm air tickled my skin. I opened my eyes and got the biggest shock of my life.

Standing before me was a dragon.

"Ahhh!" I jumped back and tripped over a rock. I flung my arms out wildly, looking like an angry tujiu bird, and plunged back into the water.

My head emerged and water sputtered out of my nose. I glanced up at the dragon. It was staring at me curiously. Well, okay, I didn't know what a curious dragon would look like, but it wasn't trying to chomp my naked butt, so I was going with that.

I tentatively climbed out of the pool, keeping my eyes on the dragon. I took in its full form. It had a long, sinuous body held up by four short legs and balanced by a lithe tail. It was a pleasing aqua color from tail to teeth, which were sharp and plentiful under a long snout. Its mane spread impressively on either side of its head and was a darker blue than the rest of its body.

It looked very much like my village's idol.

I waved awkwardly. "Um, hello Mr. or Miss Dragon. You, um, aren't planning to eat me, are you?"

"Why would I eat you?" it scoffed. "You barely have any meat on you."

I almost fell into the water again. The dragon could talk! Well, not exactly. I was hearing it in my mind.

"Hey!" I protested. "There's plenty of meat here." I was more outraged at being labeled scrawny than shocked that a dragon was talking to me. But, c'mon, I thought I had filled out okay after puberty.

That made me realize I had my hands on my hips and was flaunting my very naked bits. Oops. I tried to cover up as best I could.

The dragon seemed surprised. "You can understand me?"

"Yeah. Well, you're kind of inside my head. It's... strange."

The dragon cocked its head to the side. "I have never communicated with one of your kind before." His voice was deep and slow, as if every word had meaning.

"Oh. Um, likewise. I'm Ling Wei. But you can just call me Wei."

"Wei," the dragon drawled, as if testing out a foreign word.

"Do you... have a name?"

"It would be unpronounceable by your kind."

Great. First, the dragon called me scrawny. Now it thought I was uneducated. Stupid dragon.

"Fine. Then I'm giving you a name. How about... Hailong? Yeah, that's perfect."

"Sea dragon?" he pondered my choice. "That is acceptable. I have spent many lifetimes in the unending depths. Though something drew me here."

His large eyes bore into me. I really wished I wasn't naked. But he seemed to be gazing into my soul rather than my flesh.

"Why are you moving so strangely?"

I was hopping from one foot to the other, my hands wrapped around my chest.

"I'm a little cold."

"Really? I find it quite comfortable."

"Well, you're a dragon and I'm a human. I think we have different definitions of comfortable."

He lowered his snout and breathed out two large gusts of air from his impressive nostrils. I was bathed in the most wonderful warmth.

I put my arms out and spun in a circle, letting the sauna-like heat dry up all the wet droplets.

I turned back to face him, feeling nice and toasty. "Thanks. You're very talented."

"Of course. I'm a dragon."

I suppressed a giggle. I guess modesty wasn't a dragon's strong point.

His snout was still near me. I reached toward it. "May I touch you?"

"You may."

I stepped closer and gently put my hand on the dragon's nose. It was scaly but soft. Like running my hand along semi-hardened molasses.

"So... what's it like being a dragon?"

"It is as it should be."

I frowned. What kind of an answer was that? Okay, so maybe it was a stupid question. But, hey, I didn't know what dragons liked to talk about.

"How old are you?"

"Hundreds of your lifetimes."

"Have you met humans before?"

"Yes. But long ago and none as inquisitive as you."

I smiled. I was totally taking that as a compliment. "Thanks. You're definitely the coolest dragon I've met."

"I am the only dragon you've met."

"Oh, right. Well, you're still the coolest."

I stared at his majestic body. He was much longer than he was tall, but he still easily towered over me.

"I...actually didn't even know dragons were real."

My new buddy rose up to his full height. "You carry a dragon idol. How could you not know?"

I picked up the sacred object and ran my fingers along its aqua curves. The sunlight refracted through it, creating a kaleidoscope of brilliant blues on the cavern floor.

"We worship dragons in my village. But I just figured you were a myth my parents and the elders made up. They're always telling us tales to make sure we behave."

"Ah. So, you are a troublemaker?"

"I am not!"

The dragon gazed at me with his crystal blue eyes.

"Okay, sometimes I may get into a little trouble."

"Like how you came to possess the dragon idol?"

"Hey, some scummy warriors stole it, so I was just stealing it back. I was doing a good thing. Even though my parents will probably scold me for going off on my own."

"It was very reckless."

I scowled. Great, I was getting another disapproving parent in this dragon.

"But also very courageous," he continued.

I beamed. Getting praised by a dragon was the best!

I motioned for him to lower his head and gave him a big hug. Well, I couldn't really get my arms around him, but I kind of half-hugged the side of his face.

"What are you doing?" he asked in confusion.

"Giving you a hug. It's how we humans show affection."

"You are a strange creature. But a pleasant one to share time with."

I patted his large nose. "You're just full of compliments, aren't you?"

The shaft of sunlight faded away as the brilliant disk in the sky continued its journey westward, the cool cavern air biting my naked flesh.

"Come," the dragon said, seeing me shiver. "You may curl up with me. I will keep you warm."

I kissed him on the side of his snout, touched by his offer. "Thank you. You're a pretty friendly dragon."

"Of course. Dragons are very friendly."

I lay on his tail with the rest of his body circling around me so I was snuggled tightly on all sides. The coziest warmth emanated from him, and I nestled into his surprisingly soft skin.

His comforting breath on my face quickly lulled me into a warm slumber.

My eyes fluttered open as the sunlight hit them. I squeezed the long, comfortable pillow my body was wrapped around. And then remembered it wasn't a pillow but a dragon's tail.

I stretched, feeling the soft and scaly skin against my limbs.

"Mm, morning," I murmured.

"Good morning," the dragon replied, already very awake. "You are a very sound sleeper."

"Thanks," I yawned.

"You also make strange growling noises."

Growling noises? "Oh, you mean I was snoring? Hey, wait, I don't snore!"

"You certainly do. You are a most unusual creature."

"Well, excuse me for not being as amazing as a dragon." I lounged against his tail, in no big hurry to get up.

"That is not your fault. None can achieve that level of greatness."

I rolled my eyes. And my shifu thought I could be immodest at times. Dragons were apparently experts at it.

I hopped up and stretched my arms toward the ceiling, arching my back. The dragon studied me curiously. And then I realized I was putting two of my lovely assets on display.

I snatched my arms to my chest. "Hey! Stop peeping at me."

"What is peeping?"

"Looking. Staring. Ogling."

"I was merely curious to learn more about human behavior. I do not understand this aversion you have to me seeing you in your natural state. Are you particularly hideous for your species?"

"No, I am not hideous!" I fumed. Okay, so I wasn't the most beautiful girl in the village, but I thought I was fairly fetching.

"That is good, for you seem well-proportioned to me."

"Oh, um..." My anger melted away, replaced by slight embarrassment. Did this dragon just say I was hot? "Thanks."

I retrieved my clothes. They were nice and toasty. Hailong must have sauna-breathed them while I was sleeping.

"Um, would you mind turning around?"

"Why?"

"Because I'm getting dressed."

"Yes. You are covering up your non-hideous parts."

Great. Non-hideous is what I always hoped to be called.

"Listen, it just makes people embarrassed when others are watching them get dressed."

"You are a very strange species."

"I know, we're a bunch of weirdos. Now turn around and don't peek."

The dragon sighed, steam coming out of his nostrils. "Very well. I shall honor your unusual customs."

I slipped my robe and pants on and tied my sash around my waist.

"Okay, all done."

Hailong spun around and lay near me. I had a feeling he had been lonely and enjoyed the contact, even if it was from a strange girl.

I scratched his cheek, hoping he would like that.

He made a pleasant rumbling sound. "You are quite nice. For a human."

I scratched more vigorously. "Thanks. You're not bad for a dragon."

"Indeed. Now please use both hands."

I smiled, obliging the dragon's urge to be petted.

"So... do you think you could show me the way out of here?" I asked.

"You have tired of my company already?"

"No!" I replied quickly. "Not at all. I just need to get back to my village so my parents don't worry. I... I was actually hoping you could come with me."

"You wish me to accompany you?"

"Well, yeah. We're friends now, right?"

"Friends?" The dragon once again seemed like he was testing out the word.

"It means we like spending time together. And help each other."

"I see. Yes, we can be friends."

"Great! Lead the way."

Hailong didn't move.

"What's wrong?" I asked. I was learning to read his expressions, and the one on his face looked worried.

"I do not trust all of your kind. While some of you worship us, others wish to exploit or harm us. That is why I have spent so much time in the great depths."

I hugged his nose. "I won't let that happen. I'll protect you!"

"You will protect *me?*" He was a little incredulous at the thought of a puny human protecting a fearsome dragon.

"Hey, I'm a fierce Shou Shu warrior!" I showed off some impressive twirling moves.

"Is that a type of dance?"

"Noooo. Well, sort of. It's a way to find harmony within and defend yourself against evil people who would hurt dragons."

"Then I fully support this style of dance."

I laughed. "So, do we get out the same way I came in?"

"Yes. You'll have to hold on to me tightly."

He lay flat. I clambered behind one of the curved ridges along his fluid spine, making sure I had a firm grip on the dragon idol.

I took a deep breath just before we plunged into the water and then hung on for dear life as my dragon friend darted through the depths. Any current that had sucked me in proved no match for Hailong as he surged through the vortex.

We zipped through the curving, underwater tunnels. I clutched the idol in one hand and Hailong's ridge with the other, my body outstretched behind me.

We emerged from the passageway, the waterfall rumbling above us. We headed upward, toward the bright sunlight reflecting off the surface.

Hailong curved his body as we got closer to the light and sent me hurtling off. I breached the surface like a shayu whale and soared into the air. My shadow danced on the water's surface. The sun warmed my face before I plunged back in.

I frog-kicked underwater until I could stand, breathing in the fresh air. I tossed my wet locks behind me, the droplets sparkling in the sun as they flew out in an arc.

And that's when the lovely scene came to a grinding halt.

Standing on the shore were the warlord's soldiers. In the middle of the large group was an imposing figure on a powerful, black horse.

Li Fan.

I swallowed hard. Then realized I had something they didn't.

"I'll give you one chance to surrender," I yelled, gesturing in what I hoped was an intimidating pose. "Before me and my dragon destroy you!"

They looked at each other. Then back at me. And laughed.

"All right Hailong, time to..."

I stopped mid-sentence as I glanced behind me. No fearsome beast. Just me and the waterfall.

Stupid dragon.

The one person not laughing was Li Fan. Her dark eyes bore into me through the slits in her helmet, a red plume curving out from its top.

She made a quick motion with her arm, and her warriors charged.

"Hailong!" I yelled as I waded forward into knee-deep water. "You better get your dragon ass up here right now!"

I sensed the nearest baddie approach my flank. I ducked his blow and delivered a palm heel strike to his abdomen, focusing my jin to send him soaring backward and splashing into the water.

Then a half-dozen others were on me. I tried to block and spin away from their attacks, but the water was limiting my movement.

I got socked with two gut punches. I barely had time to groan before a wooden club walloped me in the face. The force snapped my head back and sent me airborne. Blood squirted from my nose as I got a beautiful view of the sun high above.

I splashed into the river, sinking into the depths where the bottom dropped off quickly. I knew I should probably do something, like try to swim to the surface. But my brain was having trouble processing that. Or even staying conscious, for that matter.

A blue blur darted through the water. My eyes fluttered open and shut, trying to bring the shape into focus.

I stretched my hand out and felt Hailong's nose. Then something very strange happened.

Hailong started to glow.

I started to glow.

We were both glowing.

I had no idea what was happening. Some mystical energy was forming between us, swirling all around.

Hailong turned into what looked like sinuous blue strands of mystic force, which were sucked into me. I gasped and my body seized up. It felt like Hailong's essence was permeating every fiber of my being. I felt alive, vibrant, and powerful.

I broke through the surface like I was launched from a catapult. I soared high above the river, did several flips in the air, and landed between the goons who had just attacked me. As I splashed down, the water blasted out in all directions, striking each warrior and propelling them twenty ox lengths away.

I stared in wonder. The water was no longer an impediment to my fighting, but an ally. I felt one with it. Like it was part of me and could be shaped at my command.

The rest of the warriors were equally slack-jawed. Until the warlord barked an order.

The black-clad soldiers surged toward me like locusts.

I flung my hand out and a large, circular stream of water blasted one of them like he got hit by a battering ram. I smashed two more like that, then swept my arm to the left, my fingertips grazing the surface of the water and creating a tidal wave that bowled over half the warriors and deposited them on the shore like unwanted seaweed.

I twirled around, kicking left and right, summoning rock-sized balls of water from my feet that struck the lackeys in their heads and sent them to dreamland.

The remaining dozen surrounded me. I dipped both hands into the water and raised a large, circular aqua-wall that separated us. They hacked at the water shield with their weapons but couldn't break through.

I was in tune with the water and could sense exactly where each opponent was. I lashed out, striking with my hands, feet, elbows, and knees. One by one they went down, shocked to see my limbs bursting through the seemingly impenetrable shield to strike them.

For the last lackey, I leapt through the wall of water, planted both feet into her chest, and sent her skidding across the surface like I was skipping rocks. I got her to bounce about five times before she thudded against the grassy shore.

The water collapsed behind me, like a powerful thunderstorm suddenly ending.

The only one left standing was Li Fan. I thought she might be frightened by my amazing aquatic powers. She just smiled and held up the dragon idol.

I hurled a water boulder right at her super-cute, smug face. Her body blurred and she was no longer there when my aquatic projectile arrived.

I blinked and saw her astride her steed. What the...?

She spurred her horse into a gallop.

"Hailong, she's getting away!" I screamed in frustration.

"I can see that."

I spun all around, looking for the source of his voice. "Wait, where are you?"

"Inside you, remember?"

"Oh, right. Wait, how the hell is this possible?"

"I am not sure."

"Not sure?! I thought you dragons knew everything."

"No. We just know much more than humans."

I stifled a growl. Dragons could be very annoying.

"We have to catch her. I don't suppose your dragon abilities let me fly?"

"No, but I can help in another way."

A surge of energy left my body, and Hailong emerged in front of me. I collapsed to my knees, feeling like I just lost a vital part of my essence.

"Uhhh," I moaned. "That... didn't feel good."

"Stop dawdling. Climb on and we will pursue your quarry."

I rose shakily. Hailong bent down to give me easier access. I hauled myself behind his head, straddling his neck and holding on to his impressive mane.

Hailong launched forward, nearly throwing me off. I clung to him as the landscape whisked by. He was almost as fast on land as in the water.

"This is awesome!" I screamed over the wind as it whipped my hair behind me.

The tall grass and trees became a blur as we hurtled at speeds faster than any horse could travel.

"Thank you for saving me," I told him. "You were incredible."

"We were incredible," he corrected. "You harnessed my dragon power spectacularly."

My cheeks got rosy, and not just from the wind. Hailong's praise meant a lot to me. "Oh, um... that's really sweet."

"Of course. Dragons are very nice."

I laughed and clung to him more tightly.

Soon, we had caught up to our prey. Somehow, Hailong was able to move fast but still make almost no noise, as if he was gliding along the ground. Dragons were the best!

Hailong leapt into the air, dissolving into me as we soared like a wind goddess. I tingled as my dragon friend became one with me.

As our fusion finished, I slammed into Li Fan, tackling her off her steed. We rolled along the ground, both coming up in fighting crouches.

We glared at each other. Well, she glared. I sighed. Her helmet had fallen off and her dark hair spilled loose, framing an exquisite face.

"Any chance we could just make out instead of bashing each other's face in?"

Her teeth glinted in a sinister smile. "Tempting. But I believe I will go with the latter option."

I frowned. C'mon, didn't anyone think I was adorable enough to kiss?

"Stop your awkward human social rituals," Hailong chided. "And retrieve the dragon idol."

"Okay, okay," I replied in a huff. "And I am not being awkward."

Li Fan gazed at me, probably thinking someone talking to herself was very awkward.

I stood into a relaxed, ready stance. Li Fan did the same. She was supposed to be the greatest warrior in the five realms.

In the blink of an eye, she was right in front of me, thrusting both hands against my chest and launching me off my feet.

I blinked up at the wispy cloud-filled sky. What the heck just happened? I didn't even see her move.

"I sense some mystical power within her," Hailong informed me.

"Great," I grunted. "So, what should I do?"

"I suggest getting up."

"Thanks. You're a big help."

"You are very welcome."

I groaned. Dragons obviously did not understand sarcasm.

I didn't see Li Fan when I got my bearings. But I felt her. Right behind me.

I shifted to the left, her fist barely missing me. I felt its power as it sailed through strands of my hair.

I grabbed her arm, shifted my weight, and flipped her. She turned the flip into a graceful, acrobatic maneuver, landing softly on her feet.

I launched fierce palm heels, knee strikes, and kicks. She blocked them all like she was swatting shuiguo flies.

"Hitting her may be helpful," my dragon companion suggested.

"I am trying to hit her!"

Whap! I got a foot right to the face. I stumbled and landed on my butt.

"Perhaps you should focus more on defeating her and less on imagining her ungarmented."

"Hey! Stop reading my thoughts and help me beat her."

"Find water."

"We're in the middle of a field! There's no water here."

"There's water everywhere."

I rolled out of the way of her heel stomp as I pondered that.

Water everywhere. Ooh, I had it.

I parried her next two strikes, then rammed my shoulder into her chest. She tumbled end over end on the ground.

"Yes!" I cheered as I performed several backward flips to put some distance between us.

I knelt and put my palms on the damp soil. I closed my eyes and concentrated. It had rained last night, and I could feel the moisture within the earth. Waiting for me to call it forth.

My hands and body glowed with bluish-white energy. Tiny droplets emerged from the earth, floating upward.

I stood with my arms spread, the water particles surrounding me and coalescing into larger droplets the size of acorns.

My fierce opponent got to her feet. She began her shadow technique, becoming a blur of motion.

I thrust my hand out, and the droplets shot forward like aquatic projectiles. There were so many of them that it was impossible for her to avoid them all. She came back into focus as the aqua bullets ripped into her, jerking her body as they struck her chest and limbs.

She collapsed to the ground, unmoving.

I blinked. Then hopped up and down. "Holy shit! I did it! I'm a water goddess!"

"You are a very strange goddess."

"Oh, shush and just tell me how awesome I am."

"You did well."

"Thank you. You kinda helped too, I suppose."

"Kind of?" my dragon buddy replied in a huff.

"I'm just teasing. You were great."

"Naturally. Now I suggest you retrieve the idol."

"Oh, right."

I rushed over and knelt next to Li Fan. She was unconscious but breathing rhythmically. Her wet hair stuck to her face. Her flawlessly sculpted face with...

"Weiiii," Hailong interrupted my reverie.

Oops. I was doing it again. "Right. The idol."

It rested in the dirt next to my opponent. I picked it up and cleaned it with my sash.

"Wanna give me a ride?" I asked my companion.

"Of course." He phased out of me, and I felt the communal loss again, making me fall to my knees. That was going to take some getting used to.

Hailong clenched the back of my robe in his teeth and flung me up to his neck.

I grabbed hold and pointed forward. "Onward, dragon friend!"

He snorted, which I interpreted to mean he thought I was very charming.

We galloped away.

"I have given our ability to fuse more thought," he told me in a way that I knew meant I was about to be bestowed with some amazing dragon wisdom.

"Well, don't keep it a secret," I replied, guiding him eastward toward my village.

"It may not have been chance that we met. The dragon idol may have led you to me. There are legends of Dragon Warriors, humans who can become one with dragons. I thought they were merely a myth."

"I thought dragons were a myth," I reminded him.

"Indeed. It seems we both have much to learn."

"Ooh, so you're admitting a mere human can teach you a thing or two?"

"Perhaps. If it's the right human."

I scratched his mane. I was totally the right human.

"Dragon Warrior, huh?"

"It would seem so."

"Yes! I'm the most amazing person in history!"

"That may be a tad hyperbolic. However, now that I have seen many others of your species, I can confirm you are one of the least hideous ones."

I smiled. I had gotten used to his weird compliments.

"So, you're saying I'm cute?"

"Yes."

"You're very wise."

"Of course. I'm a dragon."

I laughed as my hair whipped behind me, clinging tightly to my new best friend.

Dragon Warrior. I liked the sound of that. And liked even more that Hailong would be part of my adventures.

Jeff Burns is the writer/director of superhero comedy series *Super Knocked Up*, which has been viewed over 5 million times and which he's currently releasing as a serial fiction series. He has written several action, sci-fi, and fantasy short stories and comics and is the host of geeky improv comedy show *Super Geeked Up*. He also moderates celebrity, fan, and Tabletop RPG panels at comic cons across North America and secretly wants to live with Ewoks. Check out his geeky content at supergeekedup.com.

POISONED WATERS
by Sen R. L. Scherb

THE DRAGON LIES IN a pool of its own bloody feathers. A sharp, sour smell lingers over the dead beast—a scent that has Enau recoiling to Rayns' side when they step closer.

Rayns brushes his palm over the smooth line where Enau's apatite-green head feathers shift to glistening cerulean. Despite her apprehension, she trills quietly under his touch, shifting her weight side to side as her tail lashes behind her.

"Steady, Enau," Rayns whispers, his throat tight. The dead dragon hits too close for comfort—another Tevian hybrid, like Enau. Yet where she bears the gems and blistering breath of a Ridian alongside her Tevian feathers, this dragon is splayed in a limp tangle of six legs.

A ghostly shadow at its chest betrays where a fourth pair had been amputated in seasons' past.

Bile rises in Rayns' throat. Egret hybrids are among the least ethical of the dragon crossbreeds, if he had to rank them—certainly his least favorite to witness. So many extra legs on a body only meant to bear four...it's lucky this dragon wasn't from a two-legged variant Tevian. Rayns shudders at the thought.

He moves forward. Multiple lengths of coagulated cord wrap around the dragon's mouth, nearly hidden in damp, half-melted feathers, broken at the shafts and stained with blood.

A bait animal.

"It didn't even have the chance to fight back." Heat rises to the points of his ears and Rayns fans them out. He can't get too worked up. High emotions lead to mistakes.

Rayns pulls out a roughspun canvas from his pack. Dark stains splotch the threads. It's ragged from use, stretched at the weave, frayed at the edges.

He lays the canvas over the body of the dragon, still warm under his touch. Before its head is covered too, Rayns unsheathes the knife at the small of his back and slices the cords away.

Enau chirps, butting a smoky sapphire horn against Rayns' side.

"I know, girl," he says. "I don't know how we're going to bring it back either. I don't think you can drag this one."

Enau is large for a Tevian-Ridian hybrid. Most of the others Rayns has seen are smaller—not quite compact enough for eowains to wear around the neck like a full-blooded Ridian gem dragon, though they're often able to be carried. Enau reaches his waist, easily within hands' reach.

The dead dragon has not just the bulk, but the length. Transporting it will be difficult.

Enau *skrees*, the press of her horn turning into a jab. It's blunt enough it doesn't pierce through, but it gets his attention.

"What, *what*—" Rayns turns.

Conversation carries on the brisk air of dawn.

He swears under his breath and sprints to the tree line, Enau a whisper at his heels. The early morning birds mask his sharp inhales. Enau presses close to his legs, her long, Ridian-esque tail curling around his worn boots. Rayns sets a hand on her dark-feathered snout and eases out from around the branches.

Two other eowains approach the corpse. Their path skirts the edge of the nearby town, not quite coming from it. One carries a torch, his voice masculine when it reaches Rayns' ears, the other more neutral.

"Isn't right, sending us to do the clean-up," the empty-handed eowain says. Their voice holds the lilt of the standard Eastern trade language, rough with the undercurrent of Ridian. They are taller, leaner than their stockier companion, arms like the branches of a septa tree. "Should'a been Miyre's turn."

"Hold up," their companion says, stopping in front of the dragon corpse. He is gruffer and built more like a skila, with his thick legs and short, flat hair reminiscent of the animal's weight-bearing hindquarters and planed skull. "What's this?" He grabs the edge of the canvas with his free hand.

Rayns curses, then shushes Enau when she whines.

"Shit," 'Septa' echoes. "Someone must'a found it before we got back."

"Ah, so what?" 'Skila' yanks the canvas off the dragon and a piece of Rayns' soul tears with it. He bunches the fabric underneath his arm. "Not like anyone in this hole of a town is going to do anything about it. If it comes up, blame it on C. They're the one who told us to bring the others back first."

Sea? Or perhaps some other spelling, like Seiy. It sounds Tevian, its pronunciation soft where Ridian names are not.

"Whatever," Septa says. "Just burn it and be done with it, before anyone comes back."

Revulsion churns in Rayns' stomach. Dozens of mangled and scorched corpses that he's found over the weeks rise in his memories. He's never come across one as recently dead as the Tevian-Egret. So many lives lost in the fights. Many are sure to die in the future if he doesn't put a stop to it.

Rayns turns and closes his eyes when Skila reaches forward with the torch in his hand. It doesn't block the acrid scent of sulfur from carrying through the air, or keep Enau's quiet whine out of his ears. He buries his fingertips into her feathers and slides to the rotting leaves on the ground. She presses the crown of her head to his. She's almost too warm to the touch, the sapphire plates down her throat cool where they touch his legs.

Patience. He can't reveal himself. The two eowains will leave, and Rayns can deal with the burned corpse. Then, he can move to the next thing. Too many dragons have died here. He needs to find the source. A river can't run clear without taking out the poisoner first. His friend taught him that on Peredair.

Seiy. At least he has a name.

The shrieking howl hits him first, alongside snapping growls and teeth. The cheering comes next, racing up Rayns' spine with a bloodcurdling shudder. He refrains from petting Enau. No telling what kind of other eowains might be watching. A few hang outside the crumbling wooden building, their eyes drawn to the hybrid dragon he leads beside him. Rayns shivers despite the illunop-fur jacket he pilfered from the town.

The four moons have risen countless times since he found the Tevian-Egret. He's scoured the outskirts of the nearby town for any sign of another fight. He'd gained a location from whispers, but there's been no mention of someone named Seiy from what little he's able to gather. Anyone could be involved with the fights.

Everyone here is his enemy.

Enau looks up at Rayns, deep red tourmaline eyes meeting his brown. A trill rumbles quietly in her throat. Leather wraps around her muzzle, covering the line where her yellow face feathers turn to black at her snout.

Rayns cringes. "I know," he whispers. "I know, I'm sorry. I need you to do this for me." He knows she will. Enau would do anything for him. He just wishes it didn't have to be this. Eowains like this are less wary around contestants.

The chain in his hand rattles with every step Enau takes, clinking against her sapphire neck plates. She had balked slightly when he first put the collar and lead around her throat. It made sense. Rayns had cut one off her when they'd met.

Then she cocked her head to the side and let him fasten it.

That shouldn't have hurt the most.

Rayns shakes it off. High emotions lead to mistakes. He can't risk it. Not here.

The fight tonight is taking place in an abandoned tavern, forgotten by any travelers that come here. Most of the decorative wood embellishments have rotted or been eaten away. A few of the braver six-legged gintings, the likely culprits, cling to the sides of the pitted supports, staring at him with wide eyes.

Other eowains crowd the entrance of the tavern, the force of the cheering buffeting Rayns full on when he shoves the door open. A few eowains curse at him, then quickly part when they see him leading a dragon. Blood and sweat hang thick in the stale air. It's uncomfortably hot inside, enough so that he shucks the jacket.

"Where do I register?" he says to the closest eowain, near yelling to be heard over the snarls. The bottom half of her face is covered and hair pulled back, but her eyes hold the same sparkle as one of the shopkeepers he spoke to in the town. Rayns tries to forget it. Take away the poisoner and the river will run clear.

Rayns barely hears the eowain's answer before he walks past her. He doesn't look at the ring. Not yet.

"I'd like to enter," Rayns says. He stops in front of a burly woman, mouth pursed in a deep scowl.

She scribbles something in her book with a length of charcoal. "Don't get many newcomers around here." Her sharp eyes fix on him, taking in his Ridian-short hair yet un-Ridian complexion. He hasn't lived here for as many winters as she.

The cheers swell in volume, dulled by the ringing in Rayns' ears.

"Miyre told me the location," he says, cutting off her next words. He flashes a grin, straightens his shoulders. If this eowain is Miyre, she'll know he's lying—but he lets the risk sink in.

The woman squints at him for a moment longer, then softens slightly. "Name?"

"Klire." The name drops from his lips easily, practiced. It leaves a sour taste in its wake.

"You been doin' this a while, Klire?" she says.

"Not my first time." It isn't, technically. But he hasn't been to a fight since finding Enau at the last. Since Klire—the real Klire—died. He has to force the next words out of his dry throat. "I have the next champion. One your boss might be interested in." Rayns lifts the lead to Enau's collar.

The woman scoffs. "Yeah, you and all the other newcomers." Her sharp gaze moves to Enau. "Though you got a fine hyb there, huh?"

"Tevian-Ridian," he says. "Winning combination."

There's a laugh, which doesn't belong in a place like this. "If you've got the money, I'll get it in there."

Rayns hands over the starting fee—high for a first bet, which draws a raised eyebrow from the woman, but he knows Enau's capabilities.

Once the exchange is done, Rayns is directed down creaky wooden stairs that groan under a dragon's weight.

The basement has been completely gutted, separating walls replaced with cruelly forged iron bars. Through them, Rayns can see into the ring that's been created, as well as onto the main floor he's just come from where spectators look on. On the opposite side of the arena lay cages of dragons, spitting and howling through their chains.

He lets his eyes lower to where the snarling has finally stopped.

Blood splatters the floor and across both dragons in the ring. One of them is dead, the final dregs of life oozing from its gaping throat. The dark red liquid pools onto a canvas that has been spread on the floor of the crude arena. Rayns nearly gags when he recognizes the roughspun brown fabric.

A cleanup crew compromised of eowains and subdued dragons goes in to wrangle the remaining dragon—some sort of Lopenu hybrid, judging from the flaring fins—and drags the dead one out of the arena.

"Move out of the way, fuckin' Dair, you lookin' to get sliced?" a handler yells.

Rayns jerks away as another arena door opens in front of him.

The Lopenu hybrid spits at Enau as it passes and the short feathers on her head bristle, a growl echoing from her throat. It's been years, but Enau wouldn't forget.

Rayns hardly registers the following moments. The woman leading him speaks with another eowain and Enau is taken from him. The cords on her muzzle are cut away with a knife, fingers retreating just out of reach as she snaps at them. Her garnet eyes are wild as she fixates on Rayns, feathers spiked down her back in a Tevian threat display.

Then, she's in the ring and Rayns is against the bars of the clanging door, ignoring the eowains around him. He whispers a prayer to whichever gods might be listening—whether it's the Peren old gods, the Tevian trio, or some other entity out there. For Enau to win or for the world to forgive him for asking Enau to kill more dragons, he's unsure. Maybe both. This will all be over soon.

Hopefully.

Another dragon enters from the other side of the ring, a writhe of movement against its handlers. The gate opens and it launches into the arena, leaping at the walls. Eowains leaning over the edge jerk back in response while its eight legs scrabble for purchase.

For a hybrid, it moves smoothly on all eight fully-grown limbs. A stunted amphibious tail juts out from its hindquarters, barely scraping the ground with a fin-less edge that slices a cloud of grey dust behind it. Flared webbing lines the blunt curve of its jaw, leathery scales ragged and patchy, exposing white at the edge of its salivating mouth. Yet the dragon bears a distinct *otherness* that Rayns can't place. Something in the flash of its fangs, the way it locks eyes with Enau at the other side of the ring and begins to stalk her, hints at something else.

Offspring of two dragon species are rare enough on Tarakona—a triple lineage is practically unheard of. It's the only thing that Rayns can think of as the dragon moves from side to side with a predatory nature that Lopenu and Egrets don't traditionally possess.

"What is that dragon?" he whispers.

The beast pierces the turbulent air with a shriek that quiets the onlookers surrounding the upper rim of the arena.

"What is that dragon?" Rayns repeats, louder, to a nearby eowain. They are tall, with arms as long and lean as tree branches.

"You're in for a treat," Septa says, a wicked smile curving toward him. "Not often we let this beast out. Straight from the breeding pens on Peredair itself. Like the Dairians might say, it's an *ielca*. You speak Peren, don't you, newcomer?"

Rayns clenches his fists, trying not to strangle the eowain in a building packed with others. "*What is it?*" he snaps.

Their smile doesn't drop. "Something to challenge your so called 'champion,'" they say.

A horrible retching fills the arena. The dragon arcs its head back and lunges for Enau with a blinding speed. Cheers erupt through the tavern. Spittle flies from the dragon's mouth toward Enau, who scrabbles against the canvas floor.

She dodges—but only just. Her opponent launches past her, its shoulder slamming into the metal bars where she stood. The edge of the spittle catches her and she stumbles. The blue feathers sizzle away where it touches, eating pockmarks in the ground where it's missed.

Juna.

The dirty cheats put Enau up against an acid-spitter.

Both dragons prowl the ring, attention riveted on one another. Enau's opponent is taller than her, but her bulk is nearly double its width. If she can avoid the acid spit and get in close, she'll have the best chance at winning.

Rayns fixates on the bare patch of skin on her flank. It's a big if.

The dragon hacks again and Enau rushes forward. A low snarl accompanies her thrust up, pushing one of her blunt sapphire horns into the dragon's soft throat. It coughs, choking on the acid build up and knocks her away with its front legs. Claws score down her side. The gathered crowd frenzies at the sight of first blood.

"Come on, Enau," Rayns whispers.

She staggers up, shaking. Blood splatters onto the stained canvas floor. Red paints down her legs, muddying the line between apatite and citrine feathers. She's met with the fangs of her opponent, clamping around the underside of her throat. Enau screeches, raking her own talons down the front of the dragon.

It releases with a shriek, the gashes spurting as it backs away.

Rayns holds his breath until Enau turns. Where she was bitten, the sapphire plates protected her. Small puncture wounds line the edge of the hard gem coverings, feathers disintegrated and shafts split from the acidic saliva.

The dragons circle again, more wary now that both of them have been injured. Someone clangs against the bars, startling Enau's opponent. She takes the distraction, launching herself forward once more.

The Juna hybrid recovers quicker. It sidesteps with a grace that belies its size, jaws streaking for Enau's unprotected tail. The fangs pierce her tail. She howls. Acid corrodes the feathers, turning the blue copper, and the dragon whips its head from side to side. It drags Enau to the floor and she stills. The dragon raises onto its four back legs, retching again.

No. Rayns' hands clench the bars, as if he can push through them and go to her aid.

The dragon slams down. Then it screams.

Enau's mouth is locked onto the Juna hybrid's front leg and she yanks it back. The sharp *crack* of bone echoes through the swelling cheers.

Head tipped back, most of the acid spit falls directly onto the dragon's own head. It pulls back, trying to escape the burning as the acid eats away at its eyes.

Enau releases the dragon's leg, lunging up at its exposed throat. Its shrieks turn into a gurgling wetness as it scrabbles at Enau's chest with its remaining good legs, unable to find purchase against her smooth feathers.

It falls limp.

Her feathers streaked with blood not entirely her own, Enau drops the body. She shakes away rivulets of acid dripping down her jaws. The cheers crescendo around the tavern. Through the bars, Enau's garnet eyes meet his, still holding the wild flare of a feral champion.

The low light of candles illuminates the center of the room he's shoved into, casting the corners in shadow. It attaches to the back of the tavern, on the ground floor rather than the basement level. No one paid him any mind as he was led past them in the main room, only able to catch glimpses of Enau in the ring below. A faint floral scent carries through the air. It masks the smell of death from the ring.

"Get your hands off me," Rayns snaps. He jerks away from Skila's hold, folding his arms tight to his chest. He doesn't know why he's been brought here, only that soon after the fight another eowain approached Skila and they led him away. Enau was still in the ring. "Where's my dragon?"

"Thank you for your assistance, Velt," a smooth, rich voice says from the other side of the room. A man steps forward and nods at Skila—Velt—then fixes his light eyes on Rayns. "Tell them to bring her up next. Handled, of course."

Velt steps back and shuts the door, but Rayns hardly notices. He stares at this man, stuck between rage and apprehension. He doesn't need a name to know who this is. *What* this eowain is. The river's poisoner.

The man leans against the desk on the opposite wall. Too casual. He glances Rayns over. He's young—not much older than Rayns. "I suppose a traditional Dairian greeting won't be necessary?" The man makes a vague gesture reminiscent of curling a hand to his chest, but drops it too soon. "Klire."

Rayns breath catches in his throat, snaring like a bug caught in a piser web. High emotions lead to mistakes. He hasn't been outed yet, despite how pinned Rayns feels. "And I suppose you're Seiy?"

The man smiles. It's easy, along with the tilt of his head. "Cryft, please. We're not friends yet, Klire."

C. Not Seiy.

"Could have fooled me," Rayns says. "I wasn't aware you showed your face to every eowain that frequented the fights. *Cryft.*"

Cryft pushes off the desk, a slight screech filling the room at the movement. He laughs, the sound deep. "Oh, but you haven't been frequenting my fights at all. In fact, tonight was the first time anyone's ever seen you." He steps forward.

Rayns shifts his gaze from Cryft to the broken windows on his left. An escape route. But he can't leave Enau behind. He won't. "It's not my first," he says.

"No, I'd guess not." His light eyes, molten in the dim candlelight, look behind Rayns.

The doors open, cheers and voices swell, and he fights not to turn. Even when he hears the rasping hiss of Enau and the desperate scrabbling of her talons on the wooden floor. She hits the ground with a dull thud.

Cryft makes a hand motion. There's a pause, then the door shuts once more, voices muffling.

Rayns risks a glance back. Enau is crumpled on the floor, blood leaking from her flank and a fresh wound on her neck. Her muzzle is bound once more. She lets out a hollow keen, eyes bright with pain.

"You speak the Eastern trade dialect well, Klire," Cryft says. He's much closer when Rayns focuses on him once more. "But I know a Western farmer when I hear one." The smile returns, much sharper.

"Why bring me here then?" Rayns hisses. He doesn't have his knife, doesn't have anything he can remotely use as a weapon. Stupid. He should have been more prepared. High emotions lead to mistakes, and he'd played right into them. "You could have let me leave and I'd be none the wiser you were here."

Cryft is close enough Rayns can feel his cool breath. Then the man brushes past him, stepping toward Enau. The cold glare of a long leather lash glints in his hand.

"Get away—"

"Tevian-Ridian hybrids are common in this line of work," Cryft interrupts. Enau's attention fixates on the object in Cryft's hand. "But not many could defeat my champion. Only another champion comes close. And a sapphire and blue cawma hybrid? That seemed familiar." A knife flashes and the white cords around Enau's muzzle fall. She doesn't move. The dragon-tail whip unfurls from Cryft's other hand and she jerks. Stiffens. Her haunches raise. Cryft turns back to Rayns. "You know what happened to my sister, then?"

The whip cracks and Enau lunges forward despite her injuries. Rayns dives to the side, teeth snapping where he just stood. The solid bulk of her weight lands on him, talons scraping the skin of his chest. He gasps, eyes wide as he stares up into Enau's bared fangs, white against the black feathers of her muzzle.

Cryft steps to him and crouches, illuminated in the candlelight. "How did you come across my sister's champion? I heard there were two involved in her death, but none had survived."

The dragon above Rayns isn't the Enau he knows. She's more the *ielca* he found, blood-splattered and wild-eyed, standing above the corpse of a woman holding a black leather whip.

Cryft snaps the whip again and Enau lifts onto her back legs in a pantomime of the Juna hybrid in the ring.

Without thinking, Rayns rolls. Enau's heels slam into the floor. Rayns hears himself scream before the pain hits. His right arm lies limp at his side, burning with the fire of a Ridian's blistering breath. Red blinds him. Enau is stuck when he can see again, the pitted wood smashed under her weight and trapping her for a few precious moments.

He scrabbles to his feet, nearly collapsing once more. He can't feel his arm—no, that's wrong. It's too much. It's nearly overwhelming.

Black leather streaks through the air, wrapping around his useless wrist. The fire flares tenfold as he's yanked toward Cryft. Nausea churns in Rayns' stomach.

Cryft catches him by the throat, holding him in place, making him stare up into the cruel light of that smile. "No more words, Klire?" Cryft's whisper traces over him. The name rends through his chest, as effective as any talons. But Klire is gone and Rayns is here.

"Give me back my dragon," Rayns spits. He curls his fist and punches Cryft in the cheek as hard as he can manage. Black spots dance on the edge of his vision.

Cryft stumbles back and Rayns lunges forward. The whip is smooth as he rips it away, tossing it to the other end of the room.

Blood drips from Cryft's nose. He straightens, wiping it with the back of his hand. With a growl, he flicks it away and moves the light hair from his face. He thrusts forward and Rayns shoves himself away.

It's not fast enough to prevent the knife from slashing his thigh, cutting through the thick fabric of his pants to the vulnerable skin underneath. He staggers, dropping to the floor and the knife flashes where his throat was.

On his back, Rayns watches with wide eyes as Cryft angles the blade to him.

There's a streak of blue.

Cryft shouts. Enau stands above him, throat rasping with a sharp hiss. She sinks her fangs into his shoulder, flinging him to the side. He sails across the room, hitting the wall with a sickening crash that sends him through the crumbling wood.

Even the cheers on the other side of the door wouldn't be able to mask that.

Rayns pushes himself up. He gasps as his arm gives out under his weight, sending him to the floor again. He won't be able to get out before Cryft's supporters come in.

Enau appears in his sight. She chirps at him, butting her head into his hand. Her weight shifts from side to side in the familiar nervous gesture, casting wide-eyed glances between the door to the arena and the dragon tail whip tangled in the corner.

"Go, Enau," Rayns whispers. "Get out of here." If someone comes in and grabs the whip, she'll be taken again. Enau is strong, but years of conditioning aren't so easily forgotten.

Her chirp turns into a sharp trill, bordering on a screech. She leans down as the door rattles, feathers bristling in apprehension. Her fangs close on his shoulder, a hair's breadth from the gashes caused by her own talons. The pain turns blinding when she drags him across the floor to the opening in the wall.

His vision swims in darkness, punctuated with flashes of images. Rayns sees the wooden ceiling of the abandoned tavern turn to the four moons in a deep blue sky. Cryft's unmoving body, half-buried underneath the debris of the wall Enau pulls him through.

They're in the tree line when the first eowain comes out of the wreckage. The eowain leans over Cryft's body and shouts something. They don't see Rayns and Enau, far enough away they must look like shadows.

Enau drops him and presses her dark feathered muzzle to his cheek. He lifts his hand, burying it in the soft feathers of her jaw. "I'm okay," he says, though he doesn't feel it. "You saved me."

After attacking him.

But Cryft is dead—or so Rayns hopes. Poisoner gone, the rivers can run clear. Without him, Rayns can get the rest of the dragons out before they fall victim to the fights.

His stomach turns at the thought of the dragons in the basement level. Just how many were down there? And only the gods knew how many more elsewhere.

Enau lays down, curling her warm body against him. His shoulders shake when Rayns wraps the remainder of his shirt around his gashed arm, pulling as tight as he can with leaden fingers. The grass around him is wet and stained in blood.

They can plan their next move when the sun rises. He can find the rest of the dragons then. Cryft and his champion are dead.

Rayns releases a shuddering breath. He can still feel Cryft's hand on his throat, Enau's talons in his flesh. His dragon chirps quietly, as though sensing his thoughts and apologizing.

"It's not your fault," Rayns says softly.

She settles her head on his stomach.

One rope at a time. He'll get them out.

Sen R. L. Scherb is a nonbinary writer with a love of dragons too big to contain. They currently live in south Florida with their two cats, Salem and Wren, working on their thesis novel for their Master of Fine Arts in Writing Popular Fiction at Seton Hill University. They graduated in 2019 from the University of Iowa with a Bachelor of Arts in Creative Writing. Though they've been writing for as long as they can remember, their passion for fantasy hasn't diminished. You can find their frequent haunts at www.linktr.ee/SenRider

FORGIVENESS
BY COLTEN FISHER

TAMIRA LOCKED THE DOOR behind her. The Christmas feast was in full swing—with luck, no one would notice she had slipped away.

Stepping awkwardly, with a mug of hot cocoa in one hand and squirming bundle in the other, she walked toward the window and winced as a splash of cocoa ran down her fingers.

They were in the tallest tower. The window was open to the sky, its stone ledge easily wide enough for a girl her size to sit on and watch the world beyond.

Which was exactly what she did. Cocoa beside her, bundled blanket spread across her lap, she looked out over the castle below.

Fat, fuzzy flakes of snow drifted like dancers through the air. The courtyard garden was a gray plane, marked only by dark lumps of snow-covered plants that could just as easily have been gravestones. Red and green wreaths hung on all the doors. They and the warmly glowing windows of the feast hall were the only spots of color inside the walls. In the distance, white hills blazed ember-like from the light of the setting sun, and the far-off mountain peaks were purple like the banners that flew over her father's armies.

Piano music drifted from somewhere in the castle. The snow made it seem bigger, somehow. More full. The notes of it didn't echo, they simply drifted through the air and settled, peacefully.

An errant snowflake fell against Tamira's cheek where it quickly melted. She shivered and lifted the mug to her lips, savoring the richness on her tongue.

"Do you like Christmas?" she said.

On her lap, a blue dragon emerged from underneath the blanket. Its wings still seemed too big for its body and its horns had just begun to grow in, while its scales—a bright, gem-like blue—sparkled in the evening light. It gazed at her with icy eyes.

This is my first Christmas. How should I know?

The dragon made its thoughts known to her, though that didn't mean she ever understood it. And it was never the first to speak. It always fell to her to ask the questions. She had to work for its feelings, piece by piece.

"Right," she said, "but I meant before. Before you were young again."

Things change. The dragon laid its head down on one of her legs and closed its eyes. *I change. The world changes. Christmas isn't what it once was. How do you expect me to know what I have not experienced?*

"But you have experienced it."

That was when I was old.

The dragon's answers made sense about as often as her father said something kind. At least the dragon was pleasant to be around.

"I remember what Christmas was like last year," she prodded. "It can't have changed that much."

Yes, but last year you were young. That is different than being old.

"I don't see how it is. It can't change your memory all that much."

The dragon sighed. Its body expanded and contracted, and a misty cloud slid from its nostrils. *Perhaps I will know what words to say to you when I am older. Until then, let's talk of other things.*

"All right." The music had ceased. The only sounds were the distant feast noises of clattering dishware and intermittent laughter, and the much nearer *pfft pfft* of snowflakes striking against the tower wall. The distant hills were darkening. The sky deepened into bruised colors; the clouds lost their glow.

Soon.

She took a sip of her cooling cocoa and considered what she wished to know. "Do all dragons breathe fire?" she asked.

No.

Again, having to seek its thoughts, question by question. "Why not?"

Because they do not.

Stupid question. She reworded it. "What allows a dragon to breathe fire?"

Nothing. No dragon can breathe fire.

"But you made it seem like some could!"

Your question made it seem that way to you.

She huffed and a cloud of mist swirled from her mouth. "Can you breathe anything?"

I breathe everything that you do.

She stuck her tongue out at it.

Though its eyes were still closed, it seemed to sense her mood. *Why do you ask these questions?*

"Because I want to know about you," she said. "Don't you want to know anything about me?"

I know everything I need to. You are warm. You dislike when I bite you. When you're sleeping, you move around and bruise my wings.

"You truly are young," she said, "to be concerned with only the things that affect you."

No doubt I will think the same when I am old.

Outside, the snow had ceased, and night had fallen. The roof of clouds drifted apart, framing a glittering sheet of stars. The perfect view for Christmas.

"What of the stars?" she asked the dragon. "Don't they cause you to wonder?"

I wonder at them surely. But I do not wonder about them. I know what I need to. When it comes time for me to hunt, they will light my way, unless they are hidden by clouds. I need only know if they will shine, not why.

"Perhaps only humans wonder."

They were both silent then. When the pale moon began to rise, the dragon turned itself and lifted its head to observe. White light streamed over the castle and garden, casting long shadows and flattening the world. Not long after, the snow pinkened as the other moon rose. Red chased white tonight, and both moons would be in the sky for the spectacle.

"This world is beautiful," Tamira whispered. Then she scowled. "Do you think anything of beauty? Or is that something else that has no matter?"

It surprised her by saying, *Of course I think well of beauty. A world without beauty is a world without life. Or perhaps it is the reverse.*

"Do you think the moons are beautiful?"

Yes.

"Do you think the stars are beautiful?"

Yes.

"But they don't ignite in you a sense of wonder."

No.

"Do you think Christmas is beautiful?"

I wouldn't know.

She sighed. They had come full circle.

"Do you hate us?" The words were out before she could question their wisdom.

An icy eye cracked open. *Why would I hate you?*

"Because we came here. Because they—" she cut herself off, but still the image of the massive dragon head hanging above her father's chair in the feast hall flashed through her mind.

I have no reason to hate you. You've been nothing if not kind. The dragon narrowed its slitted eye at her. *Though occasionally annoying.*

"Do you... Do you remember?" A roar, the sound of an ancient creature dying, echoed in her ears. It was a sound she wasn't likely ever to forget.

Of course I remember. But I can do nothing to change the past. I don't need to be old to know that.

It turned away to indicate that the topic was done, but she laid a hand on its back.

"Thank you."

Then the sky lit up.

Rivers of light blazed through the air, twining like ribbons. Reds like rubies and yellows like gold, green and blue and blazing white. Behind the lights, the moons glowed like a pearl and garnet on spinning strings, and the snow on the earth reflected all the colors of the heavens.

The dragon lifted its head, stretching its neck skyward. *So, this is Christmas.*

"Every year."

The colors oscillated as if taking turns on a stage. Orange roared forth to set the sky aflame, only to be replaced by a verdant green that made Tamira feel she was on the floor of a heavenly forest. An ocean of blue laced with white shifted into a glacial cyan river.

The spectacle didn't last long. Or at least not long enough. When it finally faded, the last tendril disappearing beyond the horizon, Tamira set her empty mug on the floor and wrapped the blanket around herself and the dragon. It wriggled around on her lap, then poked its head out between the folds.

"Was it like you remembered?"

Not at all. The colors were brighter. It yawned, opening its jaws wide and letting its tongue loll out. Tamira giggled, then had to stifle a yawn of her own.

Why do you laugh?

She smiled and scratched underneath its chin. "Simply because. You make me smile."

That's hardly an acceptable answer.

"It's better than the answers you've given me."

My answers are at least answers.

"As are mine. It's no fault of mine if you fail to understand."

The dragon contorted its face. It took Tamira a moment to realize it was scowling. When she did, she couldn't help but laugh. The sound of it fell on the snow like muffled chimes.

The dragon stood up and tried to flare its wings, but they caught in the blanket. *Why do you laugh?* Its thought was loud.

"Because of what you're doing with your face! Are you trying to do what I do?"

Instantly the scowl vanished, and the dragon whipped its head around to face away from her. *I don't know what you mean.*

"It's all right. I think it's cute."

Mist rolled from the dragon's nostrils. *Dragons are not cute.*

"Of course not." She hid a smile behind a hand, and with the other reached under the blanket and tickled its belly.

Stop it! It thrashed around on her lap. Pulses of colored thought flew into Tamira's mind. They made her feel giddy. She thought she was seeing the Christmas lights again, but no, it was the dragon's laugh in her head. *Enough!* it cried in delight.

She relented. For a moment it lay motionless on her lap, panting. Then it pulled in its legs, turned itself over, and climbed its way up the blanket. It settled itself around the back of her neck, its tail coiling and uncoiling over her throat and chest. It was twice as big now as when she'd found it in the ashes and hidden it from her father and his soldiers. A bigger dragon would be harder to hide, but she pushed the thought away. They had this moment. They had now.

After a moment, she inclined her head and spoke. "What of love? Do you believe in that?"

It exhaled a deep breath, the warm air like a gentle touch on her skin. *Yes.*

"Is there anyone whom you love?"

Tenderly it slid its neck against her and pressed its face into her cheek. *I love you.*

Another wave of pleasant giddiness fluttered through her. She lifted her hand and lightly stroked its scales.

"I love you too."

Colten Alexander Farley Fisher grew up living in the Midwest and reading every story he could get his hands on (especially fantasy, and especially if it had dragons). He attended college at Washington University in St. Louis where he studied both English and accounting, and then went on to graduate from Seton Hill University's Master of Fine Arts in Writing Popular Fiction program. There he completed his first novel, *The Gift of Fire*. He currently lives in Minneapolis, Minnesota with the Monster--his oversized bookshelf that needs to be fed with new books at least once a month. There he works, writes, and quests to find the best Indian restaurant in the Twin Cities.

Five
BONUS: BEHIND-THE-SCENES

A Potent Cocktail: "Chasing the Dragon"

by Sean Gibson

AS JANE AUSTEN ONCE said, it is a truth universally acknowledged that *The Hound of the Baskervilles* is the best Sherlock Holmes story, and it is also true that dragons make everything cooler—or, perhaps hotter, on account of the fire and all.

I'm pretty sure that was Jane Austen, anyway. Could have been someone else. The point is, it's a factual statement. Or statements, more accurately.

Though Holmes himself regarded the supernatural with disdain, *Hound* was my entrée into the great detective's world, which, in conjunction with my exposure to *Dracula* at a distressingly young age, led to both a fascination with the Victorian era and an inextricable link in my mind between London particulars, gaslight, and the fantastic.

While those early forays into the wilds of Victorian London offered ample room for the unexplained to lurk in the shadows, a later sojourn as an undergraduate English lit major forced me to confront a disappointing reality: the arcane and inexplicable were about as common during Queen Victoria's reign as exposed table legs which were, of course, taboo—given that the mere sight of them might incite untoward thoughts in the minds (and loins) of otherwise upstanding gentlemen. Such structural wooden supports bore an uncanny resemblance, after all, to their flesh-and-blood counterparts that remained modestly concealed beneath the crinolines of respectable ladies. Still, in writing a story set in an age where science gradually displaced superstition, there remains enough mystery and romance to allow for flights of fancy, and I have always fancied the idea of introducing a gargantuan flying reptile into the sordid streets of London's seedier neighborhoods. Enter Marx Pyle.

In the wake of my first conversation with the estimable Mr. Pyle, I had numerous ideas for how I might contribute to his brilliant conceit. It didn't take long, however, for most of those ideas to fall prey to one that soared higher and burned hotter: the notion of a Holmesian detective (with a twist) pursuing a wicked wyrm with the very fate of Britain at stake.

I hope you enjoy the resulting foray into an alternate version of Victorian London. Will we see more of Celare and Stanley? That is entirely up to you, dear readers.

A WILD STORY OF THE WEST: "A WILD BEAST OF THE WEST"

BY MARX PYLE & JULIE SEATON PYLE

WHEN I FIRST THOUGHT of this anthology and decided on a dragon theme, I had no idea what our own short story would be. Knowing Julie's love of westerns, however, I suspected she would want a story set in that world. And honestly, it was hard *not* to get excited about a Wild West tale with dragons.

This was our first time writing fiction together, however, so there was a learning curve. We discussed plot points and characters—and then Julie insisted on what I considered to be a counter-intuitive ending. I resisted at first, but as I thought about the relationship between Sarah and Aaron—layered with Sarah's relationship and sacrifice for Baby Blue—I realized it was the perfect way to end the story, after all.

Sarah, Aaron, Blue, and even Harv (gotta love Harv!) all came to life for us, making it so much fun to write. Heck, even Doc (who was barely in the story) was fun to write. We both believe great characters are crucial for a memorable story, and we hope they feel as real to you as they do to us.

Maybe it's my screenwriting experience or my years of martial arts training, but I can't help throwing in action scenes. Luckily, Julie is great at translating my crazy action scenes. (Who *wouldn't* want to write Wild West aerial shootouts with dragons and griffins?) In the end, she ironed out my crazy fight scenes and layered in essential details.

I did a lot of the world-building, which is something I love. Creating a unique spin on how our dragons flew and how people rode them was fun. So was providing a griffen to act as their natural predator. And of course, I couldn't resist throwing in some chupacabres, Sasquatch, etc. Sometimes, even with short stories, I struggle to reign in my inner creative dragon. There are so many cool things in this world that we would have loved to explore, but who knows? Maybe one day, we'll once again encounter Sarah as she secures her status as a Wild Beast of the West...

—Marx Pyle

When Marx suggested we co-write a short story for this anthology, I instantly announced that it just *had* to be a western. After all, cowboys (and cowgirls!) riding dragons —what could be better?

While we hammered out details, there were a few key elements I felt compelled to include. One was the conclusion of Baby Blue's story, *Hidalgo*-style. Another was the ending. The final sentence was cemented in my brain, and the rest of the story was in service of that, as far as I was concerned. Thankfully, my very understanding, creative genius of a husband and writing partner was willing to work within those confines to help craft a dynamic and touching story. The inclusion of the flint quarry was due to the countless hours of my life spent watching westerns. Not only was it a convenient plot device as a handy location for rustlers to hide their ill-gotten gains, it was also an opportunity to give modern readers a glimpse into the clever ingenuity and rich history of Native Americans that is far too lacking in our current educational environment.

All in all, playing in this Wild West sandbox with Marx was a truly enjoyable and rewarding experience. He is a remarkable story-teller, patient partner, and absolute mastermind of world-creation. As a result of such a richly layered universe, I feel we've only scratched the surface of Sarah's story. So perhaps we've not heard the last of this Wild Beast of the West *or* her world...

—Julie Seaton Pyle

p.s. This one's for you, Doc. I'll forever treasure the hours we yarned away discussing our favorite westerns.

"Dragons and legends...It would have been difficult for any man not to want to fight beside a dragon."— Patricia Briggs, *Dragon Blood*

BEHIND-THE-SCENES: "THE BROOKLYN DRAGON RACING CLUB"

BY KATHARINE DOW

THREE THINGS SHAPED THE writing of this short story. The first was moving to a new neighborhood during the COVID-19 pandemic. The second was my newly discovered obsession for the much-maligned pigeons of New York City. The third was my unexpected discovery of how much fun it is to name characters.

I'll start with the pandemic--which really is about trying to connect with a place while being alone. I moved to the Bay Ridge neighborhood of Brooklyn in mid-2020, only a few weeks after recovering from a bout with COVID-19. Our lease was up, our landlord was raising the rent, so we looked online and moved from Manhattan to Brooklyn.

I didn't know anything about Bay Ridge before moving, except that it was next to Dyker Heights, which has the best Christmas lights in Brooklyn, and Coney Island, which is my favorite place to watch the sun set. Bay Ridge is basically Brooklyn's version of flyover country. It doesn't get a lot of visitors, but the locals are fiercely proud of it, and it's got a lot to offer, especially if you like to eat.

It's a challenge to get to know a neighborhood during a pandemic, but I did my best. I talked to my neighbors over the wall about soup. We've had some great soup talks. I joined a couple of local Facebook groups. I went on long walks. I became a Patreon supporter of "Radio

Free Bay Ridge," a hyper-local podcast. I read *How Bay Ridge Became Bay Ridge,* by local historian Henry Stewart, and wondered if, someday, I could manage to come up with any cool ideas and join the history club, too. I loved the idea of getting to know a small corner of the Earth on such a deeply intimate level, and I did my best while also being profoundly isolated. After a while, I started to feel proud of it, too. When Marx put out the anthology call, there was no question where my story needed to take place. I'm not sure it could have taken place anywhere else.

Names: One thing I've always been particularly bad at is naming characters. I once wrote a book with one character named Walter, and another named Walther—a name I'm fairly certain does not even exist. I decided to try a little harder this time around, and in doing so, discovered a whole world of fun I'd been missing out on. I'll share a couple of examples.

My neighborhood is home to a lot of older Italians, so for my protagonist, I wanted a very normal, ordinary sort of name for an Italian New Yorker. I wondered if there was someone I admired from history after whom I might name him. I landed on one of my husband's favorite painters, Michelangelo Merisi da Caravaggio. For the purposes of this story, the name was shortened to Angelo. Caravaggio was a passionate, highly confrontational, and determined person. He fit my Angelo's personality very well.

For my secondary protagonist, Karima, I chose another inspirational person from history: a woman who also fit the skills and personality of my character closely. Bay Ridge is home to a large Arabic-speaking community, and the best Palestinian restaurant in New York is down the street from my house. Karima was named after Karima Aboud, Palestine's "first photographer." Born in the 19th century, she is famous for bringing photography to Palestine during a time when it was seen as fairly new and strange. She was brave, creative, and enormously talented, just like my character.

I chose the name of the dragon, Odysseus, to reflect one of the themes of the story, the search for home and belonging. Odysseus is the noble hero of Homer's *The Odyssey* and is famous for his lengthy adventures as he tries to go home to recover his kingdom. He is clever and brave and driven by his love for home and family—a bit like my dragon, who begins the story lost and alone, and ends up found and loved.

Pigeons: The R train, Bay Ridge's only subway line, has the nickname "Rarely" because of its traditionally easygoing approach to arriving and departing. But during the long and difficult year before I wrote this story, I had nowhere to go, anyway. I worked from home, and when not working, I mostly stared out of my window at the Verrazzano Bridge, watching the antics of the local pigeons. The pigeons perching on my windowsill made it clear that I was an unwelcome intruder in their neighborhood, and I quickly learned to respect my place in the pecking order. I decided to educate myself, and in what was becoming a predictable pattern of behavior for my life in Bay Ridge, I read a book. *Pigeons: The Fascinating Saga of the World's Most Revered and Reviled Bird*, by Andrew D. Blechman, and fell in love. When I drove past a local pigeon "racing club," I wondered what Bay Ridge would look like if dragons took their place in New York instead. They would need to be small enough to fit in, but still big enough to make their presence known. They should be smart and scrappy, but maybe a little bit ridiculous, too. Not everyone should like them. Then I thought about Bay Ridge, and how long before Verrazzano sailed into New York, which at the time, this place was named Nyack. So, when I imagined dragons living here, I imagined them always living here, no matter what changed, hanging on, as the world around them grew increasingly hostile. I wondered if there might be a way for dragons and humans to live together. I wondered if there was hope. And that is how my story about the racing dragons of Bay Ridge, and their human friends, was born.

INSPIRATION, BACKGROUND, AND CONTEXT: "RESORTING TO REVENGE"

BY K.W. TAYLOR

"RESORTING TO REVENGE" IS part of my Sam Brody series of fiction about a dragonslaying radio show host. Sam appears in my novel *The Red Eye* and its prequel novella *The House on Concordia Drive*, both originally published in 2014. In 2020, I released *The Skittering*, another novella, under my own Dioscuri Books imprint, and I have other Sam Brody stories in various stages of completion.

I first created the character when brainstorming what to write for my first attempt at National Novel Writing Month (NaNoWriMo) way back in 2003. I'd known I wanted to write something that I could do quickly and that wouldn't cause me to have to do a lot of research. I drew on my own experiences as a college disc jockey, and set the first book in my own hometown so I wouldn't have to look a lot of things up as I raced toward a tight deadline. After many revisions and alterations—and time spent working on vastly different fiction projects, including what would become my science fiction novel *The Curiosity Killers* (Dog Star Books, 2016)—I finally got *The Red Eye* into good enough shape to submit to Alliteration Ink, a local small press that has sadly since gone out of business. Now that I have the rights back to the original Sam Brody novels, and with other story ideas percolating, I plan to release a definitive omnibus edition of all of these pieces in a few years.

The idea for "Resorting to Revenge" specifically came to me after going on a vacation in Ohio's Hocking Hills Park during the first summer of the COVID-19 pandemic. My husband and I were looking for a way to have a safe vacation, so we rented a cabin as far away from other humans as we could possibly get. Of course, the cabin turned out to have zero cell service, so while we spent a very relaxing few days, we were constantly fearful of needing help in an emergency. We didn't even have a landline, and the nearest one was literally tacked to a pole near a mud puddle half a mile from our cabin. Fortunately, we didn't encounter any emergencies, but the experience did lead me to worry about what would happen in such a place if disaster were to strike.

I based Sam and Heather's cabin on the small one-room unit we stayed in, and the lodge is based on a different Hocking Hills location, one that I'd visited for a 2015 writers' retreat hosted by Raw Dog Screaming Press/Dog Star Books. While nothing dramatic or scary happened at *that* retreat either, the combined experiences in Hocking Hills were rife with setting opportunities.

There is something spooky about being in the woods, even with other people. The locked-room-mystery-ness of it all; the classic horror movie trope; the isolation; the potential for bad weather combined with limited communication... It all has the potential to be frightening or dangerous. Add that to the fact that when Sam uses his telekinetic powers, he has the tendency to bring thunderstorms in his wake, and you have all the elements for a dangerous weekend that proves to be anything but relaxing for our erstwhile hero.

Sam was originally designed to answer a fiction question I always had: what if a "breakout" character who serves as the likable but annoying comic relief were the protagonist of their own story? Would they still be likable? By creating a protagonist like that and hearing my readers' responses, I learned that ultimately no, he is not likable, but that doesn't mean he's not an *enjoyable* character. Nobody wants to emulate Sam, but this is also what happens when an immature person closing in on middle age is granted some measure of purpose or greatness later in life. How do they cope with it? Poorly, it turns out. However, I think that through his stressful adventures, Sam is becoming more and more redeemable. At the end of the day, he may be snarky and annoying, but he always wants to do the right thing and protect the people he loves.

When I was invited to submit to this anthology, I knew the only way I could do a dragon story justice was to bring Sam in to fight one. The dragons in his world are shapeshifters, they're definitely bad, and they are usually bent on pure destruction and want to consume humans for their energy. In particular, they tend to focus on hurting the chosen modern-day knights who are created to fight them. Known as "conduits," these knights are a long line of dragonslayers with telekinetic powers, and Sam is merely the latest one.

In *The Red Eye*, Heather is kidnapped by a dragon masquerading as their coworker, a DJ called Doug, and Sam manages to defeat and kill him, rescuing Heather in the process. Now, in "Resorting to Revenge," we see that this act had consequences, and that dragons have families and a thirst for vengeance.

BEHIND-THE-SCENES: "SPIRIT OF THE DRAGON"

BY J.C. MASTRO

I'VE ALWAYS WANTED TO write a dragon story. Not that I'd call myself a dragon nut, but a sincere enjoyment of them started way back as a kid with the long-lost Rankin/Bass animated movie *The Flight of Dragons* (if you've never seen it and can somehow track it down, I highly recommend) and continued on through the books of Pern and later movies like *Dragonheart*. If there was a dragon in it, chances were very good that I'd enjoy it. So, when the chance to be a part of this awesome anthology came up, I eagerly signed on.

Then came the tough part... What would my non-conventional dragon story be about?

It took weeks of brainstorming. With untold possibilities open to me, so many hints and inklings of ideas came and went. Desperation even set in at one point that I'd have a story at all. Then something clicked, and DraggenFraggen was born.

As there are no completely original ideas anymore, I'm not afraid to share where my inspiration came from. I had recently played an older video game called *Brutal Legend*, a crazy mash-up RPG of demonic fantasy realms and heavy metal music, voiced by Jack Black. Critical side note: I'm a lifelong fan of rock and metal. Heavy distorted guitars feed my soul. Anyway, the game has an opening cut-scene where the forces of Hell take over and destroy a rock concert. My creative gears spun, dragons and heavy metal and not-so-bright rockers and real-life mystery exploration combined in what became an absolute joy to write. "Spirit of the Dragon."

Story concept roughly three quarters formed, I began by writing the song that inadvertently summons the dragon. I dabble in poetry, yet had never actually written a song. So, I tapped into and listened to many of my favorite bands to find a head-banging shredder of a tune that fit what was in my head. The first, and probably obvious place I started, was the band DragonForce. It's no surprise that more than one fellow writer in this anthology thought of them during our critique process. Those guys are great. Fast, heavy, and fun to listen to. But they weren't quite right.

Then I listened to Amon Amarth. Drop-tuned, growling, Viking-themed death metal. They were exactly what I was picturing! The full use of Nordic themes in the music, the sound, the song structure... I did however change my vision of the band itself to be more like an 80's and 90's hair metal, dynamic lead singer, with a hint of Spinal Tap, fully dragon-themed band. I had so much fun creating them!

I'd share the exact Amon Amarth song that I hear "Spirit of the Dragon" played like, but I don't want it to actually be "Spirit of the Dragon." I have a secret and likely high hope that someone out there will compose and play a version of this song and share it with us all. Perhaps some like-minded fellow geek musicians will form a DragonFraggen band. Second critical side note: The name DragonFraggen is a callback to the video game term frag. Plus, it just sounds cool. Anyway, it would be amazing, and this silly writer can dream, can't he?

Band and song created, I dove headfirst into the rabbit hole of research for some location to base their discovery of the ancient book on. I wanted it to be somewhere that made sense with dragon legends. I remembered an episode of one of my favorite shows called *Expedition Unknown*, where the host Josh Gates found himself spelunking through the vast cave systems under the country of Wales. It was an awesome setting to potentially find the book. In researching the caves in Wales, I found an absolute gift in the real-life location called King Arthur's Labyrinth. Look it up, it sounds amazing. Let's just say I will visit it one day.

The final element to this story was the ending. My writing process tends to be of discovery, finding the story as I write it rather than outlining the whole thing. Originally, I envisioned a scene of all hell breaking loose with fiery dragon mayhem and incinerated rows of headbanging fans... Dark, I know, which is why no matter how I tried to spin an ending like that, I found no joy in it. It had become very clear in writing the band and their little adventure that this story needed to be fun throughout. When the twist I actually wrote clicked into place, I knew instantly that the fun and joy I'd hoped for had been found.

"Spirit of the Dragon" is full of what I hope are fun references and musicality that capture an imaginative tale that fulfills the anthology theme of non-conventional dragons, and leaves readers with a memorable laugh or two and desire to explore the references within. And, if anyone is inspired to create a DragonFraggen song, I'd be thrilled to hear it!

DRAGONS, LISTS, AND A DRAGON ENTERING THE LISTS: "THE GEORGE"

BY TIMONS ESAIAS

WHEN I WAS ASKED if I'd consider participating in an anthology of dragon stories, I was quick to say Yes. After all, I was already writing not one, but two, dragon stories; the first such stories I'd ever written.

The actual invitation and guidelines soon followed, and I realized that neither of my existing stories would really fit in the concept of the anthology. Not even with determined twisting and squeezing.

The professional response to this dilemma is to start a new story, from scratch. I needed a brand-new idea. Finding a new idea can be an intimidating challenge, but I've been at this long enough to have a strategy: what we call, in both football and chess, *flooding the zone*.

It's easier to come up with ten ideas than just one idea. My method involves carrying a legal pad around with me for a couple of days, jotting down odds and ends of possibilities, until there are bits of several ideas. In this case I came up with quite a lengthy list. Then I started generating one-paragraph pitches, at which point a couple of the ideas lost steam. In the end I sent Marx six pitches for stories, from which he selected this one. (And yes, I've already gone on to write one of the others.)

One approach I'd taken was to imagine dragons in high-conflict roles I'd personally never heard of them in before. Dragon special agents, actual dragons in Viking dragon ships, refusenik dragons, dragon ice cream vendors. No. No I did not suggest ice cream vendors. Ridiculous.

Professional sport, and especially professional boxing, has always been a realm for outsiders. It's also a world filled with danger, exploitation, and illegality. I could see cesspools of conflict in this world, and conflict is the heart of storytelling. Possibilities just popped for that one, and that made it stand out among the six original pitches.

Once I developed the basic idea for the story—a reigning champion about to lose his title—I needed to decide where to put the camera. In the two dragon pieces I'd already started I'd used two different approaches. For the story about a dragon walker in Manhattan, the human had the most interesting job in the story, and I told it from his viewpoint, first person. For the story about the nameless dragon who can pretend to be a plush toy, I went for an omniscient observer who could read the dragon's mind.

But it seemed to me that this story would be most interesting from inside the mind and experiences of the Bipedal Heavyweight Champion of the World. He has the most to lose, and he's deliberately hiding some of what he's up to.

The trick, for this story, was how to present a world with dragons in it—and with boxing divisions that are open to more than one species—and not stop to explain it all. Nothing kills pacing like explanation, especially if you're in the mind of a character who takes much of their world for granted. (Most short fiction contains human characters, but how often do they stop to think about hominid evolution in Africa, and the diaspora of *sapiens* into an already-hominid-populated world?) My technique is to do the worldbuilding by mentioning only the things that threaten or irritate the Point-of-View character, and just implying or hinting at the rest.

BEHIND-THE-SCENES: "MASTERING AESTHETICS"
BY HEIDI MILLER

SHORT STORIES ARE ALWAYS a challenge for me. It takes me longer to write a 3000 to 5000 word, self-contained tale than it does to flesh out a chapter outline for a novel or novella with an ensemble cast, multiple POVs, and several converging plotlines. In truth, I now only write short stories when editors request them. Thus, I answered the call for Marx, a former SHUWPF mentee, and his talented wife, Julie.

When I saw their brief for a dragon story which wasn't "a typical dragon story," I knew I must revisit a particular location from my Ambasadora space opera series (published by Dog Star Books, 2012 - current). Initially I titled this story "Rushow," after the beautifully exotic territory in which it takes place, but settled on the more meaningful "Mastering Aesthetics" instead.

Rushow first appears in *Marked by Light: Ambasadora Book 1*. It just so happens that its architecture showcased what the inhabitants called fossilized sea dragons, so it was a perfect fit for the anthology. I always intended to do more with Rushow—with all my worlds in the Ambasadora-verse, really—and this opportunity came along at the right time.

Those of you familiar with *Marked by Light* may recall that Rushow is where Sara and Rainer search for a secret Fragger doctor who can implant certain markers within

Sara. She needs them to enter a restricted virtual world (V-side). It is a pivotal moment in the novel because she makes a sacrifice in order to save someone she loves...in a universe where love is considered nothing more than an emotional fallacy. It was that moment which placed the novel onto so many feminist SF reading lists. It is also the polarizing aspect of the book.

In "Mastering Aesthetics," I continue the feminist theme and expand upon it. The story takes place just after the events of *Marked by Light* and leads into an upcoming tie-in novel *Frostfall (From the World of Ambasadora)*. This is my first time writing a dragon space opera. I like to shake things up a bit. Rest assured that Xin, Olivia, and the mysterious dragon-person will be making appearances in *Frostfall*.

This is the second published short story from the Ambasadora-verse. The first was "Rainer" in *Far Worlds* (The Bolthole, 2014). The two stories take place concurrently.

BEHIND-THE-SCENES: "CATALYST"
by Kevin Plybon

"CATALYST" IS A PREQUEL set a thousand years before the events of my unpublished novel, *Dragon Star*. That book features a group of nomadic people called the Bhak who lost their planet in an invasion long ago. According to legend, the Bhak escaped destruction only by piling into the mysterious dragons that orbited their world. Now, they live permanently inside the creatures, crisscrossing the galaxy in search of their lost home. "Catalyst" portrays the beginning of their exile.

I had never tried writing a prequel before, and quickly realized there were huge challenges. How could I build up the story to stand on its own while giving (eventual) readers of *Dragon Star* an enriching glimpse into the lore? How much continuity did I really have to maintain if a thousand years had passed? Also, yikes, there were way too many world-building details to stuff into a short story. I'd have to be selective, and my biggest concern was the opening. How could I charge up the setting and stakes as fast as possible?

In my day job, I'm a technical writer. The prime directive of tech writing is clarity. Your goal is often to help the reader accomplish a task, like changing their security settings or getting quick context on a new system. In other words, your goal is to get them *out* of your documentation as fast as possible. Nobody wants to read their car manual cover-to-cover.

Fiction, on the other hand, is linear and tries to capture the reader. The author holds back key details to propel the story with emotion or mystery. It's tempting to think the two disciplines have nothing in common, but I've found that many tech writing techniques are useful in fiction. (The reverse might not be true; imagine looking up how to reinstall an app but the instructions leave out key details, hooking you to the next article with a mystery. I sense many smashed phones.)

With "Catalyst," I knew from prior feedback that people living *in* dragons *in* space was an effective hook. But I also knew there was so much setting to explain that I couldn't risk confusing the reader at the start. Clarity was critical. I needed the quickest, clearest path from opening line to dragon guts.

I decided to use a tool of technical writing and front-loaded crucial elements and context. To give a contextual anchor, I picked a familiar archetype to start: a chill dude vibing. From there, Bhak describes the Hidran Empire's space invasion, another easy-to-grasp trope, before ramping into the goods—the guts—after about 200 words.

Not bad. Tech writing can improve fiction. I hope it worked!

One last note: in the final accounting between this prequel and *Dragon Star*, there is a joke for book readers about temperament. In *Dragon Star*, the nomadic people that live in their dragons—the Bhak—are a pretty uptight, noble bunch. They would be chagrined to learn that their progenitor, the guy after whom their whole society is named, was a stoner who killed his boss. I thought that was pretty funny.

BEHIND-THE-SCENES: "THE LAST HOUR OF NIGHT"
BY G.K. WHITE

NOW FOR A LITTLE behind the scenes action. Inspiration for "The Last Hour of Night" first struck while I was reading Robert E. Howard's *God in the Bowl*. I had been trying to figure out how I wanted to write a dragon differently than the trope for a while and had gotten pretty much nowhere. So, I made the responsible decision to procrastinate by reading a Conan story. My love for heists and thrillers mixed with my admiration for Conan the Barbarian's cat-like grace. Suddenly, the urgent desire to write from the perspective of a thief was born.

As for picking the genre, I had been working on a different project at the time that was sci-fi/fantasy, and I realized that the grim and desperate feel of space would be a great backdrop for a story about a thief. I briefly considered what planet this might take place on before deciding that Earth's Moon was the best candidate for the rear-end of the galaxy. It's a place humanity's already been and would likely establish a colony or forward base on when first trying to live in space. So, it makes sense that the Moon might be left in the dust eventually, assuming Earth became uninhabitable at some point.

With that decision made, I promptly fell down a research hole for five or six hours, researching the Moon and what life would be like there. Most of the society and environment of the Hab came from the first hour or so of my research. The rest of the time spent was my inability to reign in my curiosity. Seriously, I know far too much about the Moon. More than is healthy. Anyway, one of the first things I learned is that, due to its low degree of axial tilt, there are craters on the Moon near its poles that rarely see sunlight. I also learned that the sunrise and sunset are extremely slow. You can outrun it if you are fast enough. I really liked the idea of day and night being several months long, giving my thief plenty of time to ply her trade in the dark. So, I put my society near a crater closer to the poles (I thought craters made for a decent source of water up there for the initial colony.)

I sat myself down to start writing and found that, like with most of my stories, the piece became about the importance of family, community, and communication. I wanted to create something that emphasized the power of telling those you love that you love them, something that would show how intimacy and vulnerability are things in life worth changing for. All the bones were there initially, but I didn't get the through line, Raia's real conflict, until one day when I was talking to my wife.

I was facilitating a guided prayer session for her, and she was taken back to a time when she had been depressed. She told me that had felt like being trapped in a cold, dark cave. You can see your loved ones nearby, but you can't reach them or help them. She shared how God found her there. He warmed her up, told her she wasn't alone. He touched the water of the cave and turned it gold. She knew in that moment that He would take care of her and her family. It's a powerful image born of a tragic situation, and it displays the power of loving someone and letting them know they aren't alone. Her story became Raia's story.

With one last bit of inspiration, I changed the cave to these vents I had imagined under the city. Raia would dream of this place because she was stuck there. Stuck by what she had done and who that experience made her to be. Depressed by her own cynical view of the world. Alone. Then, she let those she loved matter. She opened herself up to intimacy, despite her pain, and found the truth that she wasn't alone.

This story is the journey out of darkness, out of depression, out of loneliness. A story into love and light. At least, that's what it is to me.

To see more of my work or connect with me, visit https://gwhitestoryteller.wixsite.com/mysite

BEHIND-THE-SCENES: "WITHERWILLOW"

BY CARRIE GESSNER

ALTHOUGH I PRIMARILY WRITE fantasy stories, I read widely and like to use short stories as opportunities to explore new ideas, worlds, or genres. So, when Marx asked me to be part of an anthology whose goal was to put a new spin on dragons, I was game.

As many readers did, I grew up with stories about virtuous knights slaying evil dragons. I think fantasy storytelling has evolved in the past two decades so that we're portraying dragons as villains less often and more often as heroes in their own right. Or at least as benevolent helpers to our protagonists. "Witherwillow" certainly falls in this tradition.

While people who can shift into dragons (or dragons who can shift into humans) aren't a new idea, it was one that fit into my vision for this short story, where Iris doesn't always know who to trust because people aren't always what they seem. And the characters who might seem monstrous aren't necessarily the ones she has to watch out for.

Why did I throw noir into the mix? The simplest answer is I wanted to try something new. I've watched and read my fair share of noir stories, but I'd never written one before, and I like challenging myself to try new things. Pretty soon after I decided on noir as a genre, I envisioned a seedy city inhabited by all kinds of supernatural creatures, a city built on tension between those creatures and humans. Could they coexist? Or would the humans find themselves at a disadvantage and turn to nefarious means to keep their world to themselves?

Writing, for me, is often less about reinventing genres and more about expanding the sandboxes of the genres I enjoy. As much as I wanted to lean into certain tropes, like the bedraggled, down-on-their-luck private investigator, I also wanted to give them a little twist. So, I purposefully chose a female P.I. And since I enjoy writing down-on-their-luck characters, Iris fits that mold nicely.

Her narrative voice was a harder task. I don't often write in first-person because I think it's sometimes harder for readers to connect with the character. But in this instance, the personal connection to the P.I. that noir stories are known for made first-person the right choice. I hope I rose to that challenge.

Short stories involve packing a lot of world information into few words. That's one of the exciting things about writing them. The world has to be fully realized, but the story you're telling only scratches the surface of it. There are a few elements here, like the auction of magical artifacts and "icebreath," that add to the world and, if I choose, can be explored in more depth down the road. Until then, I hope you enjoy this foray into the world of "Witherwillow."

FOR MY SISTER: "TINY HEARTS"
BY SOPHIA DeSENSI

MY YOUNGER SISTER HAS always been my best friend. I wrote this short story for her over the summer of 2021 as she prepared to go away to college. I struggled with the idea of not seeing her for months at a time. Much like Lovlet, the protagonist of "Tiny Hearts", I, too, wasn't ready to be without a sister.

I wrote her stories in middle school, and she supported me when I decided to devote my life to writing fiction at a time when many didn't. She might be eight years younger than me, but I've looked up to her my whole life. I've always been proud of her every accomplishment and her kind heart. Throughout our childhood, we never had a single fight. We weren't the normal siblings to bicker or tease. Our bond was strong and it never wavered.

Then, she left. First, she left home. And then, she left school. And she didn't come home.

Like Lovlet's sister, she became enamored and left me and the rest of our family behind.

All I knew in my life to be true was shattered in a single instance. In a single tragic night.

She's chosen a path without me and my family. I remember sitting in the rain when she first left praying, begging, puking. I shook with pain. I couldn't fathom a life without the girl I loved more than anyone else on this earth. I've selfishly begged God to bring her back to me because I need her, even if she doesn't need me. But she's an adult and this is her choice. I fear for her future, of what may happen to her next, of living the rest of my life without her. I've been through a heap of challenges, stress, and trauma, but nothing compares to the pain of losing my sister.

I revised this story with a heart full of pain and agony. I sat at this computer as tears rolled down my cheeks. My hands shook as I typed, but I knew I had to tell this story no matter what. I couldn't give up on "Tiny Hearts" because it felt too much like giving up on my sister. I revised this story to reflect a life without her. With no means of communication, with no hope for the future, with no knowledge of her well-being. That's how I wrote this story.

To my little sister: I love you. I will always love you. Always. I hope you return. I hope you know that you are intensely loved by your family, and that you deserve so, so much more than you believe in this moment. I write this to you because when the lines of modern communication are severed, the oldest form of communication rises—storytelling.

I hope this story will be a safe place for all those who've lost a piece of their heart. There is always a spark of hope for those willing to raise their chin and live on. I hope Lovlet is an example of that sentiment.

Because in this world, all we have is tiny hearts.

BEHIND-THE-SCENES: "WEI LING AND THE WATER DRAGON"
BY JEFF BURNS

DRAGON WARRIORS UNITE! I'M not sure why I opened with that. I just wanted to shout something about dragons. Anyway, behind-the-scenes stuff time! The idea for this story came from watching the live-action *Mulan*. There aren't any dragons in that version, but the ancient China setting and wuxia elements definitely inspired me. I'm a huge fan of Eastern martial arts films, and thought it would be fun to combine kung fu and dragons.

The wushu (Chinese martial arts) style my protagonist Wei practices is Shou Shu. That is not a real style of kung fu, but I searched through the names of the many real-life styles to find inspiration for the name. Feng Shou is the actual wushu style that led me to come up with Shou Shu. Feng Shou means "Wind Hand Fist Art." I liked how that sounded, and that it was a style that used soft, circular motions. Wei's kung fu is similar to Northern styles of kung fu, which emphasize kicks and acrobatics, whereas Southern styles prefer short powerful moves and close fighting. Both are awesome, but since *Mulan* was on my mind, I was visualizing a more acrobatic fluidity to Wei's moves.

Believe it or not, I did not base Wei's dragon-infused water powers off of *Avatar: The Last Airbender*. I began watching the acclaimed series after I had written the initial draft (I know, I'm late to the game with *Avatar*). I wanted to go with an elemental connection for the dragon and use something other than fire, a power many Western-influenced dragons possess. I liked the idea of water-based powers, which would relate to the flowing style of wushu Wei practices. That being said, if you think Wei is inspired by Katara, the waterbender from *Avatar*, I'm totally cool with that. Katara rocks!

I did have a lot of fun writing the aquatic fight scene and coming up with unique ways for Wei to harness Hailong's power. The aquatic bullets she uses to defeat Li Fan are my favorite. I came up with that idea in a screenplay I wrote several years ago, but never filmed. It was nice to bring it back and use it in this story.

I used real Chinese terms in some places, such as shifu, or "master." While in others, I tried to create Chinese-influenced fantasy terms like the Qiying Mountains. The site FantasyNameGenerators.com is a great help when trying to come up with cool names for just about anything, and I used it a few times during my writing.

I liked the idea of using a Chinese dragon, which are significantly different from their Western brethren. I felt a Chinese-inspired dragon should be wise, a little arrogant, but also kind. I loved playing Hailong's high opinion of dragons off Wei's irreverence and curiosity. I enjoy creating humor by having distinct characters interact with and try to understand each other.

I'm also a huge fan of writing kick-ass, funny female protagonists, so I tried to make Wei both a fierce warrior and quirky companion who gets lovestruck a little too easily. She's definitely a unique character in Hailong's eyes, and each character's uniqueness makes them great friends.

My initial draft was almost twice the length of the final version you see in this anthology. More kung fu and dragon action! But don't worry, I plan to release a longer version of the story after the anthology's run and may even make it into a series. I really like Wei and Hailong and love writing their fun dynamic. So, you may get to see more kung fu hijinks in the future! Please feel free to write me at supergeekeduplive@gmail.com if you'd like to see more martial arts adventures with Wei and her dragon buddy, or just to let me know what you thought of the story.

I'm very grateful to my fellow writers in this anthology who were my critique partners and helped me improve and streamline the story. And to Marx Pyle for coming up with the great critique idea and including me in this deep dive into delicious dragons! Sorry, I couldn't help working in some alliteration.

But I'm most grateful to you, the readers, for checking out this book and reading our stories. Thank you so much! I hope you enjoyed these fun dragon tales. Because, as Hailong would say, dragons are very fun.

I hope you all find your own dragon buddy to join you on your adventures!

BEHIND-THE-SCENES: "POISONED WATERS"
BY SEN R. L. SCHERB

WHEN ORIGINALLY APPROACHED ABOUT writing a story with unconventional dragons, I already knew I wanted to set it within my world of Tarakona, the setting for my thesis novel in Seton Hill's Writing Popular Fiction program. It already had a lot of the monikers that the call was asking for, especially in terms of unconventional dragons, and I've always known throughout the writing of my novel that in building this world, I was creating it in a way I could explore more stories that take place in it.

What I didn't expect was the sheer amount of *possibility*.

My novel has eight continents with seven species of dragons—what kind of story would be able to convey that kind of richness and diversity within just a few thousand words? What was the most narratively interesting?

Since "Poisoned Waters" takes place before the events of my novel, I was a little more limited in terms of abilities of the dragons—however, one of the major foundational aspects of my thesis novel has always been a concept of dragon fights (as, I'll admit, a very heavily inspired and thinly veiled allegory for dog fighting rings). It's something that I've always wanted to explore further, especially as one of the main dragons in my novel comes from these fights, yet doesn't fit within the story I'm trying to tell there.

So, the idea began just with that—a foundation that I knew involved the taboo trade and breeding of hybrid dragons, and someone who wants desperately to make a difference in trying to stop it.

There was a lot to consider while crafting a story involving not only concepts from illegal dog fights, but also combining aspects of the established ideas of taboo dragon interbreeding from my own world. Yes, the dragons *can* interbreed, but that doesn't mean they should. I introduce this early on in the story, with the Tevian-Egret hybrid dragon, where the dragon's fourth pair of legs had to be cut off when it was a hatchling because it was too malformed otherwise.

Yet believe it or not, that hybrid was a lucky one. Most die before, during, or shortly after they're born because their bodies aren't made to survive. A Juna hybrid can't live if it doesn't have the natural inner resistance to its own acid saliva. A Lopenu hybrid will drown if it's too heavy or waterlogged to swim. A Ridian hybrid will rip its own flesh open if it doesn't have the hard scales to protect it.

Of course, as any good story does, the foundation began growing as I started writing this partnership between Rayns and Enau and how Rayns wanted to try and get at this dragon fight ring leader. I had known that Rayns rescued Enau from a previous fighting ring. However, Rayns' original eowain partner, Klire, didn't exist beyond a code name, and Enau was only a dragon that happened to be alive when Rayns found her. The ideas for Enau being the previous champion of the ring on the continent Peredair, the leader having been Cryft's sister, and the *actual* Klire came much later—most of them coming when I wrote the interaction between Cryft and Rayns for the first time. Cryft seemed to have *so* much resentment and suspicion for Rayns, beyond him just being able to kill Cryft's champion. Where were those emotions coming from?

It came together when Cryft pulled out the whip—Enau wasn't just another fighter, but she had been the champion, trained and conditioned by a near identical weapon now held by Cryft.

The story's end was more difficult than I'd like to admit. Quite honestly, I wasn't sure how Rayns was going to get the whip away from Cryft and break Enau out of her conditioning. As terrible as it may sound, I didn't want the more typical trope of "I know you'd never hurt me" being able to snap through Enau's feral state. We love to see it, but I didn't want that aspect of Enau's past and tangible evidence of where she came from to just be tossed aside as though it could never affect her again.

The story originally ended externally—after being injured, Rayns knocks a candle from the table and sets the tavern on fire. He escapes, barely, with Enau after the whip is destroyed but leaves everyone in the tavern, dragons included, to their death.

It didn't sit right with me. Something about it seemed wrong, ill-fitting, and not satisfactory. The next morning after sleeping on it, I immediately changed the ending, building more on the concepts of Enau having been the previous champion and playing a more active role in both conditioning and eventually saving Rayns by killing Cryft like she killed his sister.

Ultimately, I love how "Poisoned Waters" turned out. It allowed me to dabble within the aspects of my novel that I hadn't been able to go into deeper, while also solidifying concepts of how certain aspects of the world worked. I look forward to delving more into the lands of Tarakona and uncovering the stories that are hidden within.

BEHIND-THE-SCENES: "FORGIVENESS"
BY COLTEN FISHER

I WROTE THE FIRST version of this story, then titled "Inspiration," several years ago while at my grandparents' over Christmas. My goal then was to create a simple story that was just jam-packed with elements of creative inspiration. Every time I felt like a reader would be comfortable, like they had a grasp on the story, *bam!* I tossed in a new twist for the setting or characters. And so I went from describing a castle (typical medieval setting), to chocolate (only introduced to Europe after the 1400s), to a dragon, to Christmas, to two moons and on, all to confound and, hopefully, inspire a hypothetical reader.

I had no particular reader in mind, of course, when I first penned the story. This concept consisted solely of creative fodder that came to me in response to an experience I'd had a few times, and which I'm sure is shared by many other storytellers. That experience is: when watching movies, specifically fantasy movies (I believe *Battle of the Five Armies* had just come out), there would come a moment of excellent cinematography, or music, or writing/acting, or all three combined, that would leave me filled with the passionate urge to write. "Yes!" I would think, "I want to craft a story to match *this*! I want to take this unique idea they've come up with and create an even more unique idea of my own! I want to write about dragons!" Or so the thinking would go.

Whether that desire to write would stick around once I got to my notebook, though, well that was a different matter.

And so the first version of the story of Tamira and the Dragon, "Inspiration," was intended to be a written version of that same experience. It wasn't meant to be a story, per se, but rather something that would leave a writer wanting to write. The goal of crossing so many elements that don't normally intersect—a dragon, Christmas, and a different planet—was to jump start the creative process and get someone thinking, "Where can we go from here?"

This first version of the story, though, could hardly be called a story, given that nothing happened. That is, it had a premise, but no plot. So when the idea of this anthology was brought to me, I knew I wanted to adapt the story of Tamira and her dragon to be my submission, but I had to figure out how to turn it from an exercise into a story. I didn't want to leave the quiet, relationship-focused dynamic that I'd built between my two characters, but I also didn't want to leave my readers feeling confused. Or worse, bored. So I began introducing elements of plot little by little. First, by insinuating that the girl and dragon were actually hiding in the tower, creating a little conflict, and then by putting a face to that conflict: Tamira's father.

Then, like any good writer, I had people read my story and give me feedback. The results were overwhelmingly, "we want to know more." So I added more details; I tweaked how and when information was given. The core of what's on the page never changed. It always started and ended with a girl and a dragon in a tower, looking at the sky. It was around that scene that I tried to show the story, though, to tell the tale of *why* the girl and dragon were in the tower, and why their conversation was important. It was a difficult, if rewarding process, especially as a fantasy writer who's used to having paragraphs of exposition spread across chapters, rather than sentences spread across a few pages. But success or not, and inspiration or not, it is this author's hope that this girl and her dragon at least made the reader smile.

ABOUT THE EDITORS

ANNE C. LYNCH is a full-time writer of historical fiction and part-time English teacher with an MFA in Writing Popular Fiction from Seton Hill University and a BS in Secondary English Education from The University of Texas at Austin (Hook 'em, Y'all!). She lives in Austin, Texas, with her husband and two dogs—Penny the slightly defective beagle and Luna the delightfully derp-y great dane. Her debut novel is *The Mercenary's Son*. She is currently working on her second novel.

J.C. MASTRO grew up in California in the 1980's. As a child, he enjoyed science fiction and fantasy, spending sunny days outside battling invisible aliens and flying through space in oversized, cardboard ships. Evenings and lazy afternoons were spent consuming 1980's TV and movie favorites like reruns of *Star Trek,* and *Star Wars* on worn-down VHS tapes. In his teens, J.C. discovered a love of reading sci-fi and fantasy novels by authors such as Frank Herbert, Michael Crichton, Timothy Zahn, Anne McCaffrey and even Stephen King. His goal is to entertain readers through fun action and relatable characters, and to stimulate their imaginations--just like his was growing up. J.C. earned a Bachelor of Arts in Creative Writing and English from Southern New Hampshire University, and a Master of Fine Arts in Writing Popular Fiction from Seton Hill University. He is currently a visually impaired stay-at-home-geek-dad seeking publication for his first young adult sci-fi novel, *Academy Bound*. Connect with J.C. at jcmastroauthor.com or Instagram @jcmastroauthor

MARX PYLE is an author, screenwriter, filmmaker, podcaster, adjunct professor, and martial artist whose journey has been as complex as his characters and the worlds in which they live. His first degree was to save the world (Psychology), and the next to pay the bills (Computer Information Systems). His third degree (Film Production) helped him follow his storytelling dreams, but his final (Master of Fine Arts in Writing Popular Fiction) allowed him to do so without budget constraints. In addition to urban fantasy, he dabbles in science fiction, fantasy, and horror because he can't filter that "what if" voice in his head. Marx's new serial fiction urban fantasy/thriller, *Obsidian Archives*, is currently online. He enjoys relaxing at home with his supportive wife, their two cats, and albino rabbit who, while mostly cute and cuddly, occasionally seems to thrive on human flesh and blood. (We suspect she's related to The Killer Rabbit of Caerbannog).

Five words describe **VICTORIA SCOTT**'s knowledge base: "How hard can it be?" This can-do attitude inspired her to learn to speak Latin, to quilt, and to operate a blueprint machine. Sometimes what she tries can be damn hard, like learning Ancient Greek, studying karate, and taking Calculus. Those...were not as successful. Victoria writes Contemporary Fantasy, usually while hanging out with her dog, Red. She teaches Latin by day and earned her Master of Fine Arts in Writing Popular Fiction at Seton Hill University. Her bucket list is simple: drive a Zamboni, cruise down the Nile River, and get a book published. How hard can it be?

ABOUT THE PUBLISHER

Dragons of a Different Tail: 17 Unusual Dragon Tales
Published by Cabbit Crossing Publishing LLC

At Cabbit Crossing Publishing, we started as readers who love urban fantasy, epic fantasy, science-fiction, superheroes, and more. Now we are writing what we love and sharing it with the world! Like the urban legend of the cabbit (a cat rabbit hybrid) our stories are often blends of genres.

Also By Cabbit Crossing Publishing:

Obsidian Monsters (Book 1 of the Obsidian Archives) - Coming 2022

Lightning Source UK Ltd.
Milton Keynes UK
UKHW040828081221
395269UK00002B/587